Henry Montgomery

The Life of Major-General William H. Harrison

Second Edition

Henry Montgomery

The Life of Major-General William H. Harrison
Second Edition

ISBN/EAN: 9783337111892

Printed in Europe, USA, Canada, Australia, Japan

Cover: Foto ©Raphael Reischuk / pixelio.de

More available books at **www.hansebooks.com**

THE

LIFE OF MAJOR-GENERAL

WILLIAM H. HARRISON,

NINTH PRESIDENT OF THE UNITED STATES,

BY

H. MONTGOMERY.

SECOND EDITION.

NEW YORK:

C. M. SAXTON, BARKER & CO., 25 PARK ROW.

SAN FRANCISCO: H. H. BANCROFT & CO.

1860.

TO

MAJOR GENERAL WINFIELD SCOTT,

THE HERO, THE PATRIOT, AND

THE STATESMAN,

WHOSE FAME FILLS THE WORLD,

AND WHOSE EFFORTS TO

MAINTAIN PEACE

HAVE AS MUCH ENDEARED HIM TO HIS COUNTRYMEN

AS HIS GLORIOUS ACHIEVEMENTS

IN WAR,

WHOSE LIFE FROM BOYHOOD UP

HAS BEEN SPENT IN DEFENDING THE HONOR

And promoting the welfare of his Country,

THIS WORK IS

RESPECTFULLY DEDICATED,

AS A SLIGHT TOKEN OF THE ESTEEM ENTERTAINED FOR

HIS CHARACTER,

AND THE GRATITUDE FELT FOR HIS SERVICES,

BY THE AUTHOR.

PREFACE.

ANOTHER life of so eminent a general, and so unselfish a patriot, as WILLIAM HENRY HARRISON,—a man whose history is almost literally the history of the country for fifty of the seventy-five years which make up the length of our national existence,—was not undertaken with the hope of producing anything either novel or exciting. No such ambitious design prompted the compiler to the temerity of attempting what had already been done by a Hall and a Todd. His humble object has been to combine, in a single volume, as much of what is now scattered throughout many, and all over the records of the times, as he considered of sufficient interest. No memoir of General Harrison but contains something that others do not, and much, indeed, that ought to be preserved to

1*

the country, in a more durable and attractive form
than a badly printed shilling pamphlet.   Most of the
biographies, too, of the eminent soldier and civilian,
were written with the single view to promote his election to the presidency.   This destroys none of their
merit, nor diminishes the value of the many facts and
truths they contain; but it is a reason why they
contain also much that cannot claim to be preserved
in a sober, posthumous biography, written, not to advance the political fortunes nor to defend the political
character, but to do justice to the memory and faithfully to describe the acts of an eminent man.

It has elsewhere been said, that not a complete
biography of General Harrison, in a permanent form,
has ever been published.   Judge Hall's Memoirs, and
Sketches of Harrison, by Colonel C. S. Todd and
Benjamin Drake, Esq., are both admirable in many
respects.   But the first was written previous to 1835,
to promote his first nomination to the presidency, and
is therefore necessarily defective, stopping as it does
far short of the most important event in his career.
The other is much more complete, though it was
originally prepared under the supervision of a political committee, with a political design solely.   It was

much extended after his death. These comprise the only attempts of any pretension that have ever been made to present the public with even a tolerably full sketch of WILLIAM HENRY HARRISON's life. There are also many other sketches of his life of more or less merit, but all having for their aim the single object of promoting his political prospects.

And yet to these unpretending little works the compiler is indebted for much of whatever merit may be accorded to his enterprise. He is also greatly indebted to McAfee's *History of the Late War*, to Burnett's *Notes on the North-western Territory*, Monette's *Valley of the Mississippi*, Frost's *Book of the Army*, Dawson's *Historical Narrative*, Niles' *Register*, and, above all, to Brackenridge's *Late War*. He has made free use of their pages wherever he has found anything to his purpose or taste. It may be that he has not been over scrupulous in giving them credit as he went along for all the good things he has thus appropriated. The fear that he may have done them this great wrong, and the equally strong fear that he will be thought to have attempted thus to appear in borrowed plumes, has prompted him to make an acknowledgment, which he trusts is broad enough to cover all his delinquencies of this character.

He claims but little originality for his book. He might, perhaps, assume for it something more than a compilation, with as much justice as many others; but a discriminating public would discover the attempted cheat as it is discovered in other cases. Policy, therefore, as well as honesty, has induced him to claim no more than he deserves, believing that the most certain means of securing quite as much. It is not much, indeed, in regard to such a man as Harrison, that has not already somewhere and in some shape been said. If the following pages have a redeeming point it can only be that there has been grouped together within the more of them facts that make up his public life than are anywhere else to be found. As many of these facts as were accessible, which were considered necessary to complete the record of his acts, illustrate his character, and do justice to his memory, will be found there.

Some things may be found in the Appendix, which have little apparent, and indeed little real, connection with a Life of General Harrison. But still it is believed they will be admitted to occupy an appropriate place, and to possess an interest and value that entitles them to it. Some are important for the instruction they give, some for the information they contain, some for the pleasure they will afford, and others as simple matters of reference. And it may be thought, that only so many of the events of the war of 1812, as transpired within the range of General Harrison's command, should have been recorded in a Life of Harrison; but the compiler believed his name and fame sufficiently identified with the whole war to make appropriate a brief sketch of all its most remarkable incidents. This, therefore, has been done, and it is trusted the book will possess none the less interest for the innovation.

Little more need be said,—and perhaps it would have been better for the book if much less had been said. The compiler has labored to make it as deserving the great merit of its subject, and as worthy of public approbation, as his humble abilities would permit. To what degree of merit it is entitled, and how near it comes to the point at which it aspires, he is quite willing to submit to the universal umpire in all similar cases; and this he is all the more willing to do, as he has not been able to discover any alternative.

The only merit he will therefore absolutely *claim*, is
that of making a virtue of necessity, and of submitting with cheerfulness to what an inexorable necessity
imposes.

Auburn, *July* 1852.

INTRODUCTION.

THE cheapest as well as the most enduring monument that can be erected to the memory of those whose virtues and public services have endeared them to their countrymen is a true and impartial history of their lives, and a faithful record of their acts. Monuments of stone, the sculptured marble, and the animated canvas, may preserve to their posterity, for a few ages, the *names* of our statesmen, and patriots, and heroes; but it requires the ever living and speaking pages of written history to perpetuate what is far more useful to mankind, and much more worthy to be held in everlasting remembrance—their great and noble deeds, and the examples of wisdom and virtue presented in their lives. While the pyramids and other monuments of antiquity throw but the faintest possible light upon the character and history of the people, by whom they were built, and have scarcely preserved even the names of those to whose memory, or the events to commemorate which they were erected, written history has made us familiar with all we know of the men and their history, as well as the manners and customs, not only of that, but a much earlier period.

Though the monument which the American people are now erecting, at the capital of the nation, to the memory of its founder and the Father of his country, is a tribute to GEORGE WASHINGTON, most grateful to the heart of every true American, and though it may stand long after the *Union* has ceased to exist, yet if there were no more lasting record of his services to his country, and his unrivaled virtues, than that pile of crumbling marble, a few ages hence it might be a disputed point, whether it was reared by "the great American rebel" as a monument at once of his successful treason and his overweaning ambition, for a shot-tower, or as a tomb for American kings. It is only by books that the history of nations and men can be permanently preserved from oblivion. What is true of Washington is equally true of every other distinguished American, and it is as much a duty to transmit to their posterity a correct account of their acts, for its benefit and example, as it is to exhibit our gratitude for their public services, by raising to their memories lofty monuments.

It has already been said, that this is the cheapest as well as the most enduring means of honoring the memories of national benefactors, and illustrating their virtues, as it is the only means of preserving a faithful record of their lives. Biographies of the great and good are, besides one of the most interesting and agreeable, one of the most useful studies. Certain it is, at all events, that no class of books is so eagerly read by the American public as the lives of our own distinguished patriots, statesmen, and generals. Our country is not so old yet, but it may almost be said, that the life of every citizen composes a part of its history—at least, that every American can recollect much of its history, from the day it began its struggle for an independent national existence. Biographies, therefore, of the men who have contributed most towards establishing that independence, and who have participated most actively and successfully in creating for us national character and importance, are sought for more with the interest and avidity that we exhibit for an account of the scenes, and events, and men, with which and with whom we are familiar in every-day life, than with that sober and philosophical spirit of investigation, which is shown for that class of biographical writings, which more exclusively and appropriately help to form the history of the past.

Great as this demand has been for a history of the lives of those who have distinguished themselves, either in the field, the cabinet, the forum, or the pulpit, it still seems to increase in proportion to the efforts made to supply it; and the Life of one distinguished man but creates a desire for that of another, and that again for still the third. And thus the

2

public appetite is increased indefinitely by what it feeds upon, like that of the inebriate for the intoxicating cup, after he has once tasted its contents. The American press has been prompt to take advantage of this determination in the public mind, to know the history of our public men, and it annually teems with hundreds and thousands of volumes, embracing every degree of merit, from the mere hasty compilation to those displaying profound research, philosophical enquiry, and striking originality of thought. They all, however, if they but exhibit a reasonable regard for the truth of history, and a fair share of skill and industry in the use of materials, find eager, or at least abundant, readers.

It is with the hope of contributing something towards satisfying the public desire for this kind of knowledge, but more with the view of erecting a "monument," though a very humble one, to commemorate the services of a great General, a pure Patriot, and a distinguished Statesman, and to supply what is believed to be a public want, that another Life of WILLIAM HENRY HARRISON has been undertaken. As large a space as he filled in the public eye for nearly half a century, important as were the services he rendered his country, great as were his virtues, and closely as his name is identified with the history of the government, it is a singular fact, that the whole history of his life has never yet been published in a single volume.

The half century between the entrance of General Harrison upon public life, in 1791, in defence of what . was then the wild western portion of our country, and his death in 1841, embraces almost the whole period of our existence as an independent nation. Commencing his career nearly cotemporaneously with the adoption of the constitution under which we now live, he grew up with the country, and lived to see the original thirteen States of the Union multiplied into twice that number; the population of the country increased from four to seventeen millions, and instead of a weak and distracted people, but recently emerged from a long and bloody war, and just entering upon the doubtful experiment of self-government, scarcely respected at home, and openly derided abroad—a great and flourishing republic, respected and feared by the nations of the earth, affording security to its own citizens, and a refuge and protection to the oppressed of every land.

We had, to be sure, as already stated, just emerged from that glorious struggle which ended in giving us a name amongst independent nations, and in permanently establishing the only free form of government that had then ever existed. But, though we had succeeded in asserting our freedom of a foreign yoke, we could yet scarcely claim to be really independent. The country had hardly begun to recover from the exhausting effects of the war of the Revolution, and it was still suffering the curse of poverty, and the moral as well as physical debility, produced by that long and relentless contest. The government was without credit, without resources, and almost literally bankrupt.

The north-western territory, with whose history the name of General Harrison is more closely interwoven than that of any other American, was then almost one unbroken wilderness. The first emigrants, to what is now the seat of empire of the American Union, planted themselves at the mouth of the Muskingum but three years before he forsook the pleasures and comforts of home and of civilized life, to aid in defending the infant settlements from the ruthless savages, who claimed undisputed possession of that vast region.

What a change was wrought in this wild region during the fifty years that began with his military services, at the age of nineteen, and ended with his elevation to the presidency of a great and powerful nation! The wild north-western territory of 1791, in 1841 embraced several of the most powerful States of the Union, holding in their hands the destinies of a mighty republic, scattered all over with populous cities, and flourishing villages, and seats of learning, manufactures, rail-roads, canals, and every other indication of the highest state of civilization. The crack of the hunter's rifle is now nowhere heard, and the once powerful savage nations, who then held undisputed dominion over those unbroken forests, have long since wholly disappeared. Civilization reigns supreme where, but little more than half a century ago, nothing was heard but the war-whoop of the Indian, or the howl of the beasts of prey. All this almost miraculous change General Harrison lived to witness, and to contribute his full share to bring about. What in other countries and in other ages of the world would have required many generations to accomplish was here wrought during the public life of a single man. In that brief half century we made a longer stride towards greatness and power than even ancient Rome, with all her boasted progress, did in ten centuries.*

All that is physically, intellectually, or politically essential to national strength and power, is undeniably to be found in the geographical position and extent of our territory, in the character of our people, and the form of our government; or rather, these undeniable advantages of position, character, and institutions, have already given us a higher rank in the scale of nations than any other people ever reached in many centuries. The United States is now only the second power in Christendom, and before the present generation has passed away, estimating the future by the past, it will no longer occupy even a secondary position. At least, nothing but our own folly, and those intestine commotions and feuds, which have ever been the rock upon which free governments have wrecked, can snatch from us the sceptre of empire which Providence seems to have destined for our country.

* See Appendix (A).

2 *

That we owe much of our present greatness and prosperity to the wisdom of our statesmen, and to the ability and patriotism of the men who have played the most conspicuous part in the affairs of the Republic, as well as to the virtue, intelligence, and native energy of the people, is a proposition too self-evident for argument. To the sages, patriots, and heroes of the revolution, undoubtedly belongs the chief glory of founding a great and free nation, and establishing a government, which affords the blessings of civil and religious liberty to so many millions of people, and which holds out in the future so much of hope and promise to the oppressed and suffering millions of other nations. But all their labors, and sacrifices, and sufferings would have been of little avail, if the duty of carrying out the principles, and of perfecting the designs, contemplated by the noble system of government they created, had fallen upon ambitious demagogues, or narrow-minded statesmen. Fortunately for us, for our posterity, and for the world, however, what was so well begun by them, has been as wisely carried out by their successors. The spirit of patriotism, with which the founders of our government were so eminently embued, was shared by those on whom devolved the task of perfecting their noble work.

This is especially true of General Harrison. Indeed, he inherited patriotism from one of the most devoted spirits who bequeathed to us, besides their

patriotism, the inestimable blessings of the free institutions, of whose great benefits we all now partake.
Stimulated by the example of the revolutionary patriot whose name he bore, and whose blood coursed in
his veins, possessed of superior talents, and occupying
a large field for usefulness and renown, he had the
power, and he did not fail to exert it, to contribute
largely to that eminence which is the envy of other
nations, and towards securing those privileges which
are our own greatest boast. Anything like a faithful
biography of one who, for so long a portion of our
national existence, performed so prominent a part in
public affairs, and filled so large a space in the public
eye, though destitute of great skill, and marked by
no very profound ability, cannot fail to be received
with favor, if with no very warm approval. The acts
of such a man are ever of deep interest to those, to
whose services he devoted his life, however clumsily
they may be recorded.

THE LIFE

OF

WILLIAM HENRY HARRISON.

CHAPTER I.

WILLIAM HENRY HARRISON was born at Berkley, Charles City County, in Virginia, February 9th, 1773, and was the third son of Benjamin Harrison, a leading patriot of the revolution, and one of the most prominent actors in the events that lead to that glorious struggle for independence. He was a descendant of Colonel John Harrison, a distinguished officer during the civil wars of England, and one of the judges who tried and condemned the ill-fated Charles, for which, and for his active participation in the affairs of the Commonwealth, he was himself tried and executed after the Restoration.

Benjamin Harrison, the father of William Henry, was, as has already been stated, one of the leading, most devoted, and most influential of the many noble patriots, whose virtues, and talents, and self-sacrificing love of country, the occasion called into requisition. He was amongst the first to embrace the cause of the people in the contest with Great Britain, which preceded the resort to arms, and one of the last who would have yielded one hair's breadth to her tyrannical and haughty demands. The patriot cause had no more active, uncompromising, and fearless defender and advocate, nor any whose services were more important, or whose counsels were wiser, than Benjamin Harrison's.

At the early age of twenty-one years, he was elected a member of the House of Burgesses of the Colony of Virginia, in which capacity he gave such signal evidence of ability and rising distinction as to attract the immediate attention of the English government. And in order to rid themselves of one who gave promise of becoming so powerful and dangerous an opponent of British aggression, and so eloquent and effective a champion of the people's rights, they attempted to purchase his friendship, or at least his silence, by offering him a place in the Executive Council of the colony, notwithstanding he had yet scarcely reached the age of manhood. Though this was a distinction corresponding in character with that of member of the English Privy Council, and presented decided advantages, and opened future prospects of promotion and distinction, that few so young, with the necessity before them of carving out their own fortunes, ever

possessed virtue and patriotism sufficient to resist,—
young Harrison indignantly and promptly rejected it.
He had already seen enough of the grasping disposition and the grinding oppression of the British government throughout the American colonies to understand what was to be expected by a tame submission,
or passive obedience, to these incipient measures of a
tyrannical prince. Between his own interest and advancement and the submission of his country on the
one hand, and the possible fate of a rebel or the independence of his country on the other, he did not
for a moment hesitate. He decided to take sides with
the people in the approaching struggle between them
and the mother country, and to share with them the
fortune, good or ill, of the unequal contest.

From the termination of his duties as a member
of the House of Burgesses, until the imposition of the
attempted obnoxious Stamp Act, little is recorded of
the life of Mr. Harrison, beyond his continued and
zealous resistance to every attempt, on the part of
England, to abridge the liberties of the colonies. But,
in 1764, he was appointed one of a committee to prepare a remonstrance against that odious Act, a measure at that time in contemplation by the British cabinet, and which soon after actually became a law. If
anything had yet been wanting to decide the future
course of Harrison and the other patriots of the different colonies, this adoption of the principle of *tax-
ation without representation* would have left them no
longer room for hesitation. From that time he con-

tinued to exert all the energies of his strong mind and
his great influence, in connection with the other noble
spirits of the day, towards the maintenance of that
civil, religious, and political liberty, for which they
had already suffered and sacrificed so much, and in
resisting the encroachments of a profligate government.

In 1774 he was elected a member from Virginia
to the Continental Congress, which assembled at Philadelphia, in September of that year. That Congress
being unwilling quite to close the door of reconciliation, made a last attempt to bring the parent government to a sense of justice, adopted a pacific and conciliatory address to the crown, proposing such conditions of settlement as a proper regard for their honor
and the rights of the colonies would permit. After
having adopted this measure of peace, it adjourned,
patiently and calmly to await the result of the appeal.

He was also elected a member of the Continental
Congress from Virginia, in 1775. Soon after the
meeting of this Congress, his brother-in-law, Peyton
Randolph, vacated the office of Speaker of Congress,
and the duty devolved upon it of electing a new
speaker. The members were divided in their preference of a successor to Mr. Randolph, between Mr.
Harrison and John Hancock, of Massachusetts. But
Mr. Harrison, with the magnanimity of a noble mind,
promptly waived his claims in favor of Mr. Hancock.
Upon modestly hesitating to accept the office after his
election, through distrust in his capacity and ability

for the proper discharge of its responsibilities, Harrison seized him in his athletic arms, and placed him in the presidential chair, exclaiming as he did so, "We will show mother Britain how little we care for her, by making a Massachusetts man our president, whom she has excluded from pardon by a public proclamation."

On the 4th of June of the same year, he was selected a member of a committee to place the American Colonies in a state of defence. The report of that committee, which was made after a month's earnest deliberation, formed the basis of the present militia system of the United States. In the following September he was also appointed a member of a committee, in connection with the immortal Washington, who devised and perfected a plan for the support of the provincial army, and was chairman of the committee through whose agency Lafayette and his companions were induced to enlist in the American cause, as well as a member of the Board of War.*

On the 10th of June 1776, Harrison called up the resolution, offered three days before by one of his colleagues, Richard Henry Lee, declaring "that the United Colonies are, and ought to be, free and independent States; that they are absolved from all allegiance to the British Crown, and that all political connection between them and the State of Great Britain is, and ought to be, totally dissolved." Though

* Sanderson's Lives of the Signers of the Declaration of Independence.

3

this bold proposition to dismember the British Empire was received with great anxiety by all, and was strongly opposed by some, yet in Harrison it found an eloquent, able, and unflinching advocate, and after two days of very warm debate was finally passed by a bare majority. In accordance with this resolution, a committee was appointed to prepare a Declaration of Independence. They reported a draft on the 28th of June, and on the 1st of July it was adopted in committee of the whole, nine States out of the thirteen having voted for it; and on the FOURTH OF JULY it was finally passed, and published to the world.

Amongst the signers to this "Great Charter" of American liberty is the name of Benjamin Harrison. To illustrate the fearless and cheerful character of the man, and to show in how much dread he stood of British vengeance while about to take a step by which he would forfeit his life if the colonists should prove unsuccessful, a curious anecdote is recorded of him. On signing the Declaration, he turned to Elbridge Gerry, —one of the delegates from Massachusetts, who was standing beside him, and who was as slender and thin as Harrison was vigorous and portly,—and remarked to him with a pleasant smile, "When the hanging-scene comes I shall have the advantage over you, for it will be all over with me in a minute, but you will be kicking in the air half an hour after I am gone."

Mr. Harrison remained in Congress until 1778, and continued to exert all his powers and influence in behalf of the cause of his struggling country.

At the end of that time he withdrew from Congress, but not from the cause he had so ardently espoused and so zealously defended. Soon after, he was elected a member of the House of Delegates of Virginia, and speaker of that body. He continued to discharge the duties of this new and responsible position until 1782. On the resignation of Governor Nelson, in that year, he was elected Governor of Virginia, and was re-elected until the constitution rendered him ineligible, all the time exerting his whole personal as well as political influence to further the independence of the United States. In 1791 he was again unanimously elected to the Legislature, but suddenly died the next day, at the age of sixty-five years, universally known and universally regretted by those for whom he had aided to establish a free country.

Such is a brief sketch of the father of William Henry Harrison, the subject of this biography. Springing from such patriot-stock, reared amid such scenes as he must have been familiar with, and seeing the example of such patriots as must have been his father's companions and associates, he must have been much less susceptible to good impressions than most other young Americans of that period, not to have imbibed much of that spirit of freedom and love of liberty that was diffused throughout all classes and conditions. But young Harrison was no such dull student, nor such unconcerned spectator, young as he was at the close of the revolutionary struggle, of the great events of those stirring times. It was from such men and such events that he received those principles of truth and justice, and that patriotic devotion to his country which so distinguished his after-life. Here was laid deep the foundation upon which was built the superstructure of greatness which he finally attained.

Notwithstanding Mr. Harrison left an ample fortune, it was still insufficient to render all his sons independent of their own mental resources. Devoting so much of his time and means to the service of the people, he knew that his fortune had become too much shattered to place them above the necessity of relying upon their own talents and energies, and therefore wisely resolved to leave them a richer inheritance than gold and lands—sound morals, correct principles, and a good education. With this determination in view, the education of young Harrison was committed to the care of Robert Morrison, his guardian, and one of the most illustrious patriots of the revolution ; and at an early age he was placed under the best teachers in the colony,—as his brothers had previously been— when he made such rapid progress, and gave such evidence of talent, as to afford his friends the most gratifying assurances of future distinction.

At the age of fourteen he left Hampden Sidney College, where he had remained for about a year, and entered an academy there of high standing in Southampton county, where he continued to prosecute his studies with great industry and success until his seventeenth year. At the end of this time, having thoroughly qualified himself for a commencement of the study of medicine, the profession for which he was designed, he was placed in the office of Dr. Leiber, of Richmond, a physician of considerable eminence and large practice in that city. In the spring of 1791, at the age of eighteen, he was sent to Philadelphia for the purpose of completing his medical studies under the eminent Dr. Richard Rush, a revolutionary compatriot of his father, and, like him, one of the signers of the Declaration of Independence. It was while on this journey that he heard of the sudden death of his father, an event which determined him to abandon the further prosecution of his medical studies, and that, consequently, exerted an all-important influence upon his future prospects and fortune.

Upon arriving in Philadelphia, he met with the warmest and most gratifying reception from Rush, Shippen, and Wistar, the most distinguished medical professors of that day, and from Morris and other friends and revolutionary associates of his father. But though some of these gentlemen exerted all their influence to dissuade Harrison from abandoning the further study of medicine, he firmly persisted in his purpose. His inclinations as to a profession lay quite in another direction, and having entered upon it against his wishes, he felt quite free, at his father's death, to adopt one more in harmony with his own feelings. His heart had long been set upon adopting the profession of arms, and his inclination was greatly strengthened by the disasters that had overtaken the

3 *

accomplished Harmar and the north-western army in
their contest with the Indians of that region. These
events removed whatever hesitation he might have
had upon his future plans, and he at once prepared
to unite his fortunes with his unfortunate countrymen.
His wishes were strongly opposed even by Mr. Morris, his guardian, as well as by many of his other influential friends; but it was of no avail.

Possessing as he did great family influence, being
connected with Peyton, Randolph, Colonel Bassett,
Mrs. Washington, and other eminent Virginians, besides possessing the warm personal friendship of
Washington, it was no difficult matter for Harrison
to find employment in the army. In the midst of
the excitement and anxiety that the misfortunes of
Harmar's command had excited, General Henry Lee,
of Virginia, proposed to him to take a commission in
the army. The proposition was cheerfully accepted
by him as infinitely more congenial to his habits, disposition, and taste, than the profession for which he
had been designed. But fearful that his wishes might
be thwarted by his connections if his intentions should
become known, it was arranged that General Lee
should solicit his commission without communicating
the matter to either Mr. Randolph or Mr. Morris.
The latter, however, happening to receive some intimation of what was going on, sent for Harrison, with
a view of attempting to dissuade him from his purpose. Suspecting the object of the summons, he
hastened to the War Office, at the head of which was

General Knox, and procured his commission as ensign in the first regiment of United States infantry. He then repaired to the house of Mr. Morris, who expressed his decided disapprobation at the step he had taken, but said he should offer no farther opposition to his wishes.

Having remained a few days longer with his friends in Philadelphia, most of which he was employed in the recruiting service, he proceeded to join his regiment at Fort Washington, now the site of Cincinnati, and arrived there shortly after the defeat of the brave but ill-fated General St. Clair. He found the army broken, dispirited, and suffering from the effect of its late disastrous defeat. Everything looked dark and discouraging, and was especially calculated to dampen the ardor of a young and inexperienced soldier. But this was not the effect the misfortune and misery of his countrymen had upon Harrison. So far from this being the case, it convinced him still more strongly of the necessity there existed for his services. Although, when he joined his corps, he was a mere stripling, being only in his nineteenth year of age, tall and thin in his person, and, to judge from his appearance merely, but poorly qualified for the hardships and privations that a soldier's life in the wilderness is necessarily exposed to, his ardor and enthusiasm was in nowise dampened by the forlorn and wretched condition of the army.

His condition, it must be confessed, was a most trying and perplexing one. St. Clair's army was re-

duced to a mere skeleton, and consisted of only a few
hundred of half starved and half naked troops. The
time for which the militia originally enlisted had expired, the detachment of the second regiment of
Regulars which was engaged in the action under St.
Clair was nearly annihilated, and the army was
wholly inadequate to maintain the line of posts that
had been erected for the protection of the north-
western settlers. This certainly was a most gloomy
prospect for one reared as Harrison had been, amidst
all the luxuries, delicacies, and comforts that wealth
could produce, and with a frame softened by these
influences, added to the enervating effects of a southern climate. So formidable were the obstacles presented to his consideration by a friend whom he met
at Fort Washington, and so lively a picture was presented to him of the sufferings he must endure, and
of the almost certain consequence upon him of the
habits of intemperance that prevailed at that time in
the army, that no man with less firmness of character
and purpose could have resisted the strong appeals
addressed to him. But notwithstanding these appeals, backed as they were by the strong remonstrances of his other friends, he remained firm to his
purpose, influenced partly by his romantic notion of
the attractive nature of the profession he had chosen,
and his pride, but principally by the strong sympathy
that the disasters of Harmar and St. Clair's armies
had aroused in his breast he inflexibly adhered to his
design.

The name of William Henry Harrison is so closely connected with the West, from the time he arrived at Fort Washington, with an ensign's commission in his pocket, to his election to the office of chief magistrate of a great nation, that a brief reference to its situation at that time, as well as to the events that immediately preceded his arrival there, may very appropriately be here introduced; and indeed this seems in some measure quite necessary to a full understanding of many of the incidents in his life that will be narrated.

CHAPTER II.

It has already been incidentally stated that the first emigrants to the north-west territory was made, in the spring of 1788, by a colony from New England, mostly officers and soldiers of the Revolution, who settled at the mouth of the Muskingum River, and laid out the town of Marietta.* The first object of the pioneers was to erect a block-house and stockade as a means of defence against Indian attacks, after which the town was surveyed, and village lots laid out west of the Muskingum River, adjoining Fort Harmar, then recently built and garrisoned by United States troops.

Many of these founders of Ohio were men of distinction, and had held high offices, both civil and military, during the revolutionary war. Amongst their number was General Israel Putnam, who by common consent, from the necessity of having some chief head in such a colony, was selected as their leader, a position for which his character and experience particularly fitted him. Soon after the settlement at Marietta was commenced there, other companies were formed, one of whom laid out the town of Columbia,

* Burnet's Notes.

at the mouth of the Little Miami; the second founded Cincinnati, in the fall of 1788; and the third settled at North Bend, the subsequent residence of General Harrison, with the intention of founding a magnificent city there. The city was actually laid out on a most extended scale, and named Symmes, after Judge Symmes, the leader of the party by whom it was settled.

Seven years after the settlement of Cincinnati, it was but a miserable village of log cabins, except fifteen rough, unfinished frame-houses, with stone chimnies. There was not then a single brick house in a place now the Queen of the West, and containing numerous elegant and costly public edifices and many thousands of inhabitants. At this period the population of the whole north-western territory was only fifteen thousand, and in 1800, five years after, but a fraction over forty-five thousand. When Harrison reached Cincinnati, to enter upon his military career, there was probably scarcely a log cabin there, much less frame and brick houses, and the population of the whole territory could not have been more than three or four thousand, and these scattered over an immense extent of country. As late as 1796, five years after Harrison reached Fort Washington, the emigrants in the territory were represented to be few in number, and were located in different and remote settlements, between which there was little or no intercourse.* The country they inhabited was wild and uncultivated, and

* Burnet's Notes.

was separated from the Atlantic inhabitants by rugged mountains, almost impenetrable forests and impassable rivers, with hardly the semblance of a road, bridge, ferry, or any other improvement for facilitating communication with the old Atlantic settlements. The adjoining regions on every side were all equally wild and uncultivated, without commerce or the means of creating it. The country contained neither shelter nor safety for civilized man.*

Previous to the treaty negotiated by General Wayne, in 1795, with all the Indian tribes north-west of the Ohio River, known as the treaty of Greenville, by which a permanent peace with all the various tribes was established, but few improvements had been made of any kind; and the settlers, besides the dangers and sufferings to which they were subjected by their almost constant collisions with their inveterate savage foes, endured all the privations that are incident to pioneers. Though a large portion of them had been accustomed to the comforts, and many of the luxuries of civilized life, previous to their emigration to the West, they were here deprived of all the luxuries, and some of the necessaries of life. But all these inconveniences and deprivations they submitted to, not only without murmuring, but even with cheerfulness. Before they determined on selecting a home in the wilderness they had schooled their minds for the new life before them, and to endure with patience and courage whatever might chance to them. They

* Burnet's Notes.

mostly sought the West, for the purpose of recovering from the ruin brought upon them by their sacrifices in the revolutionary struggle, and partly to hide themselves from the mortifications of poverty.

Little peace, however, was given them, or little chance afforded to amend their shattered fortunes. The war they had to wage with the north-western Indians was of equal duration, and little less bloody than that which had so recently ended in establishing their independence. During the revolutionary war many of the tribes took part with the British, and when peace was concluded, some of them refused to lay down their arms, but still continued their merciless ravages upon the new settlers.

In 1790, the various north-west tribes were supposed to consist of about fifteen thousand warriors, of whom five thousand were in open war with the United States, and of the others, several tribes were by no means friendly. They were also now much more formidable than the early English colonists found them, for they no longer depended on bows and arrows for defence and attack. Under seventy years of French tuition, and the experience of the revolutionary war, they had become skilled in the use of arms and had acquired considerable knowledge of discipline. In courage and the power of endurance they had no superiors in any country or age of the world, though in physical strength they were inferior to the descendants of Europeans.*

* Frost's Book of the Army.

4

A treaty of peace was concluded with the Creek Indians, who had for some time been at war with Georgia, at New York, in August, 1790, and overtures were made to the north-western Indians, but rejected. It became necessary, therefore, for vigorous preparations to be made to meet the threatened storm, on the part of the government. It was therefore resolved by Congress to increase the military force and to destroy the Miami villages. To carry out this object, the governor of the territory, General St. Clair, was authorized to call on Pennsylvania and Kentucky for fifteen hundred militia, to join General Harmar's regiment, consisting at that time of four hundred effective men. On the 15th of July, 1790, he addressed circular letters to the proper officers of Kentucky and Pennsylvania, requesting them to proceed to Fort Harmar, at the mouth of the Muskingum, as soon after the 3rd of September as possible. The militia from Kentucky arrived at Fort Washington, without even stopping at Muskingum, on the day designated, with the exception of about one hundred and fifty. The troops of Pennsylvania were less prompt in their movements; but they joined the army, however, soon after it had marched from Fort Washington.

The troops who composed General Harmar's army were in a wretched condition, many of them being substitutes hired by those who had been drafted. Others were too old and infirm to bear the fatigues of an active campaign, and they were nearly all awkward and undisciplined. A large portion of their arms were also unfit for use, many of their muskets and rifles being without locks, and there was a state of insubordination and a disregard of military rule that gave little promise of future success.* When the troops arrived at Fort Washington, the season was too far advanced to permit of any delay for drilling them, and on the 1st of October, General Harmar took up his march for the enemies country. During the campaign, several Indian villages were destroyed, but the expedition on the whole was a disastrous one to the American army. When these towns were burnt, and their inhabitants were dispersed, the chief object of the enterprise was accomplished. General Harmar, however, considered his work unfinished, and was therefore determined to bring on an engagement with them if possible. But instead of advancing himself with the main body of his army, and forgetful also of the character of his forces, Colonel Hardin was sent forward with a detachment of three hundred men, of whom only thirty were regulars, in pursuit of the enemy. He was attacked by a body of Indians, when the militia, under his command, were seized with a panic, and precipitately fled, and the regulars were nearly all cut off. Colonel Harden was then sent out with another detachment of three hundred and sixty men, who speedily encountered another large body of the savage foe. But after a long and bloody contest, in

* Burnet's Notes.

which Colonel Hardin lost nearly half his force, he was compelled to retreat and fall back on the main body of the army. General Harmar, after these and some other less disastrous reverses, returned to Fort Washington, by easy marches, pursued for some time by the Indians; but owing to the vigilance of the General, they were unable to harrass his movements or injure the troops during the march. Soon after, the militia were disbanded, and General Harmar resigned his command, and obtained a court martial, by which he was fully acquitted.

Though this expedition is generally considered to have been a failure, General Harmar claimed for it a different and more honorable name; and in justice to the character of a brave and patriotic officer, it ought to be stated that the movement was got up in great haste, and that the troops, with the exception of three hundred and fifty rank and file, were undisciplined, insubordinated, and barely equipped.* Notwithstanding these facts, the main object of the expedition, which was the destruction of the Miami villages, was accomplished; and those places of rendezvous, where British traders resorted to poison the minds of the Indians, and excite their hostility against the settlers, were broken up. Thus far the expedition was completely successful. But in his anxiety to inflict still further injury on the enemy, he suffered what, with very little stretch of the imagination, looks much like a very decided defeat.

* Burnet's Notes.

But whether General Harmar may have been victorious or defeated, the result of his expedition had very little effect in repressing the attacks of the Indians upon the American settlements. In the winter of 1790–1, one of those attacks, by a party of four or five hundred, and headed by the notorious Simon Girty, was made upon Dunlap's station at Coleraine; but it proved unsuccessful, as a similar one subsequently did upon Fort Jefferson. But it is not necessary to enumerate all the hostile movements and outrages of the Indians. Their depredations and incursions continued more or less frequent during the whole progress of the war, and small parties were constantly lurking in the neighborhood of the white settlements, watching for opportunities to plunder and murder the settlers. So frequent were these depredations, that the inhabitants were kept constantly on their guard against them. There was no safety for any one outside their defenses: no one retired to rest with any confidence of ever seeing another day. The pioneers literally slept on their arms for years; they felt that there was no security for their lives for a single day. This condition of affairs produced its natural consequences upon their characters. They became bold, daring, and almost reckless of life; or rather, they became so accustomed to danger, that they seemed to be almost indifferent to it. This was rather a necessity of their mode of life, however, than any real disregard for life. Their apparent disregard of life even led them to hazard it when nothing was to be gained

4 *

by the risk. All the elements of true courage they possessed in the highest degree: and it is not too much to say that, by the constant exposure to danger with which they were surrounded, and the hard necessities of the life they were compelled to lead, were planted the germ from which has sprung many of these distinguishing features of their descendants, known as "Western character."

So frequent were the depredations and murders of the Indians, even after General Harmar had destroyed their towns, that in January, 1791, President Washington felt called upon to submit to Congress a statement of the condition of the western country, and to recommend the measures which, in his opinion, it was necessary and proper to be taken for its defense and security. He urged upon Congress the duty of taking prompt and efficient measures for the protection of the white settlements against the relentless and cruel warfare that was carried on against them, and recommended another expedition against the Wabash Indians as the most effectual means of putting an end to these outrages.

In consequence of the President's statements, and his urgent recommendation for some speedy action, Congress was induced to authorize him to raise an army of three thousand men ; and in the meantime, for the purpose of affording immediate relief, they authorized him to raise a corps of Kentucky volunteers, with the view of destroying the towns on the Wabash. The execution of this latter duty was intrusted to General

Charles Scott, and proved entirely successful, several villages having been burnt, the growing corn cut up, a large amount of property destroyed, thirty-two warriors killed, and fifty-seven prisoners taken, and without the loss of a single man killed, and only four wounded, on the part of the Americans; and what is more to their honor, without having permitted a single act of cruelty to mark their conduct.*

Soon after the termination of this brilliant expedition another was fitted out, under the discretionary power given to Governor St. Clair, and the command of it intrusted to Colonel John Wilkinson, who had signalized himself during the campaign of General Scott. It consisted of five hundred and fifty well mounted and equipped Kentucky volunteers. Though all the objects designed by Colonel Wilkinson were not accomplished, it was nevertheless in the main successful, and great praise was awarded the whole detachment for their perseverance and bravery.

While these military operations were going on under General Scott and Colonel Wilkinson, the War Department was engaged in raising the army of three thousand men, authorized by Congress. Of this army Governor St. Clair was appointed commander, with the rank of Major-General; and on the 28th of January, 1791, he left Philadelphia for Fort Pitt, now Pittsburgh, where he arrived on the 16th of the ensuing April, and at Fort Washington on the 15th of May. The troops which had assembled at this lat-

* Burnet's Notes.

ter fort on the last of August, amounted to about two thousand men. On the 17th day of September they took up their line of march from Ludlow's station, five miles in advance of Fort Washington, where they had been encamped for four or five weeks waiting for reinforcements, under the command of General Butler, who was the second in command.

On the 3d of November, after a fatiguing and laborious march, the army arrived at a creek which proved to be a branch of the Wabash, in the vicinity of the Miami villages for the destruction of which the expedition had been undertaken. Here General St. Clair encamped on a commanding piece of ground, having this creek in front, intending to occupy that position until the first regiment, which had been sent back a few days before to bring up the provisions in the rear, and if possible to arrest three hundred militia who had deserted.* The next day he proposed to commence fortifying his position, for the purpose of rendering himself secure from the attack of the Indians while he should be compelled to wait for the absent regiment, and until he should be prepared for active operations.

But the ever-watchful enemy had prepared for him other and far less agreeable employment for that day. They had observed his movements, and had no intention of permitting him peaceably to retrench himself in their midst. On the morning of the 4th, accordingly, a short time before sunrise, the men having but just been dismissed from parade, a fierce at-

* Burnet's Notes.

tack was suddenly commenced on the militia posted in front, who immediately gave way and rushed into the camp in great confusion, throwing the army into the most hopeless disorder, the Indians following close upon their heels. The enemy, however, were checked for a few moments by the brisk fire of the first line; but this fire was returned with equal briskness and fatal effect, and in a few minutes extended to the second. In each case the fire was principally directed to the centre, where the artillery was posted, and from which the men were frequently driven with great slaughter.

Resort was had to the bayonet in this emergency, and Colonel Darke was ordered to make the charge with a part of the second line, an order that was executed with great spirit and courage. The Indians immediately gave way, and were driven back several hundred yards at the point of the bayonet. For want of a sufficient number of riflemen, however, to preserve the advantage thus gained, they soon renewed the attack, and the Americans were in turn compelled to give way. At the same instant, they entered the American camp on the left, having forced back the troops stationed at that point. Another attack was made by Major Clark and Major Butler with great success, and several afterwards with equal success.[*] They were attended, however, with heavy loss of men, and particularly of officers. In the charge made by the second regiment, Major Butler fell mortally wound-

[*] Burnet's Notes.

ed, and every officer of the regiment was killed or mortally wounded, except three. The artillery being silenced, and half of the troops slain, the General saw no other means of saving the remnant of his forces, than to make a retreat while it was yet in his power. To accomplish this object, a charge was made on the enemy, which was so far successful as to enable him to reach the road, when the militia commenced a hasty, and soon a disorderly retreat, followed by the United States troops, commanded by Major Clark, who covered their rear. The camp and artillery were entirely abandoned. The men threw away all their arms, accoutrements, &c., in their flight, even after the pursuit, which was continued about four miles, had ceased.*

The greatest confusion and panic prevailed amongst the militia, and but for the coolness and courage of the regular troops during the retreat, the army would have been nearly annihilated. All the horses of the General were killed in the action, and he was mounted on a broken-down pack-horse that could scarcely be forced out of a walk, so that it was impossible for him to get forward in person to command a halt, and orders dispatched by others were wholly disregarded. The rout continued as far as Fort Jefferson, which they had erected in their advance, and twenty-seven miles distance from the battle-ground, where they arrived about dark. The battle lasted about three hours, and during its continuance all the troops, with one exception, acted with great bravery.

* Burnet's Notes.

The loss of the Americans in officers was even more severe than in men, thirty-nine having been killed, and twenty-two badly wounded. The loss in men amounted, in killed and wounded, to about seven hundred. Although the army amounted to two thousand three hundred men, rank and file, when it took its march from Ludlow's station, there could not have been over fourteen hundred and fifty men engaged in the action, three hundred having deserted from Fort Jefferson, and one regiment of about five hundred and fifty having been ordered back to bring up the provisions. It has been stated, that even as many as six hundred and thirty were killed, and two hundred and sixty-three wounded. But, whether the loss of the Americans was as great as this, it was undoubtedly one of the most fatally bloody battles ever fought in this country, and the great disproportion of the wounded to the killed shows with what desperate bravery they fought, as well as the folly of further resistance.

The intelligence of this melancholy and disastrous defeat, and the inglorious termination of an expedition upon which such high hopes had been placed, fell like a thunderbolt upon the government, filling the whole country with consternation, and especially the now doubly exposed settlers of the North-west. It was not difficult to foresee, that such an overwhelming defeat of an army which had inspired such strong confidence of success, would result in the dissolution of all our treaties with the various Indian tribes of the North-west, and in the formation of a general

confederacy amongst them against the United States.
This confederacy was entered into not long after St.
Clair's defeat.

Such was the discouraging situation of affairs, and
such the alarm that everywhere prevailed when Ensign Harrison arrived at Fort Washington to enter
upon his military career; and it must be confessed,
that it presented but a dark and discouraging prospect, and but a barren field for reaping laurels, or
gratifying ambition. But it was the field upon which
he voluntarily entered, at the age of nineteen years,
not simply to gratify either ambition, or reap laurels,
but in obedience to the dictates of what could only
have been patriotic duty.

CHAPTER III.

ENSIGN Harrison arrived at Fort Washington and joined his regiment just in season to witness the return of the dispirited and care-worn fragments of General St. Clair's army, and entered with cheerfulness and zeal upon the trying and dangerous duties of his new position.

The period for which the militia had enlisted had expired, and the detachment of the second regiment of United States troops, which was in the army under St. Clair, was entirely cut up. The task, therefore, of maintaining the long line of posts that had been erected, of establishing new ones, and of affording convoys for provisions, devolved upon an inconsiderable body, composed of between three and four hundred of the first regiment, and the miserable remnant of General St. Clair's shattered army. In this condition of affairs, Harrison was appointed to take command of a detachment of twenty men who had been ordered to escort a number of pack-horses to Fort Hamilton. This duty, it can be very easily understood, was one attended with great danger and exposure to hardships of every kind. It would necessarily expose him to singular difficulties, distresses, and

5

privations, as well as to the hazard of being surprised and cut off by the Indians. He was compelled to lay out unsheltered, although it was the commencement of winter, exposed to the inclemency of the weather, to rain and snow, with no protection but such as his blanket afforded, and no security against the attacks of savages but his own vigilance. Yet, in spite of every obstacle, he accomplished the hazardous enterprise so entirely to the satisfaction of General St. Clair as to receive his public thanks for the fidelity and good conduct he displayed.

The fatal termination of the expeditions under General Harmar and General St. Clair enforced upon Congress the absolute necessity of adopting some more effectual means of repressing the Indians, and of putting an end to their barbarities. It was clear that a larger and more efficient and better disciplined force must be raised, and a more cautious system of operations pursued. Accordingly, an act of Congress was passed for raising a considerable army; and in April, 1792, General Anthony Wayne, who had rendered his name illustrious during the revolutionary struggle, was nominated by President Washington to take command of it, with the title of Major-General. In order to provide against the error which had mainly contributed to the defeat of both General Harmar and General St. Clair, which was conceded to be a want of discipline,—though a want of provision also contributed its full share to those misfortunes,—the whole of the year 1792, and the winter and spring of 1793, were employed in recruiting the army, and in instructing them in military discipline. The new troops were stationed under General Wayne, at first at Pittsburgh, and then upon the banks of the Ohio, a few miles below Cincinnati. Here Harrison joined the army in June, 1793, and was appointed second aid-de-camp to the commander-in-chief, having the year before been promoted to the rank of Lieutenant in the first regiment. The negotiations which had some time before been entered into with the Indians, having entirely failed and been broken off, the army took up their march for Greenville, in September. It consisted of four thousand five hundred effective regulars, including some troops of dragoons, and of an auxiliary force of two thousand mounted militia, under the command of General Scott. But an early frost setting in, rendered it advisable to go into winter quarters. Huts were therefore built, and a system of discipline, calculated to prepare the troops for the kind of warfare they were about to enter upon, was diligently put in practice. Here Harrison devoted himself exclusively to the study and practice of his profession, and with such success as to obtain the confidence of his commander and the attachment of his associates. The army continued in their encampment until near the last of June, 1794. Having then been joined by the mounted volunteers from Kentucky, arrangements were promptly made for entering upon the campaign, by advancing into the Indian country.

So perfect were the precautions taken by General Wayne to guard against embarrassments, that no delay nor difficulty attended his march. For the purpose of deceiving the enemy in regard to his movements, he made such demonstrations as induced them to expect he would advance in a different direction from the one he had selected. By this expedient, he arrived almost in sight of Auglaize, the great emporium of the enemy, and took possession of it on the 8th of August, without the loss of a single man. All their property fell into the hands of the Americans.

The enemy were collected at the foot of the Rapids in great force. They had been joined by the militia of Detroit and a portion of the regular army, and had selected an elevated plain at that place for the contest. General Wayne advanced upon the main body on the 20th of August, which was drawn up under the cover of a British fort. A battallion of mounted volunteers, commanded by Major Price, moved in front of the legion, who marched sufficiently in advance to give timely notice for the troops to form in case of an attack. When he had proceeded about five miles, so severe a fire was opened upon him by the enemy, secreted in grass and woods, as to cause him to fall back; but the troops soon after came in view of the enemy.

The Indians held a position admirably suited to their peculiar mode of warfare, being within a thick wood of felled trees that had been torn up by a hurricane. Their line was formed in three divisions, within supporting distance of each other, and extending two miles at right angles with the river. It was at once seen by the commanding General, that an enemy thus posted could not be successfully attacked with cavalry, and that a regular fire in line must prove equally unsuccessful. He therefore determined to commence the engagement by an attack at the point of the bayonet, and for this purpose he ordered his troops to march through the woods with trailed arms, and to drive the Indians from their covert with charged bayonets. As soon as they were forced from their hiding place, he directed a close fire to be opened upon them, followed by a brisk charge, so as to prevent them from loading a second time. The cavalry, commanded by Captain Campbell, and the mounted infantry, under Major-General Scott, were ordered to turn the flanks of the enemy by circuitous routes.

These various orders were all obeyed with such spirit and promptitude,—such was the impetuosity and immediate success of the charge made by the first line of infantry, however,—that the Indians, Canadian militia and volunteers, were driven from their coverts before the second line, and General Scott, with his mounted volunteers, could possibly reach their position in time for all of them to participate in the action. The enemy were driven for more than two miles through the woods, in the course of an hour, by a force not half as numerous as their own. They were estimated to be two thousand strong of fighting men, while the American troops, who actually parti-

5 *

cipated in the action, did not exceed nine hundred; yet the savages and their allies fled in all directions in the utmost confusion, leaving the Americans in full and undisturbed possession of the field of battle. The engagement was begun, and terminated within sight of the British Fort, and under the very muzzle of their guns. They did not deem it prudent, however, openly to interfere in behalf of those whom they had so industriously and insidiously incited to take up arms against the Americans.

The victory of the Americans was decisive and complete, and attended with the most important results. As the intelligence of it was received in different parts of the country, it created the liveliest feelings of joy. The bravery and good conduct of every officer belonging to the army, as well as that of the common soldiers, received the warmest approbation of the country, as well as the special commendation of the Commander-in-chief. This was the first general action in which Lieutenant Harrison was engaged, and General Wayne paid him the very highest compliment for the efficient aid he rendered him, and for his gallantry, courage, and zeal throughout the battle. He had been appointed by the General, to assist in forming the left wing of the regular troops, a task of extreme difficulty, owing to the thickness of the woods in which they were posted, but one that he accomplished with great skill and effect. In closing his official report of this battle, General Wayne does full justice to Harrison by declaring that he

" rendered the most essential services by communicating his orders in every direction, and by his bravery in exciting the troops to press for victory."

An incident characteristic of the coolness, intrepidity, and enthusiastic efforts on the field of battle, is related by one who was a participant in the action, and an eye-witness to the gallantry of Lieutenant Harrison. The old soldier, from whose interesting narrative of the victory at the Rapids the incident is taken, says that, when the battle was raging hottest, many in that wing of the army where he was, were beginning to falter and to think of a retreat. Just at the moment that this feeling began to become prevalent, a young lieutenant who was known as the confidential aid of old Mad Anthony, galloped up to the line, and called to the men with a voice that was heard above the roar of battle, "Onward, my brave fellows! the enemy are flying—one fire more, and the day is ours." This gallant young lieutenant, it will be understood, was William Henry Harrison.

By the official returns of the adjutant-general, it appears that the number of the Americans killed in the action, including those who subsequently died from their wounds, was thirty-nine, and the number of wounded one hundred. The killed and wounded of the enemy were estimated to be more than double that of the Americans. For some distance the woods were strewed with their dead bodies. A large number fell on the prairie in attempting to gain the river, or were shot while in the act of crossing it.

The army remained on the field of battle for three days, during which time the duty was assigned to Lieutenant Harrison, and three or four other officers, by General Wayne, of accompanying him in making a critical examination of the British fort, which was found to be a regular military work of great strength. This close and daring scrutiny, however, did not precisely accord with the notions Major Campbell, the commander of the fort, had formed of the dignity of his sovereign and his own importance, and led to a correspondence so characteristic, at least on the part of General Wayne, as to deserve being extracted.

On the 21st of August, the day after the battle of the Maumee, Major Campbell addressed the following supercilious note to General Wayne:

"Sir,—An army of the United States of America, said to be under your command, having taken post on the banks of the Miami, for upwards of the last twenty-four hours, almost within reach of the guns of this, being a post belonging to His Majesty, the King of Great Britain, occupied by His Majesty's troops, and which I have the honor to command, it becomes my duty to inform myself, as speedily as possible, in what light I am to view your making such near approaches to this garrison. I have no hesitation, on my part, to say that I know of no war existing between Great Britain and America."

To this insolent demand General Wayne thus replied under the same date: "Sir,—I have received your letter of this date, requiring from me the motives which have moved the army under my command to the position they at present occupy, far within the acknowledged jurisdiction of the United States of America.

"Without questioning the authority, or the propriety, Sir, of your interrogatories, I think I may, without breach of decorum, observe to you that were you entitled to an answer, the most full and satisfactory one was announced to you from the muzzles of my small-arms, yesterday morning, in the action against the hordes of savages in the vicinity of your post, which terminated gloriously to the American arms; but had it continued till the Indians, &c., were driven under the influence of the post and guns you mention, they would not have much impeded the progress of the victorious army under my command, as no such post was established at the commencement of the present war between the Indians and the United States."

On the next day, 22nd of August, Major Campbell again addressed General Wayne, and in equally swelling terms, under the judicious pretence of wishing to avoid so dreadful an alternative as commencing hostilities against him, he says: "Sir,—Although your letter of yesterday's date fully authorizes me to any act of hostility against the army of the United States of America in this neighborhood, under your command, yet, still anxious to prevent that dreadful decision, which, perhaps, is not intended to be appealed to, by either of our countries, I have forborn,

for these two days past, to resent the insults you have
offered the British flag, flying at this post, by approaching it within pistol shot of my works, not only
singly, but in numbers, with arms in their hands.
Neither is it my wish to wage war upon individuals.
But should you, after this, continue to approach my
post in the threatening manner you are at this moment doing, my indispensable duty to my king and
country, and the honor of my profession, will oblige
me to have recourse to those measures, which thousands of either nation may hereafter have cause to
regret, and which, I solemnly appeal to God, I have
used my utmost endeavor to arrest."

Nowise alarmed by this threatening epistle, General Wayne returned the following reply the same
day: "Sir,—In your letter of the 21st instant, you
declare, 'I have no hesitation, on my part, to say,
that I know of no war existing between Great Britain
and America.' I, on my part, declare the same, and
the only cause I have to entertain a contrary idea,
at this time, is the hostile act you are now in the
commission of, i. e. by recently taking post far within
the well-known and acknowledged limits of the United
States, and erecting a fortification in the heart of the
settlements of the Indian tribes, now at war with the
United States. This, Sir, seems to be an act of the
highest aggression, and destructive to the peace and
interest of the Union. Hence it becomes my duty to
desire, and I do hereby desire and demand, in the
name of the President of the United States, that you

immediately desist from any further act of hostility or aggression, by forbearing to fortify, and by withdrawing the troops, artillery, and stores, under your orders and direction, forthwith, and removing to the nearest post occupied by His Britannic Majesty's troops at the peace of 1783; and which you will be permitted to do unmolested by the troops under my command."

The following reply of Major Campbell to the above, and bearing the same date, closed this somewhat tart correspondence: "Sir,—I have the honor this moment to acknowledge the receipt of your letter, in answer to which I have only to say, that being placed here in the command of a British post, and acting in a military capacity only, I cannot enter into any discussion, either on the right or impropriety of my occupying my present position. These are matters that I conceive will be best left to the ambassadors of our different nations. Having said this much, permit me to inform you, that I certainly will not abandon this post at the summons of any person whatever, until I receive orders for that purpose from those I have the honor to serve under, or the fortune of war should oblige me. I must still adhere to the purport of my letter, this morning, to desire that your army, or individuals belonging to it, will not approach within reach of my cannon, without expecting the consequences attending it.

"Although I have said, in the former part of my letter, that my situation here is totally military, yet

let me add, Sir, that I am much deceived if His
Majesty, the King of Great Britain, had not a post
on this river at and prior to the period you mention."

General Wayne did not deem the longer continuance of this correspondence would lead to any profitable result, and the only reply he made to it, therefore, was by laying waste the country and destroying
everything of value within view of the fort, and indeed within reach of their guns. Major Campbell
thought it the safest policy not to put in execution
the threats he had made, by seeking to resent these
indignities. From the daring character of General
Wayne, it is more than probable that his object was
to provoke the British commander to fire upon him
as a pretext for attacking his fort.

Having accomplished the object of his expedition,
and so broken the power of the confederation as to
discourage the Indians from immediately risking
another battle, General Wayne returned to Grand-
Glaize, where he arrived on the 27th of August, and
commenced fortifying his position. But signal as his
victory was over the savages, the main body of the
enemy still remained in arms,—though it had deterred
many tribes from their cause,—while his own force
was gradually growing weaker. Apprehensions were
therefore entertained that a discovery of the real
condition of the American forces would prevent the
enemy from entering into any negotiations for peace,
and the utmost caution was observed to keep them
ignorant of their real strength. Preparations were

also made to recruit the army. In the meantime there was a growing anxiety on both sides for peace. The Indians had been stunned by the blow they had received from General Wayne, and prepared by it to listen to terms. A proposition was therefore made by General Wayne, to all the tribes at war with the United States, to assemble at Greenville, with the view of agreeing upon some terms of reconciliation. After some delay and much correspondence a general council was assembled at that place, which resulted in the "Treaty of Greenville," by which universal peace was once more restored to the Northwest. This treaty was concluded on the 3rd of August, 1795, and was signed by ten of the Indian tribes who had so long waged a relentless war upon the United States.

The efficient services rendered by Lieutenant Harrison during this whole campaign, and the evidence of courage, zeal, and ability he had so often given, inspired General Wayne with such confidence in his character as an officer of prudence and judgment, as well as of ability and courage, that soon after the peace of Greenville, he was entrusted with the important and responsible command of Fort Washington, though then only twenty-three years old. He had a short time previously been promoted to the rank of Captain, an honor he had well earned by his good conduct in the recent campaign.

While in command of Fort Washington, in the autumn of 1795, Captain Harrison was married to the

6

youngest daughter of Honorable John Cleves Symmes,
one of the judges of the north-west territory, and
the distinguished founder of the Miami settlement, a
lady who still survives him, and whose mental accomplishments and private virtues gave grace and dignity
to her character as a wife and a mother, in the domestic and social circle, or presiding over the presidential mansion. An anecdote is related, in connection
with his marriage to this lady, which illustrates a remarkable trait in Harrison's character, and which, as
much as any other, was the moving principle of his
life. It was his perfect reliance on his own energies
to work out his own fortune. On applying to Mr.
Symmes for permission to address his daughter, he
was asked what were his resources for maintaining a
wife. Placing his hand upon his sword, he replied,
with as much confidence as though he were pointing
to his coffers and his title-deeds, "This is my means
of support." Mr. Symmes was so much delighted
with the cool self-reliance and daring chivalry displayed by the young soldier, that he at once yielded
a cheerful assent to the proposal.

Captain Harrison remained in command of Fort
Washington, and had the management of the large
amount of public property collected at this post, until
the spring of 1798. Peace then being restored throughout the North-west, the object which principally
prompted him to enter the army, and there being no
further use for his services, he resigned his commission and retired to his farm, at North Bend, with

the intention thereafter of devoting his time to the peaceful and more congenial pursuits of agriculture. He was not permitted long to indulge his desire, however. Almost immediately after resigning his commission he was appointed, by President Adams, secretary of the north-west territory, in the place of Winthrop Sargeant, Esq., who had been promoted to the office of Governor of Mississippi, or south-western territory. By virtue of this office he was ex-officio Lieutenant Governor, and in the absence of Governor St. Clair from the territory, the executive duties of his office devolved upon him. These he discharged in a manner so satisfactory to the people as to win their universal approbation.

The population of the north-western territory having been ascertained to amount to five thousand white male inhabitants, the territory was entitled, as a matter of right, to enter upon the second grade of territorial government under the provisions of the ordinance of 1787, and to a delegate in Congress. Measures were therefore taken to organize a territorial government, and Jacob Burnnet, James Findlay, Harvy Vanderberg, Robert Oliver, and David Vance, were appointed by the President to be members of a legislative council. They were selected from amongst a list of ten persons that had previously been chosen and sent to the President by the first general assembly of the territory elected in pursuance of the proclamation by Governor St. Clair.

This first legislative assembly of the north-western territory, assembled at Cincinnati on the 16th day of September, 1799. Of the character of the members who composed it, and of the considerations which controlled the people in electing them, it has been said by one whose position and ability gave him the means of judging more correctly than any other man in the territory,* that in choosing members of the territorial legislature, the people in almost every instance selected the strongest and best men in their respective counties. Party influence was scarcely felt, and it may be said with confidence, that no legislature has been chosen under the State government, which contained a larger proportion of aged and intelligent men than were found in that body. Many of them, it is true, were unacquainted with the forms and practical duties of legislation, but they were strong minded, sensible men, acquainted with the wants and condition of the country, and could form correct opinions of the operation of any measure for their consideration.

Upon this legislature devolved the duty of electing a delegate to represent the territory in Congress. This subject had excited much attention from the moment the proclamation of the Governor ordering an election had been published. But before the legislature met, public opinion had settled down on William Henry Harrison, and Arthur St. Clair, jr., a son of Governor St. Clair, who were the only candidates for the office. On the 3rd of October the two branches

---

* Judge Jacob Burnnet of Cincinnati.—*Burnet's Notes.*

met in convention for the purpose of proceeding to an election, and Harrison was elected on the first ballot by a vote of twelve to ten. On being furnished with a certificate of his election, he resigned the office of secretary of the territory, and proceeded to Philadelphia, where Congress was then in session.

He at once took his seat and entered actively upon the discharge of the duties of his position. He did not retain it but a single session, however, but he succeeded in that brief period in securing several important advantages for his constituents. Amongst other beneficent measures of legislation which he induced Congress to adopt for their benefit, was a law authorizing the surveys of the public lands to be subdivided, and requiring them to be offered for sale in small lots. This important act he succeeded in getting through both branches of Congress in spite of the most determined opposition of interested speculators, who had till then monopolized the whole business of selling lands to the poorer class of settlers, at their own exorbitant prices. This act was hailed as the most beneficent measure that Congress had ever adopted for the benefit of the people of the West. It put it in the power of every industrious man, however poor he might be, to become a freeholder,—to cultivate his own domain and lay a foundation for the support and future comfort of his family.* To this single act, more than to any other one measure, is to be attributed the wonderfully rapid growth and un-

* Burnet's Notes.

6 *

precedented improvement and prosperity of the West.
By putting in the power of every man to become an
independent land owner, it started such a tide of
emigration westward as the world never before
witnessed.

Another act of great importance to the western
settler was a liberal extension of the time of payment
in behalf of those persons who had procured pre-
emption rights to lands they had previously bought of
Judge Symmes, lying beyond the limits of his patent,
and for which it was not in his power to make their
titles.   The effect of this indulgence to the class of
settlers for whose relief the act was passed, enabled
them to secure undisputed titles to their farms, and
ultimately to become wealthy men and enterprising
and useful citizens.

Soon after the adoption of these salutary measures, Mr. Harrison addressed a circular to the people
of the territory, setting forth the result of his labors
in their behalf.   In this circular he states, that
amongst the variety of subjects that engaged his attention, none appeared to him of so much importance
as the adoption of a system for the sale of public
lands, which would give more favorable terms to that
class of purchasers who are likely to become actual
settlers, than was offered by the existing laws upon
that subject.   Conformably to this idea, he procured
the passage of a resolution, at an early period, for
the appointment of a committee to take the matter
into consideration, and shortly after reported a bill

containing terms for the purchaser as favorable as could have been expected. This bill was adopted by the House without any material alteration; but in the Senate, amendments were introduced, obliging the purchaser to pay interest on the money for which a credit was given, from the date of the purchase, and directing that one-half of the land (instead of the whole, as was provided by the bill from the House of Representatives) should be sold in half sections of three hundred and twenty acres, and the other half in whole sections of six hundred and forty acres. All his efforts, aided by some of the ablest members of the lower House, at a conference for that purpose, were not sufficient to induce the Senate to recede from their amendments. But still he felt that there was great cause of congratulation to the people of the territory, as the bill still contained as favorable terms as could be procured. The law, he said, promised to be the foundation of a great increase to the population and wealth of the country, an anticipation that has been realized far beyond what he could have foreseen.

Though the minimum price of lands was still fixed at two dollars, the time for making payments was so extended as to put it in the power of every industrious man to comply with them, it being only necessary to pay one-fourth of the money in hand, and the balance at the end of two, three, and four years. The odious circumstance of forfeiture which was made the penalty of failing in the payments under the old law

was also entirely abolished, and the purchaser allowed
one year, after the last payment should become due,
to collect the money.   If the land should not then be
paid for, the balance of the money, after reimburs-
ing the government, was to be returned to the purchaser.

CHAPTER IV.

It was during this session of Congress, that the North-western Territory, then represented by Harrison, was divided, and the new Territory of Indiana established. Not long after the passage of the Act creating this territory, Mr. Harrison was appointed its first governor and superintendent of Indian affairs, by President Adams, and immediately thereupon resigned his seat in Congress, with the view of entering upon the duties of the office. The region embraced within the new territory included what now constitutes the States of Indiana, Illinois, Michigan, Wisconsin, and Iowa. All this vast region, now inhabited by a hardy, enterprising population of two millions and a half of people, contained at that time, a short half century ago, only a population of five thousand souls, thinly scattered through the vast wilderness of the territory, with only three white settlements of any note within its boundaries. One of these was Vincennes, the seat of government, a beautiful town situated on the Wabash, and originally settled by the French. The second was known as Clark's Grant, at the falls of the Ohio, nearly opposite Louisville; and the other, a French settlement on the Mississippi, not far from St. Louis, and more than two hundred miles from the seat of government.

The whole territory was inhabited by warlike tribes of Indians, and the whole country overrun by their hunting-parties. It can at once be imagined how dangerous and difficult was the duty of keeping open a communication between these distant settlements. Notwithstanding the treaty of Greenville, these various tribes retained all their restless hostility towards the United States. Their natural hatred, too, was constantly stimulated by unscrupulous British agents, who constantly misrepresented the policy of the American government, and by presents of liquor and merchandise, fomented their passions, and excited them to resist the further progress of the white settlers to the North-west. Frequent robberies and other outrages were committed, and sometimes whole families were murdered, and their cabins burnt to the ground. These outrages produced retaliations, and the consequence was greatly to increase the deadly hatred that existed between the Indians and Americans.

It was under these circumstances that Harrison was appointed Governor of Indiana Territory. Few situations could be more encouraging, or surrounded with more incidents less embarrassing, than those he was to encounter in the administration of its government. With such difficulties, as have been enumerated, to be encountered at the outset of his administration, it was no less a matter of duty than of necessity, that he should be clothed with the amplest independent powers. Understanding this, he was invested by the President with civil as well as military powers of the most important nature. Amongst the powers conferred upon him, were those, jointly with the judges, of the legislative functions of the territory, the appointment of all the civil officers within the territory, and all the military officers of a grade inferior in rank to that of general, commander-in-chief of the militia, —the absolute and uncontrolled power of pardoning all offenses,—sole commissioner of treaties with the Indians, with unlimited powers, and the power of confirming, at his option, all grants of lands.

These, it will be admitted, were dangerous powers to place in the hands of one man, and nothing would have justified the government in placing the lives, liberty, and property of the people of the territory almost literally, at the disposal of Governor Harrison, but an overruling necessity created by the peculiar condition of the territory, and the undoubting confidence with which his well-tried virtue and inflexible integrity had inspired all minds. It will be seen that the people had no voice whatever in the management of their affairs, and that their interests of every kind were at his disposal.

The able, faithful, and impartial discharge of such absolute, delicate, and responsible duties as Harrison was clothed with, it is obvious, required a rare combination of moral and intellectual qualities. Yet, delicate and responsible as they were, and as independent as he was, not only of the people, but even of

the government, the high honor belongs to him of
never having abused his great power by trampling on
the rights of the people, or consulting his own interests at the expense of the public good. Though he
held this office sixteen years, having been twice reap-
pointed by Jefferson, and once by Madison, no consideration of private gain or of personal ambition
ever severed him from the straight line of his duty,
and no charge either of tyranny or corruption rests
upon his memory. The legislative council and House
of Representatives of the territory, the officers of
the militia, the citizens of St. Louis, when their connection with Indiana was about to cease, and other
public and private bodies of the people, all bore the
amplest testimony to his disinterested integrity and
patriotic devotion to the welfare of the territory.

The liberal and enlightened policy he pursued
during his administration of the affairs of the territory contributed largely to the rapid settlement and
great improvement which commenced with his appointment, and which have continued with each increasing year to the present time, and which bid fair
to increase still more rapidly for many years to come.
The moderation, good sense, and disinterestedness with
which he exercised his almost unlimited powers won
for him the friendship and esteem of the whole people. In the management of the Indian affairs of the
territory he was equally straightforward and upright,
and received the warm approval of government for
the promptness, energy, and fidelity with which he
discharged its duties.

A leading and most important object with Governor Harrison was the conciliation of the warlike tribes of the territory. By his intimate acquaintance with the Indian character, his undaunted firmness, and the reputation he had established amongst them by his justice and impartiality, as by his uniform kindness of manner and considerate forbearance, he had inspired their confidence and respect. He was, therefore, better qualified to accomplish this purpose successfully than almost any other man in the Union. Owing to the unremitting efforts of British minions, however, he did not entirely succeed in allaying the suspicions and jealousies that these agents so constantly stimulated, though his influence was sufficiently strong over them to prevent any open outbreak until 1811.

In 1805, it being ascertained that the territory contained a sufficient population, it was advanced to the second grade of government, and a legislative council was selected by the President, and a House of Assembly chosen by the people. This measure, of course, deprived Governor Harrison of much of the power he had previously possessed, by transferring it from him to the people; but, democratic in his principles and feelings, it met his hearty concurrence and approbation.

On the 30th of April, 1803, the negotiations that had been instituted with France, for the purchase of Louisiana, were brought to a termination, by which the immense region of country, known as the ter-

7

ritory of Orleans, now the State of Louisiana, and the District of Louisiana, was ceded to the United States, in consideration of the sum of fifteen millions of dollars. In the following December, our government took possession of this vast region, and the boundaries of the ancient charters of the British government to her American colonies were thus realized. This large acquisition to our territorial possessions greatly enlarged the jurisdiction of Governor Harrison, and the laborious duties and responsibilities of his position were correspondingly increased.

In his first address to the territorial legislature, two years after the annexation of Louisiana, he took occasion to refer to that important measure at length. His message on this subject displayed so many unmistakable evidences of statesmanship, and such striking indications that the important bearing of that measure upon the future destiny of the country were fully understood by him, and contained withal so many noble and enlarged sentiments, that an extract from that part of it, referring particularly to this question, will be found of interest.

"Upon a careful review of our situation, it will be found that we have much cause of felicitation, whether it respects our enjoyment or our future prospects. An enlightened and generous policy has forever removed all cause of contention with our western neighbors. The mighty river which separates us from the Louisianians will never be stained with the blood of contending nations, but will be the bond of our union, and will convey upon its bosom, in the course of many thousand miles, the produce of our great and united empire. The astonished traveler will behold upon either bank a people governed by the same laws, pursuing the same objects, and warmed by the same love of liberty and science. And if, in the immense distance, a small point should present itself where other laws and other manners prevail, the contrast it will afford will serve the useful purpose of demonstrating the great superiority of a republican government, and how far the uncontrolled and unbiased industry of freemen excels the cautious and measured exertions of the subjects of despotic power.

The acquisition of Louisiana will form an important epoch in the history of our country. It has secured the happiness of millions, who will bless the moment of their emancipation and the generous policy which has secured to them the rights of men. To us it has produced immediate and important advantages. We are no longer apprehensive of waging an eternal war with the numerous and warlike tribes of aborigines that surround us, and perhaps being reduced to the dreadful alternative of exterminating them from the earth.

By cutting off their communication with every foreign power, and forcing them to procure from ourselves the arms and ammunition and such of the European manufactures as habit has to them renderd necessary, we have not only secured their entire dependence, but the means of ameliorating their condition, and of devoting to some useful and beneficial purpose the ardor and energy of mind which are now devoted to war and destruction. The policy of the United States with regard to the savages within their territories forms a striking contrast with the conduct of other civilized nations. The measures of the latter appear to have been well calculated for the effect which has produced the entire extirpation of the unhappy people whose country they have usurped. It is in the United States alone that safety and protection from every species of injury, and considerable sums of money have been appropriated, and agents employed, to humanize their minds, and instruct them in such arts of civilized life as they are capable of receiving.

To provide a substitute for the chase, from which they derive their support, and which from the extension of our settlements is daily becoming more precarious, has been considered a sacred duty. The humane and benevolent intentions of the government, however, will forever be defeated, unless effectual measures be devised to prevent the sale of ardent spirits to those unfortunate people. The law which has been passed by Congress for that purpose has been found entirely ineffectual, because its operation has been construed to relate to the Indian country exclusively. In calling your attention to this subject, gentlemen, I am persuaded that it is unnecessary to remind you that the article of compact makes it your duty to attend to it. The interest of your constituents, the interest of the miserable

Indians, and your own feelings, will urge you to take it into your most serious consideration and provide the remedy which is to save thousands of our fellow-creatures. So destructive has been the progress of intemperance, that whole villages have been swept away. A miserable remnant is all that remains to mark the names and situation of many numerous and warlike tribes.

In the energetic language of one of their orators, it is a dreadful conflagration which spreads misery and desolation through their country, and threatens the annihilation of the whole race. Is it then to be admitted as a political axiom that the neighborhood of a civilized nation is incompatible with the existence of savages? Are the blessings of our republican government only to be felt by ourselves? And are the natives of North America to experience the same fate with their brethren of the southern continent? It is with you, gentlemen, to divert from these children of nature the fate that hangs over them. Nor can I consider that the time will be considered misspent, which is devoted to an object which is so consistent with the spirit of christianity, and with the principles of republicanism.

During this time, and for two or three years before, events had been maturing with the various Indian tribes of the North-west which produced results that were the ultimate cause of the war of 1811. This was the formation of a general league amongst them. It was not finally consummated, however,

7 *

until the following year. Various causes had transpired to keep up their irritation against the Americans. The active agency of Britsh minions in producing this state of things has already been noticed.
Other causes and other agents were still more powerful. Most prominent amongst the latter of these
were the renowned Indian warrior and celebrated orator, Tecumthe, and his cunning and hypocritical
brother Olliwachica, better known as the prophet.
The genius of the one, and the prophetical character
of the other, gave them almost an unlimited influence
amongst the savage tribes, and drew around them
large numbers of reckless followers.

A confederacya mongst the tribes, along the whole
frontier against the United States, had been repeatedly attempted before, but never with success. By
the wisdom and prudence of Governor Harrison,
aided by the respect he had inspired amongst the
savages by his courage and high character for justice
and integrity, he had always succeeded in defeating
it. But against the influence of a chief of Tecumthe's
ability, tact, and daring, backed by the fanaticism
which had been created by the prophet's incantations,
he could not contend. Tecumthe was as wary and
sagacious in council as he was bold and impetuous in
war, and in the execution of his designs of whatever
character. He possessed a capacity for commander
of the very highest order. He was, besides, familiar
with every cause of grievance of every tribe in the
North-west—with all their passions and sympathies.

This knowledge he used, with the most consummate skill, to carry out his ambitious projects. Though his brother was remarkable for little else than his cunning, he proved a powerful auxiliary, by enlisting the superstition of the tribes which they wished to mould to their views. With the view of impressing upon them the sacred calling and character of the prophet, Tecumthe affected to treat him as a being of a superior order. By this cunning artifice he succeeded in inspiring a reverence for him, which gave him an immense influence.

One of the first acts of Tecumthe, after the union between the tribes was consummated, was to induce them to abstain from using the supplies furnished by the United States. As a necessary consequence of this refusal, illicit trading followed, frequently accompanied with fraud, violence, and sometimes murder, and hostile incursions soon followed. This state of things continued until war finally commenced. The treaty of Fort Wayne, negotiated by Governor Harrison in 1809, gave especial offense to the distinguished chief, it being considered a violation of the great principle of his confederacy, which was that the Indian lands were the common property of all the tribes, and could not be sold without their unanimous consent. He was absent when the treaty was ratified, and on his return not only indignantly refused to acknowledge it, but threatened to kill the chiefs who had signed it, declaring his determination to prevent the lands, ceded to the United States by it, from being surveyed or settled.

On being apprised of this determination, Governor Harrison sent a message to Tecumthe, informing him that any claims he might have to the lands which had been ceded by the treaty of Fort Wayne, were not affected by that treaty, and inviting him to visit Vincennes and exhibit his pretensions, and if they were found to be valid, the lands would be relinquished, or an ample compensation made for it. In accordance with this invitation he went to Vincennes, in the month of August 1810, attended by four hundred warriors, notwithstanding Harrison had restricted the number to thirty. The interview took place in front of the governor's house, when Tecumthe entered into a long and elaborate statement of his many supposed or real causes of grievance, and the grounds upon which he refused to acknowledge the validity of the treaty of Fort Wayne. He alleged that the Great Spirit had created this continent exclusively for the use of the Indians,—that the white man had no right to come here and take it from them,—that no part of it was given to any tribe, but that the whole was the common property of all the tribes, and that, therefore, any sale of lands, made without their unanimous consent, was not binding upon any.

Governor Harrison's reply to this artful address was firm, and at the same time conciliatory and moderate. He stated that the Indians, like the white people, were divided into different tribes or nations, and that the Great Spirit never intended that they should form but one nation, or he would not have taught them to speak different languages, and thus precluding them from understanding each other. He also informed them that, even if the ground taken by Tecumthe was sound as a general principle, the Shawanoees, who emigrated from Georgia, could have no claims to the land on the Wabash, which had been inhabited by the Miamies far beyond the memory of man. At this point of his address the governor took his seat, for the purpose of having what he had said interpreted to the different tribes present. No sooner had it been translated into Shawanoees, than Tecum the interrupted the interpreter by indignantly declaring that the statement of the governor was all *false!* At the same time he gave the signal to his warriors, who immediately seized their weapons and sprang to their feet, ready to do the further bidding of their chief, whatever it might be.

The occasion was one, it will readily be perceived, of the most imminent peril, and calling for the exercise of all the governor's coolness, courage, and presence of mind. Great as the danger evidently was, Harrison proved equal to it, and remained as calm and self-possessed as though it was but an ordinary occurrence. Although he was almost wholly unattended in the midst of four hundred fierce and desperate savages, fully armed and ready for any outrage, he at once rose from his seat and drew his sword, and boldly faced the threatened storm. A considerable number of the citizens of Vincennes were present, entirely unarmed, however, therefore compelled to remain

mere spectators of the exciting scene. But close at
hand was a guard, composed of a sergeant and twelve
men, who were promptly ordered to take a proper position for sustaining the governor in whatever emergency might arise. But Tecumthe thought it advisable
not to carry matters to extremities. The undaunted
bearing and unruffled self-possession of the man they
had to deal with, brought Tecumthe to his senses, and
made his savage train quail before his steady valor.

The treacherous and wily chief thought to have
taken the governor by surprise, and to have forced
from him his own terms. But he soon discovered his
error, and the mistaken estimate he had made of Harrison's character. Though taken by surprise, and
entirely at the mercy of the foe, he remained unmoved
and firm in his purpose, equally incapable of violence
and fear. The moral influence of his conduct under
the critical circumstances with which he was surrounded, was at once perceptible upon the savages, and
especially upon Tecumthe. He knew how to appre-
ciate such true courage, and it at once subdued him.
When Harrison saw that all immediate danger was
passed, he told Tecumthe that he was a bad man, and
that he would have no further intercourse with him,
and at once broke up the council, directing him to
leave his camp and return to his home.

Fearing that an attack might be made upon the
town, as the savages greatly outnumbered its citizens,
two companies of militia were brought in during the
night, and a considerable number the following day.

But the next morning Tecumthe sent for the interpreter, apologized for his bad faith, and requested that another conference might be granted him. The request was complied with by the governor, but he took good care not again to trust himself to the mercy of the treacherous enemy. He therefore took with him a number of his friends well-armed, and had the troops at his command ready for action. Another conference was accordingly held the same day, at which Tecumthe explained the cause of his conduct at the previous meeting. He alleged that it had been pursued in accordance with advice given him by white persons interested in getting up a war between the Indians and the United States, but that it was not his intention to offer any violence to Governor Harrison.

In reply to his speech, the governor inquired if he had any other claim to the lands ceded to the United States by the treaty of Fort Wayne, than such as he had stated at their interview. He answered that he had not; but stated during the conference, that, if the lands in question were not relinquished to the Indians, it was his determination to wage a war against the United States, and that he would never bury the hatchet, or cease his efforts, until he had united all the tribes upon the continent into one grand confederacy, and compelled the pale faces to acknowledge their rights, and do justice to the Indian race. The council here ended, and Tecumthe withdrew.

As soon as the council of Vincennes was dissolved, and the ambitious and sagacious chief discovered that he had nothing to hope from negotiation, he set about the great object of effecting his favorite object of a confederacy amongst all the North-American tribes. It was his policy to avoid hostility until this object should be accomplished, or the anticipated war between the United States and Great Britain should break out. The next year, in pursuance of this plan, he visited the southern Indians, leaving his brother in charge of a party at Tippecanoe. In reference to these efforts, Governor Harrison thus referred in his message to the Territorial Legislature of Indiana, at its next session:

"Presenting, as we do, a very extended frontier to numerous and warlike tribes of the aborigines, the state of our relations with them must always form an important and interesting feature in our local politics. It is with regret that I have to inform you, that the harmony and good understanding, which it is so much our interest to cultivate with these our neighbors, have, for some time past, experienced a considerable interruption, and that we have indeed been threatened with hostilities by a combination, formed under the auspices of a bold adventurer, who pretends to act under the immediate inspiration of the Deity. His character as a prophet, however, would not have given him any very dangerous influence, if he had not been assisted by the intrigues and advice of foreign agents and other disaffected persons, who have for years omitted no opportunity of counteracting the measures of the government with regard to the Indians, and filling their naturally jealous minds with suspicions of the justice and integrity of our views towards them.

"The circumstance which was laid hold of to encourage disaffection, on a late occasion, was the treaty made by me at Fort Wayne, in the autumn of the last year. Amongst the difficulties which were to be encountered to obtain those extinguishments of title, which have proved so beneficial to the treasury of the United States, and so necessary as the means of increasing the population of the territory, the most formidable was that of ascertaining the tribes which were to be admitted as parties to the treaties. The object was accordingly discussed in a long correspondence between the government and myself, and the principles which we finally adopted were made as liberal towards the Indians as a due regard for the interests of the United States would permit. Of the tribes which had formed the confederacy in the war which terminated by the peace of Greenville, some were residents upon the lands which were in possession of their forefathers at the time that the first settlements were made in America by white people, whilst others were emigrants from different parts of the country, and had no other claim to the tract they occupied, than what a few years' residence, by the tacit consent of the real owners, could give. Upon common and general principles, the transfer of the title of the former description would have been sufficient to vest in the purchaser the legal right to lands so situated. But in all its transactions with the Indians, our gov-

8

ernment has not been content with doing that which was just only. Its savage neighbors have on all occasions experienced its liberality and benevolence. Upon this principle, in several of the treaties which have been concluded, several tribes have been admitted to a participation of their benefits, who had no title to the land ceded, merely because they had been accustomed to hunt upon, and derive part of their support from them. For this reason, and to prevent the Miamies, who were the real owners of the land, from experiencing any ill effects from their resentment, the Delawares, Potowatamies, and Kickapoos, were made parties to the late treaty at Fort Wayne. No other tribe was admitted, because it never had been suggested that any other could plead even the title to use or occupancy of the lands, which at that time were conveyed to the United States.

"It was not until eight months after the conclusion of the treaty, and after his design of forming a combination against the United States had been discovered and defeated, that the pretensions of the prophet, in regard to the lands in question, were made known. A furious clamor was then raised by the foreign agents among us, and other disaffected persons, against the policy which had excluded from the treaty this great and influential character, as he is termed, and the doing so expressly attributed to the personal ill-will on the part of the negotiator. No such ill-will did in fact exist. I accuse myself, indeed, of an error in the patronage and support which I afforded him on his first arrival on the Wabash, before his hostility to the United States had been developed. But on no principle of propriety or policy could he have been made a party to the treaty. The personage, called the prophet, is not a chief of the tribe to which he belongs, but an outcast from it, rejected and hated by the real chiefs, the principal of whom was present at the treaty, and not only disclaimed on the part of his tribe any title to the lands ceded, but used his personal influence with the chiefs of other tribes to effect the cession.

"As soon as I was informed that his dissatisfaction of the treaty was assigned as the cause of the hostile attitude which the prophet had assumed, I sent to inform him, that whatever claims he might have to the lands which had been purchased for the United States, were not in the least affected by the purchase; that he might come forward and exhibit his pretensions, and if they were really found to be just or equitable, the lands would be restored, or an ample equivalent given for them. His brother was deputed and sent to me for that purpose; but far from being able to show any color of claim, either for himself, or any of his followers, his objections to the treaty were confined to the assertion, that all the lands upon the continent were the common property of all the tribes, and that no sale of any part of it could be valid without the consent of all. A proposition so extremely absurd, and which would forever prevent any further purchase of lands by the United

States, could receive no countenance from any friend of his country. He had, however, the insolence to declare, that by the acknowledgment of that principle alone could the effects of his resentment be avoided."

CHAPTER V.

But, though Tecumthe was only successful to a limited extent in his mission amongst the southern Indian tribes, he relaxed none of his efforts to organize his plans for prosecuting a war against the United States, nor abated any of his deep-rooted enmity against the white "intruders." Early in the year 1811, matters had assumed so serious an aspect, that it was foreseen that the cloud of war, which had darkened the western frontier, must shortly burst, and involve the country once more in all the horrors of this most direful curse to frontier-settlers. The hostile intentions and the fierce hatred of the Indians, which had been so long and so industriously kept alive and stimulated by British spies and agents, began to assume so bold and threatening an aspect, that Governor Harrison saw the necessity of making prompt and efficient preparations for the emergency. He therefore applied to President Monroe for authority to prepare for the approaching contest. In accordance with this request an armed force, consisting of Ohio, Kentucky, and Indiana militia, was immediately furnished him, but with the strictest orders not to resort to hostilities of any kind whatsoever, and to any degree, not indispensably necessary.

8 *

His situation was now of the most delicate and embarrassing character. Although furnished with means of defense, it was crippled with such rigid conditions as seemed to leave him but little discretion. Under these trying circumstances he consulted with Governor Howard, of Missouri, and Governor Edwards, of Illinois, who advised him to break up the prophet's town, where the Indians had already begun to assemble in large force. These outrages had become so frequent, in consequence of the impunity with which they had been suffered to carry on their depredations, that any longer forbearance would have been felt to be criminal indifference to the safety of the settlers. Surmounting every difficulty, he prepared to strike a blow that, if successful, would effectually crush the savage confederation, and put an end to all further apprehensions from them. When it had become known that an attack upon the prophet's town was resolved upon, a large number of gentlemen from Kentucky volunteered their services to Governor Harrison, amongst whom where the gallant Joseph H. Daviess, an eminent lawyer of great military ambition; Major-General Samuel Wells, who had already distinguished himself in Indian wars; Colonel Owen, also a distinguished officer in those wars; Colonel Keiger, and Messrs. Croghan, O'Fallan, and others, who afterwards distinguished themselves in the war with Great Britain, as well as at the battle of Tippecanoe. The governor's army was thus increased to about nine hundred effective men, consisting of regular troops and volunteer militia.

Having completed all his arrangements, he commenced his march up the Wabash, with the best disciplined force that had ever been brought into the field against the Indians, towards the last of September 1811. Acting under the express orders of the President, to present a last opportunity to the Indians for a reconciliation, before actually commencing hostilities, Governor Harrison came to a halt at Fort Harrison, within the limits of the United States, for the purpose of attempting to induce the prophet to deliver up the murderers, who had taken refuge amongst his men, and to deliver up the many horses that had been stolen from the white settlements. But his messengers were treated with contempt; and every proposition made to him was rejected; and to put an end to all hopes of accommodation, an attack was made upon the Americans, their sentinels fired upon, and one of them severely wounded. Finding it but lost time, therefore, to hold any further intercourse with the prophet, he determined to march upon the prophet's town as soon as his army, which had suffered severely from the use of fresh food, was in a condition for active service. On the 28th of October, Governor Harrison left Fort Harrison for the head-quarters of the prophet and his army.

Well skilled in the peculiar mode of Indian warfare, and profiting by his own early experience and the example of General Wayne, his march through the wild region to Tippecanoe was conducted with so much skill and caution, that he avoided all danger of an ambuscade or surprise from the enemy, and on the 6th of November arrived within six miles of the prophet's town in perfect safety. In accordance with the instructions of the President, Governor Harrison immediately sent a flag of truce to the prophet, to endeavor once more to open an ample negotiation with the hostile Indians. A pacific, but deceitful, reply was returned to this overture, professing the most friendly intentions, and agreeing to meet the governor the next day in council with his chiefs, with the view to settle definitely the terms of peace. Harrison knew too well the treacherous character of his artful antagonist, to allow himself to be deceived by his friendly professions, or lulled into any fancied security. He carefully selected the most eligible and defensible position for his encampment, and posted his troops in a hollow square, with his cavalry drawn up in rear of the front line. His men were ordered to lie on their arms all night, that they might be in readiness at a moment's warning for any sudden attack that might be made during the night. He also surrounded his entire camp with a chain of sentinels, placed at such a distance as to give timely notice of the approach of the enemy, and the officers were required to sleep with their clothes on, and their arms by their sides. The governor himself, too, was ready to mount his horse at any moment. All these careful preparations to guard against a surprise were necessary, not only from their well-known treacherous character, but from certain intimations Governor Harrison thought he discovered in the sinister conduct and proceedings of the prophet. He felt confident from these indications that an attack would be made upon his encampment before morning.

The order was given the army, in case of a night attack, for each corps to maintain its ground at all hazards until relieved. The dragoons were directed, in such a case, to parade dismounted with their swords on and their pistols in their belts, and thus to wait for orders. The guard for the night consisted of two companies of forty-two men and four non-commissioned officers, each under the command of a field officer.

The two columns of infantry occupied the front and rear of the position he had chosen, at the distance of about one hundred and fifty yards from each other on the left, and something more than half that distance on the right flank. These flanks were filled up, the first by two companies of mounted riflemen, amounting to about one hundred and twenty men, under the command of Major-General Wells, of the Kentucky militia, who served as a major; the other by Spencer's company of mounted riflemen, which amounted to eighty men. The front line was composed of one battalion of United States infantry, under the command of Major Floyd, flanked on the right by two companies of militia, and on the left by one company. The rear line was composed of one battalion of United States troops, under the command of Captain Baen, acting as major, and four companies of militia infantry, under Lieutenant-Colonel Decker. The regular troops of the line joined the mounted riflemen, under General Wells, on the left flank, and Colonel Decker's battalion formed with Spencer's company on the left.

Two troops of dragoons, amounting in the aggregate to sixty men, were encamped in the rear of the left flank, and Captain Parker's troop, which was larger than the other two, in the rear of the front line. The order of encampment varied but little from the above described, except when some peculiarity of the ground made it necessary. For a night attack the order of encampment was the order of battle, and each man slept immediately opposite his post in the line. In the formation of his troops, Governor Harrison used a single rank, or what is called Indian file, because in Indian warfare, where there is no shock to resist, experience has shown that one rank is nearly as efficient as two, and in that kind of warfare the extension of line is of the utmost importance. Raw troops also manœuvre with much more facility in single than in double ranks. In the evening he assembled all his field officers, and gave them the watchword and their instructions for the night.

On the morning of the 7th of November, Governor Harrison had risen at a quarter before four o'clock, with the intention of ordering out the men, and the signal for that purpose was on the point of being given. The orderly drummer had already been roused for the reveille. The morning was dark, in consequence of the moon being overshadowed with clouds. After four o'clock, General Wells, Colonel Owen, and Colonel Daviess had all risen and joined the governor, when the treacherous foe, notwithstanding their appointment to meet them in council the next morning, for the purpose of listening to terms of peace, had crept up so near the American lines as to hear the sentries challenged when relieved. It was their intention to rush upon them and kill them before they could fire. But one of the sentries discovered an Indian creeping towards him in the grass, and fired upon him. This was immediately followed by the Indian warwhoop, and a desperate attack upon the left of the American line.* But a single gun was fired by either the sentinel or guard in the direction of the attack. They made not the least resistance, but abandoned their officers and fled into the camp in the wildest confusion, and the first intimation the troops of that flank had of the attack was from the yells of the savages within a short distance of the line. But though thus taken by surprise, through the bad conduct of the sentinels and guard, they promptly rallied and behaved with the most distinguished gallantry. Many of them were not yet awake, but upon the first alarm they seized their arms and took their stations. Those who were more tardy met and contended with the enemy in the doors of their tents. The storm first fell upon Captain Barton's company of the fourth United States

* McAfee's History of the Late War.

regiment, and Captain Geiger's company of mounted riflemen, which formed the left angle of the rear line. The fire upon these companies was most galling and destructive, and they suffered severely before relief could be brought to them. Some few Indians passed into the encampment near the angle, and one or two even penetrated some distance before they were killed.

All the other companies were under arms and formed in line before the attack was commenced upon them. The camp fires, which afforded a partial light in the darkness of the morning, for the Indians to take a sure aim, and which was therefore more advantageous to them than to the American army, were at once extinguished. Under all these discouraging circumstances, so well calculated to produce a panic even amongst veteran soldiers, the governor's troops, although nineteen-twentieths of them had never before been in an action, exhibited the utmost coolness and bravery, and fought with a gallantry that entitled them to the highest honor. They took their places, too, with less noise and confusion than might have been expected from veteran troops in similar circumstances.

As soon as Governor Harrison could mount his horse, he rode to the angle where the attack commenced, and found that Captain Barton's company had suffered severely, and that Captain Geiger's was entirely broken. He immediately ordered Captain Cook's company, and the late Captain Wentworth's, under Lieutenant Peters, to be brought up from the centre of the rear line, where the ground was much more defensible, and formed across the angle in support of Barton's and Geiger's companies. He then discovered that a heavy fire was kept up on the left of the front line, where a small company of United States riflemen, armed however with muskets, were stationed, and also the companies of Captains Baen, Snelling, and Prescott, of the fourth regiment. Colonel Daviess immediately formed the dragoons in the rear of these companies. Understanding that the heaviest part of the fire proceeded from a small thicket, fifteen or twenty rods in front of them, Harrison directed him to dislodge them with a part of his dragoons. Unfortunately the order was not distinctly heard by his men, and but few of them accompanied him in the charge, amongst whom were Messrs. Mead and Sanders, who afterwards rendered signal service in the army of the United States. This enabled the enemy to avoid him in front and attack his flanks. The charge, therefore, though executed with great gallantry, was entirely unsuccessful, and the brave Colonel Daviess, as chivalrous an officer as ever drew a sword in his country's defence, fell mortally wounded. The Indians, however, were immediately dislodged from their advantageous position by Captain Snelling, at the head of his company.

In the course of a few minutes after the commencement of the attack, the fire extended along the left flank, the whole of the front, the right flank, and part of the rear line. Upon Spencer's mounted rifle-

9

men, and the right of Captain Warwick's, the latter of which was posted on the right of the rear line, the fire was excessively severe. Captain Spencer and his first and second lieutenant were killed, and Captain Warwick was mortally wounded. Their companies, however, still bravely maintained their posts, but Captain Spencer's Company had suffered so severely, and having originally too much ground to occupy, was reinforced with Captain Roble's company of riflemen. This company had been driven from their position, or ordered from it by mistake. They fought bravely, however, during the whole action, and especially after they had been ordered to the support of Spencer's company, having seventeen men killed in the battle.

The great object of Governor Harrison was to keep the lines entire and unbroken, in order to prevent the enemy from penetrating into the camp until daylight, when a general and more effectual charge could be made. With this view he had reinforced every part of the line as fast as it had become weakened, and as soon as the approach of morning was discovered, Captain Snelling's company, Captain Posey's, under Lieutenant Albright's, and Captain Scott's, were withdrawn from the front line, and Captain Wilson's from the rear line, and drawn up upon the left flank; and at the same time Captain Cook's and Captain Baen's companies, the former from the rear, and the latter from the front line, were ordered to reinforce the right flank, the governor foreseeing

that all the enemy would make their last efforts.
General Wells, who commanded on the left flank, not
knowing the intentions of the governor precisely, had
taken command of these companies, and with the aid
of some mounted dragoons, commanded by Captain
Park, and charged the enemy before the governor had
completed his arrangements for the attack. But the
charge was entirely successful, however, and the Indians were driven by him and the infantry, at the
point of the bayonet, and forced by the dragoons into
a marsh, where they could not be followed.

Captain Cook and Lieutenant Larebee had, in the
meantime, agreeably to the governor's orders, marched
their companies to the right flank, and formed them
under the fire of the enemy. Being then joined by
the riflemen of that flank, they had charged the Indians, killed a number, and put the rest to a precipitate flight. The decisive success of this charge, and
the overwhelming defeat of the enemy at this point,
terminated the battle, and gave the victory to the
American arms.

The whole of the infantry was under the command
of Colonel Boyd, who acted as Brigadier-General,
during the engagement, and formed a small brigade.
Throughout the action he manifested equal zeal and
bravery in carrying into execution the orders of Governor Harrison, in keeping the men at their posts and
stimulating their courage and exertions. His brigade,
Major Clark, and his aid-de-camp, Croghan, also rendered valuable service by their coolness and courage

during the battle. The conduct of Colonel Joseph Bartholomew, a brave officer, who commanded the militia infantry, under General Boyd—,Major G. R. C. Floyd, the senior of the fourth United States regiment who commanded the battalion of that regiment,—Colonel Decker, who commanded on the right of the rear line, and Major-General Wells of the fourth division of Kentucky militia,—all likewise received the highest praise from the commander-in-chief for their gallant conduct and good services. Indeed, every officer of the army, as well as the rank and file, discharged their whole duty like brave men and true soldiers. Several of the militia companies acted with the steady courage and firmness of veteran troops.

Amongst the killed, the brave and accomplished Colonel Joseph H. Daviess, of Kentucky, has already been mentioned, as have also Captains Spencer and Warwick, and Lieutenants McMahon and Berry, all accomplished and excellent officers. In addition to these, Colonel Abraham Owen, commandant of the eighteenth Kentucky regiment, who joined the army as a volunteer a few days before the action, and who acted as an aid to Governor Harrison during the battle, also fell early in the action. He was a noble-minded and brave man, and a much-esteemed citizen. Captain Baen, of the fourth United States regiment, another gallant officer and brave soldier, was killed, too, early in the action. In the death of these brave officers, the United States suffered a great loss, as they possessed the characteristics of true soldiers.

and displayed the most chivalrous devotion, even after they had been mortally wounded. Even after Captain Spencer had been shot through the head, he exhorted his men to fight on. Being next shot through both thighs, he still continued to encourage his men, and even requested to be taken back after he had been carried off the field, and when it was evident he had but a short time to live. Other similar acts of self-sacrificing devotion might be recorded.

The whole loss of the Americans, in killed, was sixty-two, and one hundred and twenty-six wounded. The Indians left thirty-eight, and their whole loss, in killed, was supposed to have been between fifty and sixty; but from their practice of carrying their dead off the field when in their power, their loss was unknown. The number of Indians engaged in the action were estimated at six hundred. Three weeks before the battle, the prophet was known to have had four hundred and fifty followers; and his force was daily augmented by the arrival of lawless adventurers. Not an American was taken prisoner during the action.

This was probably one of the most desperate battles ever fought with the Indians, and but for the caution and efficiency of Governor Harrison, might have terminated as fatally to the American army as the night attack upon General St. Clair, just twenty years before. Resolutions were passed by the legislatures of Kentucky and Indiana, highly complimentary to Governor Harrison and the officers and men

9 *

under his command. It established the reputation of
the commander-in-chief on the most solid and permanent basis, and created a feeling of confidence and
security amongst the frontier settlers that had never
before been experienced.*

An incident occurred the evening before this action admirably illustrative of his character for magnanimity. A negro, named Ben, who was attached
to his camp, deserted to the Indians, and entered into
a conspiracy to assassinate his old general as soon as
the attack upon him should commence. Being ap-
prehended while lurking about Governor Harrison's
marquee, waiting for an opportunity to execute his
bloody purpose, he was tried by a court-martial and
sentenced to be shot. The execution of the sentence
was delayed for a short time, in consequence of the
troops being engaged in fortifying the camp. In the
meantime, the negro was put into Indian stocks, that
is, a log split open, notches cut in it to fit the cul-
prit's legs, and when placed in it, firmly staked to the
ground. Governor Harrison interposed his authority
and pardoned the guilty wretch, assigning as a reason
for the undeserved act of clemency the following :—
"The fact was," said he, to a friend afterwards, " that
I began to pity him, and could not screw myself up
to the point of giving the fatal order. If he had
been out of my sight he would have been executed.
The poor wretch lay confined before my fire, his face
receiving the rain that occasionally fell, and his eyes

* Brackenridge's History of the Late War.

constantly turned upon me as if imploring mercy.   I could not withstand the appeal, and determined to give him another chance for his life.

Though the conduct of Governor Harrison, both preceding and during this action, has been as severely criticised as any battle ever fought between the Americans, whether Indians, English, or Mexicans, yet it has received the universal approval of military men, and of every man competent to form a correct judgment, who has given the subject any investigation. Amongst others who have paid the highest commendation to his prudence, judgment, and military genius, were most, if not all, the gallant officers who served under him on that occasion, especially the brave and gallant O'Fallan, Wells, General Scott, Major Larribee, and Captain Snelling. A defence of his conduct, therefore, would now be as out of place as it would be unnecessary. The charges were originally made by his personal enemies, and renewed with equal bitterness by his political opponents, when a candidate for a high office many years after, not to be permanently believed, but to effect a temporary disaffection. The battle has been fought over again many times, and, after years of altercation, public opinion has permanently settled the question in favor of the military skill, prudence, and caution, displayed by Governor Harrison. All the accusations of his personal enemies have been disproved, and those of his political opponents abandoned.

In regard to the personal bearing and gallant conduct of the commander-in-chief during the engagement, cotemporaneous testimony is equally clear, and public opinion equally decided.   Mutual confidence existed between him and his officers and soldiers to an extent rarely equaled.   Wherever his presence was required, there he was found urging on his troops by cheering words and his personal example.* He shared every danger and fatigue to which his army was exposed.   In the battle he was in more peril than any other officer, as he was personally known to every Indian, and exposed himself fearlessly on horseback at all points of attack during the whole engagement. Every important movement was made by his express order.†   His self-possession, too, was as remarkable as his courage and personal exertions throughout the battle. Though shrouded in almost impenetrable darkness almost the whole time the action lasted, he seemed to understand, as if by intuition, where his presence was most needed, and there he was sure to be found.

* Dawson's Life of Harrison.

† Hall's Memoirs of Harrison.

CHAPTER VI.

THE battle of Tippecanoe was but the precursor of more important events, and only preceded the war with Great Britain, which it had been long foreseen must soon burst upon the country,—as the shadow precedes the substance. If anything were required to inflame the country to a still higher pitch of exasperation than had been produced by the well-known efforts of British agents to incense the Indians against the United States, and their positive encouragement to repeated outrages, and the insolent aggressions of the British government on our commerce, it was found in this battle.   It was, indeed, the beginning of the war. There was little doubt that the Indians had previously received assurances of aid from Great Britain in case of hostilities, and they immediately began to threaten all the American border-population in the Michigan, Indiana, and Illinois Territories, as well as the north-western confines of New York, Pennsylvania, and Ohio.*   The whole of the western frontier was thrown into a state of alarm, and many of the inhabitants removed to the older settlements for safety.

* Monette's Valley of the Mississippi.

Besides the efforts of Great Britain to stir up a war amongst the Indians against us, and her impressment of American seamen, an affair between an American and English vessel of war, on the 16th of May, 1811, served greatly to complicate matters between the two governments. This was an attack upon the United States frigate President, Commodore Rogers, by the British ship-of-war Little Belt, commanded by Captain Brigham, under the following circumstances: When off Cape Henry, the President fell in with the Little Belt, and having come within speaking distance after a long chase, hailed her, and was hailed in turn as the only answer to Commodore Rogers. Believing himself entitled to the first answer, as he hailed first, he hailed a second time after a few seconds pause, and before he took the trumpet from his mouth, the Little Belt fired upon him, cutting off one of the main-top back-stays, and the ball entering the main-mast of the President, and immediately after another, and then three more in quick succession. Hereupon, being determined neither to be the aggressor, nor suffer the American flag to be insulted without impunity, he gave a general order to fire. In the course of ten minutes the Little Belt was entirely disabled and silenced, when Commodore Rogers ceased firing. From twenty to thirty of her men were killed or wounded. A court-martial, called to examine the conduct of Commodore Rogers, fully acquitted him of going beyond his most imperative duty to his country. But the affair was made a pretext, on the part of the Brit-

ish government, for still further outrages and insolence, and great efforts were made to prove that the
President was the aggressor, but without success.

The United States government was unwilling to
resort to war, as l ng as there was any hope of an
honorable adjustment, and therefore exhibited great
forbearance. But this very proper apprehension of
venturing upon the experiment of resorting to arms,
and involving the country in a long and bloody war,
was looked upon by Great Britain as proceeding from
pusillanimity rather than a humane desire to avoid
bloodshed, and subjected us to new insults. This state
of things could not and was not long to continue. The
public mind was gradually becoming not only prepared,
but anxious for the contest. Dreadful as the alternative
of war was, and anxious as the American government
and people were to avoid it, they nevertheless felt
that there were other things worse even than that,—
that a peace purchased at the price of dishonor was
far more to be deprecated. The first session of the
Twelfth Congress assembled under the influence of
this state of the popular feeling, and was protracted
to an unusual length by the exciting and momentous
question of peace or war.

On the 5th of June, 1812, President Madison laid
before Congress the correspondence between the
American Secretary of State and the British Minister
near this government, which seemed to preclude all
probability of a satisfactory adjustment.* At length,

* Breckenridge's Late War.

on the 18th of June, 1812, after having sat with closed
doors for seven days a declaration of war was declared against Great Britain. This act, terrible as it
was, received the approbation of the people, or a
large majority of them.*

After the battle of Tippecanoe, Governor Harrison proceeded, with his usual energy and regard for
the public interests, to put the frontier in a state of
defense, as well against the Indian incursions, as to be
prepared for the approaching war with England. He
held interviews with the governors of several of the
western States, at which plans of defense were arranged, measures taken for enrolling and equipping
troops and preparing munitions of war. From the
large military experience of Governor Harrison, as
well as from his well-known abilities and patriotism,
the most unlimited confidence was felt in his opinions
and judgment, and his advice in all matters relating
to the defenses of the country was never unheeded
by the people of the West.

When he had aided Governor Edwards, of Illinois, in putting the exposed portions of that State in a
posture of defense, he was invited by the distinguished General Charles Scott, of Kentucky, then
governor of the State, to hold a conference with him
in relation to the disposition of the Kentucky troops
who were destined to protect the western frontier.
He at once proceeded to Frankfort, where he was received with public honors, the governor appearing in

* See Appendix (B).

person at the head of the troops, amidst the firing of cannon and the acclamations of the people.*

The highest civil and military honors were paid him as a mark of respect for his distinguished public services and private virtues, and marks of the ardent attachment and unbounded confidence of the people whom he had so triumphantly defended from their savage enemy.

After having remained at Frankfort some days, he was actively engaged in maturing plans for the protection of the lives and property of the people of the West, and giving to that object all the energies of his active mind. During this visit to Kentucky, an incident occurred which may not be without sufficient interest to deserve recording:—One day Governor Harrison dined in Lexington, in company with a large party of gentlemen of that town and its vicinity, all of them ardent friends of the war. The conversation turning upon the north-western campaign, and the governor delivering his sentiments similar to those in a letter afterwards written, the company were so struck with the wisdom and justice of his remarks that he was urged to communicate them to the Secretary of War. To this he objected on the ground that it might be interfering with matters which were foreign to his own duty, and might not therefore be considered entirely free from presumption. But being assured by Mr. Clay, who was one of the party, and who was always alive to the true interests and honor of his country, that it

* Hall's Life of Harrison.

10

would be well received by the government, the letter was written.

In this letter, besides suggesting a system of operations, in which he displayed his intimate acquaintance with the military art as with the actual condition of affairs throughout the whole western country, he evinced the sagacity of a strong and penetrating mind by predicting events, which, unhappily for the country, had not been anticipated by the government.* He expressed his fear that the capture of Macinac would give the British and Indians arms, that the northern tribes would pour down in swarms upon Detroit, oblige General Hall to act entirely on the defensive, and meet, and perhaps overpower, the convoys and reinforcements that might be sent to him. He considered it highly probable that the large detachment which was destined for his relief, under Colonel Wells, would have to fight its way; but he expressed his confidence in their valor, though he was apprehensive that the event might be adverse to the Americans, and that Detroit might fall, and with it every hope of re-establishing our affairs in that quarter until the next year. These considerations induced him strongly to recommend the Secretary of War to send a reinforcement to General Hall.

War having now commenced in earnest, the eyes of the whole West were turned upon Governor Harrison as the ablest General, and one of the most popular men of the nation. Governor Scott, of Kentucky,

* Dawson's Life of Harrison.

had levied an armed force of five thousand militia, commanded by some of the most experienced officers of the State. Two thousand of these were designed for immediate service. No sooner had they learned their destination, than they expressed the most earnest desire to be placed under the command of Governor Harrison, and this feeling met a cordial response from the people of the entire State.

But there seemed to be an insuperable difficulty in the way of such an arrangement in the laws of Kentucky, which prohibited any other man than a citizen of the State from holding a command in her militia. In this dilemma, Governor Scott held a consultation with the venerable Isaac Shelby, Governor elect,— Henry Clay, then Speaker of the United States House of Representatives,— Thomas Todd, United States Judge,—and several other most distinguished individuals,—by whom it was unanimously decided that Governor Harrison should receive a brevet commission of Major-General, from the Governor of Kentucky, in the militia of that State.

This was a distinction as unusual as it was honorable, and did infinite credit to the judgment and foresight of the authorities and people of Kentucky. It was received with the most lively satisfaction by the people of the West, and inspired a feeling of confidence that nothing else, short of a defeat of the enemy, could have produced.

The appointment was made on the 25th of August, 1812, and shortly after he marched to the relief of the frontier posts, especially Fort Harrison, on the Wabash, and Fort Wayne, situated on the Miami of the lakes. He reached Cincinnati on the 27th of the same month. At the same time, Brigadier-General James Winchester, of the army of the United States, was recruiting at Lexington; and having written to the Secretary of War, that he intended to assume the command of that portion of the Kentucky troops then under General Payne, on their march to Detroit, he accordingly set off and overtook the detachment at Cincinnati. Upon General Harrison's arrival at that place, he informed General Winchester of the authority he had received to take the command of the Kentucky troops, but invited him to continue with the army. Winchester, however, immediately returned to Lexington. On the 28th, he wrote the letter to the Secretary of War, suggesting a plan of operations for the campaign, an incident in connection with which has already been noticed. On the 30th, he left Cincinnati, and joined his troops the next day about forty miles north of that city.

In the meantime, the Secretary of War, not having yet been advised of the appointment conferred upon Governor Harrison by the executive of Kentucky, had appointed General Winchester to take command of the same troops. The information of this appointment, in reality superseding Harrison, created no little excitement and disapprobation throughout the army; and the venerable Shelby at once wrote to the Department, remonstrating against the proceeding, as a measure not only very unpopular, but likely to prove highly injurious to the country. But General Harrison, ever ready to submit to the laws, and cheerfully to yield his own wishes and interests to the public good, at once wrote to General Winchester, from Piqua, where he arrived on the 3rd of September, to come to that place and assume the command of the detachment.

While waiting the arrival of General Winchester, however, he determined to destroy the Indian towns on the Wabash Elk Hart, and for that purpose General Wells led a body of troops to the latter place, and General Harrison himself headed those destined for the former. Both of these expeditions were successful; and after having destroyed several towns and large quantities of corn, they returned to Fort Wayne, where General Winchester shortly arrived and took command of that portion of the army designed for him. This consisted of the regiments of Colonels Allen, Lewis, and Scott, of the Kentucky troops,— Garrard's troops of cavalry, also of Kentucky,—and a part of the 17th United States regiment of infantry, under General Wells.

In consequence of this supersedure, General Harrison, on the 19th of September, took leave of the army in a very affectionate manner, and set out for the Indiana Territory, with a body of troops, to break the settlements of the savages. In his general order of that date, he closes by adding, that " if anything could soften the regret which the General feels at

10 *

parting with troops which have so entirely won his
confidence and affection, it is the circumstance of his
committing them to the charge of one of the heroes
of the glorious revolution, a man distinguished as
well for the services he has rendered the country as
for the possession of every qualification which constitutes the gentleman."

So great was the dissatisfaction created by the
appointment of Winchester over Harrison, that it required all his influence, as well as that of the officers
of the detachment, to recommend the soldiers to the
change. But the President of the United States,
seeing the confidence that the western people reposed
in General Harrison, and anticipating the dissatisfaction that his withdrawal from the army would produce, appointed him commander-in-chief of the whole
western department. On the 24th of September, he
received a letter from the War Department, in answer
to his communication from Cincinnati upon his appointment by the Governor of Kentucky, in which
the Secretary informing him that in taking command
of the north-western army, he had only anticipated
the wishes of the President. A few days after, he
received another dispatch, dated on the 17th day of
September, officially announcing to him his appointment to the command from which he had been dis-
placed.

A messenger was therefore dispatched for him,
and he accordingly returned and resumed the command of the army. The most extensive powers were

conferred upon General Harrison by the President. He was authorized to command all such means as might be practicable, to exercise his own discretion, and act in all cases according to his judgment. Such unlimited power had rarely before been conferred upon any American commander, and never perhaps, except upon Washington and Greene. General Harrison, however, had already proved himself worthy of such confidence, and shown that power in his hands never would be abused, and never used except for the public good, and to promote the designs of the government. In communicating the appointment of General Harrison to Congress, he expressed the most unlimited confidence in his skill and ability.

At the same time that this appointment conferred upon him powers of the most delicate kind, it also imposed upon him responsibilities, requiring the exercise of all his great talents. The services he was required to perform were, in the opinion of old, experienced able officers, the most extensive and arduous that were ever required of any commander in America. The endless number of posts and scattered settlements which he was obliged to maintain and protect, and numerous and scattered bands of Indians, while he was contending with difficulties almost insurmountable, in the main expedition against Malden, were sufficient to employ all the time and talents and resources of the greatest military genius at the head of a well-appointed army.*

* McAfee's History of the Last War.

The day before General Harrison returned to Fort Wayne to take upon himself once more the command of the army, General Winchester had marched for Fort Defiance on his way to the Rapids, the ultimate destination of the forces under his command. It consisted of a brigade of Kentucky militia, four hundred regulars, and a troop of horse—in all, about two thousand men. The march was one of great difficulty and embarrassment, and to facilitate it, each man was compelled to carry provisions for six days. General Harrison now proceeded in person to Fort St. Mary's, for the purpose of organizing the ultimate movements of the army. A detachment was ordered to proceed with supplies, under Major Jennings, to the Auglaize river.

The army was obliged to advance with great caution, in order to avoid surprise, in a country so highly favorable for Indian warfare. Owing to the closeness of the thicket, the troops were compelled to cut out a road as they proceeded, and were unable to proceed more than seven or eight miles a day. They took the precaution to send in advance a party of spies, and also an advance guard of about three hundred men. During the march, they fell in with a party of Indians, whom they succeeded in dislodging from an ambush they had formed for the Americans; and when near Fort Defiance, they found them encamped in great force within two miles of that fort. A messenger arrived on the 29th of September from Colonel Jennings, with the information that, on having discovered the British and Indians in possession of Fort Defiance, he had landed about forty miles above that place, and erected a blockhouse, where he was awaiting further orders. He was ordered to join the army with the provisions, and the order was promptly obeyed, and the exhausted army was once more recruited in body and spirits. In the meantime the British and Indians precipitately abandoned the fort, and the American army took immediate possession of it.

While at this fort, news was received that General Harrison had been appointed to the command of the north-western army. This intelligence was received with the liveliest satisfaction by the soldiers, and went far to reconcile them to the severe hardships they were called upon to endure. In announcing the appointment, he expressed his earnest hope that General Winchester might remain with the army. On the 3rd of October he yielded up his command to General Harrison. In his general order of that date, relinquishing the command of the army to his successor, he expressed a high opinion of the great military skill and reputation of General Harrison, and declared his belief that his appointment would be hailed with universal satisfaction. As General Winchester preferred the service in the north-west to that on the Niagara frontier, General Harrison immediately appointed him to the left wing of the army.*

The charge has been preferred against General

* Sketches of the civil and military services of General Harrison.

Harrison, by the friends of General Winchester, of having procured his appointment to the command of the north-western army by unworthy means. But there was not the slightest ground for the accusation to rest upon, and it has been so triumphantly disproved by gentlemen of the highest character and the amplest means of information, that it left no impression on the public mind injurious, in the slightest degree, to the reputation of General Harrison.

General Harrison left Fort Defiance on the 4th of October, and returned to Fort St. Mary's, with the view of organizing and bringing up the centre of the army. General Tupper was ordered to proceed immediately to the Rapids, by the commander-in-chief, with about one thousand men, for the purpose of driving the enemy from that place. But the expedition proved a failure, in consequence of the delays caused by the damaged state of the ammunition and the requisite time necessary to prepare the provisions for the troops. They were also totally insensible to everything like military discipline or subordination. So literally true was this, that upon Major Bush being ordered to disperse a body of Indians lurking in the vicinity, the whole camp broke up in bodies of twenty and thirty, and joined in the chase without the slightest regard for order or even common prudence. If they had been attacked, they must inevitably have been cut to pieces.

General Tupper was, immediately after this occurrence, ordered to go in pursuit of the Indians, and,

if possible, to ascertain their strength.   But he represented to General Winchester the disorganized
state of his troops, and requested that the order might
be countermanded.   The commanding general, however, peremptorily persisted in it, and General Tupper
attempted to execute it.   But this resulted in a misunderstanding between the two officers, that led to
the appointment of Colonel Allen to supersede General Tupper, and the consequent refusal of the Ohio
troops to submit to the command of the former.   The
expedition, therefore, was broken up and abandoned.

Nothing more could now be done until the arrival
of the other wing of the army, either against the
Rapids or Detroit.   General Tupper having returned
to Urbana, after his misunderstanding with General
Winchester, with his mounted men, was dispatched
with the division of the centre, consisting of a brigade of Ohio volunteers and militia, and a regiment
of regulars, to Fort M'Arthur, while the right wing,
consisting of a Pennsylvania and a Virginia brigade,
was ordered to Sandusky.*   On his arrival there, he
organized another expedition to proceed against the
Rapids, consisting of about six hundred men.   The
expedition marched on the 10th of October, and arrived within thirteen miles of the Rapids on the 13th,
which was still in the hands of the British and Indians.   General Tupper marched immediately for the
fort, intending to cross the river and attack it at
once.   But he found the river too rapid to effect this,

* Brackenridge's History of the War.

and therefore attempted to induce the enemy to cross by resorting to a stratagem. This was only partially successful, though a considerable number finally crossed over, and a brisk skirmish ensued, which finally resulted unfavorably to the Americans, and they were compelled hastily to return to Fort M'Arthur.

After the failure of General Tupper's attempt to cross the river, he dispatched an express to General Winchester for reinforcements, and upon the arrival of his second express he found that a detachment of four hundred men had been sent out under the command of Colonel Lewis, to march to his support. On the 15th, this reinforcement proceeded on their march, and during the night Ensign Charles S. Todd, afterwards minister to Russia, under General Taylor's administration, was sent with a few men to apprise General Tupper of his approach. But he found General Tupper's camp evacuated. He therefore returned, and Colonel Lewis at once retreated to General Winchester's camp. Though this expedition was in some degree a failure, it was of service in one particular, which was in inducing the detachment of British and Indians to fall back to the river Raisin, and to abandon the design of removing the corn from the farms that had been abandoned at the Rapids, the principal object of their expedition to that place.*

Events of considerable importance, meanwhile, were transpiring further West. A large army had

* M'Afee's History of the late War.

assembled at Vincennes, and early in October proceeded to Fort Harrison, under the command of General Hopkins, and sanctioned by Governor Shelby, of
Kentucky. This army reached Fort Harrison about
the 10th of October, and proceeded soon after against
the Kickapoos and Peoria towns. But after a march
of only four days, evident signs of discontent began
to exhibit themselves, and every man seemed to feel
at liberty to act upon his own responsibility, and the
army became little more than an ungovernable mob.
They demanded to be led back, and everything was
in disorder; and after every effort on the part of
General Hopkins to awaken in his men some little
sense of duty had failed, the crowd returned to Fort
Harrison, against his orders, and left him to bring up
the rear. Not long after, he led another expedition
against the towns at the head of the Wabash, with
more success, which he destroyed. The principal
camp of the Indians was also discovered, which they
were compelled to evacuate, though they occupied an
exceeding strong position.

Some time previous to the termination of this expedition, an attack was made on Fort Harrison, then
in the command of Captain Zachary Taylor, afterwards President of the United States. This was a
rude and weak stockade, garrisoned by only fifty
men, most of whom, like Captain Taylor himself, were
worn down and disabled by their long and severe service. Almost in the midst of an enemy's country,
surrounded on all sides by a sleepless savage foe, and

11

kept constantly on the alert, night and day, for weeks together, Taylor and his men had nearly sunk under the fatigue and labor they had been compelled to endure.

While in this wretched condition, with scarcely a dozen men fit for service, he was attacked on the night of September 5th, after an ineffectual attempt to get possession of the fort by stratagem, by a force of four hundred and fifty Indians. The attack was commenced about eleven o'clock at night, amidst the excitement and confusion occasioned by the burning of the lower blockhouse, containing the property of the contractor, which they had previously fired. The Indians, confident of victory, had completely surrounded the garrison, and commenced their fire upon all sides, simultaneously with the firing of the blockhouse. Captain Taylor, however, was prepared for the attack, and was neither dismayed by that nor the even more dangerous enemy they had called to their aid. He calmly gave his orders for extinguishing the flames, but for a long time all efforts were fruitless. The fire communicated with the roof, in spite of all their exertions to check it. Finally, however, by his great presence of mind, and the well-directed efforts of his men, the flames were subdued.

Having extinguished the fire, and erected a temporary breast-work, the fire of the enemy was returned with redoubled vigor during the whole night, and with such success that, at six o'clock in the morning, the Indians gave up the contest in despair, and withdrew their forces. In this gallant defense, Captain Taylor lost only two men killed, and two wounded. The Indians must have suffered severely: but they were in sufficient force to take off all their killed and wounded. Soon after, he was reinforced by Colonel Russell, with several companies of rangers and Indiana volunteers. In consequence of his gallant conduct on this occasion, he was promoted to the rank of major.

Soon after Colonel Russell had relieved Fort Harrison, he undertook an expedition against the Peoria towns, and destroyed a populous village, and killed twenty Indians. About the same time, Lieutenant Campbell marched with a small detachment against the towns on the Mississinewa River, a branch of the Wabash, which resulted in defeating a body of Indians, by whom they were furiously attacked, killing fifty of their warriors and taking thirty prisoners. They also destroyed several of their villages, in various expeditions of less importance, but in which the militia of Indiana, Illinois, and Missouri Territories greatly distinguished themselves. During these various expeditions, the Indians had been so harassed, and their means of subsistence so effectually cut off, that they began seriously to doubt whether they had acted wisely in taking up arms against the United States, and even to repent having done so. The only prospect before them now was to be compelled to remove to distant British settlements.

CHAPTER VII.

THOUGH the season had now considerably advanced, and the weather had become extremely cold, General Harrison did not retire into winter quarters, nor abandon any of his vigilance. When the troops composing the left wing of the army had completed Fort Winchester, they were directed by him, early in December, to proceed to the Rapids as soon as provisions for a few weeks could be provided. And on the 12th of the same month, he wrote to the Secretary of War, that if there were not some important political reason urging an immediate attempt to capture Malden, and recover Michigan Territory, he would suggest that an effort first be made to obtain command of Lake Erie, and that Malden, Detroit, and Mackinaw will then fall into the hands of the Americans, almost as a matter of course. The necessity of securing the naval ascendancy of Lake Erie had been forcibly pointed out to the government by him as early as the year 1809. He established his head quarters at Upper Sandusky, on the 20th of this month. Whilst here, he received a communication from Lieutenant-Colonel Campbell, giving him official information of the result of his expedition to the Mississinnewa River, and immediately started for Chillicothe to consult with Governor Meigs about another expedition against the Indians in the same quarter.

General Harrison's plan of operations for the campaign was to occupy the Miami Rapids, and to deposit as much provision there as it was possible for him to procure, and to move from thence with a choice detachment of the army, and with as much provision, artillery, and ammunition as the means of transportation would allow. His design also was to make a demonstration from this point towards Detroit, and by a sudden passage of the straits of Detroit upon the ice, an actual investiture of Malden. Should his offensive operations be suspended until spring, he strongly advised, as the most effectual as well as the cheapest plan, would be to obtain the command of the lake. This being once effected, he believed that every difficulty would be removed, and that an army of four thousand men landed on the north side of the lake, below Malden, would soon reduce that place, retake Detroit, and, with the aid of the fleet, proceed down the lake to co-operate with the army from Niagara.

On General Harrison's arrival at Sandusky, he expected to be met by an express from General Winchester, with information of his advance to the Rapids, in conformity with advice that had previously been given him. But as no such information had arrived, he dispatched Ensign Todd to Winchester's camp, on

11*

the Miami, below Fort Defiance. He performed the journey with great secrecy and dispatch, having completely eluded all the scouts of the enemy. He was instructed to communicate to General Winchester the following directions and plans from the commander-in-chief: that as soon as he had accumulated provisions for twenty days, to advance to the Rapids, where he was to commence the building of huts to induce the enemy to believe that he was going into winter quarters there, and to construct sleds for the main expedition against Malden. He was to impress it upon his men, however, that they were for transporting provisions from the interior. The different lines of the army were to be concentrated at that place, and a choice detachment from the whole would then be marched rapidly upon Malden. In the meantime he was to occupy the Rapids, for the purpose of securing the provisions and stores forwarded from the other wings of the army.

A tolerable supply of provisions having been received, General Winchester took up his march for the Rapids, and at the same time Leslie Combs, a volunteer in the army, was sent to inform the commander-in-chief of the movements. While on his march to the Rapids, General Winchester received a dispatch from General Harrison, recommending him to abandon the movement to the Rapids and fall back to Fort Jennings. The recommendation, however, was disregarded, and on the 10th of January the detachment reached the Rapids. A despatch was sent to the commander-in-chief of the arrival of the troops at that place, but was not received by him, in consequence of various delays, until his arrival himself at the Rapids. On the 12th another despatch was forwarded to General Harrison, advising him that no reliance could be placed on retaining the Kentucky troops after the expiration of their term of service in February. This was received by the commander-in-chief on the 16th, and was the first information he had of the arrival of General Winchester at the Rapids.

Information was received by General Winchester, on the 13th of January, that the Indians were threatening an attack upon the settlement on the River Raisin, and asking assistance from him. In accordance with this request, Colonel Lewis was dispatched by him on the 17th, at the head of six hundred troops, to protect Frenchtown on that river, and at once moved down to Presque Isle, a distance of twenty miles from the Rapids. Here he received information which should have induced him to request a reinforcement; but, instead of this, he pushed on his command to Frenchtown, where he arrived the next day. On the same day he attacked the combined forces of British and Indians, and defeated them with great loss, having driven them for two miles at the point of the bayonet.

News of this victory was sent to General Winchester on the night after the engagement, who at once marched to the Rapids, and reached Frenchtown on

the night of the 20th.   He encamped on the right of
Lewis' detachment, which was defended by some garden pickets.   The reinforcement was commanded by
General Wells.   General Winchester himself established his head-quarters at a house on the other side of the
river, more than half a mile distant from his troops.
The day after the arrival of Winchester, a spot was
selected for the encampment of the army, intending
to fortify it the next day.*

No sooner was the news of the defeat of the British and Indians by Colonel Lewis known at Fort Malden, a British fort, it will be recollected, near the
mouth of the Detroit River, or straits, in Canada,
than a large reinforcement was sent from that post,
and preparations were made for an immediate attack
upon the Americans.   On the 22nd, accordingly, at
reiville, the attack was commenced by a considerable
British and Indian force, with six pieces of artillery.
The troops being completely surprised, and the ground
unfavorable, had but little opportunity of forming to
advantage.   They were entirely surrounded, and broke
in twenty or thirty minutes.   One major, a captain,
and twenty or thirty privates, were all that effected
their escape.

When General Harrison received information that
the action had commenced, he was three miles above
the Rapids, with only three hundred and sixty men.
He immediately ordered them to march to the relief
of Winchester, and set out himself and staff to over-

* Sketches of the Life of General Harrison.

take a detachment of three hundred men that had a few hours before started for the River Raisin. He overtook them at the distance of six miles, but before the troops that had set out with him had come up, he ascertained that Winchester had met with a disastrous defeat. It was the unanimous opinion of General Payne, General Perkins, and the field officers, that these two detachments should now return. But a detachment of one hundred and seventy picked men was sent forward, with orders to proceed as far as possible, for the purpose of assisting those who were so fortunate as to escape. Very few, however, succeeded in reaching the American camp, the snow being so deep that the fugitives became entirely exhausted in running a few miles—not more than forty or fifty who got a mile from the scene of action, and the greater part of them were overtaken and massacred.

Until this disastrous defeat, the American army was in a most prosperous condition, the result solely of the unfortunate step of marching to the River Raisin, not only without the authority of the commander-in-chief, but in opposition to his views and even his express advice. Even if Colonel Lewis had been satisfied to return after his defeat of the Indians and British, everything would have been well, notwithstanding the original error of General Winchester. But in resolving to hold Frenchtown, a measure sanctioned by Winchester, they brought upon their troops the fatal calamity which befell them on the 22nd.

Everything was done by General Harrison to avert the disaster, after he had discovered the false step General Winchester had taken, and reinforcements were pushed on with all possible rapidity. Major Congreve's battalion, the finest body of troops in the army, was within fourteen miles of the action, and three hundred regular troops were also on their way, when they heard of the defeat, leaving him with but a single regiment at the Rapids.

The British troops in this action were commanded by the notorious General Proctor, and the savages by Round Head and Split Log, two famous chiefs. Their forces, united, amounted to about fifteen hundred, while the American numbered only one thousand. The American right wing was either cut to pieces or surrendered themselves prisoners to the British, under promise of protection. But the left wing continued to fight with desperate courage, and in attempting to rally the right, General Winchester and Colonel Lewis were taken prisoners. They repulsed every assault of the enemy with unsurpassed gallantry, making dreadful slaughter in his ranks.

The British commander at length attempted to secure, by fraud and treachery, what he either could not by force of arms, or what must be secured at too great a sacrifice. General Winchester was informed by Proctor, that unless his men surrendered, they would be delivered over to the fury of the savages, or at least that he would not be responsible for their conduct, and that the village would be burnt. These threats, or rather the promises of protection made by Proctor, induced General Winchester to agree to a surrender of his troops as prisoners of war on condition of being protected from his savage allies. It was not, however, until these flags of truce had passed that the remnant of the little army, then consisting of thirty-five officers and four hundred and fifty non-commissioned officers and men, would consent to the terms of the surrender*. They did agree to the terms of the surrender, after the most solemn assurances from Proctor that he would faithfully adhere to all its conditions, and not only protect their lives, but respect private property.

No sooner had they laid down their arms, however, than it was discovered that they had been fully betrayed by the infamous and blood-thirsty Proctor, and that they were to be butchered in cold blood by their brutal and savage conquerors. The work of scalping and stripping the dead, and of murdering the wounded, who had previously fallen into their hands, had already commenced. And the barbarous outrage was suffered to go on without the least attempt to restrain it on the part of the infamous Proctor. Indeed, so far from this being the case, or from his exhibiting any inclination to arrest his savage fiends in the work of carnage, he seems to have encouraged and advised it; and when they could find no other victims of this class to vent their thirst for vengeance and blood upon, they begun to butcher the

* Breckenridge's Late War.

brave men who had laid down their arms under the
pledged faith of the British commander.

He, as well as his equally infamous officers, turned
a deaf ear to the remonstrances of their now unre-
sisting and defenceless victims, and they were toma-
hawked and scalped by dozens and scores. The few
that survived this first wholesale slaughter were placed
in the rear of their forces in charge of the Indians,
to be marched to Malden. But long before they
reached that post they, too, were murdered, one by
one, as they became too weak to walk, either from
their wounds or exposure to the inclemency of the
season. Those who were not thus inhumanly butchered were reserved for the more horrible fate of
being roasted at the stake.

The night after the action, from fifty to sixty of
the prisoners who had been badly wounded, most of
them officers of distinction, were permitted to take
shelter with the citizens of Frenchtown, and Proctor's
surgeons suffered to dress their wounds. They were
promised, too, a sufficient guard to protect them from
the scalping knife of the savages. But this was only
the refinement of cruelty; no such guard was provided. On the contrary, they were probably pointed
out to the savage hell-hounds, by the infamous wretch
who employed them for such infernal objects, as easy
victims of their fiend-like hatred; and, as has been
foreseen and designed, they fell upon them the same
night, plundered them of their clothing and every
article of value in their possession, murdered the most

of them in the most horrible manner, and then set fire to the houses, consuming alike the few remaining and the bodies of the slain in the flames.

Infamous as these acts of infernal barbarity were, and as eternally infamous as they must render the memory of the blood-thirsty monster who permitted them, both were increased, if it were possible to add to the cruelty of such acts and the infamy of such a monster, by his treatment of the bodies of his slaughtered victims. It would seem that the innocent blood he had shed would have satisfied the most unrelenting and sanguinary; but not so with Proctor; he even refused to permit those rites which every civilized country held sacred. The inhuman wretch refused to permit the citizens of Frenchtown to bury the bodies of the murdered soldiers, on pain of death! These bodies were suffered to lie on the ground exposed to ferocious beasts of prey, or the more horrible pollution of domestic animals.

There were many scenes of individual suffering which created even a stronger feeling of sorrow for this bloody tragedy, and increased the melancholy interest felt for its numerous victims. Amongst those was the case of Captain Hart, a near relative of Henry Clay, an accomplished gentleman and ripe scholar, who particularly distinguished himself during the action. Upon being surrendered, he was recognized by Colonel Elliot, who was a citizen of the United States, with whom he had been a class-mate at Princeton, but who had become an officer in the

12

British army, and an ally of the savages. Elliot
voluntarily offered his old friend his protection, but
subsequently either changed his mind or was forbidden to keep his promise by the savage Proctor, for he
gave himself no further concern in regard to Captain
Hart. The next day a party of savages came into
his room and tore him from his bed. He was taken
to another room by some brother officers, when he was
again subjected to the same barbarity. By the offer
of a large sum of money, he induced some Indians to
take him to Malden; but when they had proceeded a
short distance, he was dragged from his horse, shot
and scalped. The same tragedy was enacted respectively in the case of Colonel Allen, Captains Hick-
man, Woolfolk and M'Cracken; also, Mr. Simpson, a
member of Congress from Kentucky, and Captains
Bledsoe, Watson, Hamilton, Williams and Kelly, and
Majors Madison and Ballard, from the same State,
were amongst the victims.*

Becoming restless under the load of infamy which
his conduct had brought upon him, Proctor sought to
wipe out some little portion of the stigma by offering
the very few prisoners who had escaped the Indian
tomahawk, *for sale*, instead of permitting them to be
murdered; and in pursuance of this impulse of humanity, prisoners of the highest respectability were
literally hawked about the streets of Detroit like
beasts of prey, by their captors, in search of purchasers. The conduct of the people of Detroit, in re-

* Brackenridge's History of the Late War.

gard to those unfortunate prisoners, was of the most humane and noble character. Many of them parted with everything in their possession to procure means for purchasing them, and all vied with each other in acts of benevolence, women taking the lead in the good work. They gladly gave their shawls, and even the blankets from their beds, when nothing else was left them to give.* But these horrible details need not be pursued farther. The voice of the civilized world has assigned to the principal actors in the barbarities, that have been but faintly portrayed above, a depth of degradation from which no length of time and no power of sophistry can rescue them, and their crimes have been so indelibly stamped upon the history of the times, that no effort can erase the damning stain.

In pursuance with the unanimous advice of his general and field officers, upon hearing Winchester's defeat, General Harrison fell back to the Rapids, and immediately set about constructing a fort, which, in honor of Governor Meigs, of Ohio, for his patriotic efforts in behalf of the American army, he named Fort Meigs. Fortifications were also constructed at Upper Sandusky, by General Crooks, who commanded the Pennsylvania militia. Excepting some other partizan excursions of little moment, the first campaign may be considered as having ended. The movements of General Winchester and his overwhelming defeat had so entirely deranged all his plans, that it was

* Brackenridge's History of the Late War.

necessary to organize a new system, and make new
preparations for the approaching campaign. He accordingly returned to Ohio for the purpose of obtaining reinforcements from that State and Kentucky.*

General Harrison had continued to flatter himself
with the hope that he might find an opportunity during the winter to carry into execution his long-cher-
ished enterprise of attacking Fort Malden. The barbarities of Proctor had stimulated his desire, as well
as that of his troops, to get possession of that post.
For this purpose he had ordered up all his troops in
the rear, except such as were necessary to maintain
the forts on the Auglaize and the St. Mary's. He
had intended to advance against Malden by the 15th
of February, disperse the Indians, destroy the shipping, and establish a post near Brownstown, and remain there until the weather should become sufficiently cold to freeze the lakes and swamps, so as to
permit the artillery to be brought up. It continued
so rainy, however, and the period for which the Kentucky and Ohio troops had engaged to serve being
about to expire, he was reluctantly compelled to
abandon for the season his contemplated attack upon
Malden. All further thoughts were now abandoned
by the commander-in-chief of continuing a campaign
which had virtually ended with the defeat of Winchester.

* Brackenridge's Late War.

CHAPTER VIII.

BEFORE following General Harrison into the next campaign, a hasty glance will be taken at events that had in the meantime transpired upon other portions of the theatre of war. A short time preceding the declaration of war, William Hull, then governor of the Territory of Michigan, a revolutionary officer of distinction, and then recently appointed a brigadier-general in the regular army, was placed in command of twelve hundred Ohio volunteers, a regiment of United States infantry, and some detachments of other regiments, with which he arrived at Detroit on the 5th of July, 1812. Before taking the command, he had received discretionary power to act offensively in case of war. He therefore determined on an invasion of Canada, and great preparations were made for the enterprise, and on the 12th of July the main body of the army crossed into Canada. General Hull issued a proclamation to the inhabitants, which induced a considerable number of them to join the American standard, and favorably inclined the most of them towards the Americans.

Immediately after the army entered Canada, an expedition was sent out under Colonel M'Arthur,

12*

with the view of reconnoitering the country, and on the 16th another, for the same purpose, under Colonel Cass. Both these enterprises were highly successful, and proved that, had the army of invasion been entrusted to a bold, skilful and patriotic officer, it would most certainly have succeeded in subduing to our arms the whole of Lower Canada. Malden, situated at the junction of Detroit River with Lake Erie, and then the key to that province, might have been reduced with scarcely an effort. But General Hull remained comparatively idle at Sandwich, and the favorable opportunity for striking a blow that would have ended the war in that quarter permitted to pass unimproved. While waiting here for cannon in order to attack Malden, news was received that Mackinac had been surprised and taken by the British on the 17th of July, the garrison, through the criminal neglect of Hull, not even having been advised of the declaration of war. By the fall of this important post, the British were enabled to collect such a force at Malden as put it out of the power of an army, under such a leader as Hull, to accomplish anything against it. He accordingly abandoned Canada, with the exception of a small detachment left to protect the inhabitants who had taken up arms for the Americans, and arrived at Detroit, where he had determined to concentrate his force, on the 8th of August.

The evacuation of Canada, after so prosperous a parade, without accomplishing anything of real advantage to our arms, created not only loud murmurs against General Hull, but even suspicion of treachery. After his arrival at Detroit, two attempts were made to open a communication with the River Raisin—one by Colonel Miller with six hundred men, and another by Colonels M'Arthur and Cass at the head of three hundred men. Colonel Miller met and was attacked by a superior body of British and Indians. He, however, defeated them, after a severe engagement, with great loss ; but he was compelled to return to Detroit, in consequence of the great fatigue his troops suffered during the action. The other detachment set off on the 14th of August, six days after Colonel Miller.

The day following the departure of Colonels Cass and M'Arthur, General Brock, the British commander, dispatched two officers with a flag of truce, from Sandwich, demanding of Hull the immediate surrender of Detroit, as the only means of preventing a general massacre by the Indians in his army. Hull replied that he was prepared to meet any force that could be sent against him, and was prepared to abide the consequence. On the return of the flag, the British opened a brisk fire from their batteries at Sandwich, which was as vigorously returned by the Americans. The firing was kept up till ten o'clock at night, and resumed early the next morning.

During the night the British ships of war had moved up the river in order to protect the landing of the troops. About ten o'clock on the morning of the 16th of August, accordingly, the landing was effected, and immediately they advanced upon the fort. The

American forces had, in the meantime, been judi
ciously posted, and had placed several pieces of can
non so advantageously as to command the approach
of the enemy and sweep the whole of his line as he
advanced. The enemy, however, fearlessly advanced,
and all was anxiety amongst the American army, expecting every moment that the fire would commence,
when General Hull, to the mortification, amazement
and indignation of his whole army, ordered a whig
flag to be hoisted and the firing to be suspended. The
firing from the British side also was immediately suspended. A treaty was at once entered into, and
terms of capitulation agreed to by Hull, by which the
whole territory, with all the American forts, and Detroit, with all the American troops, public stores, and
everything else of a public nature, as well as the detachment under Colonels M'Arthur and Cass, who
were absent, were surrendered to the British. By
this shameful surrender, twenty-five pieces of iron and
eight pieces of brass ordinance, the latter taken from
Burgoyne, just thirty-five years before, fell into the
hands of the British, also twenty-five hundred muskets and rifles, and a large quantity of ammunition.
General Hull was tried by a court-martial on a charge
of treason, imbecility and cowardice. He was virtually acquitted of treason, and sentenced to be shot
on the other charges, though he was recommended to
mercy in consideration of his revolutionary services.
The sentence was remitted by the President, but his
name stricken from the rolls of the army.

This event, so disgraceful to our arms, and so mortifying to our national pride, was received with one burst of indignation throughout the whole Union, and an army at once sprung up at the West, almost as if by magic, determined to avenge their lost friends and retrieve their tarnished honor. This army, as has been seen, was placed under the command of Governor Harrison.

The American forces on the frontier were stationed at Plattsburgh, under General Bloomfield; at Buffalo under General Smith, and at Sacket's Harbor and Black Rock and Ogdensburgh—the whole being under the command of General Dearborn. The militia of the State of New York, under General Van Rensselaer, amounting to three thousand five hundred, were stationed at Lewistown. Owing to an armistice that had been entered into between General Dearborn and Sir George Provost, it was late in the season before any movement of importance was made by either commander. The time was therefore employed by the American officers in drilling and disciplining their troops and in preparing for active service.

As the season for military operations was now so far advanced that the militia began to display great impatience and anxiety to be led against the enemy, General Van Rensselaer, therefore, determined to make an attack upon Queenstown, a British post, situate on the Canada side of the Niagara River, directly opposite his quarters at Lewistown. The attempt was to be made on the 13th of October. The troops were to cross over in two divisions, one under the command of Colonel Solomon Van Rensselaer, and the other under Lieutenant Colonel Chrystie; but, owing to a deficiency of boats, only a portion of each detachment could pass over; and even such as could be procured did not all reach the opposite side. The attack, however, was immediately commenced by the troops who succeeded in landing, and the enemy gradually gained ground in front of Colonel Van Rensselaer. He, as well as Colonel Fenwick, had both been so severely wounded as to be compelled to quit the field. Each company now fought on his own responsibility, there being no one entitled to command. The enemy, however, were soon driven from the great height, called the "mountain," having previously carried a battery in their ascent. The enemy fled precipitately to Queenstown, where they were met and rallied by General Brock. He instantly led them to the charge, but when at the distance of an hundred paces, fell mortally wounded. His troops were again dispersed.

At this moment Lieutenant Colonel Winfield Scott arrived on the heights, having been ordered over to take the command of the whole force. General Wadsworth claimed to command the militia, however, and he was therefore only permitted to command the regular troops, only about two hundred and thirty in all. But with this small force he made prompt arrangements for meeting the enemy. With the assistance of Captain Totten, of the engineers, Colonel

Scott drew up his men in the most judicious manner. His position was the strongest that could be chosen, and so selected, that he could protect the boats as they landed from the other side with additional troops, and also receive the enemy at the best advantage.

The firing in the morning had attracted the attention of the British garrison at Fort George and the Indians collected there. The Indians, amounting to four hundred strong, arrived first at the scene of action, and a sharp conflict at once ensued. Colonel Scott received the enemy with his regulars in gallant style, and routed them with considerable loss. He pursued them as far as the main design of protecting the landing of troops would permit, and then resumed his position. On account of their great superiority, the enemy was induced to renew the attack. He drove in the pickets and forced his way into the midst of the American camp. All was now confusion. Defeat and massacre seemed almost inevitable. At this critical moment, Colonel Scott, who had been everywhere in the thickest of the fight, stimulating his men by his presence and example, by great exertions brought the retreating line to stand to face the enemy. They at once caught the spirit of their brave and chivalrous leader. With a burst of enthusiasm, as sudden as the panic of the moment before, the line charged upon their pursuers with such impetuous zeal, and the movement was so instantaneous with all, that the enemy at once broke and fled in confusion, leaving a considerable number of dead and wounded on the field. They were pursued a considerable distance. In these affairs the militia, with individual exceptions, behaved very badly, and indeed with little else than cowardice.*

Having been so frequently defeated by a greatly inferior force, the Indians and light troops were resolved to await the arrival of the garrison from Fort George, already in sight, and amounting to nearly nine hundred strong, under general Sheaffe. Information was at the same time brought to Colonel Scott that no aid was to be expected from Lewistown. General Van Rensselaer had done everything in his power to induce the militia to go to the assistance of their gallant countrymen on the other side. But the sight of General Sheaffe's reinforcement excited in their minds the liveliest constitutional scruples. Nothing could induce them to relinquish their constitutional rights by setting their feet on foreign soil. The sight of their countrymen being cut down, one after another, for want of the aid they had the power to give them, had no other influence than to strengthen their determination not to hazard their own lives.

It was now discovered that retreat was as impossible as succor was hopeless, as the boats were all on the American side. The gallant Scott, therefore, and his brave little army, resolved to receive the enemy on the ground they occupied, and that if any of them survived it would be time enough to surrender. The British general approached to the attack with great

* Frost's Book of the Army.

caution, finding that such an enemy as he had to meet were not to be easily subdued, even by a force three times as large. He feared, too, that the small body he saw in view of American troops were only a small part of the army he had to encounter, and designed to decoy him to his ruin. At length, however, the conflict commenced. The action was sharp, bloody and desperate, and continued for nearly half an hour. The Americans being nearly surrounded on every side, and finding longer resistance against such fearful odds little else than madness, surrendered prisoners of war.

Through this whole engagement, in each of the fierce contests with the enemy, Colonel Scott fought with desperate bravery, though he acted with the coolness and discretion of a veteran. He exposed his person in the most fearless manner in every quarter where the fire was the thickest and the danger the greatest. Being in full uniform, his remarkably tall and commanding person was observable towering far above all others, and was singled out as a mark by the enemy's sharp shooters. He was advised by a brother officer to throw aside his uniform, or cover it so as to escape observation. "No," said he, smiling, "I will die in my robes." Captain Lawrence fell by his side, dangerously wounded, immediately after. When the action was over and the Americans had surrendered themselves prisoners of war, an Indian came up to Colonel Scott, and, attentively surveying him, said, "Sair, you are not born to be shot—so

13

many times—(holding up all the fingers of both hands, to indicate ten)—so many times have I leveled and fired my rifle at you." From Queenstown Colonel Scott was sent to Quebec. In about a month after he embarked for Boston, and was exchanged in the following January.

In the engagement the Americans, especially the regulars who were actually in the battle, acted with a gallantry that reflected the highest credit on themselves and on their country. But for the cowardice of the militia in refusing to cross the river, the result would have been quite different. The most of them who did participate in the action behaved with great coolness and bravery. The loss of the Americans in the battle was believed to be full one thousand in killed, wounded and prisoners. The loss of the British is not known, though it must have been very considerable, as they were twice repulsed.

Soon after the battle of Queenstown, General Van Rensselaer resigned his commission, and General Smith was appointed to succeed him in his command. Another invasion was projected by General Smith, and great promises made to the "men of New York." If they would come to his standard in his contemplated invasion of Canada, they were assured that they should have an opportunity not only to cover themselves with glory and renown, but of retrieving the tarnished honor of the country, which he believed to have been very seriously wounded by the previous failure under his predecessor. After a large number of volunteers had been collected by these bright visions of fame and fortune, and the most imposing preparations made for the conquest of Canada, the troops having been twice actually embarked in the boats for the great enterprise, the whole magnificent expedition was suddenly abandoned, the troops ordered to be withdrawn from the boats and to go into winter quarters. This enterprise, terminating thus unfortunately to the country, and dishonorably to a portion of the militia and to General Smith, ended the operations of the "Army of the Centre," as the battle of Queenstown begun them, to the equal dishonor of another portion of the militia, though to the everlasting renown of Colonel Scott and the officers and men under his command. Two years after, the same gallant officer, on the same field of battle, added new laurels to his own fame, and did much to wipe out whatever of disgrace to their country there was in his previous defeat.

While many of our operations by land during the first campaign brought but little honor and less advantage to the nation, our naval exploits can be pointed to with pride and exultation by every patriotic American. Our victories at sea, while they did much to inspire confidence and hope at home amongst ourselves, also did more to humble the pride, if not to destroy the confidence, of our haughty enemy, in their boasted invincibility in what they claimed as their native element. The capture of the frigate "Guerriere," one of the finest vessels in the British navy, by the "Constitution," Commodore Hall, after an action of only thirty minutes, was probably the severest blow to the national vanity of England that she had ever received, either on land or by sea. It is doubtful whether even her overwhelming defeat at New Orleans, at a subsequent period, produced so deep a feeling of mortification as the capture of one of their favorite frigates. This was more particularly the case, as the "Guerriere" had been sent out to revenge the insult to the "Little Belt." This action took place on the 19th of September, 1812. The "Guerriere" was so much shattered, that a few broadsides must have sunk her, and it was impossible to carry her into port: she was therefore blown up the day after the action. Her loss was fifteen killed and sixty-three wounded; while the "Constitution" had only seven killed and seven wounded. The joy which this brilliant achievement produced throughout the United States was only equalled by the depression and chagrin produced by the same result in England.*

* The following account of the capture of the "Guerriere," which was communicated to the New York *Evening Post* by an American gentleman who was a prisoner on board that vessel during the action, will be found to be excitingly interesting, and to deserve a place amongst the historical records of the country: —

Having been an American prisoner on board the "Guerriere," during the famous battle between that frigate and the United States frigate "Constitution," I propose giving you an account of that important action which took place in June, 1812.

About two weeks previous to the engagement, I left Boston in an American ship, which was captured by the "Guerriere" some five days before she fell in with the "Constitution."

Almost immediately after this victory of the "Constitution," news was received of the capture of the

It was about ten o'clock in the morning when the "Constitution" was discovered. The "Guerriere" hove to, to enable her to come up. As the "Constitution" neared us, Captain Dacres handed me his glass, and asked what I took her to be. My reply was, "She looks like a frigate." Very soon she came within reach of the long guns of the "Guerriere," which were fired, but with no effect, as the sea ran high. The "Constitution" made no reply, but, as I saw, was manœuvring for a position, during which Captain Dacres said to me, "Do you think she is going to strike without firing?" I replied, "I think not, Sir."

At this moment, seeing a severe contest was about commencing, in which I could take no part, being only a prisoner, I raised my hat to Captain Dacres, and said to him—"With your permission, sir, I will go below, as I can take no part." "O certainly," said he, "and you had better go into the cock-pit; and should any of our men chance to get wounded, I shall feel obliged if you will assist the surgeons in dressing them. "Certainly, sir," said I, and then descended into the cock-pit. There were the surgeons, and surgeons' mates, and attendants, sitting round a long table, covered with instruments and all necessaries for dressing the wounded, as still as a funeral. Within one moment after my foot left the lower round of the ladder, the "Constitution" gave that double broadside, which threw all in the cock-pit over in a heap on the opposite side of the ship.

For a moment it appeared as if heaven and earth had struck together; a more terrific shock cannot be imagined. Before those in the cock-pit had adjusted themselves, the blood run down from the deck as freely as if a wash-tub full had been turned over, and instantly the dead, wounded, and dying, were handed down as rapidly as men could pass them, till the cock-pit was filled, with hardly room for the surgeons to work. Midshipmen were handed down with one leg, some with one arm, and others wounded in almost every shape and condition. An officer, who was on the table having his arm amputated, would sing out to a comrade

13 *

British sloop of war, "Alert," by Commodore Porter,
of the "Essex." Following fast upon the heels of

coming down wounded—"Well, shipmate, how goes the battle?"
another would utter some joke, that would make even the dying
smile; and so constant and freely were the playful remarks from
the maimed and even dying, that I almost doubted my own senses.
Indeed, all this was crowded into a space of not over fifteen or
twenty minutes before the firing ceased. I then went upon deck,
and what a scene was presented, and how changed in so short a
time.

The "Constitution" looked perfectly fresh; and even at this
time, those on board the "Guerriere" did not know what ship
had fought them. On the other hand, the "Guerriere" was a
mere rolling log, almost entirely at the mercy of the sea. Her
colors all shot away, her main-mast and mizen-mast both gone by
the board, and her fore-mast standing by the mere honey-comb
the shot had made. Captain Dacres stood, with his officers, surveying the scene—all, all in the most perfect astonishment. At
this moment, a boat was seen putting off from the hostile ship for
the "Guerriere." As soon as within speaking distance, a young
gentleman (Midshipman Reed, now Commodore Reed) hailed and
said—"I wish to see the officer in command of the ship." At this,
Captain Dacres stepped forward, and answered. Midshipman
Reed then said—"Commodore Hull's compliments, and wishes to
know if you have struck your flag?" At this, Captain Dacres
appeared amazed, but recovering himself, and looking up and
down, he deliberately replied, "Well, I don't know—our mizzen-
mast is gone, our main-mast is gone—and, upon the whole, you
may say we have struck our flag!"

"Commodore Hull's compliments, and wishes to know if you
need the assistance of a surgeon or surgeon's mate?" Captain
Dacres replied: "Well, I should suppose you had on board your
own ship business enough for all your medical officers." Midshipman Reed replied, "O, no, we have only seven wounded, and they
were dressed half an hour ago."

Captain Dacres then turned to me, deeply affected, and said, this victory, followed those of the "United States" over the "Macedonian," and of the "Wasp" over

"How have our situations been suddenly reversed? You are now free, and I a prisoner."

All the boats of both ships were now put in requisition to remove the wounded on board the "Constitution;" so dreadful was the condition of many of them that two days were nearly consumed in the removal, after which the "Guerriere" was burned, with all her stores, armament, &c. The "Constitution," having recently come out of port, had no room to take scarcely an article.

Who can imagine the joy I experienced in finding myself again under American colors—or the pride I felt at finding, from Commodore Hull down to the most humble man on board, an entire absence of everything like a boastful or even a triumphant look at their wonderful victory. Captain Dacres kept his state-room till we arrived in port. About two hundred of his men were necessarily ironed, as the ship was so crowded. Charles Morris (now Commodore), the first officer of the "Constitution," had a ball through his body, and for several days his recovery was doubtful —during which he sent for me to come to his room; and I well remember his perfect unconcern for himself, although the surgeon had apprised him of his danger. Every courtesy and kindness was by Captain Hull and his officers extended to their prisoners.

On Sunday, about noon, the "Constitution" arrived in Boston harbor. I was sent on shore in the boat. The harbor between the ship and wharves was now covered with boats to learn the news. To the first boat that we neared we hailed, "The 'Constitution' has captured the 'Guerriere.'" Instantly, the two men in the boat took off their hats, and violently struck them on the side of the boat, and rising, gave cheer upon cheer. They hailed other boats, and thus the air was rent with cheers, and the victory passed along until it reached the wharf, and then spread like wildfire all over the city and country.

It is now nearly forty years since the transaction of that day proved to the Americans that British frigates were not invincible. Who can remember that day without feeling a glow of pride, that the British brig "Frolic," the first of which took place on the 25th of October, and the other on the 20th of the same month. When the "Frolic" surrendered, she had but four of her crew alive on deck. She had thirty-eight killed and fifty wounded. On board the "Wasp" there were but five killed and five wounded. This was the most decisive action fought during the war, and was more fatal to the enemy in proportion to the number engaged. On board the "Macedonian" there were thirty-six killed and sixty-eight wounded, while the "United States" lost but five in killed and seven wounded. In addition to these victories, so mortifying to British arrogance, they had to submit to another quite as humiliating to their pride. This was the capture of the British frigate "Java" by the "Constitution," Commodore Bainbridge, on the 29th of December. The "Java" carried forty-nine guns, and had on board, when captured, four hundred soldiers and one hundred seamen, whom she was carrying out to the East Indies. She had on board, also, despatches of an important character for St. Helena, the Cape of Good Hope, and for their different establishments in the East Indies and

so early in the war, and in a manner so unpretending, a victory so perfect should have been achieved! I write this statement without notes, but believe it to be, in the main, accurate.

In justice to Captain Dacres, I add, that there was none of the boasting on his part, before the action, which has to him been attributed, as he did not know the ship till Midshipman Reed announced her name and commander.

                                                            O. W.

China, besides the Governor of Bombay, and a large number of officers, civil, military and naval. The "Constitution" had nine men killed and twenty-five wounded. The killed on board the "Java" were sixty, and one hundred and twenty wounded. The capture of the "Java" was of little if of any less importance than the capture of the "Guerriere," by the same ship. The conduct of all the officers of the "Constitution" towards their prisoners was as remarkable for its humanity and courtesy as it had been during the action for courage and good conduct, and they received the public acknowledgments of the Governor of Bombay, Lieutenant General Halsop, upon their arrival at St. Salvador.

The exploits of some of the American privateers were little less humiliating to British pride, and gratifying to the American people, than those of our legitimate naval ships. One of the first to sail was the " Atlas," commanded by Captain Moffat, who on the 3rd of August fell in with two armed ships, and, after a severe action, captured them both. The "Dolphin," Captain Endicot, in the course of a few weeks, captured fifteen ships of the enemy, but had the mortification to be captured herself by an English squadron. The achievements of Commodore Barney, who sailed from Baltimore, carried destruction throughout the British merchant trade, and did more injury to her commerce than it had received for years before from French cruisers. These repeated disasters carried consternation throughout the British nation, as our privateers had throughout her commerce. Its *signi-fication* was more terrible to England than the defeat of her ships of war or the ruin to her trade, for it told her that omnipotence upon the seas was about to be destroyed.

CHAPTER IX.

It has already been stated that, after the termination of the campaign, General Harrison had gone to Cincinnati for the purpose of procuring a reinforcement from that State and Kentucky. Early in the spring, while prosecuting this object, he received information that the British were making extensive preparations and concentrating a large force of regular soldiers, Canadians and Indians, for the purpose of laying siege to Fort Meigs. In consequence of this intelligence, he immediately returned to that post and commenced the most energetic and judicious arrangements to be prepared for the threatened attack.

As the new levies had not arrived, the Pennsylvania brigade, although its term of service had expired, generously volunteered for the defence of Fort Meigs. His arrival had inspired the troops with fresh confidence, and strong hopes were rekindled in all hearts that an opportunity would soon be presented them, not only of avenging their murdered countrymen at the River Raisin, but vindicating the honor and establishing the supremacy of the American arms.

Fort Meigs was situated on a rising ground, a few

hundred yards from the river, on both sides of which the country was chiefly natural meadows.* The garrison was amply supplied with the means of defence, and Harrison labored night and day to improve its capacity for resisting the anticipated attack. With the assistance of Captains Wood and Gratiot, his principal engineers, his fortifications were so improved and strengthened, that he felt confident of being able successfully to resist any force that could be brought against him. The troops in the fort were in excellent spirits, and determined to defend themselves to the last.

On the 28th of April, one of the parties of observation, that was constantly kept out for the purpose of discovering the advance of the enemy, returned with information that the enemy were in great force only about three miles distant. Shortly after a few British and Indians made their appearance on the opposite side of the river, but a few shots from an eighteen pounder soon compelled them to disperse.

General Harrison now determined to dispatch an express to General Clay, commanding the Kentucky reinforcements, amounting to twelve hundred militia, to hasten his march. For the discharge of this dangerous and responsible duty, requiring an intimate knowledge of the country and great intrepidity and firmness, he selected Captain William Oliver. These qualities he possessed in an eminent degree. He was accompanied by one Indian and one white man, and

* Brackenridge.

performed the hazardous duty assigned him with signal success, having found him at Fort Winchester, and urged upon him the importance of forwarding the reinforcement with all possible dispatch.

For three days after the enemy was first discovered in the vicinity of the fort, he was occupied in selecting a suitable position for erecting his batteries, from whence he might the more successfully annoy it. Their labors were greatly impeded, however, by the brisk fire that was kept up upon them by General Harrison during the day. On the first of May they had succeeded in mounting their batteries, and they immediately commenced a heavy fire upon the fort from several of their guns. No material injury, however, was done on either side, though General Harrison made a narrow escape, a ball having struck a bench on which he was sitting. On the following morning, after the fort had been fully invested, the commander-in-chief issued a general order to his troops, appealing to their patriotism in the most eloquent terms. He closed by saying,—"Can the citizens of a free country, who have taken up arms to defend its rights, think of submitting to an army composed of mercenary soldiers, reluctant Canadians, goaded to the field by the bayonet, and of wretched naked savages? Can the breast of an American soldier, when he casts his eyes to the opposite shore, the scene of his country's triumphs over the savage foe, be influenced by any other feelings than those of glory? Is not this army composed of the same materials with that which

14

fought and conquered under the immortal Wayne?
Yes, fellow-soldiers, your general sees your counten-
ances beam with the same fire that he witnessed on
that glorious occasion; and although it would be the
height of presumption to compare himself to that
hero, he boasts of being that hero's pupil. To your
posts, then, fellow-soldiers, and remember that the
eyes of your country are upon you."

By the time the enemy were prepared to open their
batteries upon the fort, the American troops had completed a grand tower, about twelve feet high, upon a
base of twenty feet, three hundred yards long, on the
most elevated ground, through the middle of the camp,
calculated to ward off the shot from the enemy's batteries. Orders were given for all the tents in front
to be instantly moved into the rear, which was effected
in a few moments. The enemy's efforts, therefore, to
bombard and cannonade the American lines was entirely thwarted, and all their immense labor in erecting their batteries was rendered useless. The em-
bankment of earth behind which our troops now retired entirely obscured the whole army, while it served
as a perfect protection against the British fire. Not
a tent nor a soldier was to be seen; but, notwithstanding the futility of the attempt, Proctor still kept
up a tremendous fire upon the fort, and continued it
for five days, at great expense of powder and ball,
but little injury to the American troops, only one man
being killed and four wounded during the whole time.

On the 3rd of May, Proctor sent a flag to the fort

by Major Chambers, and very coolly summoned General Harrison to surrender. Chambers assured him that the great anxiety of the British commander, in thus summoning him to surrender, was to spare the effusion of human blood! and that his force was so numerous, that it would be impossible to withstand it. He also assured him that, unless the Americans at once surrendered at discretion, and throw themselves upon the tender mercies of the author of the butcheries at the River Raisin, they might expect to be indiscriminately massacred in cold blood.

As might have been expected, from the character for courage and gallantry which General Harrison had acquired and so well sustained, this insolent summons was treated with the contempt anything from the infamous Proctor so well deserved. He, as well as every officer and soldier under his command, preferred instant death to the ignominy of surrendering to such a monster, even if they had any faith in his promises of protection. But they had none. He had already forfeited his honor, as well as all claims to the respect of mankind, for his infamous barbarities. To look for mercy at the hands of a man who had thus outraged every principle of truth and every feeling of humanity, required a degree of credulity that his conduct had not inspired in General Harrison.

He expressed his surprise at the demand, especially under the circumstances in which it was made, looking upon it as an intentional insult on the part of

Proctor. This, however, Major Chambers disclaimed
in behalf of the British commander, but intimated to
him at the same time that he was in sufficient force to
compel his demand. To this General Harrison replied, that he believed he had very correct information as to Proctor's force, and that it was not such as
to create the least apprehension for the result of the
contest, whatever shape he might thereafter be pleased
to give to it. He desired Major Chambers to assure
him, however, that the fort would never be *surrendered* to him, and that should it fall into his hands,
it would be in a manner calculated to do him more
honor and to give him a larger claim upon the gratitude of his government than any capitulation could
possibly do.

Finding how little he had to hope, either from his
threats or from the force of his arms, the siege was
renewed with redoubled vigor, and the firing was
kept up on both sides with great energy. The savages
even mounted into the tops of trees with the object
of firing down into the fort, and by this means succeeded in killing and wounding several men. General
Harrison now began to feel the most anxious solicitude to receive intelligence of the approach of General Clay, to whom, it will be recollected, he had
some days before dispatched a special express for the
purpose of urging him to forward the Kentucky volunteers with all possible speed. But his anxiety was
soon to be relieved, for late in the night of the 4th
of May, a small party under Major Trimble and Cap-

tain Oliver, reached the fort, with the gratifying information that General Clay was but a few miles above the Rapids, with a considerable reinforcement.

Immediately upon receiving this intelligence, General Harrison dispatched orders to him, requesting him to detach eight hundred men for the purpose of landing on the other side and attacking the enemy's batteries. In the meantime, he embraced the favorable opportunity given by the timely arrival of General Clay's reinforcements, for completing the arrangements for a sortie he had planned some time before. The sortie was designed to be made upon the side of the fort commanded by Lieutenant Colonel Miller, of the nineteenth United States infantry, simultaneously with the attack to be made upon the enemy's batteries by the detachment under Colonel Dudley, from General Clay's reinforcement. The attack was admirably planned, and should it prove successful, the enemy would be compelled to raise the siege immediately. The duty assigned to Colonel Dudley was executed with ability, and he landed his men in good order. He then advanced at once to the enemy's cannon, and with such determined bravery, that four of their batteries were carried almost instantly, and the British regulars and Indians were at once put to flight.

The victory of Colonel Dudley seemed to be complete and decisive; but it was soon turned into a defeat. A large body of Indians, under the celebrated Tecumthe, were on their route to the British

14 *

camp, when they met the fugitives whom Dudley had
so signally beaten. This body was immediately ordered to form an ambush, and to await the approach
of the Americans, while a few Indians were to act as
decoys. After having executed his orders, Colonel
Dudley ordered a retreat; but his men, flushed with
victory, and desirous of avenging their murdered fellow-soldiers at Frenchtown, pushed on in pursuit of
the flying foe with an impetuosity that nothing could
resist. Their commander attempted in vain to check
their headlong career, and even threatened them with
summary punishment, but without effect, and in a few
moments they found themselves drawn into the snare
that had been set for them, surrounded by a force
three times their number. A dreadful battle now ensued, in which the Kentuckians fought with their
usual desperate courage; but they were fighting
against tremendous odds, both in numbers and position, and were finally slaughtered, with the exception
of one hundred and fifty, who succeeded in making
their escape. Colonel Dudley, in attempting to cut
his way through the enemy to the river, was killed,
having fought with great gallantry throughout the
bloody engagements.*

The misfortune that befel Colonel Dudley in some
measure disconcerted the plan of the sortie under
Colonel Miller, though it did not deter him from sal-
lying forth at the head of three hundred men and as-
saulting the whole of the British works, manned by

* Brackenridge.

three hundred and fifty regulars and five hundred Indians. In this attack, which was made with an impetuosity that overcame every obstacle, he drove the enemy from their principal batteries, spiked their cannon, and returned to the fort with forty-two prisoners. When the great disparity of force between the Americans and British, and the advantageous position of the enemy are considered, the sortie of Colonel Miller must be looked upon as one of the most successful and gallant actions of the whole war. Every man fought with the courage of a hero, and indeed every man made himself a hero by his noble conduct.

The attack was commenced against the Canadians and Indians by Major Alexander's battalion, and was followed by Colonel Miller in a gallant and irresistible charge against the British regulars. Amongst the officers in these two attacks were Captains Croghan, Langham, Bradford and Waring, and Lieutenants Gwynne and Campbell. A company of Kentuckians, commanded by Captain Lebree, who had distinguished himself at Frenchtown, won new honors by their brave conduct in this gallant action.*

Though Colonel Dudley was finally defeated by being drawn into an ambush, the complete success of his attack upon the British batteries, and Colonel Miller's equally successful sortie, had taught Proctor a profitable lesson, and proved to him that, in anything like an equal contest, the Americans were more

* Brackenridge.

than a match for his blood-thirsty allies and his almost equally ferocious regulars. He was therefore quite willing for a cessation of hostilities, which took place for the three days following the sortie. Flags frequently passed between the besiegers and the besieged during this temporary calm, and arrangements were entered into for the exchange of prisoners. Tecumthe agreed to release his claims to the persons taken by the Indians, provided some Wyandots, to the number of forty, were delivered up. Proctor also promised to furnish a list of the killed, wounded and prisoners; but he again forfeited his word; the promise was never fulfilled.*

Thus terminated this siege at the end of thirteen days. It had not only reflected honor on General Harrison and his brave little army, and the American character, but convinced the butcher Proctor that, whatever victims he might thenceforth procure to feed his own and the appetites of his savage auxiliaries upon, he must fight for, and that they would be dearly purchased. His speedy retreat from Fort Meigs, after all his vaunted parade and impudent threats, were as disgraceful to his generalship, and as mortifying to his vanity, as his previous butcheries of defenceless men and his want of truth were dishonorable to him as a soldier and a gentleman.

The loss of the Americans in the fort was eighty-one killed and one hundred and eighty-nine wounded, seventy of whom were Kentucky volunteers. This

* Brackenridge.

does not include the killed and wounded under Colonel Dudley. The force under Proctor was reported at five hundred and fifty regulars, eight hundred militia, and fifteen hundred Indians,—the latter of whom fought with great courage, frequently saving their allies from total destruction.

After the cessation of hostilities, the savages returned to their homes, in accordance with an almost universal custom, and in spite of all the influence Tecumthe could exert. Proctor was so much weakened by this defection of his allies, that he was compelled precipitately to retreat, and to leave behind him, in his haste to make his escape, many valuable articles.

In reflecting upon the siege of Fort Meigs, a judicious writer * expresses the opinion that it was fortunate for the American cause that the enterprise of General Proctor against that fort was delayed so long. Had he been ready to sail as soon as the lake became navigable, and so timed his movements as to arrive at the fort during the first week in April, immediately after the last militia of the winter campaign had been discharged, and before General Harrison arrived with reinforcements, he must have succeeded against that post. The garrison was then left very weak, being considerably less than five hundred effective men. The works, too, were then very incomplete, and entirely too large for that of soldiers successfully to defend, as the fortified camp included seven or eight acres of land.

* M'Afee.

The capture of Fort Meigs would have been a most serious loss to the country, as it contained nearly all the artillery and military stores of the north-western army, besides a large amount of provisions. General Harrison repeatedly pressed upon the attention of the government, during the winter, the necessity of preparing a force to take the place of the militia then in service. But instead of this, the new Secretary of War, John Armstrong, who had been appointed to that office the preceding February, in place of William Eustis, at the critical moment when the last of those troops were disbanded, restricted General Harrison to the use of regulars, which were still to be levied in a country where it was almost impossible to raise a regiment of regulars through the whole year. Without the aid of the Ohio and Kentucky militia, which the general called into service without the authority and contrary to the views of the War Department, it is highly probable that the important post at the Rapids would have fallen into the hands of Proctor, and the bloody scenes of French-town been re-enacted.

CHAPTER X.

WITH the raising of the siege of Fort Meigs were suspended offensive operations on both sides for a considerable time. The troops were to remain at that post and Upper Sandusky until the completion of the naval preparations on Lake Erie, whichwere then in a considerable state of forwardness. Without the command of that lake, little of consequence could be accomplished, and any attempt either to recover Detroit or subdue Malden, objects which General Harrison as well as the government had much at heart, would be worse than useless, while it was in the hands of the enemy. The troops, therefore, must necessarily remain in a state of inactivity a great part of the summer, awaiting the completion of the fleet designed to co-operate with the army in those favorite objects.

While awaiting this event, therefore, General Harrison returned to Franklington for the purpose of organizing the forces which were to be concentrated at that place. In the course of the summer, deputies from the various Indian tribes residing in

Ohio, and from some of those in the territories of Indiana and Illinois, waited upon him at Franklington, and volunteered their services for the campaign into Canada. It had been the general policy of the government not to employ any of the friendly Indians in the service of the United States. The only exception to this human policy was in employing a small body under the command of the celebrated Logan, a nephew of Tecumthe. But the advice to them to remain neutral could not be comprehended, as they looked upon it as an indirect imputation upon their courage. General Harrison finally consented to receive them into his service, but only upon the condition that they should spare their prisoners, and not make war upon defenceless women and children.

He informed Tarke, the oldest Indian in the western country, who was at the head of the deputation, that he would be able to judge by the conduct of the Indians who might enter his service, whether the British could restrain those in their army from the horrible cruelty they had perpetrated. If the Indians under him would forbear such conduct, it would satisfy him that Proctor could also restrain them if he wished to do so. He humorously told the deputation that he had been informed that Proctor had promised to deliver him into the hands of Tecumthe, if he had succeeded at Fort Meigs, to be treated as that warrior might think proper. As a fair offset to this liberal offer, he promised them that, if Proctor should fall into his hands, they should have him as their prisoner, on condition that they would agree to treat him as a *squaw*, and put petticoats on him, for he must be a coward, deserving only such treatment, who would kill a defenceless prisoner.*

There is little doubt that the promise to deliver General Harrison, and all who fought at Tippecanoe, over to Tecumthe, if the attack on Fort Meigs should prove successful, with the understanding that they were to be burned at the stake, was true. Major Ball ascertained this fact from the prisoners, deserters and Indians, all of whom agree as to its truth; and besides, it is sustained by the previous conduct and well-established character of Proctor, though inconsistent with the conduct of Tecumthe after the treaty of Vincennes.†

Though the failure of the expedition against Fort Meigs, and the consequent dispersion of many of the British allies, had to a considerable extent checked the depredations of the savages upon the more thickly inhabited parts of the country, they still continued to attack the settlements along the borders of the lake from Frenchtown to Erie. Their inroads, however, received a temporary check from a squadron of horse under Major Ball, a brave and valuable officer. As he was descending the Sandusky with only twenty-two men, he was fired upon by about the same number of savages, from an ambuscade. He promptly charged upon them, drove them from their hiding places, and after an obstinate contest, in which both

* Sketches of Harrison.   † Dawson.

15

parties fought with great courage, the Indians were
defeated, and the whole band killed to a man. The
Indians fought with the ferocity of despair, but discipline prevailed over their savage desperation.

A hasty glance at the operations of the northern
army under General Dearborne. The British Government during the past winter had made extensive
preparations for the defense of Canada, and had sent
a large number of troops to Halifax, for the purpose
of being employed in that object. Great care and
energy had also been used in disciplining the militia of
Canada for the same purpose, while little had been
done on the American side toward the conquest of
that Province. In consequence of the unpopularity
of the war in the northern part of the union, it was
difficult to prevail on the States to call out the militia.
The favorable moment for the conquest of Canada,
therefore, seemed to have passed, though the hope
was still indulged that something might still be
done, if a proper spirit could be roused in the northern States, especially if the command of the lakes
could be obtained; there was no doubt entertained
that the whole of Upper Canada, at least, must fall.

Several acts of hostility took place, also, during
the winter on the northern frontier. In February,
a small party of British passed over from Canada, os-
tensibly in search of deserters, during which they committed many wanton depredations upon the houses
and property of American citizens. Determined to
avenge these injuries, Major Forsyth, who commanded

at Ogdensburgh, took part of a company of riflemen, with several volunteers, and entered Canada with such celerity that he surprised the British general at Elizabethtown, took fifty-two prisoners and a considerable amount of public property, after which he returned to Ogdensburgh without the loss of a man. Shortly after this exploit, on the 21st of February, the British made an attack upon Ogdensburgh, with a force of twelve hundred men, and succeeded with the vastly superior force in expelling Major Forsyth from the town, but not until after a sharp contest, in which the Americans lost twenty men in killed and wounded, and the enemy twice that number.

It was determined by the commander-in-chief to make a descent upon Canada, by such a force as should at least make itself felt. For this purpose General Zebulon Pike, one of the most accomplished officers and bravest men in the army, and a gentleman who was as highly beloved by the soldiers for his noble qualities of heart as he was respected and honored for his bravery and accomplishments, was selected for this responsible enterprise. After a conference between the commander and chief, it was determined that the contemplated expedition should be directed against York in Upper Canada. The fleet under Commodore Chauncey was ordered to co-operate with General Dearborne, in his plans of whatever character. On the 27th of April he landed his troops, destined for the attack about two miles from York, in spite of the most obstinate efforts of the British and Indians

to prevent him.   Having succeeded in landing all his
troops, in the midst of a destructive fire, he gallantly
charged the enemy and drove them all from their positions at the point of the bayonet.   They then fled
to the fort in all speed.

He at once formed his lines and commenced the
attack, carrying several of the batteries and driving
the enemy within the garrison.   Suspecting that some
stratagem was designed from the fact that the British
appeared to have deserted their barracks, he dispatched Lieutenant Riddle to learn the situation of
the enemy.   While waiting the return of Riddle he
seated himself upon the stump of a tree, after having
humanely removed a wounded British soldier to a
place of security, when suddenly an explosion took
place that shook the very earth.   The magazine had
blown up, and instantly the air was filled with huge
stones and fragments of wood which were rent asun-
der and whirled aloft with tremendous force.   The
magazine contained five hundred barrels of powder.
This was the treacherous and cowardly stratagem
General Pike had feared, but the precise nature of
which he could not have foreseen.

Immense quantities of these broken and blackened
fragments fell amongst the victorious columns of the
Americans, causing a havoc which the arms of the
enemy could not effect in a fair and honorable contest.   Upwards of two hundred Americans were thus
killed and wounded in a manner scarcely more credit-
able or less barbarous than the Frenchtown massa-

ere. Amongst the number slain was the beloved and heroic Pike. But though for a moment confounded by the shock and the dreadful havoc in their ranks, the brave troops almost instantly rallied, closing up their broken columns and giving, in their turn, three loud cheers. General Pike, though mortally wounded, preserved his undaunted spirit. With his last breath he addressed them in words of cheerful confidence. "Move on," he exclaimed, "my brave fellows, and avenge your general." The appeal was instantly obeyed, and with such irresistible impetuosity and gallantry as to overwhelm their treacherous foes, and soon the British flag was presented to Pike. At four o'clock the Americans were in possession of the town; and all the troops of the garrison, regulars and militia, naval officers and seamen, were surrendered prisoners of war. All the public stores were given up, but private property and the rights of the citizens were strictly respected.

The American loss, until the blowing up of the magazine, was inconsiderable. By this characteristic act of base treachery and cowardice, the number was increased to three hundred in killed and wounded. About three hundred British surrendered prisoners of war, besides the killed and wounded. But, as might have been expected from the treachery displayed by the British general in attempting to blow up the whole American force, the terms of the stipulation were not faithfully observed, for a large amount of public property was destroyed after the capitulation.

15*

The next enterprise of importance was an attack
upon Fort George and Fort Erie.   Both these forts
were captured, and all the British fortifications along
the shore fell into the hands of the Americans on the
27th of May.   In these operations Colonel Scott,
now commander-in-chief of the army of the United
States, and then an accomplished officer, distinguished himself, as he had the year before at Queenstown,
as did also General Boyd.   Commodore Chauncey,
who commanded our little navy on the lake, co-ope-
rated with the land forces and added greatly to the
success of the American arms.   Commodore Oliver
H. Perry also signalized himself in these various
movements.   The day after the battle, Lieutenant
Perry was dispatched to Black Rock with fifty men
for the purpose of taking five vessels to Erie, and to
prepare the squadron at that place for commencing
operations, in conjunction with General Harrison, as
early as the 15th of June.

A few days after the battle of Forts George and
Erie, the battle of Stoney Creek was fought.   Though
this action resulted in the accidental capture of both
General Chandler and General Winder, two American officers of distinction and acknowledged bravery,
they were nevertheless beaten in the action, with
great loss.   Their killed and wounded amounted to
more than double that of the Americans, besides one
hundred prisoners captured by the Americans.   But
these movements of General Dearborne against the
British fortifications on the Niagara had well nigh

cost the Americans dear. Taking advantage of the absence of the troops and fleet, the British made an attack upon Sacket's Harbor, the depository of all our naval and military stores, both those captured at York and those accumulated for a year past for the contemplated operations against Canada, and a place, therefore, of the utmost importance. The attack, however, proved unsuccessful, through the judgment and well-managed stratagem of General Brown. As usual, Sir George Provost, who commanded the attack, boastfully claimed a victory after his return to Canada.

The next enterprise of the British was a predatory incursion to the village of Sodus, principally with the view of destroying some stores that had been deposited there. But their stores being concealed in the woods upon their approach, and exasperated at their disappointment, they set fire to the most valuable part of the village, and continued their devastations until they were compelled precipitately to retreat. Shortly after this, Lieutenant Colonel Berstler was defeated in an attempt to dislodge the enemy from La Couse's house, about seventeen miles from Fort George. After having been attacked by a greatly superior force, while in the execution of this object, he and his whole party were compelled to surrender.*

The British, having been greatly reinforced a few days after, invested the American camp. During the remainder of this and the ensuing month a war of posts was kept up between the two armies. On

* Brackenridge.

the 8th of July a severe skirmish took place, in which nearly the whole force on both sides was engaged; but it ended in no important result. The British, however, succeeded in capturing Lieutenant Eldridge, an accomplished young officer, and ten men, who were never afterwards heard of. They were undoubtedly handed over to the savages, and by them inhumanly murdered. Three days after they attacked Black Rock, but were compelled to betake themselves to their boats, in great haste, almost immediately after landing. On the 28th of July, Colonel Winfield Scott undertook another expedition against York, which had been recaptured by the British. He landed suddenly at the head of three hundred men, destroyed the public stores, released a number of prisoners, and returned to Sacket's Harbor, with but a trifling loss.

The enemy's ambition seem to have been quite satisfied by this kind of warfare, during June and July, and they pursued it with a zest which showed that their hearts were in the cause. They continued their war upon such peaceable citizens, and their outrages upon such private property, as they could reach without too much exposure. They laid waste the country along the borders of Lake Champlain. All the public buildings at Plattsburgh were wantonly burnt, and a large amount of private property carried. Similar outrages were also committed at Swanton, in Vermont. On the lakes, little of importance to either side was accomplished during these months. Commodore Chauncey attempted to bring Sir James

Yeo to an engagement on Lake Ontario, but without success.

At the South, in the meantime, the enemy had prosecuted the war with even less of the usages of civilized nations than at the North; cruelty and destruction marked their course. Sometime in February, an attack was made upon Lewistown, on the Delaware, by Commodore Beresford; but the town making a gallant resistance, he was compelled to abandon the enterprise. But, on the Chesapeake, they were more successful. It was here that the notorious Cockburn, who commanded the British blockading squadron, acquired the reputation which has rendered his name infamous throughout the world, and given him a standing, in the eyes of all civilized countries, second only to that of Proctor. This miserable creature commenced operations as a rear-admiral in the British navy, by attacking and robbing detached farm-houses, wantonly slaughtering cattle that he could carry off, and by arming slaves against their masters. Emboldened by his success in robbing hen-roosts, and decoying women and children, he next turned his attention to objects offering richer plunder.

His first achievement on a large scale was against the village of Frenchtown, containing six dwelling-houses, two store-houses, and a few stables, which he gallantly captured, carrying off as usual a considerable amount of private property stored there. This exploit was followed by the still bolder one of burning Havre de Grace, a village of thirty houses, situ ated on the Susquehanna. Amongst other acts of bravery, during the burning of this town, they offered the grossest insults to the women, tearing their clothes from their backs, and subjecting them to almost every outrage. Having stolen all the private property that had been spared from the flames, and laying waste the country for miles around, they suspended the work of destruction for the work of something else to destroy. Following these victories over unarmed citizens and defenceless women and children, was the destruction of Georgetown and Frederickton, Maryland, both of which were plundered of everything valuable before being burned. Not long after these achievements, so honorable to the British arms, and so much in keeping with the chivalry and humanity of British officers, their fleet was greatly increased by the arrival of Admiral Warren from the West Indies.

It was soon ascertained that the first formidable enterprise of the English, after the reinforcement of their fleet, was an attack upon Norfolk. But before this could be successfully undertaken, it was necessary to subdue the forts by which it was protected. Craney Island was the first of these, and it was attacked with great fury on the 22nd of May; but they were repulsed with loss, several of their boats sunk, and their whole force compelled to make a precipitate retreat. To revenge themselves, however, for this defeat, they proceeded to pillage the town of Hampton, about eighteen miles from Norfolk; but they met with a warm reception, and, but for the immense superiority of force, would have been defeated. After they had got possession of the town, the most shocking outrages were committed upon the inhabitants. Full license was given the soldiers to gratify their passions; and such acts of brutality and blood-thirsty cruelty were perpetrated as never before disgraced the soldiers of any civilized nation.

Having satiated his thirst for blood and plunder, or rather having exhausted the means of gratifying it on the Chesapeake, the hen-roost robbing admiral proceeded farther south in search of new objects to display his gallantry upon. He commenced his career there by various depredations in North Carolina, quite as honorable as those by which he had already distinguished himself.

Though all the legitimate evils of war were experienced north of the Chesapeake, none of the barbarities which disgraced Cockburn's career were perpetrated. Nor, indeed, were there any very important movements or exploits of any kind on the northern coast. An attempt of considerable pretension was made upon New London, or rather an attempt was threatened, but the place was so well fortified that it was abandoned.

While these events were transpiring,—events that were, in the main, as dishonorable to the British name as they were annoying to the Americans,—our gallant little navy had been running a career of glory that filled the breast of every American with pride, and the hearts of our enemies with mortification. One of the most brilliant of this series of victories was the capture of the "Peacock," Captain Peake, by the "Hornet," Captain Lawrence, on the 23rd of February, 1812. The "Peacock" was of somewhat superior force to the "Hornet." The action only lasted fifteen minutes, during which the enemy was literally cut to pieces, and went down before her crew could be rescued by the utmost efforts of Captain Lawrence and his crew.

This brilliant victory, however, was more than counterbalanced by the capture of the "Chesapeake," commanded by the victor of the "Peacock," by the British frigate "Shannon," on the 21st of June following. This calamity was owing, not to the want of courage and good conduct in Captain Lawrence, but must be attributed to the character of his crew, most of whom had but just been enlisted. Many of his officers were also sick; and, worse than all, several foreigners had crept into the ship's crew, who had succeeded in poisoning their minds. This victory made the British nation almost wild with joy, as it seemed to afford them some hope that the American navy was not quite invincible, a fact about which they were beginning to have their doubts. This hope was considerably strengthened by the capture of the "Argus," after having for two months committed great havoc upon the shipping of the enemy in the English channel.

On the 5th of September, these misfortunes were

partly compensated by the brilliant victory of the American brig "Enterprise," Lieutenant Commandant William Burrows, over the British frigate "Boxer," of superior force. But this victory was purchased with the life of the brave Burrows, the only man killed on board the "Enterprize." The commander of the Boxer was also killed. On the 26th of the same month, Commodore Rogers returned after a most successful cruise of five months, having captured a large number of British merchant vessels, and the British war schooner, "Highflier," a tender to Admiral Warren. The "Congress," Captain Smith, which put to sea with the "President," returned on the 12th of December, having also captured a large number of the enemy's vessels and two armed brigs.

Besides these brilliant achievements, — for even the actions in which the "Chesapeake" and "Argus" were captured added to our naval renown,—on the part of our vessels of war, the American private cruisers rendered valuable service to the country, and aided to convince our proud and powerful enemy that America would, at no distant day, dispute the claim of Great Britain to mistress of the sea. In the engagement between the "Comet" and a Portuguese brig and three armed merchantmen, Captain Boyle, the commander of the "Comet," after fighting them all for several hours, compelled the brig, though double his own force, to make her escape, and captured one of the merchantmen. Little less brilliant

16

was the action between the privateer "Decatur" and the British vessel of war "Dominica," in which the latter was captured, after a hard contest. Many other actions equally honorable to our brave seamen, and equally beneficial to the American cause, we fought during the summer, and immense damage was done to British commerce.

CHAPTER XI.

HAVING thus given a very meagre glance at some of the leading events transpiring at the North, along the Atlantic course, and on the ocean, during this second year of the war, the history of operations with which General Harrison was more immediately connected will be resumed. In these occurrences, important preparations were being made by him at the West. Public attention was directed to that quarter with great anxiety, and the northern army remained almost with folded arms, awaiting the campaign upon which he was about to enter, and of the daily anticipated contest for the command of Lake Erie. The British labored with equal diligence to strengthen themselves, fully alive as they were to the fatal consequences of defeat either on the lake or by land. Troops were therefore constantly arriving to reinforce Proctor's army, and to enable him to follow up any advantage that might be obtained over our fleet.*

On the other hand, the people of Ohio and Ken-

* Brackenridge raising reinforcements and organizing.

tucky were making the most patriotic sacrifices in seconding the efforts of General Harrison. One universal feeling of excitement prevailed amongst the people; and had the exigencies of the country required it, every man capable of bearing arms would cheerfully have marched to her defence at whatever sacrifice. Fifteen thousand men, — three times the number required,—promptly responded to the call of the patriotic Governor Meigs of Ohio; and the noble-hearted Shelby, Governor of Kentucky, declared his intention of putting himself at the head of the volunteers of that State, whose number he limited to four thousand, with the determination of avenging their murdered friends and brothers.

General Harrison, who, it will be recollected, was left at Franklinton with his army for active operations, received information in June that Fort Meigs was again invested. But this proved to be a false alarm; and, after satisfying himself that the enemy had no such immediate intention, he returned to Lower Sandusky. From that place, he set off for Cleveland, on business connected with the public stores accumulated there, and to hasten the completion of boats designed for transporting the army across the lake. On the 23rd of July, a body of eight hundred Indians passed Fort Meigs, and it was supposed they contemplated an attack upon Fort Winchester. Two days afterwards, a large body of Indians and British, amounting to not less than five thousand men, mostly Indians, passed in the same direction. This was the largest army of Indians ever assembled on any occasion during the army.

General Harrison, however, came to the conclusion that this movement against Fort Meigs was designed to divert his attention from Lower Sandusky, the real object of attack. The result proved the remarkable accuracy of his judgment. He immediately removed his head quarters to Seneca, nine miles above that place. He could thus fall back upon Upper Sandusky, should circumstances render it necessary, and move to the relief of Fort Meigs, as these two points were of far more importance than Lower Sandusky. Major George Croghan, with one hundred and sixty regulars, was left at the latter place for the defence of Fort Stephenson. The number of troops at Seneca amounted to only six hundred, a force entirely too small to advance upon Fort Meigs. Captain Mc Cune was sent back to General Clay, then in command of that post, with information that, as early as the commander-in-chief could collect a sufficient number of troops, he would relieve that fort. But the day after the return of the express, the enemy raised the siege, and, as had been foreseen by General Harrison, the British sailed round into Sandusky Bay, while the Indians marched across the country to aid in the attack upon Lower Sandusky, now satisfactorily ascertained to be the real object against which their efforts were to be directed.*

On the 21st of April of this year, General Har-

* Sketches of General Harrison.

16 *

rison had written to the Secretary of War, advising him
that he should cause the movements of the enemy to be
narrowly watched; but that in the event of his landing at Lower Sandusky it could not, in his opinion,
be saved, and he should cause it to be evacuated and
the arms there removed. Shortly before the express
from Fort Meigs reached General Harrison, he, in
company with Major Croghan and other officers, had
examined Fort Stephenson, and come to the conclusion that it could not be defended against heavy artillery, and that it then must be abandoned and burnt,
provided a retreat could be safely effected. In the
orders given Major Croghan, he was immediately to
retreat in case he could discover the approach of the
enemy with cannon, in season to do so, and to destroy
all the public stores. It was suggested that the attempt to retreat in the face of an Indian force would
be vain, and that against such an enemy, however
great, the garrison would be safe.

Immediately upon information being received by
the commander-in-chief, a council of war was held,
composed of McArthur, Cass, Bull, Wood, Holmes,
Hukill, Paul, and Graham, who were unanimously of
opinion that Fort Stephenson was untenable against
heavy artillery, and that the garrison should be withdrawn and the place destroyed, upon the approach of
the enemy. An order was therefore forthwith sent to
him, requiring him at once to abandon the fort, set
fire to it, and repair with his command to head quarters. This order did not reach Major Croghan until

the next day, the 30th of July. By this time he was of opinion that he would not retreat with safety, as the Indians had surrounded the fort in considerable numbers.

In this opinion a majority of his officers concurred. They were equally decided in the opinion that the fort would be maintained, at any rate, until further instructions could be received from head quarters. Major Croghan therefore promptly acknowledged the receipt of this order, informing the commander-in-chief that it had been received too late to make good his retreat, and then laconically adding, "we have determined to maintain this place; by heavens, we can!" Not understanding the motives which induced this apparent disobedience of orders, nor the considerations which prompted the use of such strong language,—the fear it might fall into the hands of the enemy,—next morning sent General Wells, under the escort of Colonel Ball and a detachment of dragoons to relieve Major Croghan of his ordering him to repair to head quarters. On his arrival there, he explained his motives to the satisfaction of General Harrison, and was immediately after directed to resume his post, and fully authorized to defend the fort to the last.

The next day it was supposed that the British were within twenty miles of Fort Stephenson, approaching the place by water. It was not till after twelve o'clock on the 1st of August, when the scouts that had been sent out by General Harrison communicated this information to Major Croghan. In a few hours after, the fort was actually invested by the British and Indians. The force of the enemy amounted to five hundred regulars and seven hundred Indians, under the command of the despicable General Proctor. After he had made such a disposition of his troops as rendered it impossible for the garrison to escape, he sent a flag of truce by Colonel Elliot and Major Chambers, demanding the surrender of the fort, accompanied with the usual threat of butchery and massacre of the garrison should it persist in holding out.

Major Croghan, finding that all his companions— who, like himself, were mere striplings—would support him to the last, declined the summons, assuring the bearers that "when the garrison surrendered, there would be none left to massacre, as it would not be given up while there was a man able to fight." When the flag returned, bearing this Spartan-spirited reply, a brisk fire was opened from six-pounders in their boats, and from a howitzer, which was kept up during the night. The next morning it was discovered that three sixes had been planted, under cover of the darkness, within two hundred and fifty yards of the pickets, which shortly after commenced firing, with little effect. About four o'clock in the afternoon, the enemy having concentrated his fire against the north-west angle of the fort, with the intention of making a breach, it was immediately strengthened by means of bags of flour and sand. At the same time, the six-pounder, the only piece of artillery in the fort, was carefully concealed in the bastion which covered the point to be assailed, and loaded with slugs and grape shot.

About five hundred of the enemy now advanced to attack the part where it was supposed the pickets had been injured, at the same time making several feints to draw the attention of the besieged from the real point to be assailed. Their force being thus disposed, a column of three hundred and fifty men, who were so completely enveloped in a density of smoke as not to be seen until they approached within twenty paces of the lines, advanced rapidly to the assault. A fire of musketry from the fort threw them for a moment into confusion; but they were quickly rallied by Colonel Short, who sprung over the outer works into the ditch, and commanded them to follow, character- istically exclaiming, " Give the d——d Yankees no quarter." Scarcely had the profane and inhuman order been uttered, when the six-pounder opened upon them a most destructive fire, killing their barbarous leader and twenty others, and wounding as many more. A volley of musketry was discharged upon the assailants with fatal effect.

The officer who succeeded Colonel Short in the command, exasperated at meeting such opposite re- sistance from a parcel of boys, formed the broken columns anew, and again rushed to the onset with re- doubled fury. The six-pounder was again played upon them with the same terrible success as before, and the volleys from the musketry were poured in upon them in such rapid succession, and with such unerring certainty, that they were once more thrown into confusion, and, in spite of the exertion of their officers, fled to an adjoining wood with even more speed than they had, but a few moments before, exercised to gain, as they thought, so easy and so certain prey. Their savage allies immediately followed them, and shortly after the assailants abandoned the attack in despair. Panic struck, they retreated to their boats in sullen silence, scarcely daring to cast their eyes towards the spot where so many of their companions had found a bloody grave, and where they had met with so ignominious a defeat from an enemy they held in so much contempt, and scarcely one-tenth their own number.*

Glorious as was the conduct of the heroic Croghan and his brave companions in this gallant defence of a post decided by a council of war to be *fenceless*, it reflects scarcely more honor on the noble little band than their treatment towards their wounded enemies who had been left at their mercy by the British in their flight. Regardless of the fact that they were doomed to an indiscriminate massacre had they fallen into the hands of Proctor's butchers, and of every other consideration save the impulses of their own noble souls, they directed their whole efforts to relieving the sufferings of their wounded foes. Provisions and water were handed over the

* Brackenridge.

pickets to them during the night; and although a firing was still kept up upon them, an opening was made, and many of them were removed within the fort where they were immediately supplied with surgical aid and every kindness and attention within the power of the victors shown them. The fabled eastern prince, who offered the hand of his daughter to the man who would do the noblest and most disinterested act, would have awarded the prize to Croghan, had he lived in that age. No fairer wreath can adorn the brow of a soldier than such conduct, under such circumstances. It was not so much that the objects of his humane treatment were his own and his companion's chosen and willing executions, as that they were the perpetrators of the Frenchtown massacre, that renders this act of magnanimity so truly noble.

In this brilliant defense, the Americans' loss amounted to one killed and seven wounded. The enemy lost one hundred and fifty in killed and wounded, more than one-third of whom was killed. Upwards of fifty were found in and about the ditch after the enemy had fled. The next morning it was discovered that the enemy had retreated, and with so much precipitation that they left behind them one boat, a considerable quantity of military stores, and upwards of seventy stands of arms. During the day, the Americans were engaged in burying their dead, with the honors of war, and in providing for their wounded.

This achievement, so honorable in every respect to

the gallant defenders of Fort Stephenson, or Fort Sandusky, called forth, as it deserved, the admiration of the whole American people. Major Croghan, together with Captain Hunter, Lieutenants Johnson and Baylor, and Ensigns Shipp and Duncan (the latter afterwards governor of Illinois), of the seventeenth regiment, as well as several other officers and volunteers, were highly complimented by General Harrison. They also, afterwards, received the thanks of Congress. Major Croghan was promoted to the rank of Lieutenant-Colonel, and was presented with an elegant sword by the patriotic ladies of Chillicothe. In General Harrison's official report of this brilliant affair, he said: "It will not be among the least of General Proctor's mortifications to find that he has been baffled by a youth who has just passed his twenty-first year. He is, however, a hero worthy of his gallant uncle, George R. Clark." *

When General Harrison was informed of the attack upon Fort Stephenson, he hesitated, very naturally, before going to its relief. He was hourly expecting considerable reinforcements, but had not then a disposable force of more than eight hundred men, one-fifth of whom was cavalry, who would have been of little service in the thick woods between Seneca and Lower Sandusky. The remainder of this force was raw recruits, upon whom he did not consider it safe to rely in such an emergency. He feared that to have marched against an enemy several thou-

* See Appendix (C).

sand strong, with such a force, would have resulted in its total destruction. He would also in that case be compelled to leave one hundred and fifty sick soldiers in his camp at Seneca, exposed to the ruthless foe, while the public stores at Upper Sandusky, in which were included ten thousand barrels of flour, which were indispensable to the main objects of the campaign, would be equally exposed to the attack of Tecumthe and his horde of savages.

This renowned chief was then lying between Seneca and Fort Meigs, ready to fall upon either the former place or Upper Sandusky the moment General Harrison should march to the relief of Fort Stephenson. He was bound, therefore, on correct military principles, to retain that position in which he could with the most certainty accomplish the best results.[*] Confidently relying upon reinforcements before the fort could be reduced, he determined to await the progress of events for a time, at least. On the night of the 2nd of August, that the enemy was retreating, and having in the meantime received a reinforcement of three hundred Ohio militia, he set out for the fort early the next morning, attended by the dragoons, and directing the remainder of his disposable force to follow under Generals Cass and McArthur. Upon arriving at the fort, he was informed by a wounded British sergeant, that Tecumthe was in the swamp, south of Fort Meigs, ready to attack Upper Sandusky, upon the first opportunity. This information

* Sketches of General Harrison.

17

corroborated what he had before heard, and induced him to direct General McArthur, who had not yet reached the fort, to return to Seneca with all possible dispatch.

The conduct of the commander-in-chief, in regard to the defense of Fort Stephen, having been subject to severe criticism by his enemies, the testimony of the gallant Major Croghan himself, in reply to these disingenuous charges, may be here appropriately introduced. In a letter to a friend in Cincinnati, dated at Lower Sandusky, August 27th, 1813, he wrote as follows:

"I have, with much regret, seen in some of the public prints such misrepresentations respecting my refusal to evacuate this post as are calculated not only to injure me in the estimation of military men, but also to excite unfavorable impressions as to the propriety of General Harrison's conduct relative to this affair.

"His character as a military man is too well established to need my approbation or support. But his public services entitle him at least to common justice: this affair does not furnish causes of reproach. If public opinion has been hastily misled respecting his late conduct, it will require but a moment's cool dispassionate reflection to convince them of its propriety. The measures recently adopted by him, so far from deserving censure, are the clearest proofs of his keen penetration and able generalship. It is true that I did not proceed immediately to execute his order to evacuate the post; but this disobedience was not (as some would wish to believe) the result of a fixed determination to maintain the post contrary to his most positive orders, as will appear from the following detail, which is given to explain my conduct.

"About ten o'clock, on the morning of the 30th ult., a letter from the Adjutant-General's office, dated Seneca Town, July 29, 1813, was handed me by Mc Conner, ordering me to abandon this post, burn it, and retreat that night to head quarters. On the reception of the order, I called a council of officers, in which it was determined not to abandon the place, at least until the further pleasure of the general should be known, as it was thought an attempt to retreat in open day, in the face of a superior force of the enemy, would be more hazardous than to remain in the fort, under all its disadvantages. I therefore wrote a letter to the general, couched in such terms as I thought were calculated to deceive the enemy, should it fall into his hands, which I thought more than probable, as well as to inform the general, should it be so fortunate as to reach him, that I would wait to hear from him before I should proceed to execute his order. This letter, contrary to my expectations, was received by the general, who, not knowing what reasons urged me to write in a tone so decisive, concluded, very rationally, that the manner of it was demonstrative of a most positive determination to disobey his orders under any circumstances. I was therefore suspended from the command of the fort, and ordered to head quarters. But on explaining to the general my reasons for not executing his order, and my object in using the style I had done, he was so perfectly satisfied with the explanation that I was immediately reinstated in the command.

"It will be recollected that the order above alluded to was written on the night previous to my receiving it. Had it been delivered to me, as was intended, that night, I should have obeyed it without hesitation. Its not reaching me in time was the only reason which induced me to consult my officers on the propriety of waiting the general's further orders.

"It has been stated also that, 'upon my representation of my ability to maintain this post, the general altered his determination to abandon it.' This is incorrect; no such representation was ever made. And the last order I received from the general was precisely the same as that first given; viz., that if I discovered the approach of a large British force by water (presuming they would bring heavy artillery), and had time enough to effect a retreat, I was to do so; but if I could not retreat with safety, to defend the post to the last extremity.

"A day or two before the enemy appeared at Fort Meigs, the general had reconnoitered the surrounding ground, and being informed that the hill on the opposite side of Sandusky completely commanded the fort, I offered to undertake, with the troops under my command, to remove it to that side. The general, upon reflection, thought it best not to attempt it, as he believed that if the enemy again appeared on this side of the lake it would be before the work could be finished.

"It is useless to disguise the fact, that this fort is commanded by the points of high ground around it. One single stroke of the eye made this clear to me the first time I had occasion to examine the neighborhood, with a view of discovering the relative strength and weakness of the place.

"It would be insincere to say that I am not flattered by the many handsome things which have been said about the defense which was made by the troops under my command: but I desire no plaudits which are bestowed upon me at the expense of General Harrison.

"I have at all times enjoyed his confidence, so far as my rank in the army entitled me to it, and on proper occasions received his marked attention. I have felt the warmest attachment for him as a man, and my confidence in him as an able commander remains unshaken. I feel every assurance that he will at all times do me ample justice; and nothing could give me more pain than to seize upon the occasion to deal out their unfriendly feelings and acrimonious dislike; and so long as he continues (as in my humble opinion he has done) to make the wisest arrangements and most judicious disposition which the forces under his command will justify, I shall not hesitate to unite with the army in bestowing upon him that confidence

17 *

which he so richly merits, and which has on no occasion been withheld.

"In addition to the above unqualified and magnanimous approval of General Harrison's conduct by one more nearly interested, personally, in the charges against him, all the field officers of the army united in a cordial approval of his conduct, and in an unqualified denial of the truth of those charges. Amongst others who thus unequivocally and indignantly repudiated everything like improper conduct in the commander-in-chief, in reference to this affair, were General Lewis Cass, Colonel Samuel Wells, Colonel T. D. Owen, Colonel George Paul, Colonel J. C. Boatless, and Lieutenant-Colonel Ball. These two documents spontaneously given, and from the highest possible authority, must for ever put at rest, at least with all generous minds, the censures which partizan illiberality attempted to cast upon his fair name, and his military fame."

CHAPTER XII.

IMMEDIATELY after the termination of the brilliant defense of Fort Stephenson, and the disgraceful repulse of the enemy, Tecumthe raised the siege of Fort Meigs, and followed Proctor to Detroit, all hopes being given up by the enemy of reducing the American forts, until they could gain the ascendancy on the lake. The utmost exertions had been made in the meanwhile, by Captain Perry, to complete the naval arrangements on Lake Erie. By the 2nd of August, the fleet was fully equipped, though some time was lost in getting several of the vessels over the bar at the mouth of Erie harbor. On the 4th, Captain Perry sailed in quest of the enemy, but not meeting him, he returned on the 8th. But after receiving a reinforcement of sailors, he again sailed on the 12th, and on the 15th anchored in the Bay of Sandusky. Here he took in a few volunteer marines, and again sailed in search of the enemy, and after cruising off Malden a short time, retired to Put-in-Bay, a distance of thirty miles.

The fleet of Captain Perry consisted of the brig "Lawrence," his flag ship, of twenty guns; the "Niagara," Captain Elliot, of twenty guns; the "Caled...nian," Lieutenant Turner, of three guns; the schooner "Ariel," of four guns; the "Scorpion," of two guns; the "Somers," of two guns and two swivels; the sloop "Trippe," and the schooners "Tigris" and "Porcupine," of one gun each, amounting in all to nine vessels, fifty-four guns and two swivels.

On the morning of the 10th of September, the enemy was bearing down upon the American squadron, which immediately got under way, and stood out to meet him. The Americans had three vessels more than the British; but this advantage was fully counterbalanced by the size and number of guns of those of the enemy. The fleet of the latter consisted of the "Detroit," Commodore Barclay, of nineteen guns; the "Queen Charlotte," Captain Finnis, of seventeen guns; the schooner "Lady Provost," Lieutenant Buchan, of thirteen guns and two howitzers; the brig "Hunter," of two guns; the sloop "Little Belt," of three guns; and the schooner "Chippewa," of one gun and two swivels; in all, six vessels, sixty-three guns, four howitzers and two swivels.

When the Americans stood out, the British fleet had the weather gage, but the wind soon after changed and brought the American fleet to the windward. The line of battle was formed at eleven o'clock, and at fifteen minutes before twelve the enemy's flag-ship, and the "Queen Charlotte," opened the fire upon the "Lawrence," which she sustained for ten minutes before she was near enough to return the fire. She continued to bear up, making signals for the other vessels to hasten to her support. At five minutes before twelve she brought her guns to bear upon the enemy. The wind being light, unfortunately the smaller vessels could not come up to her assistance, and she was, therefore, compelled to contend single-handed for two hours with two ships, each nearly equal to her in force. But the contest was maintained by her with unshaken courage, and with a coolness which won the highest admiration.

By this time the "Lawrence" had become entirely unmanageable, every gun in her being dismounted, and with the exception of four or five, the whole crew either killed or wounded. Perry, therefore, determined to leave her. With a presence of mind and courage that showed forth the praise of the gallant officer to whom he was opposed, he sprung into his boat, and heroically waving his sword passed with his flag unharmed to the "Niagara." At the moment he reached the "Niagara," the flag of the "Lawrence" came down. She was utterly disabled and could make no further resistance. Captain Elliot now left the "Niagara" with the view of bringing up the rest of the fleet, while Perry again bore down upon the enemy in a ship that had as yet taken no part in the action. As he passed ahead of the "Detroit," "Queen Charlotte" and "Lady Provost," he poured into each a broadside from his starboard side, and from his larboard poured a broadside into the "Chippewa" and "Little Belt." The fire upon the "Lady Provost," was so destructive that the men were compelled to take refuge below.

At this moment the wind freshened, and the "Caledonian" was enabled to come into action, opening a heavy fire. Several of the other vessels were soon after able to follow her example. For a time this action, the result of which was to have so important a bearing upon the whole campaign, raged with indescribable violence. The command of a sea, and the honor of two rival nations, as well as the result of a campaign, hung upon the issue. But the contest was not long doubtful. The "Queen Charlotte" lost her Captain, and all her principal officers, and by some mischance ran foul of the "Detroit," and thus the greater part of the guns were rendered useless. The two ships were now in turn compelled to sustain a heavy and incessant fire from the "Niagara," and the other vessels of the American squadron. The flag of Captain Barclay soon struck, and the "Queen Charlotte," the "Lady Provost," the "Hunter," and the "Chipppewa," surrendered in immediate succession. The "Little Belt" attempted to escape, but was pursued by two gun-boats and was captured.*

Thus terminated the first naval action between an American and a British fleet. Our ships had often met and conquered the enemy in single combat, but we had never before beaten Great Britain in squadron. Every vessel of the enemy was captured, and the Americans, by this brilliant victory, had acquired

* Brackenridge.

absolute command of Lake Erie, and rendered the fall of Malden, and the recovery of Detroit, and consequently of Michigan, almost certain. If anything could enhance the brilliancy of this victory, and add to the fame of the heroic Perry, it was the modest and ever memorable terms in which he announced the splendid achievement. *" We have met the enemy and they are ours,"* has become and will remain the watchword of victory, while the Union lasts, and will do little less to render immortal the name of Oliver Hazzard Perry, than the victory the language was designed to announce.

The loss on both sides, in this engagement, was unusually severe, compared with their respective forces, though much the heaviest in the British fleet. The Americans had twenty-seven killed and ninety-six wounded. Amongst the former were Lieutenant Brooks of the marines, and Midshipman Laub; and amongst the latter, Lieutenant Yarnall, Sailing-master Taylor, Purser Hamilton, and Midshipmen Claxton and Swartwout. The loss of the British amounted to about two hundred, in killed and wounded, many of whom were officers; and the prisoners, who amounted to six hundred, exceeded the whole number of Americans engaged under Perry. After the victory had been decided, Commmodore Perry's humane conduct to the wounded British soldiers, and his kind consideration to his prisoners, was as honorable to his nature as his coolness and bravery during the action was to him as an officer. It called forth their warmest thanks. Captain Barclay declared that "his conduct towards the captive officers and men was enough to immortalize him."

Having now by this signal victory over the British, and the destruction of their whole fleet, obtained undisputed possession of the lake, active preparations were immediately made for expelling Proctor from Malden, and for the recovery of Detroit. General Harrison called on Governor Meigs for a portion of the Ohio volunteers, who, it has previously been stated, had tendered their services to General Harrison; the whole of whom had not yet been disbanded. On the 17th of September, four thousand volunteers, the flower of Kentucky, with the venerable and patriotic Governor Shelby, the hero of King's mountain, at their head, arrived at General Harrison's camp.

Thus reinforced, the commander-in-chief determined at once to embark the infantry on board the fleet for Malden; and he directed Colonel Richard M. Johnson to proceed with his mounted regiment of Kentuckians to Detroit by land. The latter accordingly took up their line of march, and arrived at the point of destination on the 30th of September, the day after the infantry. On the 27th, the other troops embarked on board the vessels, and the next day arrived at a point below Malden. But the British general, brave as he was, in making war upon ·unarmed men, declined to wait the approach of the Americans at that point. He had therefore destroyed the fleet and public stores, and retreated along the Thames

towards the Moravian villages, together with his savage allies under Tecumthe.   Upon arriving at Malden, a number of females came out to implore the
protection of the commander-in-chief; but he had
already given orders that even Proctor himself, if
taken prisoner, should not be harmed, much less innocent and unprotected women.   Governor Shelby had
also issued an address to the Kentucky troops, enforcing it upon them to treat the inhabitants with justice
and humanity, and to respect private property.   On
the 29th, the army reached Detroit, and took possession of that town.   It was resolved by General
Harrison and Governor Shelby to proceed immediately in pursuit of General Proctor.

On the 2nd of October, they marched with a force
of three thousand selected men, consisting chiefly of
Colonel Ball's dragoons, Colonel Johnson's mounted
regiment, and other detachments of Governor Shelby's Kentucky volunteers.   Commodore Perry and
General Cass accompanied General Harrison on this
enterprise as volunteer aids.   On the first day the
army moved with such rapidity that it traveled twenty-six miles.   The same day they captured a Lieutenant of dragoons and eleven privates, from whom it
was ascertained that Proctor had no certain knowledge of the approach of General Harrison.   While
repairing a bridge across a branch of the Thames,
which the enemy had partly destroyed, they were
attacked by a body of Indians from the other side.
But they were soon dispersed, and two thousand stand

18

of arms and a quantity of clothing taken. They then pursued the enemy four miles up the Thames, taking several pieces of cannon, and compelling them to destroy several vessels containing public stores. The following day they reached the place where the enemy had encamped the night before.

General Harrison ascertained shortly after that the British army had made a stand a few miles distant, and was preparing for action. General Proctor had drawn up his regular forces across a narrow strip of land covered with hearth trees, flanked on one side by a swamp, and on the other by the River Thames. Their left rested on the river, supported by the larger portion of their artillery, and their right on the swamp. Beyond the swamp, and between it and the other morass, still further to the right, were posted the Indians under Tecumthe. This position was skilfully chosen by Proctor; but he committed a fatal error in neglecting to fortify his front, and drawing up his troops in open order. His whole force consisted of eight hundred regular soldiers, and two thousand Indian warriors.*

The troops, at General Harrison's disposal, amounted to about three thousand. But when it is recollected that the enemy had chosen his own position, effectually securing his flank, and that Harrison could not present to him a line more extended than his own, this disparity of force will be admitted to be nearly or quite compensated for, and the superior bravery of

* Brackenridge.

the American troops made apparent. They consisted of about one hundred and twenty regulars, of the twenty-seventh regiment; five brigades of Kentucky volunteer militia infantry, under Governor Shelby, averaging less than five hundred men; and Colonel Johnson's mounted infantry. No disposition of an army, opposed to an Indian force, can be safe, unless it can be secured on the flank and in the rear. General Harrison formed his men in conformity with this idea.

General Trotter's brigade, of five hundred men, formed the front line; his right up the road, and his left upon the swamp. General King's brigade formed the second line, one hundred and fifty yards in the rear of General Trotter's; and General Child's brigade, as a corps reserve, in the rear of it. These three brigadiers formed the command of Major-General Henry. The whole of General Desha's division, consisting of two brigades, were formed *en potence* on the left of General Trotter.

While General Harrison was engaged in forming the infantry, he had directed Colonel Johnson's regiment, which was still in front, to be formed in two lines opposite to the enemy; and, upon the advance of the infantry, to take ground to the left, and fixing upon that flank, endeavor to turn the right of the Indians. But from the thickness of the woods, and swampiness of the ground, he was convinced that they would be unabled to do anything on horseback, and there was no time to dismount and place their horses

in security. He, therefore, determined to refuse his
left to the Indians, and to break the British lines, at
once, by a charge of the mounted infantry. This was
a novel movement in military tactics, suggested by
General Harrison's good judgment, and one that
he was satisfied would succeed, from the fact that
American backwoodsmen ride better in the woods
than any other people. He was persuaded, too, that
the enemy would be quite unprepared for the shock,
and would be unable to resist it.

In accordance with this plan, General Harrison
directed the regiment to be drawn up in close columns,
with its right at a distance of fifty yards from the
road, that it might be, in some measure, protected by
the trees from the artillery; its left upon the swamp,
and to charge at full speed as soon as the enemy
delivered their fire. The few regular troops of the
twenty-seventh regiment, under Colonel Paul, occupied, in columns of sections four, the small space,
between the road and the river, for the purpose of
seizing the enemy's artillery, and some ten or twelve
friendly Indians were directed to move under the
bank. The crotchet formed by the first line, and General Desha's division, was an important point. At that
place Governor Shelby was posted.

General Harrison placed himself at the head of
the front line of infantry to direct the movements
of the cavalry, and to give them the necessary
support. The army had moved on in this order, but
a short distance, when the mounted men received the

fire of the British line and were ordered to charge.
The horses in the front column recoiled from the fire.
Another fire was immediately given by the enemy,
and the cavalry at length, getting in motion, broke
through them with irresistible force.   In one minute
the contest in front was over.   The British officers,
seeing no hope of reducing their broken and panic-
struck ranks to order, and the American mounted
men wheeling upon them and pouring in upon them a
steady and destructive fire, immediately surrendered.
Upon the left, however, the contest was more severe
with the Indians.   Colonel Johnson, who commanded
on the flank of his regiment, received a most galling
fire from them : but it was returned with great effect.
The Indians, still further to the right, advanced and
fell in with our front line of infantry, near its junction with General Desha's division, and for a moment
made an impression upon it.   Governor Shelby, however, brought up a regiment to its support, and the
enemy receiving a severe fire in front, and a part of
Colonel Johnson's regiment having gained their rear,
retreated with precipitation.

During the action the Indians, under their distinguished leader, Tecumthe, fought with a courage and
determination which the British troops did not exhibit.   The voice of their great chief could be distinctly heard, even above the roar of battle, encouraging his warriors to increased efforts ; and although
beset on every side, except that of the morass, they
fought with more obstinate bravery than they had

18*

ever exhibited before. Indeed, they only ceased their
efforts after the fall of Tecumthe, who was killed near
the close of the action. Colonel Johnson having observed the desperation with which he and a body
of warriors who had gathered around him fought,
charged into the midst of them. His uniform and
the white horse he rode made him a conspicuous mark
for Indian rifles, and he almost immediately fell badly
wounded. Tecumthe meanwhile was killed in the
mêlée; but the Indians continued to fight as fiercely
as ever for some time, until no longer hearing the
voice of their great leader, they gave way on all
sides. The contest was now closed, and the Americans had obtained an overwhelming victory over the
marauder Proctor and his far greater and more magnanimous ally, Tecumthe.

The loss of the British in this engagement was
nineteen killed, fifty wounded, and six hundred taken
prisoners. The Indians left one hundred and twenty
on the field. The American loss, in killed and wounded, amounted to upwards of fifty, seventeen of whom
were Kentuckians. Several pieces of brass cannon,
the trophies of the revolutionary war, and which had
been surrendered by General Hull at Detroit, were,
retaken. General Proctor basely deserted his troops,
almost at the very commencement of the action, thus
confirming beyond a doubt the proof of his cowardice
already given by his conduct in murdering disarmed
prisoners.

General Harrison immediately ordered Colonel

Payne to pursue the fugitive with a part of his battallion, which was promptly done, and the pursuit continued for a distance of six miles beyond the Moravian towns, where some Indians were killed, and a large amount of public property captured. The pursuit was still continued by several officers, with their privates, for several miles, but was arrested by the darkness of night. His pursuers, however, pressed him so closely that he was obliged to abandon his carriage, which, together with his sword and papers, fell into their hands, and conceal himself in the forest.

In communicating to the Secretary of War his report of this action, he commended, in the warmest terms, the conduct of his officers and men on the occasion. Of Governor Shelby especially he spoke in terms of the highest admiration, and scarcely less warmly of Generals Henry, Desha, Allen, Caldwell, King, Chiles, and Trotter; of his aids O'Fallen, Todd, Perry, Cass, Smith and Chambers; of Colonel Johnson, Payne and Thompson, and of Major Wood and Captain Butler, all of whom rendered their country good service on that day, as did every officer and private in the engagement. Commodore Perry repayed the important aid General Harrison had rendered him in the battle of Lake Erie.

It has been well said that, in the signal victory gained over Barclay's fleet and Proctor's army, it is impossible to separate the brave and victorious commanders. The circumstances are indeed very striking. General Harrison sent reinforcements to assist

Perry, and the action terminated in the capture of the whole British fleet. In return, Commodore Perry volunteered with General Harrison, and assisted him in the capture of the British army. Perry, himself, in writing to General Harrison, bears cheerful testimony to the valuable aid received from him. He says, "the very great assistance, in the action of the 10th, rendered by these men, you were pleased to send on board the squadron, renders it a duty to return you my sincere thanks for so timely a reinforcement. In fact, sir, I may say, that without those nine, the victory could not have been achieved."

Having now, in conjunction with Commodore Perry, taken quiet possession of Upper Canada, on the 17th of October, they issued a proclamation, setting forth, that as the combined land and naval forces under their command, those of the enemy in the upper district of Upper· Canada, had been captured or destroyed,—and as the said district was then in the quiet possession of their troops,—it became necessary to provide for its government. Therefore, they proclaimed and made known that the rights and privileges of the inhabitants, and the laws and customs of the country as they existed, or were in force, before their arrival, should continue to prevail. All magistrates, and all other civil officers, were to resume the exercise of their functions, previously taking an oath to be faithful to the government of the United States, as long as they shall be in possession of the country.

The authority of militia commissions was suspended in said districts, and the officers required to give their parole in such way as the officer, who may be appointed by the commanding-general to administer the government, shall direct.

The inhabitants of said districts were promised protection to their persons and property, with the exception of those cases embraced by the proclamation of General Proctor, which was declared to be in full force, and the powers therein assumed were transferred to the officer appointed.

An anecdote is related in connection with the battle of the Thames, by an eye witness, and indeed by one of the parties, showing the painful degree of anxiety that the barbarities of Proctor and his Indian bloodhounds had created, and the wild enthusiasm that the news of the victory caused. In those days mails were few and uncertain; and our citizens eagerly hailed every traveler from the West for some intelligence of our army. Such was the delay and uncertainty, that it was generally believed that Harrison and his army had, like those before him, been defeated and massacred. The narrator of this circumstance was, at the time referred to, attending school in a log cabin, in Washington, Pennsylvania, taught by an honest and patriotic Irishman.

One day while his eyes were wandering out of the window, as the eyes of the best disposed scholars sometimes will wander, he espied the mail boy, from the West, coming at full speed. Soon he reached the log cabin school-house, and as he passed it, he called out, "Harrison has whipped the British and the Indians!" The Irish tutor, with as true an American heart, as ever beat in human bosom, immediately sprang from his seat as the tomahawk of Tecumthe was about to be hurled at his head, his eyes flashing fire, and exclaimed at the top of his voice, "*Boys, do you hear that!*" Then siezing his hat, he rushed madly out in pursuit of the mail boy, his scholars all at his heels, and all exclaiming in the delirium of happy excitement, "Hurrah for General Harrison!" "God bless General Harrison!" In a few moments the whole village joined in the glad shout—"Hurrah for General Harrison! He has whipped the British and Indians!"

CHAPTER XIII.

The defeat and capture of the British army at the battle of the Thames was attended with the most important results. It, in reality, finished the work which Commodore Perry had so well begun, by his glorious victory on Lake Erie, and enabled the commander-in-chief to rescue the whole north-western territory from the depredations of the savages, and the horrors of war. The national gratitude burst out in one loud voice of applause; General Harrison was complimented by Congress, and by various public bodies, and his victory was declared by Langdon Cheves, on the floor of Congress, that the victory was such as would have secured to a Roman general, in the best days of the republic, the honors of a triumph, and that it put an end to the war in Upper Canada. And President Madison, in his next annual message, declared, in equally emphatic language, that the result was signally honorable to Major-General Harrison, by whose military talents the victory was won. And again, Governor Snyder, in his annual message to the Legislature of Pennsylvania, said, the blessings of thousands of women and children rescued from the scalping-knife of the ruthless savage of the wilderness, and from the still more savage Proctor, rest on Harrison and his gallant army. Such was the unanimous opinion of the country upon General Harrison's conduct, and of the consequences that must flow from the victory of the Thames.

General Harrison was now in a condition to proceed to the Niagara frontier without the risk of a repetition of Proctor's outrages, which he accordingly did, taking McArthur's brigade; the rifle regiment, under Colonel Wells; and the battalion, under Colonel Ball. In this he anticipated the wishes of the government. Though he had received no instructions from the War Department, since the preceding July, his own intricate acquaintance with the condition and wants of the country, as well as his superior knowledge of the movements of the enemy, and his correct military judgment, led him to transfer his disposable force to the Niagara straits after he had so successfully accomplished the main objects of the campaign. The want of necessary provisions, and the advanced state of the season, had previously induced him and Commodore Perry to abandon, for the present, the expedition against Mackinac. General Cass was stationed at Detroit, with his brigade, and the civil government of Michigan, and the military occupation of Upper Canada was committed to his charge.*

On the 22nd, General Harrison reached Erie, in Commodore Perry's fleet, and Buffalo on the 24th of

* Sketches of General Harrison.

October, and proceeded immediately to Newark, where he assumed the command of the troops at that place, and also at Forts George and Niagara, then under the command of General McClure, of New York. While at Newark, he received from General Armstrong, the Secretary of War, a copy of the despatch of 22nd September, which had been lost by Captain Brown in attempting to pass up the Detroit in October. This letter suggested to General Harrison the propriety of proceeding to the Niagara straits after he had secured Malden and the army under Proctor. Another letter received from him, about the same time, under date of October 20th, adds the weight of his opinion in favor of the course adopted by General Harrison, in his operations against Proctor, a subject about which there had been some controversy. In a letter dated the 30th of the same month, the Secretary of War recommended to General Harrison, to move against the enemy at Burlington Heights, near the head of Lake Ontario, the capture or destruction of which, he says, would be a glorious *finale* to the campaign.

Greatly to the surprise of every one, however, four days after this letter was received, he was, in effect, suspended from his command by the same administration which had, up to that time, given him so many proofs of its approval of his conduct. On the 3rd of November, he received a despatch from General Armstrong, requiring him to send General Mc Arthur's brigade to Sacket's Harbor, and concluding

19

with the declaration, that he would be permitted to make a visit to his family. This General Harrison very naturally understood as an order to retire to his own district. His letters to General McClure, of November 15th, show that he regarded it in this light; and that he believed it left him no alternative as to the disposal of General McArthur's brigade. Immediately upon the receipt of this intimation, he accompanied the troops to Sacket's Harbor, and thence returned to Cincinnati, resuming early in January, 1814, the command of the eighth military district.

Shortly before his departure from Fort George, an interesting correspondence took place between General Harrison and the British General Vincent, in regard to the treatment of prisoners of war. General Harrison, after assuring him that he had taken every precaution in regard to the prisoners in his hands, he adds, with equal force and justice, that he wished it distinctly understood, that in these assurances his conduct had been directed solely by motives of humanity, and not by a belief that it could be claimed on the score of reciprocity of treatment towards the American prisoners who had fallen into General Proctor's hands. He continues, that the unhappy description of persons who have escaped from the tomahawk of the savages, in the employment of the British government, who fought under the immediate orders of that inhuman and cowardly officer, had suffered all the indignities and privations which human nature is capable of enduring. He insisted that there was not a single instance in which the property of the officers had not been respected.

Having thus briefly referred to the past treatment of American prisoners, and to the horrid barbarities committed by the savages, under the command of Proctor, he demanded from General Vincent an explicit declaration as to the future, and whether the same species of warfare which they had, up to that time, practiced against the American troops, and against the peaceable inhabitants of our frontiers, was to be continued. He recounted a long list of barbarities of this kind, many of them perpetrated under the very eyes of British officers.

To retaliate, he proceeds to say, upon the subjects of the king, would have been justifiable by the laws of war, and the usages of the most civilized nations. To do so has been most amply within my power. The tide of fortune has changed in our favor, and an extensive and flourishing province opened to our arms, nor have the instruments of vengeance been wanting. The savages, who sued to us for mercy, would gladly have shown their claims to it by re-enacting upon the Thames the bloody scenes of Frenchtown, Fort Meigs and Cold Creek. A single sign would have been sufficient to have poured upon the subjects of the king their whole fury. The future conduct of the British officers will determine the correctness of mine in withholding it. If the savages should again be let loose upon our settlements, I shall with justice be accused of sacrificing the interests and honor of my country, and the lives of our fellow-citizens to feelings of false and mistaken humanity. You are a soldier, sir, and, as I sincerely believe, possess all the honorable sentiments which ought always to be found in men who follow the profession of arms. Use then, I pray you, your authority and influence to stop that dreadful effusion of innocent blood, which proceeds from the employment of those monsters whose aid is so little to be depended upon, when most needed, and which can have so trifling an influence upon the issue of the war. The effect of their barbarities will not be confined to the present generation. Ages to come will feel the deep-rooted hatred and enmity which they must produce between the two nations.

I deprecate most sincerely the dreadful alternative which will be offered to me should it be continued; but I solemnly declare that if the Indians, who remain under the influence of the British government, are suffered to commit any depredations upon the district that is committed to my protection, I will remove the restrictions which have hitherto been imposed upon those who have offered their services to the United States, and direct them to carry on the war in their own way. I have never heard a single excuse for the employment of savages by your government, unless we can credit the story of some British officers, having dared to assert that, as we employ Kentuckians, you had a right to make use of the Indians.

If such injurious sentiments have really prevailed, to the prejudice of a brave, well informed, and virtuous people, they will be removed by the representations of your officers who were lately taken upon the River Thames. They will inform you, sir, that so far from offering any violence to the persons of their prisoners, *these savages* would not suffer a word to escape them which was calculated to wound or insult their feelings, and this, too, with the sufferings of their friends at the River Raisin and the Miami fresh upon their recollection.

In answer to this letter, General Vincent admitted that the captured British officers bore full testimony to the kind and humane treatment they had received from their American captors, but he declined giving General Harrison the assurances he required, that he would thereafter prevent a repetition of those atrocities which had rendered Proctor's name forever infamous, though he pledged himself to *endeavor* to alleviate as much as possible those who, by the chances of war, might fall into his hands. He also expressed his desire that no such acts of cruelty might be thereafter committed, under any pretext. His reply was cautious and non-committed. Either he felt that he could not, or did not wish, wholly to suppress the outrages of which General Harrison so indignantly and so justly complained.

General Harrison, it has been seen, returned to Cincinnati, after the very extraordinary letter of the Secretary of War to him, of December 3rd, and resumed the command of his military division. The course of public opinion, during the winter succeeding

19 *

his virtual suspension from the command of the north-western army, indicated very decidedly the choice of the victor of Tippecanoe, Fort Meigs and the Thames, as the most suitable officer to be invested with the chief command of the army in the next campaign. Commodore Perry, General McArthur and other gallant and experienced officers, expressed the most earnest desire that he might be appointed commander-in-chief for the ensuing campaign. But from causes which can neither be explained nor justified, General Armstrong's feelings and opinions had undergone a remarkable change in regard to General Harrison, or at least, his conduct towards him had undergone a change not dictated by a regard for the interests of the country, or by any sudden light he had received in regard to his character and public services. His conduct, therefore, in regard to an officer, who had so faithfully, so ably, and, above all, so successfully discharged his duty to the country, and who was, besides, the idol of the army, must be attributed as dishonorable to General Armstrong, as the consequences growing out of their indulgence was injurious to the public service. Nor is the administration entirely from just censure for permitting and indeed sanctioning an act of such glaring injustice to a great and successful, and a pure patriot.

General Armstrong's plan of the campaign, submitted to the President, on the 30th of April, 1814, left no doubt that General Harrison would not be assigned a command in the active operations of the year. All the troops in the eighth military district, excepting garrisons for Detroit and Malden, were to be held in readiness to move down the lake to Buffalo, and General McArthur was designated for the command of those corps, including the 17th, 19th, 24th and 28th regiments of regulars. This arrangement of all the disposable force in the north-west, while it left General Harrison to remain in the eighth military district, was made after the receipt of his letter at the War Department, of the 13th of February, 1814, in which he expressed his views and feelings in regard to his suspension from his command of the north-western army. That letter concludes with the declaration, that apart from the considerations of his duty to his country, he had no inducements to remain in the army, and that if the prerogatives of his rank and station, as the commander of a district, be taken from him, being fully convinced that he could render no important service, he should much rather be permitted to retire from public life.

But the Secretary of War was not content with the degredation he had inflicted upon the brave Harrison, in withdrawing him from his command, and withholding him from active service, during the approaching campaign. He still persisted in interfering with his prerogatives, as the commander of the district. His next unworthy act was to dispatch to Major Holmes, a subordinate officer at Detroit, an order to take two hundred men from that port, and proceed on board of Commodore Sinclair's fleet, destined for Mackinac. This proceeding on the part of the Secretary of War was a gross invasion of military propriety, as well as a direct insult to General Harrison, whatever may have been the design.

The order not only passed by the General, but was also derogatory to Colonel Croghan, the immediate commander of the post. The gallant young officer spoke of this conduct without reserve, and in a letter to General Harrison, he wrote as follows :— "Major Holmes has been notified by the War Department, that he is chosen to command the land troops which are destined to co-operate with the fleet against the enemy's force on the upper lakes. So soon as I may be directed by you, to order Major Holmes on that command, and to furnish him with the necessary troops, I shall do so. But not till then shall he or any other part of my force leave the sod." In another letter to General Harrison, he said, " I know not how to account for the Secretary of War's assuming to himself the right of designating Major Holmes for this command to Mackinac. My ideas on the subject may not be correct, yet for the sake of the principle, were I a general, commanding a district, I would be very far from suffering the Secretary of War, or any other authority, from interfering with my internal police."

This order to Major Holmes, would authorize the inference, that the Secretary of War may have had other correspondence with him or other inferior officers of the district. At any rate it was a course of conduct, the most insulting and derogatory to a high spirited, honorable and patriotic officer, that could have been devised, and was, besides, both impolitic and indelicate. Immediately upon receiving notice of this order, he acted as any officer, having a proper regard for his honor would have done, and resigned his commission in the army. Accompanying his resignation, was a letter to the President, explaining his motives for the step he had taken, at the same time assuring him of his continued devotion to the interests of the country, and personal and political friendship for himself.

"This measure," he says "has not been determined on without a reference to all the reasons which should influence a citizen who is sincerely attached to the honor and interests of his country; who believes that the war in which we are engaged is just, and necessary, and that the crisis requires the sacrifice of every private consideration which could stand in opposition to the public good. But after giving the subject the most mature consideration, I am perfectly convinced, that my retiring from the army is as compatible with the claims of patriotism as it is with those of my family, and a proper regard for my own feelings and home.

"I have no other motives in writing this letter, than to assure you that my resignation was not produced by any diminution of the interest I have always taken in the success of your administration, or of respect and attachment to your person. The former can only take place when I forget the republican principles in which I have been educated, and the latter when I shall cease to regard those feelings which must actuate every honest man, who is conscious of favors which it is out of his power to repay."

As soon as Governor Shelby understood that General Harrison had forwarded his resignation, he addressed a letter to the President, urging him to decline its acceptance. The President was on a visit to Virginia, to which place the letters from General Harrison and Governor Shelby were forwarded. But that of the latter was not received until after the Secretary of War, without the previous consent of the President, had taken upon himself the high prerogative of accepting the resignation. President Madison expressed his great regret that the letter of Governor Shelby had not been received at an earlier date, as in that case the valuable services of General Harrison would have been preserved to the nation in the ensuing campaign.*

The letter from this venerable man, and distinguished soldier, so truly reflected the public sentiment of the times, and is withal so highly expressed, and so pregnant with patriotic sentiments, that it well deserves the consideration it has received, and to be preserved as a permanent record in favor of the conceded military genius and pre-eminent public services of General Harrison. After stating his motives for

* Sketches of Harrison.

writing to the President, to be the interest he felt for our beloved country, and his desire to promote the public good by all practicable means, he proceeds to say :—

"It is not my intention to eulogize General Harrison. He is not in need of that aid ; his merits are too conspicuous not to be observed. But it is my intention to express to you, with candor, my opinion of the general, founded on personal observation.

"A rumor has reached this State which, from the public papers, appears to be believed, that the commanding general of the northern army, may be removed from that command. This circumstance has induced me to reflect on the subject, and to give a decided preference to Major-General Harrison, as his successor. Having served a campaign with him, by which I have been enabled to form some opinion of his military tactics, and capacity to command, I feel no hesitation to declare to you, that I believe him to be one of the first military characters I ever knew ; and, in addition to this, he is capable of making greater personal exertions than any officer with whom I have ever served. I doubt not, but it will hereafter be found, that the command of the north-western army, and the various duties attached to it, has been one of the most arduous and difficult tasks ever assigned to any officer in the United States ; yet he surmounted all.

"Impressed with the conviction, that General Harrison is fully adequate to the command of the northern army, should a change take place in that division, I venture thus freely to state my opinion of him, that he is a consummate general, and would fill this station with ability and honor, and that if, on the other hand, any arrangement should take place in the war department which may produce the resignation of General Harrison, it will be a misfortune which our country will have cause to lament. His appointment to the command of the northern army would be highly gratifying to the wishes of the western people, except some who may, perhaps, be governed by sinister views.

"I confess the first impressions on my mind, when informed of the defeat of Colonel Dudley's regiment, on the 5th of May last, were unfavorable to General Harrison's plans. But on correct information, and a knowledge of his whole plans, I have no doubt but they were well concerted, and might with certainty have been executed, had his orders been strictly obeyed. I mention this subject because Mr. H. Clay informed me that he had shown you my letter, stating the impressions which that affair made on my mind on information that was not correct."

Thus was lost to the country the services of *the first military character of the day*—a general who never lost a battle, and in whom not only the army, but the whole nation, had the most unlimited confidence. And this deep injury was inflicted upon the country, from no other motive, that has ever been discovered, than to the jealousy of a small-minded and malevolent man. But while his attempts to pull a great man down to his own level, proved a signal failure, he sunk himself · so low that his name is almost forgotten, or only remembered to be despised.

CHAPTER XIV.

BEFORE proceeding with a record of General Harrison's civil and political career, it may be proper to complete the chain of military events, transpiring in other parts of the country, than upon the theatre of his immediate operations. General Wilkinson had been appointed commander-in-chief of the American forces upon the resignation of General Dearborne. The force under his command, on the Niagara, amounted to eight thousand regulars, besides those under General Dearborne, which were expected to arrive in the course of the month of October. General Wade Hampton was appointed to the command of the army of the North, encamped at Plattsburgh, and amounting to four thousand men.

Extensive preparations had been made for the invasion of Canada, by General Wilkinson, and on the 2nd of October, 1813, he left Fort George with the principle body of troops, for Grenadier's Island, a point of rendezvous convenient for embarkation. On the 6th of November, the army landed a few miles above Fort Prescott, in Canada, on the St. Lawrence. They met with some opposition, and had frequent skirmishes with the enemy between their landing and the 11th, when a sharp action was fought at a place called Chrystler's Field. Both parties claimed the victory, though, in reality, neither had the right to claim it, and it may properly be called a drawn battle, as the enemy soon after retired to their camp, and the Americans to their boats. The loss of each was also about equal. The Americans had one hundred and two killed, and three hundred and thirty-nine wounded. Amongst the wounded was the brave General Covington, who died two days after, and but for whose fall the victory would undoubtedly been with the Americans. Several other valuable officers were also badly wounded. From the fact that the British never again attacked the Americans, it may not be too much to say that the advantage of the battle was on the side of the Americans.

At Barnhart, where the army arrived on the 12th, information was received which at once put an end to all further designs upon Montreal, the main object for which the invasion of Canada was undertaken. A few days before the battle of Chrystler's Field, the commander-in-chief had sent orders to General Hampton, to meet him at St. Regis. But this order he declined to execute, owing to the scantiness of General Wilkinson's supply of provisions, and the impossibility of his transporting a larger quantity of provisions than a man could carry on his back. He therefore determined to open a communication with the St. Lawrence and Chateaugay. With a view to a readier

co-operation with the commander-in-chief in his contemplated attack upon Montreal, he had descended the
Chateaugay River from Plattsburgh with the forces
under his command. But he was thwarted in his attempt by General Provost, and, by the advice of his
officers, determined to retreat to a place he had occupied some days before, called the Four Corners,
where he arrived on the last day of the month. Having by this movement diverted the attention of the
enemy from the army of General Wilkinson, he fell
back to a position where he could with greater facility
make his way to the St. Lawrence. It was from this
point that he dispatched the letter to the commander-
in-chief already mentioned.

Upon the receipt of this information, a council of
officers was called by General Wilkinson, by whom it
was determined that the objects of the campaign were
no longer attainable. It was therefore resolved to
quit the Canada side of the St. Lawrence, and
go into winter quarters at French Mills, on Salmon
River. General Hampton followed his example, and
soon after, in consequence of indisposition, resigned
his command to General Izard. Thus terminated
a campaign which had excited the highest expectations of the country, and which created disappointment and dissatisfaction in proportion to these sanguine hopes. The failure of the enterprise was
attributed to inability of General Hampton to co-operate with General Wilkinson, and the mischievous
interference of the Secretary of War, who was on the

ground, superintending the operations of the campaign, ambitious to prove to the country how much more competent he was to bring the war to a glorious termination than General Harrison, whom his envy had driven from the service.

Commodore Chauncey, meanwhile, was not idle on Lake Ontario. He used all his exertions to bring the British squadron, Sir James Yeo, to an engagement, but was unable to do so, owing to the poor sailing qualities of his vessels. On the 7th of September, however, he got within sufficient distance of the enemy to open a running fire upon him by which considerable injury was effected. He then took refuge in Amherst Bay, and was there blockaded until the 17th. About the middle of October, he captured five British armed schooners, on board of which were a considerable number of soldiers. The same day the British fleet took refuge in Kingston, and Commodore Chauncey remained master of the lake during the remainder of the season.

On the 19th of December, the British surprised Fort Niagara, through the shameful negligence of Captain Leonard, the commanding officer, and put the whole garrison, amounting to three hundred, principally invalids, to the sword. This act of barbarity was alleged to have been committed in retaliation for the burning of Newark, a village on the Canada side of the Niagara, which was destroyed a short time before. The destruction of Lewistown, Buffalo and other places, followed rapidly upon the heels of this

20 *

outrage, all in retaliation for an act that had promptly been disavowed by the American government. And even if it had not been, there was no further outrage committed at Newark than simply burning the village after the inhabitants had been given notice to remove their effects. Thus virtually closed the campaign at the North.

At the South the war was prosecuted during the summer, principally by the Indians, with great ferocity—or rather they had *began* hostilities with a determination to wage it to the knife. They had been induced to declare war, especially the Creeks, through the machinations of the British. Their first act of hostilities was against Fort Mims, one of a line of posts, that the inhabitants had hastily thrown up on the various branches of the Mobile. This place was surprised towards the last of August. After a bloody contest, however, they withdrew, but soon again renewed the attack, the fort was carried and every person in it put to death. Not a man, woman, or child was spared. In retaliation for this wholesale massacre, General Coffee, of Tennessee, was sent against Tullushatches, a Creek town, and two hundred of the warriors were killed, and three hundred women and children taken prisoners. On the 8th of November, five days after, another action took place between General Coffee and a large body of Indians, at Fort Talladega. The Indians were defeated with a loss of about three hundred more. On the 17th, he surprised a town containing three hundred warriors, sixty of whom were killed, and the rest taken prisoners. The Georgia militia, under General Floyd, also advanced into the Creek country, and defeated them in several engagements.

On the 17th of January, 1814, General Andrew Jackson, with a view of making a diversion in favor of General Floyd, marched to the relief of Fort Armstrong. On the 21st, his camp was vigorously attacked by a large force. But they were soon repulsed, and compelled to fly. Finding himself but poorly supplied with provisions, General Jackson thought it advisable to retreat. The next morning he fell into an ambuscade. But he had anticipated it, and made such admirable arrangements for meeting it, that the Indians were repulsed at great loss. He now continued his retreat without molestation.

General Floyd in the meanwhile continued his operations against the savages. On the 27th of January, he was attacked at Fort defiance, by a very large body of them; but he repulsed them with severe loss. Often as they had been defeated, however, and desperate as their condition seemed to be, they determined to make one more desperate effort to change the fortune of war; and they accordingly made their last stand at a place called Horse Shoe Bend, on the Tallapoosa River. Across the neck of the peninsula, formed by the curve of the river, they erected a breast-work, five feet high, and of great strength, with a double row of port-holes artfully arranged. Here they imagined themselves perfectly

secure; but they were doomed to a sad disappointment.   After a dreadful conflict, as bloody as it was
short, the Indians were totally defeated and cut to
pieces.   So well had General Jackson taken his measures, that not more than fifty made their escape, while
five hundred and fifty-seven were killed, besides those
who were thrown into the river by their friends or
drowned in attempting to fly.   Jackson's loss in killed
was only forty-nine, including twenty-three friendly
Indians, and one hundred and fifty-two wounded, including forty-seven friendly Indians.   This decisive
victory ended the Creek war.   In the course of the
following summer General Jackson dictated a peace
to the Creeks, on severe terms.

The campaign of 1814 was opened at the North
by an unsuccessful attack, under General Wilkinson,
upon a considerable body of British at La Colle Mill,
three miles from Rouse's Point.   In this affair the
Americans lost one hundred and forty in killed and
wounded.   The disastrous termination of this attack,
together with the complete failure of the last campaign, brought General Wilkinson into such disrepute
that the administration yielded to the popular voice,
and suspended him from his command.   The army
was placed under the command of General Izard.
General Wilkinson was subsequently tried and honorably acquitted.

A warm contest was now begun for superiority on
Lake Ontario.   The British had commenced the construction of a large ship for the purpose of inclining

it to their side. For the purpose of maintaining as near as possible an equality of force, Commodore Chauncey had also commanded the construction of an additional one. Frequent attempts were made by each party to destroy these vessels, but they all failed. The British then attempted to destroy the rigging designed for the American ship, which was at Oswego. For this purpose they made a desperate attack on this place, on the 6th of May, but were gallantly repulsed. The following day the attack was renewed from their fleet, and two thousand men marched under General De Waterville, who succeeded in gaining the shore, though bravely resisted by Lieutenant Pierce. The Americans, finding that further resistance would be useless, fell back to Oswego Fall, whither the naval stores, for which the British had been to so much trouble, had previously been removed. The English lost in the attack two hundred and thirty-five men, in killed and wounded. To compensate them for so much blood they obtained the cannon of the fort, a few barrels of provisions, and some whiskey. The next morning the enemy evacuated the place.

After an attack upon Pultneyville, in which they were repulsed by General Swift, of the New York militia, the enemy's fleet blockaded Sacket's Harbor, cutting off all communication between that port and other places on the lake. But when he heard that the new American ship, "Superior," had received her equipment from the interior, he raised the blockade and returned to Kingston.

On the 28th of May, a large party of British were drawn into Sandy Creek, where they were suddenly attacked by Captain Woolsey, several gunboats and articles captured, and several naval officers, and one hundred and thirty men, taken prisoners. They had been sent out to capture a quantity of naval stores, bound for Oswego, and destined for the "Mohawk," another new American ship. This loss was the more severe to the British, as it gave the Americans once more the command of Lake Ontario. This was the only event of much consequence that transpired either on Lakes Erie, Ontario, or Champlain, until late in the season.

The operations on land were of comparatively little consequence, until near mid-summer, though several skirmishes took place, and some enterprises in which great gallantry and good conduct was displayed. In a skirmish on the border of Lake Erie, Major Forsyth, a valuable officer, lost his life. He made an invasion to Oldtown, and attacked a body of British, killing nineteen of them, but lost his own life. Another affair was an incursion into Canada, by Colonel Campbell, who destroyed a number of private dwellings, together with some mills and distilleries. For this act he was court-martialed and censured.

But the most gallant affair that signalized the opening of the campaign was the defense made by Captain Holmes against a greatly superior force of British and Indians. On the 21st of February, 1814, he was dispatched by Captain Butler, who was in

command at Detroit, at the head of one hundred and
sixty rangers, against a body of the enemy who had
assembled at a village about fifteen miles from Detroit.
Not knowing the strength of the enemy, he took up
a strong position, which he felt confident of being able
to defend until he should ascertain. He was soon
after attacked on all sides by the British and Indians.
But he and his men defended themselves with a courage, judgment and resolution, scarcely, if any, inferior
to that of Fort Stephenson by Major Croghan. After
several ineffectual efforts to dislodge him, the enemy
finally retreated in disorder, having lost sixty-five in
killed and wounded, besides Indians.

The British kept up a formidable squadron before
the ports of New York, New London and Boston, and
the whole eastern coast was exposed to their ravages.
Eastport was captured by Sir Thomas Hardy, and
the inhabitants compelled to take the oath of allegiance to the British crown. It was afterwards decided,
however, that they should be considered and treated
as conquered people, and placed under a military
government. The place was soon after strongly fortified, and remained in the possession of the enemy
until the close of the war. During the summer the
British conquered, or rather entered upon the peaceable possession of all that part of Maine, east of the
Penobscot, and was, like Eastport, retained until the
end of the war.

Our gallant little navy won even higher honors
this year than since the war commenced. Commo-

dore Porter completed his successful course in the
Pacific. From April until October 1813, he captured
twelve armed British whale ships, carrying in all one
hundred and seven guns, and three hundred and two
men. Having after these exploits thoroughly repaired his ship, the "Essex," he arrived at Valpa-
raiso, on the 12th of January, 1814. While here,
Commodore Hillyer arrived off the harbor in the
"Phœbe," accompanied by the "Cherub," in pursuit
of him. After trying in vain to bring these vessels
into action singly, Commodore Porter attempted to
escape. But he failed in the effort, and was finally
captured, after making the most desperate resistance
on record. His ship was almost literally cut to pieces,
and a large portion of his crew were killed, wounded
or missing. He was permitted to return to the United States on parole. But upon arriving off the port
of New York he was brought to by a British vessel,
and his parole taken from him. He, however, succeeded in effecting his escape, and arrived safely in
New York.

On the 29th of April, an engagement took place
between the American sloop of war "Peacock," and
the British brig of war, "Epervier." After an action
of forty-two minutes she struck her flag. In July
following, the American sloop of war, "Wasp," captured the British brig "Reindeer," after a desperate
engagement, in which the "Reindeer" lost half her
crew, and the ship was nearly destroyed. Not long
after the "Wasp" had an engagement with the British

brig "Avon," which sunk almost before her crew could be removed. On the 21st of September she captured another prize, a British brig of eighteen guns. This was the last ever heard of the "Wasp," or her gallant commander, and she undoubtedly foundered at sea, carrying down with her every soul on board.

A single check to the almost uninterrupted series of naval victories, which had crowned our efforts at sea, occurred in the loss of the "President," Commodore Decatur, by a British fleet of three ships of war. But this loss was more than compensated by the capture of the "Cayenne" and "Levant," by the "Constitution," Commodore Stewart, on the 20th of February, 1815, and the capture of the British brig "Penguin," by the "Hornet," captain Biddle.

Several gallant exploits signalized the American privateers. Amongst the most remarkable of these was the defense made by the privateer "Armstrong," in the Spanish port of Fayal, where she had taken refuge from a British squadron. The "Armstrong" was first attacked by four boats filled with men, and upon these being compelled to haul off, a second attack was made with twelve or fourteen boats, manned by several hundred men. They were suffered to approach almost along side, when so destructive a fire was opened, that in forty minutes scarcely a man of them was left. The next day, finding it useless to continue the contest, the captain of the "Armstrong" removed his men to the shore, and sunk his vessel. For

21

her loss a claim was preferred by our government against Spain, which came near involving the two countries in a serious difficulty in 1850, and which has but recently been adjusted. The British loss amounted to one hundred and twenty killed and one hundred and thirty wounded.

CHAPTER XV.

On the Niagara frontier, the first important movement was the recapture of Fort Erie by General Scott. The next movement was against General RiaH, who occupied an entrenched camp at Chippewa. General Brown succeeded in drawing the British General into an engagement on the plains of Chippewa, on the 5th of July. The field was bravely contested on both sides, but the Americans carried off the palm of victory; and after an action of something over an hour, the enemy retired, first, until he reached the sloping ground that lead to Chippewa, and from that point he fled in confusion to his intrenchments. In proportion to the numbers engaged in the battle, the loss on both sides was very severe. That of the Americans in killed, wounded and missing, was three hundred and thirty-eight. The total loss of the British amounted to five hundred and five. In this action, which filled the country with the greatest joy, General Scott especially distinguished himself, and contributed very largely to the brilliant result of the battle.

Immediately after this victory, the American army moved forward and encamped at Queenstown At his own request, he was detached from this point with one hundred and twenty men to reconnoiter Fort George. On his arrival in the neighborhood he surprised and captured a small body of British, one of whom, after having asked and received quarter, suddenly raised his piece and mortally wounded General Swift. He instantly killed the assassin.

After remaining a short time at Queenstown, General Brown retreated to Chippewa. General Riall immediately took post at that place, upon the American army's evacuating it. The British General was extremely mortified at the disgraceful defeat he had met with at Chippewa, and was resolved, if possible, to retrieve his credit; and, with this view, he had collected a large reinforcement from Burlington and other points. The American commander was not unwilling to afford him a speedy opportunity to prove his boasted superiority. General Scott was accordingly dispatched towards Queenstown. He discovered General Riall on the Niagara, at Lundy's Lane, a position of great strength, where he had planted a battery of nine pieces of cannon. He was immediately attacked, with consummate bravery, by General Scott and the force under his command, though the British force was more than double that of his.

The battle that followed was one of the most fiercely and obstinately contested of any during the whole war, or perhaps that ever was fought. The enemy felt that he had a shattered reputation to recover, and the Americans that they had their country and their honor to defend, and both therefore fought as though the last hopes of either depended upon the issue. The action lasted for several hours, and only terminated when the two armies had become so exhausted that they could fight no longer. The number of the British engaged in the action amounted to about five thousand, while the Americans was less than three thousand.

The loss was about equal on each side, that of the Americans being eight hundred and fifty-one in killed and wounded, while the enemy's was eight hundred and seventy-eight, being a difference of only twenty-seven. The victory was claimed by the British, as usual, but with little show of reason. Their artillery was captured, and they were three times repulsed in attempting to recover it, and were finally compelled to abandon them altogether. They were afterwards abandoned by the Americans, for want of ability to remove them, and upon this circumstance the enemy founded his claim to a victory. But it is clear that many such victories would have totally ruined the British cause in America. In the action, General Brown and also General Scott were badly wounded; and the British General Riall, and the aid to General Drummond, were taken prisoners. The next day the Americans retreated to Fort Erie, having only fifteen hundred men left fit for service, while the British force, who had received a reinforcement of one thousand, amounted to five thousand strong.

The enemy now prepared to attack Fort Erie, which was little more than an unfinished redoubt, and consid-

21 *

ered almost indefensible. On the 3rd of August, little more than a week after the battle of Lundy's Lane, or Niagara, he appeared before that port with his whole force, amounting to more than five thousand. On the night of August 14th, an assault was made upon the Fort. The enemy, however, were repulsed at all points with great slaughter. Three days after, the assault was renewed with more ferocity than ever. On the 28th, having been in the meantime considerably reinforced, the siege was continued with great zeal until the 17th of September, when General Brown resolved upon making a sortie for the purpose of destroying the enemy's works. The design was executed, and proved abundantly successful, and in a few hours the labor of the enemy was entirely destroyed, their cannon captured, and upwards of a thousand of the enemy killed, wounded, and taken prisoners. This was so severe and expensive a lesson for the British, that they immediately after raised the siege and retreated to Fort George.

Some time in October, General Bissel was detached with nine hundred men to the enemy's stores, at Cook's Mills, or Lyon's Creek. While on his march to perform this duty, his camp was assailed by the Marquis of Tweeddale, at the head of twelve hundred men. But he met with so severe a reception that he retreated in great confusion, after a brief contest, leaving his dead and wounded in his flight. Immediately after this repulse, it was resolved to destroy Fort Erie and evacuate Upper Canada in consequence of the advanced state of the season. This was accordingly done, and the American army went into winter quarters at Buffalo, Black Rock, and at Batavia. Thus ended the third invasion of Canada.

On the Atlantic coast and towards the South, events of considerable importance meanwhile had transpired. The enemy had for some time been threatening Baltimore and Washington, the defense of which was committed to General Winder. On the 19th of August, the enemy, under General Ross, landed at Benedict, the head of frigate navigation on the Patuxent, to the number of six thousand, and on the 21st, took up his march for Washington, the point now ascertained to be his destination. The British were first encountered at Bladensburgh, and some stand made against them. But after an irregular sort of a contest, in which the militia acted very badly, the Americans were defeated. A portion of the American troops, however, fought with great bravery, especially the Washington City and Georgetown militia, as the loss of the British will attest. Their killed, wounded and missing, on the occasion, was but little short of one thousand men, while the Americans had less than one hundred killed, and one hundred and twenty taken prisoners.

The defeat of General Winder placed the American metropolis at the mercy of General Ross, and on the 24th of August he arrived in Washington. Immediately after he reached the city, he ordered the President's house and the national capitol, two of the most beautiful specimens of architecture in America, to be burned. The great bridge across the Potomac was also destroyed. This act of Vandalism reflected eternal disgrace on the character of General Ross and Admiral. Cockburn, by whose order it was perpetrated, and little less dishonor on the British name for virtually sanctioning so barbarous and wanton an outrage. In this conflagration the valuable library of Congress was wholly consumed. All the public buildings, except the Patent Office, shared the same fate as the Capitol and the President's House. On the following day, after this chivalrous performance, the vandal perpetrators retreated from the city, while a small division of his army plundered Alexandria, and committed sundry other depredations. In one of their skirmishes at Moor's Fields, with some militia, Sir Peter Parker was mortally wounded, and died shortly after.

The capture of Washington filled full to overflowing the cup of indignation against General Armstrong, the Secretary of War, and he was soon after forced to resign, to avoid being removed, a punishment richly deserved for his treatment of General Harrison, as well as for his neglect to guard against the calamity that befel the Capitol.

Active preparations were now made for the defense of Baltimore. The disgraceful conduct of the British, at Washington, was received with one feeling of indignation throughout the country, and all sections of it resolved to lay aside the differences until they

had punished the insolent invader.   It was clear that
the next object of attack would be Baltimore, as on
the 11th of September, Admiral Cockran appeared at
the mouth of the Patapsco, about fourteen miles from
that city.   On the next day, General Ross landed at
North Point, at the head of six thousand troops, and
took up his march for Baltimore.   An action took
place the same day, in which the Americans were
worsted, and compelled to retreat, though the British
General Ross was killed.   The next day the British
appeared before Baltimore, in front of the American lines.   On the 13th, the enemy had brought sixteen pieces of cannon within a sufficient distance of
Fort McHenry, which commanded the entrance to
the harbor, to commence a tremendous bombardment,
which continued until the next morning.   Having signally failed in their attack upon the fort, all further
attempt upon Baltimore was abandoned, and the
enemy commenced a retreat even while the bombardment was continued.

Admiral Cockran soon after retired to the West
Indies with his whole fleet, with the view of awaiting
reinforcements from England.   He not only abandoned the idea for the present of attacking any other
cities or large towns, but withdrew all the vessels of
his squadron which had been engaged in marauding
expeditions into the country along the coast.

The operations of the American army at the North
were attended with some results of a most brilliant
character.   At the beginning of September, the Brit-

ish invaded New York, for the purpose of destroying the American army at Plattsburgh, and the subjugation of the country as far as Crown Point and Ticonderoga. Early in September the enemy occupied Plattsburgh, opposite the American works, where they calmly awaited the co-operation of the British fleet on Lake Champlain. But the fleet soon found other matters to attend to than aiding to capture the American army. On the 11th of September the American fleet, under Commodore McDonough, and the British fleet under Captain Downie, were moored abreast of each other in Cumberland Bay. The number of guns in the battle amounted to ninety-five, and one thousand men, while in the American fleet the number of guns was only eighty-six, and eight hundred men. The action commenced a little past nine o'clock, on the morning of the 11th, and continued to rage for two hours, when the guns of the enemy were silenced, and most of his vessels surrendered to Commodore McDonough. The loss of the Americans was fifty-two killed and fifty-eight wounded; and that of the enemy eighty-four killed and one hundred and ten wounded.

About the same time the action between the two fleets commenced; the British General at Plattsburgh commenced a vigorous bombardment upon the American works, which was returned with equal vigor by the Americans. The action continued until dusk. But after witnessing the surrender of their fleet on the lake, their efforts somewhat slackened, and, as soon as night set in, they commenced a hasty retreat, leaving behind their sick and wounded, besides a large quantity of military stores. The loss of the British in killed, wounded and deserters, in this action, was fifteen hundred, and their loss in the naval action was little less than a thousand men. The American loss was very trifling, compared with that of the enemy. By the glorious termination of these two actions, the Americans obtained the complete command of Lake Champlain, and the British invasion of New York was happily defeated. With the defeat of het enemy at Plattsburgh, and the entire destruction of his fleet on the lake, closed the campaign and the war at the North.

While these events were taking place at the North, and along the Atlantic coast, the war was prosecuted with vigor at the South. In the month of August, several British ships of war arrived at Pensacola, then a Spanish port, and took possession of the forts with the assent of the authorities, and fitted out an expedition against Fort Bowyer or Mobile Bay, and commanding its harbor. But after the loss of a ship of war, and a large number of men, the armament returned to Pensacola. General Jackson, who then commanded at the South, after having in vain remonstrated with the authorities for affording shelter to the enemies of the United States, marched against the town, captured it, and compelled the British to evacuate Florida. Upon returning from this enterprise, he ascertained that the enemy was making extensive preparations for invading Louisiana, and attacking New Orleans. He immediately repaired to that city, and by his energetic efforts put it in a complete state of defense, restored confidence amongst the citizens, organized the militia, and finally proclaimed martial law, a measure justified by necessity, though clearly a violation of the constitution.

On the 5th of December, a large British squadron appeared off the harbor of Pensacola, and on the 10th, entered Lake Borgue, the nearest avenue of approach to New Orleans. Here a small squadron of American gun-boats was attacked, and after a brave resistance compelled to surrender. On the 22nd of the same month, two thousand five hundred of the enemy reached the Mississippi, nine miles below New Orleans. Here they were surprised and lost four hundred men, though they succeeded in repelling the attack. General Jackson now retired to his intrenchments, which were vigorously cannonaded on the 28th of December, and the 1st of January, but without success.

General Packenham, the British commander-in-chief, however, advanced with his whole force, amounting to twelve thousand men, against the American lines on the 8th of January, 1815.

Entrenched behind his breastwork of cotton bales, General Jackson, at the head of six thousand troops, principally militia, calmly awaited the onset of this vastly superior force, reserving his fire until the enemy should approach within reach of his battery.

Then, however, he opened upon them a most terribly destructive fire from his cannons, cutting wide openings in their ranks. But they continued steadily to advance, until within reach of the American musketry and rifles, when even a more fatal shower of balls was poured in upon them than from the batteries, and they were literally mowed down by scores and by hundreds. The plain was covered with the dead and dying, and the enemy finally gave way. No flesh and blood could stand such dreadful volleys. In attempting to rally them, General Peckenham was killed, and General Gibbs, the second in command, fell mortally wounded, and General Keene severely.

The enemy now fled in the wildest confusion from this certain death, and no attempt was made to rally them a second time. General Lambert, upon whom the command now devolved, therefore retreated to his camp, leaving seven hundred dead on the field, and one thousand wounded. The Americans lost six in killed and seven wounded. The whole British army, immediately after this terrible defeat, hastily withdrew to their ships. In this whole expedition the British loss amounted to full three thousand men. The battle of New Orleans was the only action of any importance that was fought, and may be said to have ended the war in a blaze of glory, as it ended the campaign at the South, as Plattsburgh and Champlain had at the North. News of the peace which was concluded by the treaty of Ghent, on the 24th of

22

December, 1814, was soon after received, and hostilities ceased.

The commissioners on the part of Great Britain, by whom the treaty was concluded, were Lord Gambier, Henry Goulburn and William Adams; and John Quincy Adams, James R. Bayard, Henry Clay, Jonathan Bissel and Albert Gallatin, on the part of the United States. According to its stipulations, all places taken during the war, or after the signing of the treaty, were to be mutually restored, and all captures at sea made with a certain time thereafter, according to the latitude in which they were made. Every attempt was to be made by the two governments to put a stop to Indian hostilities, and to extinguish the traffick in slaves. The greater part of the treaty, however, related to the adjustment of the boundaries between the United States and the British territories, which were imperfectly defined by the treaty of 1783. The subject of impressment, which was one of the leading causes of the war, paper blockades, orders in council, and the rights of neutral flags, were passed over in silence.

But though these questions were left unsettled, the right of impressment was virtually abandoned by the British Government, and has never been asserted since she had been made to feel our strength, and to respect our power. Especially had she been taught that she was no longer the undisputed mistress of the seas. The loss of two thousand merchant ships, the many millions added to her public debt, the numerous vessels of war that had been compelled to strike their flags to the Americans, as well as the battles of the Thames, Queenstown, Chippewa, Niagara, Plattsburgh, New Orleans, and numerous other bloody fields, had effectually checked her insolent bearing towards the United States. It is probably the last attemp that Great Britain will make to recover the "jewel" that was torn from the crown of George III, by his own folly and the wickedness of his ministers.

The history of General Harrison's career will now be resumed.

CHAPTER XVI.

Upon resigning his commission in the army, for causes which have been fully explained, and which amply justified him in the eyes of the country, he retired to his farm at North Bend, fifteen miles below Cincinnati, in 1814. Here he resumed those peaceful pursuits which were so much more congenial to his tastes and inclinations than the strife and turmoil of war. If he had preferred his own interests to that of his country, he might have retained his position in the army, and continued to receive the emoluments attached to his command of the eighth military division. But when he could no longer render active service to the country, he refused the reception of pay for services not permitted to be performed, as he had previously upon the peace of Greenville.

He was not long suffered to remain in seclusion, however. During the summer of the same year he was appointed, in connection with General Cass and General Adair, to treat with some of the tribes of northwestern Indians, with whom a treaty was soon after concluded at Greenville. The following year he was appointed at the head of another commission, and concluded a treaty at Detroit with nine important tribes, which were highly advantageous to the United States. In 1816, other and still more important and honorable duties awaited him. He was during that year nominated as a candidate for Congress, in the district in which he resided, and though he had six competitors for the same office, he had an aggregate majority over all of them of one thousand. He was elected to succeed the Honorable John McLean, who had resigned the office shortly before. No stronger evidence of the strong hold General Harrison had upon the affections of the western people, and how little the unjust treatment he had received at the hands of General Armstrong had affected him in their estimation can be had than this triumphant endorsement of his character and patriotism by those most competent to judge of each.

While a member of Congress, and shortly after he took his seat, a charge was made against him by an army contractor, whose high expectations of large profits were blighted by his rigid supervision of the commissary's department, of misconduct or improper connection with that department while in command of the army at the West. General Harrison boldly met the charge, and demanded an investigation. A committee was accordingly appointed, at the head of whom was Colonel Richard M. Johnson, and after a thorough and impartial investigation, a report was made by him on the 23rd of January, 1817, in which they say, that "The committee are unanimously of opinion that General Harrison stands above suspicion

22 *

as to his having had any pecuniary or improper connection with the officers of the commissariat for
the supply of the army; that he did not wantonly
or improperly interfere with the rights of contractors,
and that he was, in his measures, governed by a proper
zeal and devotion to the public interests."

When this report was read, Mr. Hulbert of Massachusetts, who was a member of the committee, said,
that he as well as the committee considered the subject an important one, as well as interesting to the
public, and especially so to General Harrison. The
character of that gentleman had been impeached, and
the committee, therefore, determined to make the investigation as full and thorough as should be in their
power. They had received the testimony of the gentleman who made the charge, had read and considered
all the documents and papers they could obtain, and
had examined many respectable witnesses; after all
this the investigation resulted in a firm conviction and
unanimous opinion of the committee, that the insinu-
ations and complaints that had been made against
General Harrison were unmerited, groundless and unjust.

Mr. Hulbert said, it gave him pleasure to make
these declarations, as he considered himself doing an
act of justice to an individual. He admitted that he
had entered upon the investigation with impressions
very unfavorable to General Harrison. The complaint which had been made against him had spread
far and wide. The bane and the antidote had not

gone together. He rejoiced that this investigation had been made, and he had no hesitation in saying, that so far as the report of the committee should defend the character and conduct of General Harrison before the public, it would promote the cause of truth and justice. In regard to the charge of oppressive and unjust conduct towards the contractors in the army under his command, he was entirely satisfied that he had interfered only in those cases where he thought his duty to the public imperiously demanded it.

The most serious charge that had been preferred against General Harrison was that, while he was commander-in-chief of the north-western army, regardless of his country's good, he was in the habit of managing the public concerns with a view to his own private interests. This, Mr. Hulbert said, he could not refrain from pronouncing a false and cruel accusation, and that there was the most satisfactory evidence that he had, in the exercise of his official duties, and in his devotion to the public interests, neglected his private concerns to his material detriment and injury. In a word, he added, he felt himself authorized to say, that every member of the committee was fully satisfied that the conduct of General Harrison, in relation to the matter under inquiry, had been that of a brave, honest and honorable man, and that instead of deserving censure, he merited the thanks and applause of his country.

At a subsequent state of the inquiry, the matter

was referred to the Secretary of War, who reported
that General Harrison had been guilty of no impropriety of conduct; that upwards of a million and a
half of dollars had passed through his hands, during
the war, no part of which had been applied to his own
use; that from the evidence furnished him, it appeared that General Harrison was poorer at the end
of the war than he was at the beginning of it.

On the 6th of December, four days after he took
his seat in Congress, and previous to the investigation into the charges against his official conduct, he
offered a resolution instructing the military committee
to enquire into the expediency of providing by law
for the relief of such of the officers and soldiers who,
having faithfully served in the armies of the United
States, are now in distressed circumstances, and who,
not having received wounds or disabilities whilst in
actual service, are excluded from the benefits of the
pension laws, and that the said committee report by
bill or otherwise. This resolution led the way for an
act of justice to those who had sacrificed some of their
best years in the service of the country, and thus, in
many instances, entirely blighted their worldly prospects, but who had hitherto been entirely neglected
by their government, because they had not the good
fortune to lose a leg or an arm.

On the 30th of January, on his motion, the military committee was instructed to enquire into the expediency of granting a bounty of one hundred and
sixty acres of land to all non-commissioned officers

and soldiers of the army, who, having been enlisted previous to the 24th of December, 1811, are not entitled to said bounty, but who, having served faithfully through said war, have obtained an honorable discharge. These two propositions were the foundation of a system of legislation that has resulted in a vast benefit not only to a large class of soldiers, but to the widows and orphans of those who had perished gallantly fighting in defense of their country.

At the following session a bill was introduced to increase the pay of members of Congress from six to nine dollars a day. In discussing a proposition to strike out six and insert nine, which took place on the 6th of January, 1818, General Harrison said that in explaining what would otherwise appear an inconsistency in the vote he was about to give, he was aware that in order to preserve in Congress talents of a proper grade, and to enable men of moderate property to come to Congress without loss, a higher compensation was necessary than had heretofore been allowed to members of Congress. But, notwithstanding he entertained these views, he was opposed to increasing the pay of members until they had done justice to others whose claims were much stronger. Whenever justice should be done to sufferers in the war of the revolution, he should be willing to vote for the measure in question, and not till then. The revolutionary pension bill became a law before the close of the session.

This bill being under discussion the next day, on

its third reading, General Harrison said he was persuaded that the members of the House, who had voted for a compensation beyond the ancient allowance of six dollars, had voted under great embarrassment, possessed as they were on the one hand by a sense of duty and justice, and on the other by that delicacy which must be felt when they were acting as judges in their own case. He thought, however, that there was a mode by which their feelings might be saved, and which, if adopted, would be as highly acceptable to them as it would be honorable to their representatives. It would evince a disinterestedness and magnanimity which could not fail to produce the most happy effects, and finally fix the compensation at the sum which their disinterested judgment should deem right. Being satisfied that it was a question to be determined rather by feeling than argument, he would simply submit a resolution to re-commit the bill, with instructions to amend it so far as to fix the compensation for the present Congress at six dollars, and for the ensuing Congress at eight dollars. The motion, however, was lost and the bill passed.

On the 20th of January, of the same Congress, General Harrison introduced a resolution, providing that a committee be appointed jointly with such committee as may be appointed by the Senate, to consider and report what measures it may be proper to adopt to manifest the public respect for the memory of General Thaddeus Kosciusko, formerly an officer in the service of the United States, and the uniform and distinguished friend of liberty and the rights of man. Upon this resolution he made the following admirable remarks :—

"The public papers have announced an event which is well calculated to excite the sympathy of every American bosom. Kosciusko, the martyr of liberty, is no more! We are informed that he died at Soleure, in France, some time in October last. In tracing the events of this great man's life, we find in him that consistency of conduct which is the more to to be admired as it is so rarely to be met with. He was not at one time the friend of mankind, and at another the instrument of their oppressions, but he preserved throughout his whole career those noble principles which distinguished him in its commencement, which influenced him at an early period of his life to leave his country and his friends, and in another hemisphere, to fight for the rights of humanity.

"Kosciusko was born and educated in Poland, of a noble and distinguished family, a country where the distinctions in society are perhaps carried to greater lengths than in any other. His creator had, however, endowed him with a soul capable of rising above the narrower prejudices of caste, and of breaking the shackles which a vicious education had imposed on his mind. When very young he was informed by the voice of fame that the standard of liberty had been erected in America; that an insulted and oppressed people had determined to be free or perish in the attempt. His ardent and generous mind caught with enthusiasm the holy flame, and from that moment he became the devoted soldier of liberty.

"His rank in the American army afforded him no opportunity greatly to distinguish himself. But he was remarked throughout his service for all the qualities which adorn the human character. His heroic conduct in the field could only be equaled by his moderation and affability in the walks of private life. He was idolized by the soldiers for his bravery, and beloved and respected by the officers for the goodness of his heart, and the great qualities of his mind. Contributing greatly by his exertions to the establishment of the independence of America, he might have remained and shared the blessings it dispensed, under the protection of a chief who loved and honored him, and in the bosom of a grateful and affectionate people.

"Kosciusko, however, had other views. It is not known that, until the period I am now speaking of, he had formed any distinct idea of what could, or indeed what ought to be done for his own. But in the revolutionary war he drank deeply of the principles that produced it. In his conversations with the intelligent men of our country, he acquired new views of the science of government and the rights of man. He had seen, too, that to be free, it was only necessary that a nation should will it, and to be happy, it was only necessary that a nation should be free. And was it not possible to procure these blessings for Poland? For Poland, the country of his birth, which had a claim to all his efforts, to all his services? That

unhappy nation groaned under a complication of evils,
which has scarcely a parallel in history. The mass
of the people were the abject slaves of the nobles;
the nobles, torn into factions, were alternately the instruments and the victims of their powerful and ambitious neighbors. By intrigue, corruption and force,
some of its fairest provinces had been separated from
the republic, and people, like beasts, transferred to
foreign despots, who were again watching for a favorable moment for a second dismemberment. To regulate a people thus debased, to obtain for a country
thus circumstanced the blessings of liberty and independence, was a work of as much difficulty as danger.
But to a mind like Kosciusko's, the difficulty and
danger of an enterprise served as stimulants to undertake it.

"The annals of those times give us no detailed accounts of the progress of Kosciusko in accomplishing
his great work, from the period of his return from
America to the adoption of the new constitution of
Poland, in 1791. This interval, however, of apparent
inaction was most usefully employed to illumine the
mental darkness which enveloped his countrymen.
To stimulate the ignorant and bigoted peasantry with
the hope of future emancipation—to teach a proud
but gallant nobility that true glory is only to be found
in the paths of glory and patriotism—interests the
most opposed, prejudices the most stubborn, and
habits the most inveterate were reconciled, dissipated,
and broken by the ascendency of his virtues and ex-

23

ample. The storm which he had foreseen, and for which he had been preparing, at length burst upon Poland. A feeble and unpopular government bent before its fury, and submitted itself to the Russian yoke of the invader. But the nation disdained to follow its example; in their extremity every eye was turned on the hero who had already fought their battles—the sage who had enlightened them, and the patriot who had set the example of personal sacrifices to accomplish the emancipation of the people.

"Kosciusko was unanimously appointed Generalissimo of Poland, with unlimited powers, until the enemy should be driven from the country. On his virtue the nation reposed with the utmost confidence; and it is some consolation to reflect, amid the general depravity of mankind, that two instances in the same age have occurred where powers of this kind were employed solely for the purposes for which they were given.

"It is not my intention, Sir, to follow the Polish chief throughout the career of victory which for a considerable time crowned his efforts. Guided by his talents, and led by his valor, his undisciplined, poorly armed militia charged with effect the veteran Russians and Prussians; the mailed cuirassiers of the great Frederick, for the first time, broke and fled before the lighter and more appropriate cavalry of Poland. Hope filled the breasts of the patriots. After a long night the dawn of an apparently glorious day broke upon Poland. But to the discerning eye of Kosciusko, the

light which it shed was of that sickly and porten-
tous. appearance indicating a storm more dreadful
than that which he had resisted.

"He prepared to meet it with firmness, but with
means entirely inadequate. To the advantages of
numbers, of tactics, of discipline and inexhaustible
resources, the cornelian despots had secured a faction
in the heart of Poland, and if that country can boast
of having produced its Washington, it is disgraced
also by giving birth to a second Arnold. The day at
length came which was to decide the fate of a nation
and a hero. Heaven for wise purposes determined
that it should be the last of Polish liberty. It was
decided, indeed, before the battle commenced. The
traitor Pouiski, who covered with a detachment the
advance of the Polish army, abandoned his position
to the enemy and retreated.

"Kosciusko was astonished but not discouraged.
The disposition of his army would have done honor
to Hannibal. The succeeding conflict was terrible.
When the tablets of the General could no longer direct the mingled mass of combatants, the arm of the
warrior was brought to the aid of his soldiers. He
performed prodigies of valor. The feeble powers of
Ajax in defending the Grecian ships was realized by
the Polish hero; nor was he badly seconded by his
troops. As long as his voice could guide, or his
example fire their valor, they were irresistible. In
this unequal contest Kosciusko was long seen, and
finally lost to their vision.

'Hope for a season bade the world farewell,
And freedom shrieked as Kosciusko fell.'

"He fell covered with wounds, but still survived. A Cossack would have pierced his breast, when an officer interposed. 'Suffer him to execute his purpose,' said the bleeding hero. 'I am the devoted soldier of my country, and will not survive its liberties.' The name of Kosciusko struck to the heart of the Tartar like that of Marius upon the Cimbrian warrior. The uplifted weapon dropped from his hand.

"Kosciusko was conveyed to the dungeons of Petersburgh—and, to the eternal disgrace of the Empress Catharine, she made him the object of her vengeance, when he could no longer be the object of her fears. Her more generous son restored him to liberty. The remainder of his life has been spent in virtuous retirement. Whilst in this situation in France, an anecdote is related of him which strongly illustrates the command which his virtues and his services had obtained over the minds of his countrymen.

"In the late invasion of France, some Polish regiments, in the service of Russia, passed through the village in which he lived. Some pillaging of the inhabitants brought Kosciusko from his cottage. 'When I was a Polish soldier,' said he, addressing the plunderers, 'the property of the peaceful citizen was respected.' 'And who art thou,' said an officer, 'who addresses us with this tone of authority.' 'I am Kosciusko.' There was magic in the word. It ran from corps to corps; the march was suspended; they gathered around him and gazed with astonishment and awe upon the mighty ruin he presented. Could it indeed be their hero whose fame was identified with that of their country? A thousand interesting reflections burst upon their minds, they remembered his patriotism, his devotion to liberty, his triumphs, and his glorious fall. Their iron hearts even softened, and the tear of sensibility trickled down their weather-beaten faces. We can easily conceive, Sir, what would be the feelings of the hero himself in such a scene. His great heart must have heaved with emotion to find himself once more surrounded by the companions of his glory, and that he would have been upon the point of saying to them :—

'Behold your general, come once more
To lead you on to laurel'd victory—
To fame, to freedom !'

"The delusion could have lasted but for a moment. He was himself, alas! a miserable cripple, and for them, they were no longer the soldiers of liberty, but the instruments of ambition and tyranny. Overwhelmed with grief at the reflection, he would retire to his cottage to mourn afresh over the miseries of his country.

" Such was the man, Sir, for whose memory I ask from an American Congress a slight tribute of respect. Not, Sir, to perpetuate his fame, but our gratitude. His fame will last as long as liberty remains upon the earth—as long as a votary offers incense

23 *

upon her altar, the name of Kosciusko will be invoked. And if by the common consent of the world, a temple should be erected to those who have rendered most service to mankind, if the statue of our great countrymen shall occupy the place of the "most worthy," that of Kosciusko will be found by his side, and the wreath of laurel will be entwined with the palm of virtue to adorn his brow."

Though the great merits of Kosciusko was universally admired, yet this resolution met with so much opposition that General Harrison finally withdrew it, together with another testifying the respect of the brave for his memory by wearing crape. It was shown that no such respect as it proposed had been paid to any of the departed worthies, native or foreign, who had aided in the achievement of our independence, except in the single instance of Washington, which was claimed to be an exception to all general rules. The occasion, however, was happily seized upon by General Harrison to bring the great merits of the noble patriot and martyr before the country, and to pay the eloquent and touching tribute to his memory which has been quoted above; a speech containing sentiments as honorable to the heart and head of the man by whom they were uttered as to the patriot whose glorious deeds and eminent virtues they were designed to commemorate.

In 1816, a resolution was offered in the Senate of the United States, voting a gold medal and the thanks of Congress to General Harrison and Governor Shelby.

But the enemies of the late war were almost, as a matter of course, the enemies also of the man who had done so much to carry the country honorably through it as General Harrison had. A motion was therefore made by Mr. Lacoch, from Pennsylvania, to strike his name from the resolution. This motion prevailed by a vote of thirteen to eleven; but on the 20th of April, one week after, the resolution was called up again, and General Harrison's name restored by a vote of fourteen to thirteen. The subject was re-committed to the military committee where it rested until 1818. When Governor Shelby heard of the attempt to strike the name of General Harrison from the resolution, with the magnanimity of a great mind, he wrote to his old commander, praying him not to let the conduct of the Senate disturb his mind. He said, " I hope their resolution has been laid over as to both of us. The moment I heard of the course it was likely to take, I wrote instantly to Mr. Clay, and expressed my regret that it had been introduced, and how mortified I should feel to be noticed, if you were not included, who had rendered ten times more service to the nation than I had."

The subject was again brought before the Senate, on the 24th of March, 1818, by Mr. Dickinson, of New Jersey, subsequently the Secretary of the Navy under General Jackson's administration. On that day he asked leave to introduce a resolution offering the thanks of Congress, and providing that a gold medal be struck and awarded to General Harrison and

Governor Shelby, for their distinguished bravery and good conduct in capturing the British army under General Proctor, on the Thames, in Upper Canada, October 5th, 1813. Mr. Dickinson prefaced the introduction of this resolution with the following chaste and appropriate remarks :—

"I should not," he said, "at this late day, highly as I think of the merits of those officers, who, in cooperation with the hero of Lake Erie, turned the tide of war in our favor, bring forward the present resolution if no similar attempt had heretofore been made in their favor, but would leave their fame to rest upon the testimony of impartial history which has already done ample justice to their characters.

"Two years ago a resolution like the present was reported in this House, by the chairman of the committee on military affairs, by direction of that committee. This resolution was opposed on two grounds, applying solely to General Harrison, as I have been informed (for I had not then the honor of being a member of this body)—the first, that an inquiry was at that time pending before the House of Representatives, into the official conduct of General Harrison, as a commander-in-chief of the north-western army, upon charges which, if well founded, were calculated essentially to injure his character; the second, that a rumor prevailed that General Harrison had discovered some reluctance in pursuing Proctor and his army, after Perry's victory on Lake Erie, and that he had been forced to the pursuit by the remonstrance of Gov-

ernor Shelby, and that this information had been derived from the declarations of Governor Shelby.

"These charges, utterly unfounded as they turned
out to be, were deemed a sufficient reason for postpon-
ing a decision of the report of the committee until the
result of the inquiry, before the House of Representatives should at least be known.   *   *   *   As the
friends of General Harrison have it in their power completely to obviate every objection heretofore made to
the passage of this resolution, it is their duty to bring
the subject again before Congress, more especially as
the journals of this house, if left unexplained, imply
a censure upon the conduct of General Harrison,
which certainly was not intended.   I will confess for
one, from a perusal of the journal of this house, the
military reputation of General Harrison sunk in my
estimation.   And I believe this confession might be
made by three-fourths of the citizens of the United
States who read the proceedings of Congress, and
who had not an intimate knowledge of the character
and conduct of General Harrison.   I should reproach
myself for having suffered such an impression to be
made upon my mind if the means of correcting it
had also been found upon our journals; those journals did not then afford the means of correct information upon this subject, nor do they till this day.

"As to the first objection that an investigation
was depending in the House of Representatives, into
the official conduct of General Harrison, the result of
that investigation was in the highest degree honorable

to his character.   The committee were unanimously of
the opinion that General Harrison stood above suspicion of being implicated in the charges exhibited
against him, and that in his whole conduct, as commander-in-chief of the north-western army, he was
governed by a laudable zeal for and devotion to the
public service and interests.

"The second objection made to the passage of the
resolution, if well founded, was calculated to give to
Governor Shelby the entire and exclusive merit of
having urged the pursuit of Proctor and his army.
But Shelby, generous as he is brave, disclaims this
exclusive merit in a letter, which I beg leave to read;
denies, in the most positive terms, having used the
language ascribed to him, and he gives General Harrison the highest praise for his promptitude and vigilance in pursuing Proctor; for the skill with which
he arranged his troops for meeting the enemy, and
for his disinterested bravery during the action."

The resolution passed both branches of Congress
unanimously, or so nearly so that the exception was
but a single vote in the House, and on the 4th of
April, 1818, was approved by James Madison, President of the United States. So triumphantly had
General Harrison's character been vindicated from
the charges, of whatever kind, which had been preferred against him by his enemies, that scarcely an
objection was raised to the passage of a resolution conferring upon him the highest honor in the power of
Congress to bestow.

CHAPTER XVII.

It was during General Harrison's first regular term in Congress, that the celebrated and important debate was had on the resolution to censure General Jackson for his conduct in the Seminole War. Upon this subject he felt a very deep solicitude, and between his warm sympathy and disinterested friendship for a brave and patriotic fellow-soldier, and honest determination to let no considerations come between him and his duty to his country, he necessarily felt painfully embarrassed. His speech on this question was equally admired, therefore, for its ingenuity, ability and eloquence, and was pronounced one of the finest efforts elicited by that interesting occasion. It was even more admired, however, for its impartial and patriotic spirit than for its eloquence and ability; for while he disapproved the course of General Jackson, and commented on his conduct with the manly independence of a freeman, he defended such of his acts as he believed right, and did full justice to his motives.* In concluding his remarks he said :—

"If the highest services could claim indemnity for crime, then might the conqueror of Platæa have

* Hall's Life of Harrison.

been suffered to continue his usurpations until he had erected a throne upon the ruins of Grecian liberty. Sir, it will not be understood that I mean to compare General Jackson to these men. No; I believe that the principles of the patriot are as firmly fixed in his bosom as those of the soldier. But a republican government should make no distinctions between men, and should never relax its maxims of security for any individual, however distinguished. No man should be allowed to say that he could do that with impunity which another could not do. If the father of his country were alive, in the administration of the government, and had authorized the taking of the Spanish ports, I would declare my disapprobation as readily as I do now. Nay, more, because the more distinguished the individual, the more salutary the example. No one can tell how soon such an example may be beneficial. General Jackson will be faithful to his country. But I recollect that the virtues and patriotism of Fabius and Scipio were soon followed by the crimes of Marcus and the usurpations of Sylla.

"I am sure, Sir, that it is not the intention of any gentleman upon this floor to rob General Jackson of a single ray of glory, much less to wound his feelings or injure his reputation. And whilst I thank my friend from Mississippi (Mr. Poindexter), in the name of those who agree with me, that General Jackson has done wrong, I must be permitted to decline the use of the address which he has so obligingly prepared for us, and substitute the following as more consonant to our views and opinions. If the resolution pass I would address him thus : In the performance of a sacred duty, imposed by their construction of the constitution, the representatives of the people have found it necessary to disapprove a single act of your brilliant career; they have done it in the full conviction that the hero who has guarded her rights in the field, will bow with reverence to the civil institutions of his country—that he has admitted as his creed that the character of the soldier can never be complete without eternal reference to the character of the citizen.

"Your country has done for you all that a country can do for the most favored of her sons. The age of deification is passed; it was an age of tyranny and barbarism; the adoration of man should be addressed to his Creator alone. You have been feasted in the prétoires of the cities. Your statue shall be in the capitol, and your name be found in the song of the virgins. Go, gallant chief, and bear with you the gratitude of your country! Go, under the full conviction that, as her glory is identified with yours, she has nothing more dear to her but her laws—nothing more sacred but her constitution. Even an unintentional error shall be sanctified to her service. It will teach posterity that the government which could disapprove the conduct of a Marcellus, will have the fortitude to crush the vices of Marius.

"These sentiments, Sir, lead to results in which all must unite. General Jackson will still live in the

24

hearts of his fellow-citizens, and the constitution of your country will be immortal.''

General Harrison remained in Congress until he had served out the unexpired term of Mr. McLean, and the full term for which he was returned. He then declined a re-election. During his brief legislative career, he exhibited the same aptness for the new duties and responsibilities thus imposed upon him that he had previously shown for those of the soldier and the general. His familiar acquaintance with the wants of the country, and his extensive acquirements, peculiarly qualified him for an enlightened and useful discharge of the duties of the law-maker. As a debater, he was ready, fluent and forcible. Always courteous and dignified, and possessing a vigorous and cultivated mind, he not only made himself a most useful member, but was enabled to exercise an influence far greater than that exerted by many much older members. Many of his speeches will bear a favorable comparison with most members of the same Congress.

The following year after his withdrawal from Congress he yielded to the solicitation of his friends, and became a candidate for the Senate of Ohio, to which he was elected in the fall of 1819. In that body he rendered important services to the State. Earnestly as he labored for the public good, and advantageous as were his services to his constituents, his conduct did not escape the criticism of the censorious, nor even the open condemnation of disingenuous partizans.

His vote in the Senate, in favor of selling the services of convicts sentenced for larcenies of sums under fifty dollars, as a punishment less injurious to them and less burdensome to the State than confinement in the State prison, was made the pretext for charging him with voting to sell poor white men to pay their debts. In relation to this charge, General Harrison himself has given at once the clearest explanation and the most convincing refutation. After referring to an attack of this character that had been made upon him, he proceeds to say that no such act as one authorizing the sale of a poor debtor's services was either voted for him or passed by the legislature of which he was a member.

"The act in question has no more relation to the collection of 'debts,'" continues General Harrison, "than it has to the discovery of longitude. It was an act for the punishment of offenses against the State; and that part of it which is so bitterly assailed was passed by the House of Representatives, and voted for by the twelve senators, under the impression that it was the most mild and humane mode of dealing with the offenders for whose cases it was intended. It was adopted by the House of Representatives as a part of a general system of criminal law which was then undergoing a complete revision and amendment. The necessity of this is evinced by the following facts: For several years past it had become apparent that the Penitentiary system was becoming more and more burdensome at every session. A large appropriation was called for to meet the excess of expenditure above the receipts of the establishment. In the commencement of the session of 1820, the deficit amounted to nearly twenty thousand dollars.

" This growing evil required the immediate interposition of some vigorous legislative measure. Two were recommended as likely to produce the effect: first, placing the institution under better management, and, secondly, lessening the number of convicts who were sentenced for short periods, and whose labor was found, of course, to be most unproductive. In pursuance of the latter principle, thefts to the amount of fifty dollars or upwards were subjected to punishment in the Penitentiary, instead of ten dollars, which was the former minimum sum. This was easily done; but the great difficulty remained to determine what should be the punishment of those numerous larcenies below the sum of fifty dollars. By some, whipping was proposed; by others, punishment by hard labor in the county jails; and by others it was thought best to make them work on the highways.

" To all these there appeared insuperable objections. Fine and imprisonment was proposed by the House of Representatives as the only alternative, and as it was well known that these vexatious pilferings were generally perpetrated by the most worthless vagabonds in society, it was added that when they could not pay the fines and costs, which are always part of the sentences and punishments, their services should be sold out to any persons who should pay their fines and costs for them. This was a clause which was passed, as I believe, by an unanimous vote of the House, and stricken out in the Senate, in opposition to the twelve who have been denominated. A little further trouble in examining the journals would have shown that this was considered as a substitute for whipping, which was lost in the Senate and in the House, by a small majority after being once passed.

"I think I have said enough to show that this obnoxious law would not have applied to "unfortunate debtors of sixty-four years," but to infamous offenders who depredate upon the property of their fellow-citizens, and who by the constitution of the State, as well as the principle of existing laws, were subject to involuntary servitude. I must confess I had no very sanguine expectations of beneficial effects from this measure, as it would apply to convicts who had attained the age of maturity. But I had supposed that a woman or a youth who was convicted of an offense, and remained in jail for the payment of the fine and costs imposed, might with great advantage be transferred to the residence of some decent, virtuous private family, whose precept and example would greatly lead them back to the paths of virtue. * * * I think that imprisonment for debt, under any circumstances but those where fraud is alleged, is at war with the best principles of our constitution, and ought to be abolished."

General Harrison remained in the Senate of Ohio two years, during which he devoted the energies of

24 *

his mind and his great capacity for public business to
the promotion of such measures as he believed best
calculated to promote the general welfare. During
the time he was a member of the State Senate, he
was elected as one of the Presidential electors for
Ohio, and voted for James Madison for President, and
Daniel D. Tompkins for Vice President. He was
subsequently again chosen as one of the electors of
that State, and voted for Henry Clay for President.

He was nominated for Congress again in 1822,
but was defeated in consequence of his vote against
the Missouri Restriction.* Upon being nominated,
he issued an address to the people of his district, at
the conclusion of which he thus succinctly sets forth
his political principles: "I believe that upon the
preservation of the Union of the States depends the
existence of our civil and religious liberties, and that
the cement which binds it together is not a parcel of
words written upon paper or parchment, but the broth-
erly love and regard which the citizens of the several
States possess for each other. Destroy this, and the
beautiful fabric which was reared and embellished by
our ancestors, crumbles into ruin. From its disjointed
parts no temple of liberty will again be reared. Discord and wars will succeed to peace and harmony;
barbarism will again overspread the land; or, what is
scarcely better, some kindly tyrant will promulgate
the decrees of his will from the seat where a Washington and a Jefferson dispensed the blessings of a

* Hall's Life of Harrison.

free and equal government. I believe it therefore to be the duty of a representative to conciliate, by every possible means, the members of our great political family; and always to bear in mind that as the Union was effected only by a spirit of mutual concessions and forbearance, so only can it be preserved."

Having served two years in the Senate of his adopted State with honor and distinction to himself, and advantage to the people, he once more sought for that happiness and repose in the midst of his family at North Bend, which was so congenial to his disposition, but of which for so many years he had been deprived. He was once more to be disappointed in these agreeable anticipations. In the year 1824 he was elected to the United States Senate by the legislature of Ohio. Soon after taking his seat in that body he was appointed chairman of the military committee, in place of General Jackson, who had just resigned.

Acting upon the principle that had ever influenced his conduct, he warmly advocated the passage of a bill giving the preference in the appointment of cadets to the Military Academy at West Point, to the sons of those who had fallen in defense of their country's rights. While a member of the other house of Congress, he lost no opportunity of enforcing the necessity of giving not only to those who had shed their blood in their country's services, but also to the widows and orphans of those who had fallen in battle, some practical evidence of the country's gratitude.

His course in relation to the appointment of cadets was in accordance with his whole conduct towards these and the descendants of those who have periled and lost their lives in fighting for the rights of the whole people.

The eccentric and extraordinary John Randolph, of Roanoke, occupied a seat in the Senate at the time General Harrison represented Ohio in that body, and like every one else whose fortune led him into contact with the fierce genius from Virginia, he had to pay the penalty such contact imposed. True to his uniform practice, and the instinct of his nature, the Roanoke orator commenced one of his furious philippics against Harrison, renewing an old charge of having been a black cockade federalist, and an advocate of the Alien and Sedition laws which were adopted during the administration of the elder Adams. In reply to a virulent and unprovoked attack of this character, General Harrison replied with promptness and good temper, that the extraordinary manner in which his name had been brought before the Senate by the Senator from Virginia, probably required some notice from him, though he scarcely knew how to treat seriously such a charge as had been advanced against him.

To the charge that he had the stain of federalism upon his skirts, and had voted for a standing army and the Alien and Sedition laws, he said that he had not so fertile an imagination as the gentleman from Virginia, nor could he at command call up all the transactions of nearly thirty years ago. He could say, however, that at the time alluded to, he was not a party man in the sense the Senator from Virginia used. He was a delegate of a territory which was just then rising into importance, and having no vote upon the general questions before Congress, it was neither his duty, nor the interest of those whom he represented, to plunge into the turbulent sea of general politics which then agitated the nation.

There were questions of great importance to the north-west territory then before Congress—questions upon the just settlement of which depended the future prosperity of that now important portion of the Union. Standing as he did, the sole representative of that territory, his greatest ambition was to prove himself faithful to his trust by cherishing its interest; and nothing could have been more suicidal or pernicious to those he represented than for him to exasperate either party by becoming a violent partizan without the power to aid it, because he had no vote on political questions. This was his position, and although he had his political principles as firmly fixed as those of the gentleman from Virginia, it was no business of his to strike where he could not be felt, and where the blow must recoil upon himself and those whom he represented.

He wore no cockade, black or tri-colored, at that time, and never wore one but when he was in the military service of his country. But he was seriously charged with the heinous offense of associating with federal gentlemen. He plead guilty; he respected the revolutionary services of President Adams, and had paid him that courtesy which was due to him as a man and a chief magistrate. He also associated with such men as John Marshall and James A. Bayard: was the acknowledgment of such guilt to throw him out of the pale of political salvation?

On the other hand, he was on intimate terms with Mr. Jefferson, Mr. Gallatin, and with the whole Virginia delegation, among whom he had many kinsmen and dear friends. They were his principal associates in Philadelphia, in whose mess he had often met the gentleman who was now his accuser, and with whom he had spent some of the happiest hours of his life. It was true, as the senator alleged, he had been appointed governor of the north-western territory by John Adams; so had he been by Thomas Jefferson and James Madison.

But he was not in Congress when the standing army was created and the Alien and Sedition laws were passed, and if he had been he could not have voted for them, and would not if he could. It was not in his nature to be a violent or proscriptive partisan, but he had given a fine support to the republican administrations of Jefferson, Madison and Monroe. He hoped the senator from Virginia was answered; he was sure the Senate must be wearied with this frivolous and unprofitable squabble.

CHAPTER XVIII.

GENERAL HARRISON remained in Congress only three years, having been appointed by President John Quincy Adams, in 1828, Minister Plenipotentiary to the republic of Colombia. He sailed from New York on his mission on the 10th November of that year, in the ship Erie, and arrived at Bogota on the 5th of February ensuing. On the 27th he presented his credentials and was received with flattering attentions. The official journal of the government, in announcing his arrival, congratulated Colombia on beholding the interest which was manifested by the government of the United States, to cultivate friendly relations with that republic by sending among them so distinguished a citizen as General Harrison.

On the 4th of March following, twenty-eight days after General Harrison arrived at the capitol of Colombia, General Jackson was inaugurated President of the United States. On the 8th of March, thirty-one days after his arrival, he was recalled, and Thomas P. Moore, of Kentucky, appointed his successor. A recollection of this circumstance will aid in forming an opinion as to the correctness of the charge that General Harrison was recalled in consequence of his interference with the internal affairs of the republic. The government of the United States could not have been advised of his arrival at Bogota until some time after he had been recalled, and Mr. Moore appointed to succeed him. The pretext upon which this charge of interference was based, was a letter written by him to Bolivar, the President of the republic, containing some patriotic admonition as to his future course.

Unfortunately, however, for those who sought to justify the injustice done to General Harrison and the injury to the country, by his hasty recall, that letter was written six months after the appointment of his successor, and when he had ceased to be an officer of the government. The charge, however, served its purpose for the time, and has long since ceased either to be believed or repeated. The letter which was used as an attempted justification of an act that met with the almost universal disapprobation of the country, contained sentiments alike so noble and patriotic, and is withal so pregnant with the true spirit of republicanism, that it deserves to be perpetuated in every practicable form. Few papers emanating from a private citizen have ever been more admired or commanded more general respect for their patriotic principles and their beauty and energy of style. The letter is dated at Bogota, on the 27th of September, 1829. The motive by which it was dictated is best explained by the letter itself, as follows:

"If there is anything in the style, the matter or the object of this letter, which is calculated to give offense to your excellency, I am persuaded you will readily forgive it, when you reflect on the motives which induced me to write it. An old soldier could possess no feelings but those of the kindest character towards one who has shed so much lustre on the profession of arms; nor can a citizen of the country of Washington cease to wish that in Bolivar the world might behold another instance of the highest military attainments united with the purest patriotism and the greatest capacity for civil government.

"Such, Sir, have been the fond hopes not only of the people of the United States, but of the friends of liberty throughout the world. I will not say that your excellency has formed projects to defeat these hopes, but there is no doubt that they have not only been formed, but are at this moment in progress to maturity, and openly avowed by those who possess your entire confidence. I will not attribute to these men impure motives, but can they be disinterested advisers? Are they not the very persons who will gain most by the proposed change? who will, indeed, gain all that is to be gained, without furnishing any part of the equivalent? That the price of their future wealth and honors is to be furnished exclusively by yourself? And of what does it consist? Your great character. Such a one, that if a man were wise, and possessor of the empire of the Cæsars in its best days, he would give all to obtain. Are

25

you prepared to make this sacrifice for such an object?

"I am persuaded that those who advocate these measures have never dared to induce you to adopt them by any argument founded on your personal interests, and that to succeed it would be necessary to convince you that no other course remained to save the country from the evils of anarchy. This is the question, then, to be examined.

Does the history of this country, since the adoption of the constitution, really exhibit unequivocal evidence that the people are unfit to be free? Is the exploded opinion of a European philosopher of the last age, that in the new hemisphere man is a degraded being, to be renewed and supported by the example of Colombia? The proof should indeed be strong to induce an American to adopt an opinion so humiliating.

"Feeling always a deep interest in the success of the revolutions in the late Spanish America, I have never been an inattentive observer of events, pending and posterior to the achievements of its independence. In these events I search in vain for a single fact to show that in Colombia, at least, the state of society is non-suited to the adoption of a free government. Will it be said, that a free government did exist, but being found inadequate to the objects for which it had been instituted, it has been superseded by one of a different character with the concurrence of a majority of the people?

" It is the most difficult thing in the world for me to believe, that a people in the possession of their rights, as freemen, would ever be willing to surrender them and submit themselves to the will of a master. I say such instances are on record; the power thus transferred has been in a moment of extreme public danger, and then limited to a very short period. I do not think that it is by any means certain that the majority of the French people favored the elevation of Napoleon to the throne of France. But if it were so, how different were the circumstances of that country from those of Colombia, when the constitution of Cucutor was overthrown! At the period of the elevation of Napoleon to the First Consulate, all the powers of Europe were the open or secret enemies of France; civil war raged within her borders. The hereditary king possessed many partisans in every province; the people, continually betrayed by the factions which murdered and succeeded each other, had imbibed a portion of their ferocity, and every town and village witnessed the indiscriminate slaughter of both men and women of all parties and principles. Does the history of Colombia, since the expulsion of the Spaniards, present any parallel to these scenes? Her frontiers have never been seriously menaced; no civil war raged; not a partisan of the former government was to be found in the whole extent of her territory; no faction contended with each other for the possession of power; the executive government remained in the hands of those to whom it had been committed by the people, in a fair election. In fact, no people ever passed from under the yoke of a despotic government to the enjoyment of entire freedom with less disposition to abuse their newly-acquired power than those of Colombia. They submitted, indeed, to a continuance of some of the most arbitrary and unjust features which distinguished the former government. If there was any disposition on the part of the great mass of the people to effect any change in the existing order of things,—if the Colombians act from the same motives and upon the same principles which govern mankind elsewhere and in all ages,—they would have desired to take from the government a part of the power which, in their experience, they had confided to it. The monopoly of certain articles of agricultural produce, and the oppressive duties of the Alcabala, might have been tolerated until the last of their tyrants were driven from the country. But when peace was restored, when not one enemy remained within its borders, it might reasonably have been supposed that the people would have desired to abolish these remains of arbitrary governments, and substitute for them some tax more equal and accordant with republican principles.

" On the contrary, it is pretended that they had become enamored with these despotic measures, and so disgusted with the freedom they did enjoy, that they were more than willing to commit their destinies to the uncontrolled will of your excellency. Let me assure you, Sir, that these assertions will gain no credits with the present generation, or with posterity. They will demand the facts which had induced a people, by no means deficient in intelligence, so soon to abandon the principles for which they had so gallantly fought, and tamely surrendered that liberty which had been obtained at the expense of so much blood. And what facts can be produced? It cannot be said that life and property were not as well protected under the republican government as they have ever been; nor that there existed any opposition to the constitution and laws too strong for the ordinary powers of the government to put down.

"If the insurrection of General Paez, in Venezuela, is adduced, I would ask by what means was he reduced to obedience? Your excellency, the legitimate head of the republic, appeared, and in a moment all opposition ceased, and Venezuela was restored to the republic. But it is said that this was affected by your personal influence, or the dread of your military talents, and that to keep General Paez and other ambitious chiefs from dismembering the republic, it was necessary to invest your excellency with the extraordinary powers you possess. There would be some reason in this if you had refused to act without these powers, or having acted as you did, you had been unable to accomplish anything without them; but you succeeded completely, and there can be no possible reason assigned why you would not have succeeded with the same means against any future attempt of General Paez or any other general.

25 *

"There appears, however, to be one sentiment in which all parties unite; that is, that as matters now stand, you alone can save the country from ruin—at least from much calamity. They differ, however, very widely as to the measures to be taken to put your excellency in the way to render this important service. The lesser and more interested party is for placing the government in your hands for life, either with your present title, or with one which, it must be confessed, better accords with the nature of the powers to be exercised. If they adopt the less offensive title, and if they weave into their system some apparent checks to your will, it is only for the purpose of masking, in some degree, their real object, which is nothing short of the establishment of a despotism. The plea of necessity, that eternal argument of all conspirators, ancient or modern, against the rights of mankind, will be resorted to, to induce you to accede to their measures, and the unsettled state of the country which has been designedly produced by them, will be adduced as evidence of that necessity.

"There is but one way for your excellency to escape from the snares which have been so artfully laid to entrap you, and that is to stop short in the course which unfortunately has been already commenced. Every step you advance under the influence of such counsels will make retreat more difficult, until it will become impracticable. You will be told that the intention is only to vest you with authority, to correct what is wrong in the administration, and to put down

the factions, and that when the country once enjoys
tranquillity, the government may be restored to the
people.   Delusive will be the hopes of those who rely
upon this declaration.   The promised hour of tranquillity will never arrive.   If events tended to produce it, they will be counteracted by the government
itself.   It was the strong remark of a former president of the United States, that sooner will the lover
be contented with the first smiles of his mistress than a
government cease to endeavor to extend and preserve
its powers. With whatever reluctance your excellency
may commence the career ; with whatever disposition
to abandon it when the objects for which it was commenced have been obtained; when once fairly entered, you will be borne along by the irresistible
force of pride, habits of command, and, indeed, of
self-preservation, and it will be impossible to recede.

"But it is said that it is for the benefit of the
people that the proposed change is to be made ; and
that by your talents and influence alone, aided by
unlimited power, the ambitious chiefs in the different
departments are to be restrained, and the integrity
of the republic preserved.   I have said, and I most
sincerely believe that from the state into which the
country has been brought, that you alone can preserve it from the horrors of anarchy.   But I cannot
conceive that any extraordinary powers are necessary.
The authority to see that the laws are executed ;
to call out the strength of the country ; to enforce
their execution, is all that is required, and is what

is possessed by the chief magistrate of the United States, and of every other republic, and is what was confined to the executive by the constitution of Cucuta. Would your talents or your energies be impaired in the council or the field, or your influence lessened when acting as the head of a republic?

" I propose to examine very briefly the results which are likely to flow from the proposed change of government : first, in relation to the country ; secondly, to yourself personally. Is the tranquillity of the country to be secured by it ? Is it possible for your excellency to believe that when the mask has been thrown off, and the people discovered that a despotic government has been fixed upon them, that they will quietly submit to it ? Will they forget the pass-word which, like the cross of fire, was the signal for rallying to oppose their former tyrants ? Will the virgins at your bidding cease to chant the songs of liberty which so lately animated the youth to victory ? Was the patriotic blood of Colombia all expended in the fields of Vargas, Bayaca and Carebobo ? The schools may cease to enforce upon their pupils the love of country, drawn from the examples of Cato and the Bruti, Harmodius and Aristogiton ; but the glorious example of patriotic devotion, exhibited in your own hacienda, will supply their place. Depend upon it, Sir, that the moment which shall announce the continuance of arbitrary power in your hands, will be the commencement of commotions which will require all your talents and energy to suppress. You may succeed. The disciplined army at your disposal may be too powerful for an unarmed, undisciplined and scattered population. But one unsuccessful effort will not content them, and your feelings will be eternally racked by being obliged to make war upon those who have been accustomed to call you their father, and to invoke blessings on your head, and for no cause but their adherence to principles which you yourself had taught them to regard more than their lives.

" If by the strong government which the advocates for the proposed change so strenuously recommend, one without responsibility is intended which may put men to death, and immure them in dungeons without trial, and one where the army is everything and the people nothing, I must say that if the tranquillity of Colombia is to be preserved in this way, the wildest anarchy would be preferable. Out of that anarchy a better government might arise. But the chains of military despotism once fastened upon a nation, ages might pass away before they could be shaken off.

" But I contend that the strongest of all governments is that which is most free. We consider that of the United States as the strongest, precisely because it is the most free. It possesses the faculties equally to protect itself from foreign force or internal convulsions. In both it has been sufficiently tried. In no country upon the earth would an armed opposition to the laws be sooner or more effectually put down. Not so much by the terrors of the guillotine and the gibbet as from the aroused determination of the nation, exhibiting their strength, and convincing the factions that their cause was hopeless. No, Sir, depend upon it, that the possession of arbitrary power by the government of Colombia will not be the means of securing its tranquillity; nor will the danger of disturbances solely arise from the opposition of the people. The power and the military force which it will be necessary to put in the hands of the governors of the distant provinces, added to the nature of the country, will continually present to those officers the temptation and the means of revolt.

"Will the proposed change restore prosperity to the country? With the best intentions to do so will you be able to recall commerce to its shores, and give new life to the drooping state of agriculture? The cause of the constant decline in these great interests cannot be mistaken. It arises from the fewness of those who labor, and the number of those who are to be supported by that labor. To support a swarm of luxurious and idle monks, and an army greatly disproportioned to the resources of the country, with a body of officers in a tenfold degree disproportioned to the army, every branch of industry is opprressed with burdens which deprive the ingenious man of the profits of his ingenuity, and the laborer of his reward. To satisfy the constant and pressing demands which are made upon it, the treasury seizes upon everything within its grasp—destroying the very germ of future prosperity: is there any prospect that these evils will cease with the proposed change? Can the army be dispensed with? Will the influence of the monks be no longer necessary? Believe me, Sir, that the support which the government derives from both those sources will be more than ever requisite.

"But the most important inquiry is the effect which this strong government is to have upon the people themselves. Will it tend to improve and elevate their character, and fit them for the freedom which it is pretended is ultimately to be bestowed upon them? The question has been answered from the age of Homer. Man does not learn under oppression those noble qualities and feelings which fit him for the enjoyment of liberty. Nor is despotism the proper school in which to acquire the knowledge of the principles of republican government. A government whose revenues are derived from diverting the very sources of wealth from its subjects will not find it the means of improving the morals and enlightening the minds of the youth, by supporting systems of liberal education; and if it could, it would not.

"In relation to the effect which this investment of power is to have upon your happiness and your fame, will the pomp and glitter of a court, and the flattery of venal courtiers, reward you for the trouble and anxieties attendant upon the exercise of sovereignty everywhere, and those which will flow from your peculiar situation? Or power supported by the bayonet for that willing homage which you were wont to receive from your fellow-citizens? The groans of a dissatisfied and oppressed people will penetrate the inmost recesses of your palace, and you will be tortured by the reflection that you no longer possess that place in their affections which was once your pride and your boast, and which would have been your solace under every reverse of fortune. Unsupported by the people, your authority can only be maintained by the terrors of the sword and the scaffold. And have these ever been successful under similar circumstances? Blood may smother for a period, but can never extinguish the fire of liberty which you have contributed so much to kindle in the bosom of every Colombian.

"I will not urge as an argument the personal dangers to which you will be exposed; but I will ask if you could enjoy life which would be preserved by the constant execution of so many human beings— your countrymen, your former friends, and almost your worshipers? The pangs of such a situation will be more acutely reflecting on the hallowed motives who could aim their daggers at your bosom; that, like the last of the Romans, they would strike, not from hatred to the man, but love to the country.

"From a knowledge of your own disposition and present feelings, your excellency will not be willing to believe that you could ever be brought to commit an act of tyranny, or ever to execute justice with unnecessary rigor; but trust me, Sir, there is nothing more corrupting—nothing more destructive of the noblest and finest feelings of our nature—than of unlimited power. The men who, in the beginning of such a career, might shudder at the idea of taking away the life of a fellow-being, might soon have his conscience so seared by the repetition of crime, that the agonies of his murdered victims might become music to his soul, and the drippings of his scaffold afford "blood enough to swim in." History is full of such examples.

"From this disgusting picture permit me to call the attention of your excellency to one of a different character. It exhibits you as the constitutional chief magistrate of a free people, giving to their representatives the influence of your great name, to reform the abuses which, in a long reign of tyranny and misrule, have fastened upon every branch of the government. The army and its swarm of officers reduced within the limits of real usefulness, placed on the frontiers, and no longer permitted to control public opinion, and be the terror of the peaceful citizen. By the removal of this incubus from the treasury, and the establishment of order, responsibility and economy in the expenditures of the government, it would soon be enabled to dispense with the odious monopolies and the duty of the *alcavala*, which have operated with so malign an effect upon the commerce and agriculture; and, indeed, upon the revenues which they were intended to augment. No longer oppressed by these shackles, industry would everywhere revive; the farmer and the artisan, cheered by the prospect of ample reward for their labor, would redouble their exertions; foreigners, with their capital and skill in the arts, would

26

crowd hither to enjoy the advantages which could scarcely elsewhere be found; and Colombia would soon exhibit the reality of the beautiful fiction of Fenelon—Labutum rising from misery and oppression to prosperity and happiness, under the counsels and direction of the concealed goddess.

"What objections can be urged against this course? Can any one acquainted with these circumstances of the country doubt its success in restoring and maintaining tranquillity? The people would certainly not revolt against themselves, and none of the chiefs who are supposed to be factiously inclined would think of opposing the strength of the nation when directed by your talents and authority. But it is said that the want of intelligence amongst the people unfits them for the government. Is it not right, however, that the experiment should be fairly tried? I have already said that this has not been done. For myself, I do not hesitate to declare my firm belief that it will succeed. The people of Colombia possess many traits of character suitable for a republican government. A more orderly, forbearing, well-disposed people are nowhere to be met with. Indeed, it may be asserted, that their faults and vices are attributable to the cursed government to which they have been so long subjected, and to the intolerant character of their religion, whilst their virtues are all their own. But admitting their present want of intelligence, no one has ever doubted their capacity to acquire knowledge; and under the strong motives which exist to obtain it, supported by the influence of your excellency, it would soon be obtained.

"To yourself the advantage would be as great as to the country; like acts of mercy the blessings would be reciprocal, your personal happiness secured, and your fame elevated to a height which would leave but a single competition in the estimation of posterity. In bestowing the palm of merit the world has become wiser than formerly. The successful warrior is no longer entitled to the first place in the temple of fame. Talents of this kind have become too common and too often used for mischievous purposes to be regarded as they once were. In this enlightened age the now hero of the field and the successful leader of armies may, for the moment, attract attention; but it will be such as is bestowed upon the passing meteor, whose blaze is no longer remembered when it is no longer seen. To be esteemed eminently great it is necessary to be eminently good. The qualities of the general and the hero must be devoted to the advantage of mankind, before he will be permitted to assume the title of their benefactor; and the station which he will hold in their regard and affections will depend, not upon the number and the splendor of his victories, but upon the results and the use he may make of the influence he acquires from them.

"If the fame of Washington depended upon his military achievements, would the common consent of the world allow him the pre-eminence he possesses?

The victories of Trenton, Monmouth and York, brilliant as they were—exhibiting as they certainly did, the highest grade of military talents—are scarcely thought of. The source of the veneration and esteem which is entertained for his character by every description of politicians—the monarchist and aristocrat, as well as the republican—is to be found in his undeviating and exclusive devotedness to the interests of his country. No selfish consideration was ever suffered to intrude itself into his mind. For his country he conquered; and the unrivaled and increasing prosperity of that country is constantly adding fresh glory to his name. General, the course which he pursued is open to you, and it depends upon yourself to attain the eminence which he reached before you.

"To the eyes of military men the laurels you won on the fields of Vargas, Bayaca and Carobobo, will be forever green; but will that content you? Are you willing that your name should descend to posterity amongst the names of those whose fame has been derived from shedding human blood, without a single advantage to the human race; or shall it be united to that of Washington, as the founder and the father of a great and happy people? The choice is before you. The friends of liberty throughout the world, and the people of the United States in particular, are waiting your decision with intense anxiety. Alexander toiled and conquered to obtain the applause of the Athenians; will you regard as nothing the opinions of a nation which has evinced its superiority over that celebrated people in the science most useful to man, by having carried into actual practice a system of government, of which the wisest Athenians had but a glimpse in theory, and considered as a blessing never to be realized, however ardently to be desired. The place which you are to occupy in their esteem depends upon yourself. Farewell."

Immediately upon the arrival of General Harrison's successor he took his departure from Bogota, and arrived at New York on the 16th of February, 1830. He proceeded at once to his residence at North Bend, and again entered upon his favorite pursuit of agriculture with all the zeal of former years. A short time after his return he partook of a public dinner, tendered him by the citizens of Cincinnati, as a mark of their high respect for his private virtues and distinguished public services. The next year he delivered the annual address before the Hamilton County Agricultural Society. This address gave convincing evidence of General Harrison's familiar acquaintance with the theory as well as the practice of agriculture, and of the deep interest he felt in that most important of all branches of industry. An extract from it will illustrate the truth of this statement :

" The encouragement of agriculture, gentlemen, would be praiseworthy in any country ; in our own it is peculiarly so, not only to multiply the means and enjoyments of life, but as giving greater stability and security to our political institutions. In all ages and

26 *

in all countries, it has been observed, that the culti-
vators of the soil are those who were least willing to
part with their rights, and submit themselves to the will
of a master. I have no doubt, also, that a taste for
agricultural pursuits is the best means of disciplining
the ambition of those daring spirits who occasionally
spring up in the world for good or for evil, to defend
or destroy the liberties of their fellow-men, as the
principles received from education or circumstances
may tend. As long as the leaders of the Roman
armies were taken from the plow, to the plow they
were willing to return; never in the character of
general forgetting the duties of the citizen, and ever
ready to exchange the sword and the triumphal purple, for the homely vestments of the husbandman.

"The history of this far-famed republic is full of
instances of this kind; but none more remarkable
than our own age and country have produced. The
facinations of power, and the trappings of command,
were as much despised—and the enjoyment of rural
scenes and rural employments as highly prized—by our
Washington as by Cincinnatus or Regulus. At the
close of his glorious military career, he says, 'I am
preparing to return to that domestic retirement which
it is well known I left with the deepest regret, and for
which I have not ceased to sigh through a long and
painful absence.'

"Your efforts, gentlemen, to diffuse a taste for
agriculture amongst men of all descriptions and professions may produce results more important, even,

than increasing the means of subsistence, and the enjoyments of life. It may cause some future conqueror for his country to end his career

' Guiltless of his country's blood.'

* * * "To the heart-cheering prospect of herds and flocks feeding on unrivaled pastures, fields of grain exhibiting the scriptural proof that the seed had been sown on good ground, how often is the eye of the philanthropic traveler disgusted with the dark unsightly manufactories of a certain poison —poison to the body and the soul. A modern Æneas or Ulysses might mistake them for entrances into the infernal regions; nor would they greatly err. But, unlike those passages which conduct the Grecian and Trojan heroes on their pious errands, the scenes to which these conduct the unhappy wretch who shall enter are those exclusively of misery and woe. No relief to the sad picture; no Tartarus *there*, no Elysium *here*. It is all Tartarian darkness, and not unfrequently Tartarian crimes. I speak more freely of the practice of converting the material of the ' staff of life' (and by which so many human beings yearly perish) into an article which is so destructive of health and happiness, because in that way I have sinned myself; but in that way I shall sin no more."

CHAPTER XIX.

GENERAL HARRISON's time and attention now and
for several years after continued to be almost exclusively devoted to agricultural pursuits,—not so exclusively, however, that he was not ever ready to aid to
the extent of his abilities, and in any way his services might be required in every useful and benevolent enterprise. His expensive literary attainments
subjected him to frequent demands of this character.
Frequent addresses, speeches and orations of his,
written or spoken, during this period, are productions
of no mean literary merit, and evincing a range of
intellect and a depth of research which place General
Harrison in the front rank of American orators and
statesmen as well as writers.

Passing over several of these productions, an extract will be given from a speech delivered at Vincennes, in May, 1835, at a dinner given him by the
citizens of that place, for the purpose of showing his
opinions upon a question which then, as now, excited
the deepest interest in the public mind. Though his
opinions on the subject of slavery may not command
the same attention now that they did when the public
mind first began to be directed towards him as an

aspirant for the highest office in the nation, they are nevertheless entitled to that respect which everything emanating from a man of his character, talents and patriotism, should ever receive. Many of his sentiments will, probably, scarcely find a response amongst a large number of the people in one section of the Union. After having briefly referred to the movements of emancipation societies, and denounced them in terms that proved with how good a will it was done, he proceeds :—

"Am I wrong in applying the terms weak, presumptious and unconstitutional to the measures of the emancipators ? A slight examination will, I think, show that I am not. In the vindication of the objects of a convention lately held in one of the towns of Ohio, it was that nothing more was intended than to produce a state of public feeling which would lead to an amendment of the constitution of the United States. Now can an amendment of the constitution be effected without the consent of the southern states? What then is the proposition to be submitted to them? * * * But the course pursued by the emancipationists is unconstitutional. I do not say that there are any words in the constitution which forbid the discussions they are engaged in ; I know that there are not. Any citizens have the right to express and publish their opinions without restriction. But in the construction of the constitution it is always necessary to refer to the circumstances under which it was framed, and to ascertain its meaning by a comparison of its provisions with each other, and with the previous situation of the several States who were parties to it. In a portion of these, slavery was recognized, and they took care to have the right secured to them; to follow and reclaim such of them as were fugitives to other States. The laws of Congress, passed under this power, have provided punishment for any one who shall oppose or interrupt the excercise of this right. Now can any one believe that the instrument which contains a provision of this kind which authorizes a master to pursue his slave into another State, take him back, and provide punishment for any citizen of that State who should oppose him, should at the same time authorize the latter to assemble together, to pass resolutions, and adopt addresses, not only to encourage the slaves to leave their masters, but to cut their throats before they do so.

"I insist, that if the citizens of the non-slaveholding States can avail themselves of the article of the constitution, which prohibits the restriction of speech, or the press to publish anything injurious to the rights of the slave-holding States, that they can go to the extreme that I have mentioned, and effect anything further which writing or speaking could effect. But, fellow-citizens, these are not the principles of the constitution. Such a construction would defeat one of the great objects of its formation, which was that of securing the peace and harmony of the States which were parties to it. The liberty of speech and the press were given as the most effectual means to preserve to each and every citizen his own rights, and to the States the rights which appertained to them, at the time of their adoption. It could never have been expected that it would have been used by the citizens of one portion of the States for the purpose of depriving those of another portion of the rights which they had reserved at the adoption of the constitution, and in the exercise of which none but themselves have any concern or interest. If slavery is an evil, the evil is with them. If there is guilt in it, the guilt is theirs, not ours, since neither the States where it does not exist, nor the government of the United States, can, without usurpation of power, and the violation of a solemn compact, do anything to remove it without the consent of those who are immediately interested. But they will neither aid nor consent to be aided, whilst the illegal, persecuting and dangerous movements are in progress, of which I complain; the interest of all concerned requires that these should be stopped immediately. This can only be done by the force of public opinion, and that cannot too soon be brought into operation. Every movement which is made by the abolitionists in the non-slave-holding States is viewed by our southern brethren as an attack upon their rights, and which, if persisted in, must in the end eradicate those feelings of attachment and affection between the citizens of all the States, which was produced by a community of interests and dangers in the war of the revolution, which was the foundation of our happy

union, and by a continuance of which it can alone be
preserved. I entreat you, then, to frown upon the
measures which are to produce results so much to be
deprecated. The opinions which I have now given
I have omitted no opportunity, for the last two years,
to lay before the people of my own State; I have
taken the liberty to express them here, knowing that
if they should unfortunately not accord with yours,
they would be kindly received.

In relation to these opinions of General Harrison,
it may be said that public opinion in the free States
has taken a long stride forward in the sixteen years
since their delivery and the present period. Then
they were up with the sentiment of the northern
people on the subject of slavery; now they are far
behind it, at least, on some points. While the great
body of the citizens of the free States will cordially
agree with him that neither they nor Congress have
any right to interfere with slavery in the States, where
it exists, they still claim the right to investigate it in
all its relations to the North, and to use every proper
means to prevent its extension beyond its present
limits.

For a long time the attention of the people of several of the States had been concentrating upon General
Harrison as the most suitable man as the whig candidate for President, at the ensuing presidential election.
By a spontaneous movement in his behalf, he was nominated, on the part of the people, in the autumn of
1835; and the nomination thus virtually made by the

people was confirmed by various State conventions opposed to the re-election of Mr. Van Buren, held the same autumn or the ensuing spring. Several of the States, however, either made no nomination, or nominated another candidate; and this want of unanimous and harmonious action between all the opponents of Mr. Van Buren, in every part of the Union, and the late period to which the canvass was deferred, led to the defeat of General Harrison. The result proved, however, that had he been brought before the people with the advantages which a national nomination and a national organization would have given him, and the confidence it would have inspired in his friends, he might have been elected; and especially it proved that he possessed the elements of future success in his character. Though he received but seventy-two electoral votes, in the fifteen States in which he and Mr. Van Buren were the only candidates, he received five hundred and fifty-two thousand votes, and Mr. Van Buren five hundred and eighty, being a majority for the latter of the popular vote of only twenty-eight thousand.

In 1837, General Harrison was selected to deliver a discourse before the Philosophical and Historical Society of Ohio, a duty that he discharged with consummate ability. The subject of this address was on the Aborignies of the valley of the Ohio. It displays a very considerable degree of research, and a perfect familiarity with the ancient works and the Aborigines on the Ohio. It is written, too, with force and ele-

gance, and is as ingenious as it is profound. A single extract or two will illustrate this; and also afford
both pleasure and interest to the enquirer after both:
—" The process by which nature restores the forest
to its original state, after being once cleared, is extremely slow. In our rich lands, indeed, it is soon
covered again with timber, but the character of the
growth is entirely different, and continues so through
many generations of men. In several places on the
Ohio, particularly upon the farm which I occupy,
clearings were made in the first settlements, abandoned, and suffered to grow up. Some of them, now
to be seen, of nearly fifty years' growth, have made so
little progress towards attaining the appearance of
the immediately contiguous forest, as to induce any
man of reflection to determine that at least ten times
fifty years would be necessary before its complete
assimilation could be affected. The sites of the ancient works on the Ohio present precisely the same
appearance as the circumjacent forest. You find on
them all that beautiful variety of trees which gives
such unrivaled richness to our forest. This is particularly the case on fifteen acres, included within the
walls of the neck at the mouth of the Great Miami;
and the relative proportions of the different kinds of
timber are about the same. The first growth on the
same kind of land, once cleared, and then abandoned
to nature, on the contrary, is more homogenious—
often stinted to one or two, or at most to three, kinds
of timber.

"If the ground had been cultivated, yellow locust, in many places, will spring up as thick as garden peas. If it has not been cultivated, the black and white walnut will be the prevailing growth. The rapidity with which these trees grow, for a time, smothers the attempt of other kinds to vegetate and grow in their shade. The more thrifty individuals soon overtop the meeker of their own kind, which sicken and die. In this way there are soon only as many left as the earth will support to maturity. All this time the squirrel may plant the seed of those trees which serve them for food, and by neglect suffer them to remain,—it will be in vain; the birds may drop the kernels, the external pulp of which have contributed to their nourishment, and divested of which they are in the best state for germinating, still it will be of no avail; the winds of heaven may waft the winged seeds of the sycamour, cotton-wood and maple, and a friendly shower may bury them to the necessary depth in the loose and fertile soil; but without success. The roots below rob them of moisture, and the canopy of limbs and leaves above interrupt the rays of the sun and the dews of heaven: the young giants in possession, like another kind of aristocracy, absorb the whole means of subsistence, and leave the mass to perish at their feet; this state of things, however, will not always continue. If the process of nature is slow and circuitous in putting down usurpation and establishing the equality which she loves, and which is the great characteristic of her principles, it is sure and effectual. The pref-

erence of the soil for the first growth ceases with its
maturity; it admits of no succession on the principle
of legitimacy. The long undisputed masters of the
forest may be thinned by the lightnings, the tempest,
or by diseases peculiar to themselves; and whenever
this is the case, one of the oft-rejected of another
family, will find between its decaying roots shelter
and appropriate food, and, springing into vigorous
growth, will soon push its green foliage to the skies
through the decayed and withering limbs of its blasted
and dying adversary; the soil itself yielding it a
more liberal support than any scion from any occu-
pant. It will be conceived what a length of time it
will require for a denuded tract of land, by a process
so slow, again to clothe itself with the amazing variety
of foliage which is the characteristic of the forests of
this region. Of what immense age, then, must be
those works, so often referred to, covered, as has been
supposed by those who have the best opportunity of
examining them, with the second growth after the
second forest state had been regained.   *   *   *

"An erroneous opinion has prevailed in relation
to the character of the Indians of North America.
By many they are supposed to be stoics, who willingly
encounter deprivations. The very reverse is the fact;
if they belong to either of the classes of philosophers
which prevailed in the declining ages of Greece and
Rome, it is to that of epicureans; for no Indian
will forego an enjoyment, or suffer an inconvenience,
if he can avoid it, but under peculiar circumstances,

—when, for instance, he is stimulated by some strong passion; but even the gratification of this he is ever ready to postpone, whenever its accomplishment is attended with unlooked for danger, or unexpected hardships. Hence their military operations were always feeble—their expeditions few and far between, and much the greater number abandoned without an efficient stroke, from whim, caprice or an aversion to encounter difficulties. But if the Indian will not throw off 'the pomps and pleasures' with which his good fortune furnishes him,—when evils come which he cannot avoid—when 'the stings and arrows of outrageous fortune' fall thick upon him,—then will he call up all the spirit of a man into his bosom, and meet his fate, however hard, like 'the best Roman of them all.'   *   *   *

"It may be proper that I should say something more as to the character of the now scattered and almost extinct tribes which so long and so successfully resisted our arms, and who, for many years after, stood in the relation of dependents, acknowledging themselves under our exclusive protection. Their character as warriors has been already remarked upon; their bravery has never been questioned, although there was certainly a considerable difference between the several tribes in this respect. With Wyandots, flight in battle, when meeting with unexpected resistance or obstacle, brought with it no disgrace. It was considered rather as a principle of tactics; and I think it may be fairly considered as having its source in that

27 *

peculiar temperament of mind which they often manifested of not pressing fortune under any sinister circumstances, but patiently waiting until the changes
of a successful issue appeared to be favorable.   With
the Wyandots it was otherwise; their youth were
taught to consider anything that had the appearance
of an acknowledgment of a superiority of an enemy
as disgraceful.   In the battle of the Miami Rapids,
of thirteen chiefs of that tribe who we represent, one
only survived, and he badly wounded.

"As it regards their moral and intellectual qualities the difference between the tribes was still greater.
The Shawanees, Delawares, and Miamis were much
superior to the other members of the confederacy.
I have known individuals among them of very high
order of talents, but these were not generally to be
relied on for sincerity.   The Little Turtle, of the Miami tribe, was of this description, as was the Blue
Jacket, a Shawanee chief.   I think it probable that
Tecumthe possessed more integrity than any other of
the chiefs who attained to much distinction.   But he
violated a solemn engagement which he had freely
contracted, and there are strong suspicions of his
having formed a treacherous design which an accident
only prevented him from accomplishing.   Sinister instances are, however, to be found in the conduct of
great men in the history of almost all civilized nations.   But these instances are more than counterbalanced by the number of individuals of high moral
character which were to be found amongst the princi

pal and secondary chiefs of the four tribes above mentioned. This was particularly the case with Tache or the Crane, the Grand Sachem of the Wyandots, and Black Hoof, the chief of the Shawanees."

The opinions of General Harrison upon the subject of dueling may not be without interest, and possibly they exert some slight influence even in an age when the barbarous custom has almost been driven from respectable society. In 1838, he addressed a letter to A. B. Howell, Esq., of New Jersey, on this subject, from which an extract will be made. He illustrates the dreadful effects of the practice, and its demoralizing tendency, principally by giving one or two instances of his own experience in such matters :—

"I believe," he says, "that there were more duels in the north-western army between the years 1791 and 1795 than ever took place in the same length of time, and amongst so small a body of men as composed the commissioned officers of the army, either in America or any other country, at least in modern times. I became an officer in the first-mentioned year, at so early an age, that it is not wonderful that I implicitly adopted the opinions of the older officers, most of whom were veterans of the revolution, upon this as well as upon other subjects connected with my conduct and duty in the profession I had chosen. I believed, therefore, in common with the large portion of the officers, that no brave man would decline a challenge, nor refrain from giving one whenever he considered his rights or feelings had been trespassed upon. I must confess, too, that I was not altogether free from the opinion that even honor might be acquired from a well fought duel. Fortunately, however, before I was engaged in a duel, either as principal or second, which terminated fatally to any one, I became convinced that all my opinions upon the subject were founded in error, and none of them more so than those which depicted the situation of the successful duelist, as either honorable or desirable. It could not be honorable, because the greater portion of that class of mankind, whose good opinion of an individual confers honor upon him, were opposed to it; and I had the best evidence to believe that in the grave of the fallen duelist was frequently buried the peace and happiness of the survivor; the act which deprived the one of existence in planting a thorn in the bosom of another which would continue to rankle and foster there to the end of his days. The conviction that such was the case with men of good feelings and principles was produced by witnessing the mental sufferings of an intimate and valued friend by whose hand a worthy man had fallen. * *

"In the summer of the year 1793, Lieutenant Drake, of the infantry of the second sub-legion, received a marked insult from another officer. Manifesting no disposition to call him to an account, some of those who wished him well, amongst whom I was one, spoke to him on the subject, expressing our fears that his reputation as an officer would greatly suffer if he permitted such an insult to pass unnoticed. The answer that he gave me was that he cared not what opinion the officers might form of him; he was determined to pursue his own course. That course was so novel in the army that it lost him, as I supposed it would, the respect of nearly all the officers. The ensuing summer, however, gave Mr. Drake an opportunity of vindicating most triumphantly his conduct and his principles. He had been stationed in a small fortress, erected by General Wayne, during the winter, upon the spot in which they had the previous day deposited a quantity of provisions, and which had been rendered remarkable by the defeat of General St. Clair's army three years before. The garrison consisted of a single rifle company and thirty infantry, and of the latter Drake was the immediate commander. In the beginning of July, a detachment of the army, consisting of several hundred men, under the command of Major McMahon, being encamped near the fort, were attacked early in the morning by about three thousand Indians. The troops made a gallant resistance, but being turned on both flanks, and in danger of being surrounded, they retreated to the open ground around the fort.

"From this, too, they were soon dislodged by the over-powering force of the enemy. In their retreat many wounded men were in danger of being left, which being observed from the fort, the commandant, Captain Gibson, directed his own lieutenant to take the infantry (Drake's particular command) and a por-

tion of the riflemen and sally out to their relief. To
this Drake objected, and claimed the right to command his own men, and, as a senior to the other lieutenant, his right also to the whole command. 'O,
very well, Sir,' said the captain, 'if such is your
wish, take it.' 'It is my wish, Sir, to do my duty,
and I will endeavor to do it now and at all times,'
was the modest reply of Drake. He accordingly
sallied out, skillfully interposed his detachments between the retreating troops and the enemy, opened
upon them a hot fire, arrested their advance, and gave
an opportunity to the wounded to effect their escape,
and to the broken and retreating companies of our
troops to reform, and again to face the enemy.
Throughout the whole affair Drake's activity, skill
and extraordinary self-possession, was most conspicuous. The enemy of course observed, as well as his
friends, the numerous shots directed at him, however,
like the arrows of Tenar aimed at the heart of Hec-
tor, were turned aside by providential interference,
until he had accomplished all that he had been sent
to perform. He then received a ball through his
body, and fell; a faithful corporal came to his assistance, and with his aid he reached the fort, and those
two were the last of the retreating party that entered
it. Drake made it a point of order that it should be
so. He was rendered unfit for service for a long time
by his wound. He had not, indeed, recovered from
t in the summer of 1796, when he was my guest
at Fort Wayne, where I was in command, while

on furlough, to visit his native State, Connecticut.
IIis friends, however, enjoyed his presence but a short
time.   Having, as I understood, taken the yellow
fever in passing through Philadelphia, he died a few
days after he reached home.   *   *   *

"I acknowledge, then, that the change of my
opinions which I have admitted in relation to dueling
have no other influence on my conduct than to determine me never to be the aggressor.   But although
resolved to offer no insult nor to inflict any injury, I
was determined to suffer none.   When I left the
army, however, and retired to civil life, I considered
myself authorized greatly to narrow the ground upon
which I would be willing to resort to a personal combat.   To the determination which I had previously
made, to offer no insult or to inflict any injury, to give
occasion to any one to call upon me in this way, I resolved to disregard all remarks upon my conduct which
could not be construed into a deliberate insult, or any
injury which did not affect my reputation, or the happiness and peace of my family.   When I had the honor
to be called upon to command the north-western army,
recollecting the number of gallant men that had fallen
in the former war in personal combat, I determined
to use all the authority and all the influence of my
station to prevent their recurrence.   And to take
away the principal source from which they sprung, in
an address to the Pennsylvania brigade, at Sandusky,
I declared it to be my determination to prevent, by
all the means the military laws placed in my hands,

any injury or even insult which should be offered by the superior to the inferior officers. I cannot say what influence this course upon my part may have produced in the result; but I state with pleasure that there was not a single duel, nor, as far as I know, a challenge given, whilst I retained the command.

"The activity in which the army was constantly kept may, however, have been the principal cause of this uncommon harmony. In relation to my present sentiments, a sense of higher obligation than human laws or human opinions can impose, has determined me never, on any occasion, to accept a challenge, or seek redress for a personal injury, by a resort to the laws which compose the code of honor."

CHAPTER XX.

In the fall of 1838, an Anti-Masonic National Convention assembled at Harrisburgh, and after a calm and careful survey of the whole ground, nominated General Harrison as the candidate of that party for the Presidency in 1840. The proceedings of this convention were communicated to him by the Honorable Harman Denny. In December of the same year, General Harrison replied to this official announcement, laying down his views of the duty of the chief executive of the nation, and the principles by which he should be governed if elected.

Having expressed his gratitude to the convention for the honor conferred upon him, he proceeds thus to develope his political creed. Among the principles proper to be adopted by an executive sincerely desirous to restore the administration to its original simplicity and purity, he laid down the following as of the most prominent importance:

I. To confine his services to a' single term.

II. To disclaim all right of control over the public treasury, with the exception of such part of it as may be appropriated by law to carry on the public

28

service, and that to be applied precisely as the law may direct, and drawn from the treasury agreeably to the long-established forms of that department.

III. That he should never attempt to influence the elections, either by the people or the State legislatures, nor suffer the federal officers under his control to take any other part in them than by giving their own votes when they possess the right of voting.,

IV. That, in the exercise of the veto power, he should limit his rejection of bills to,—1st. Such as are, in his opinion, unconstitutional; 2nd. Such as tend to encroach on the rights of the States or individuals; 3rd. Such as involving deep interests, may, in his opinion, require more mature deliberation or reference to the will of the people, to be ascertained at the succeeding elections.

V. That he should never suffer the influence of his office to be used for purposes of a purely party character.

VI. That in removals from office of those who hold their appointments during the pleasure of the executive, the cause of such removal should be stated, if requested, to the Senate, at the time the nomination of a successor is made.

And last, but not least in importance,

VII. That he should not suffer the executive department of the government to become the source of legislation; but leave the whole business of making laws for the Union to the department to which the constitution has exclusively assigned it, until they have assumed that perfected shape, where and when alone the opinions of the executive may be heard.

A community of power in the preparation of the laws between the legislative and executive departments must necessarily lead to dangerous combinations, greatly to the advantage of a President desirous of extending his power. Such a construction of the constitution could never have been contemplated by those who propose the bills, and will always take care of themselves or the interests of their constituents; and hence the provision in the constitution, borrowed from that of England, restricting the originating of revenue bills to the immediate representatives of the people.

Referring to the appointment of members of Congress to office by the President, he says the constitution contains no prohibition of such appointments, no doubt because its authors could not believe in its necessity for the purity of character which was manifested by those who possessed the confidence of the people at that period. It is, however, an opinion very generally entertained by the opposition party, that the country would have escaped much of the evil under which it has suffered for some years past, if the constitution had contained a provision of that kind.   *   *   *

"To the duties I have enumerated, so proper, in my opinion, to be performed by a President, elevated by the opposition to the present administration (and which are, as I believe, of constitutional obligation),

I will add another, which I believe also to be of much importance; I mean the observance of the most conciliatory course of conduct towards our political opponents. After the censure our friends have so freely and so justly bestowed upon the present chief magistrate for having, in no inconsiderable degree, disfranchised the whole body of his political opponents, I am certain that no oppositionist, true to the principle he professes, would approve a similar course of conduct in the person whom his vote has contributed to elect. In a republic, one of the surest tests of a healthy state of its institutions is to be found in the community with which every citizen may, upon all occasions, express his political opinions, and even his prejudices, in the discharge of his duty as an elector.

"The question may be asked of me, what security I have in my power to offer, if the majority of the American people should select me for their chief magistrate, that I would adopt the principles which I have herein laid down as those upon which my administration would be conducted, I could only answer by referring to my conduct, and the disposition manifested in the discharge of the duties of several important offices which have heretofore been conferred upon me. If the power placed in my hands has, on even a single occasion, been used for any purpose other than that for which it was given, or retained longer than was necessary to accomplish the objects designated by those from whom the trusts were received, I will acknowledge that either will constitute a sufficient reason for discrediting any promises I may make under the circumstances in which I am now placed.

"The time had now arrived for selecting a Presidential candidate in opposition to Martin Van Buren, who was almost the only man the democratic party had spoken of for that office. Though General Harrison was defeated in 1836, by causes heretofore hastily glanced at, his friends were far from being discouraged by the event. On the contrary, the vote that he received, in spite of the unfavorable circumstances under which he entered the contest, more than ever satisfied them that he might be elected if once the whole opposition could be united upon him, and their hopes were greatly strengthened by the universal dissatisfaction that prevailed throughout the country against the administration of Mr. Van Buren. Hitherto the whig party in each State of the Union had nominated their own candidate in their own way; but the necessity had gradually made itself apparent that some mode must be adopted by which the sentiment of the whole whig party could be concentrated upon one point. Accordingly a caucus of the whig members of Congress was held at Washington on the 15th of May, 1838, to devise some plan of combining the strength of the opposition against Mr. Van Buren. They finally resolved upon a national convention as the organ through whom the will of that party should be expressed, and it was decided that it should be held at Harrisburgh, on the first Wednesday in December, 1839, each State to be entitled to as many

28 *

delegates as it had senators and representatives in Congress.

" The convention met at Harrisburgh, in accordance with this appointment. Delegates were in attendance from twenty-two of the twenty-six States. It undoubtedly combined more talent and patriotism, and a larger number of the eminent men of the nation than any body of any kind that ever before assembled in this country, with the single exception of the old continental Congress, and the convention which framed our national constitution. Amongst them were sixteen ex-governors, United States senators and ex-senators, members of Congress and ex-members, and some of the highest officers and most distinguished citizens from every State in the Union that was represented. And they assembled with motives as patriotic and purposes as pure as their characters were high. They saw, or thought they saw, that the best interests of the country required a change in the administration, and they entered upon the discharge of the duty with which they had been delegated with a disposition to sacrifice every personal consideration, and relinquish all personal preferences to the general good.

Mr. Webster having requested that his name should not be brought before the convention, the only candidates were William Henry Harrison, Winfield Scott and Henry Clay. The friends of each urged their favorite with all the zeal and warmth their high characters, great talents, and important public services were so well calculated to inspire. The choice,

after an ardent contest, fell upon General Harrison;
and then it was that the real patriotism of the convention exhibited itself in all its force, and in its true
colors.   The moment the nomination was known, all
the warmth of feeling that had been engendered by
an exciting canvass was forgotten, and the States, one
after another, through one or more of their delegates,
cordially, eloquently, nobly, responded to it; the only
rivalry being who should be the first to show that if
he had preferred either General Scott or Mr. Clay
to the successful candidate, it was not because they
had any doubt of his patriotism, his abilities or his
honesty.

The generous cordiality with which this nomination was received by the convention was but the pre-
monitory symptoms of the deep satisfaction which it
created amongst the people themselves.   They were
already ripe for a revolution in the administration,
and when the name of a man who had not only distinguished himself as one of the first captains of the
day, but who had proved himself an accomplished
statesman, and, above all, an honest man and a well-
tried patriot, the popular feeling broke out in such
exhibitions of enthusiasm as this nor any other country ever before witnessed.   There was undoubtedly
some little disappointment amongst the friends of the
unsuccessful candidates, but it was comparatively only
momentary.   The canvass gave rise to a system of
immense mass meetings, at which the people met by
tens and twenties, and fifties of thousands, to listen

to the discussion of party principles, and to a mode of electioneering as novel as it was exciting.

At such times as the several States had determined the election took place, and General Harrison received the electoral vote of twenty of the twenty-six States, and two hundred and thirty-four electoral votes of the two hundred and ninety-four, Mr. Van Buren receiving the vote of six States and sixty electoral votes. There were two millions, three hundred and ninety-five thousand, nine hundred votes polled, of which General Harrison received one million, two hundred and sixty-nine thousand, seven hundred and sixty-three; and Mr. Van Buren one million, one hundred and twenty-six thousand, one hundred and thirty-seven, giving Harrison a majority of one hundred and forty-three thousand, six hundred and forty-six of the popular vote. The vote of the electoral colleges was opened in Congress, and the election of General Harrison as President of the United States was officially declared.

CHAPTER XXI.

On the 4th of March, 1841, General Harrison was inaugurated as eleventh President of the United States, with the usual ceremonies of that important occasion. The oath of office was tended him by Chief Justice Taney. The event drew together an immense concourse of citizens from every party of the Union, to witness the simple, yet imposing and sublime ceremony; and he entered upon the duties of his high position with as bright anticipations, as honest purposes, and as firm resolves on his own part, and with the confidence of the American people to as great an extent as any man who had occupied the position since Washington. The inaugural address was read by the President, from the steps of the capitol, in a voice so clear and distinct as to have been clearly heard by the vast multitude of spectators present. Though of great length, it is entitled to a place in a work of this character, aside from its important declaration of principles, and the lesson of political wisdom it contains. It is given below:

"Called from a retirement which I had supposed was to continue for the residue of my life, to fill the

chief executive office of this great and free nation, I
appear before you, fellow-citizens, to take the oath
which the constitution prescribes as a necessary qualification for the performance of its duties; and in
obedience to the custom coeval with our government,
and what I believe to be your expectations, I proceed
to present to you a summary of the principles which
will govern me in the discharge of the duties which I
shall be called upon to perform.

"It was the remark of a Roman consul, in an early
period of that celebrated republic, that a most striking
contrast was observable in the conduct of candidates for
offices of power and trust, before and after obtaining
them—they seldom carrying out in the latter case the
pledges and promises made in the former. However
much the world may have improved in many respects
in the lapse of upwards of two thousand years since
the remark was made by the virtuous and indignant
Roman, I fear that a strict examination of the annals
of some of the modern elective governments would
develop similar instances of violated confidence.

Although the fiat of the people has gone forth
proclaiming me the chief magistrate of this glorious
Union, nothing on their part remaining to be done, it
may be thought that a motive may exist to keep up
the delusion under which they may be supposed to
have acted in relation to my principles and opinions,
and perhaps there may be some in this assembly who
have come here either prepared to condemn those I
shall now deliver, or, approving them, to doubt the

sincerity with which they are uttered; but the lapse of a few months will confirm or dispel their fears. The outlines of principles to govern and measures to be adopted, by an administration not yet begun, will soon be exchanged for immutable history; and I shall stand, either exonerated by my countrymen, or classed with the mass of those who promised that they might deceive, and flattered with the intention to betray.

"However strong may be my present purpose to realize the expectations of a magnanimous and confiding people, I too well understand the infirmities of human nature and the dangerous temptations to which I shall be exposed, from the magnitude of the power which it has been the pleasure of the people to commit to my hands, not to place my chief confidence upon the aid of that Almighty Power which has hitherto protected me, and enabled me to bring to favorable issues other important, but still greatly inferior, trusts heretofore confided to me by my country.

"The broad foundation upon which our constitution rests, being the people—a breath of theirs having made, as a breath can unmake, change, or modify it —it can be assigned to none of the great divisions of government but to that of democracy. If such is its theory, those who are called upon to administer it must recognize, as its leading principle, the duty of shaping their measures so as to produce the greatest good to the greatest number. But, with these broad admissions, if we would compare the sovereignty acknowledged to exist in the mass of our people, with the power claimed by other sovereignties, even by those which have been considered most purely democratic, we shall find a most essential difference; all others lay claim to power limited only by their own will. The majority of our citizens, on the contrary, possess a sovereignty with an amount of power precisely equal to that which has been granted to them by the parties to the national compact, and nothing beyond. We admit of no government by divine right—believing that, so far as power is concerned, the beneficent Creator has made no distinction among men; that all are upon an equality; and that the only legitimate right to govern is an express grant of power from the governed. The Constitution of the United States is the instrument containing this grant of power to the several departments composing the government. On an examination of that instrument it will be found to contain declarations of power granted, and of power withheld. The latter is also susceptible of division into power which the majority had the right to grant, but which they did not think proper to entrust to their agents, and that which they could not have granted, not being possessed by themselves. In other words, there are certain rights possessed by each individual American citizen, which in his compact with the others he has never surrendered. Some of them, indeed, he is unable to surrender, being in the language of our system inalienable.

The boasted privilege of a Roman citizen was to

him a shield only against a petty provincial rule, whilst
the proud democrat of Athens could console himself
under a sentence of death for a supposed violation of
national faith which no one understood, and which, at
times, was the subject of the mockery of all; or of
banishment from his home, his family and his country, with or without an alleged cause, that it was the
act, not of a single tyrant or hated aristocracy, but
of his assembled countrymen. Far different is the
power of our sovereignty. It can interfere with no
one's faith, prescribe forms of worship for no one's
observance, inflict no punishment but after well ascertained guilt, the result of investigation under rules
prescribed by the constitution itself. These precious
privileges, and these, scarcely less important, of giving
expression to his thoughts and opinions, either by
writing or speaking, unrestrained but by the liability
for injury to others, and that of a full participation
in all advantages which flow from the government,
the acknowledged property of all, the American citizen derives from no charter granted by his fellow-
man. He claims them because he is himself a man;
fashioned by the same Almighty hand as the rest of
his species, and entitled to a full share of the blessings with which he has endowed them. Notwithstanding the limited sovereignty possessed by the people of
the United States, and the restricted grant of power to
the government which they have adopted, enough has
been given to accomplish all the objects for which it
was created. It has been found powerful in war, and,

29

hitherto, justice has been administered, an intimate union effected, domestic tranquillity preserved, and personal liberty secured to the citizen. As was to be expected, however, from the defect of language, and the necessarily sententious manner in which the constitution is written, disputes have arisen as to the amount of power which it has actually granted, or was intended to grant. This is more particularly the case in relation to that part of the instrument which treats of the legislative branch. And not only as regards the exercise of powers claimed under a general clause, giving that body the authority to pass all laws necessary to carry into effect the specified powers, but in relation to the latter also. It is, however, consolatory to reflect that *most* of the instances of alleged departure from the letter or spirit of the constitution have ultimately received the sanction of a majority of the people. And the fact, that many of our statesmen, most distinguished for talent and patriotism, have been, at one time or other of their political career, on both sides of each of the most warmly disputed questions, forces upon us the inference that the errors, if errors there were, are attributable to the intrinsic difficulty, in many instances, of ascertaining the intentions of the framers of the constitution, rather than the influence of any sinister or unpatriotic motive.

"But the great danger to our institutions does not appear to me to be in a usurpation, by the government, of power not granted by the people, but by the accumulation, in one of the departments, of that which was assigned to others. Limited as are the powers which have been granted, still enough have been granted to constitute a despotism, if concentrated in one of the departments. Many of the sternest republicans of the day were alarmed at the extent of the power which has been granted to the federal government, and more particularly of that portion which has been assigned to the executive branch. There were in it features which appeared not to be in harmony with their ideas of a simple representative democracy or republic; and knowing the tendency of power to increase itself, particularly when exercised by a single individual, predictions were made that, at no very remote period, the government would terminate in virtual monarchy. It would not become me to say that the fears of those patriots would not have been already realized. But as I sincerely believe that the tendency of measures and of men's opinions, for some years past, has been in that direction, it is, I conceive, strictly proper that I should take this occasion to repeat the assurances I have heretofore given of my determination to arrest the progress of that tendency, if it really exist, and restore the government to its pristine health and vigor, as far as this can be affected by any legitimate exercise of the power placed in my hands.

" I proceed to state, in as summary a manner as I can, my opinion of the sources of the evils which have been so extensively complained of, and the con-

nectives which may be applied. Some of the former
are unquestionably to be found in the defects of the
constitution; others, in my judgment, are attributable
to a misconstruction of some of its provisions. Of the
former is the elligibility of the same individual to a second term of the presidency. The sagacious mind of Mr.
Jefferson early saw and lamented this error, and attempts have been made, hitherto without success, to
apply the amendatory power of the States to its correction.

"As, however, one mode of correction is in the
power of every President, and consequently in mine,
it would be useless, and perhaps invidious, to enumerate the evils of which, in the opinion of many of our
fellow-citizens, this error of the sages who framed the
constitution may have been the source and the bitter
fruits which we are still to gather from it, if it continues to disfigure our system. It may be observed,
however, as a general remark, that republics can
commit no greater error than to adopt or continue
any feature in their systems of government which may
be calculated to create or increase the love of power
in the bosoms of those to whom necessity obliges them
to commit the management of their affairs. And,
surely, nothing is more likely to produce such a state
of mind than the long continuance of an office of high
trust. Nothing can be more corrupting, nothing more
destructive, of all those noble feelings which belong to
the character of a devoted republican patriot. When
this corrupting passion once takes possession of the

human mind, like the love of gold, it becomes insatiable. It is the never-dying worm in his bosom, grows with his growth, and strengthens with the declining years of its victim. If this is true, it is the part of wisdom for a republic to limit the service of that officer, at least, to whom she has intrusted the management of her foreign relations, the execution of her laws, and the command of her armies and navies, to a period so short as to prevent his forgetting that he is the accountable agent, not the principal—the servant, not the master. Until an amendment of the constitution can be effected, public opinion may secure the desired object. I give my aid to it by renewing the pledge heretofore given, that under no circumstances will I consent to serve a second term.

"But if there is danger to public liberty from the acknowledged defects of the constitution, in the want of limit to the continuance of the executive power in the same hands, there is, I apprehend, not much less from a misconstruction of that instrument, as it regards the powers actually given. I cannot conceive that, by a fair construction, any or either of its provisions would be found to constitute the President a part of the legislative power. It cannot be claimed from the power to recommend, since, although enjoined as a duty upon him, it is a privilege which he holds in common with every other citizen. And although there may be something more of confidence in the propriety of the measures recommended in the one case than in the other, in the obligations of ultimate

29 *

decision there can be no difference. In the language of the constitution, 'all legislative powers' which it grants 'are vested in the Congress of the United States.' It would be a solecism in language to say that any portion of these is not included in the whole.

"It may be said, indeed, that the constitution has given to the executive the power to annul the acts of the legislative body by refusing to them his assent. So a similar power has necessarily resulted from that instrument to the judiciary, and yet the judiciary forms no part of the legislature. There is, it is true, this difference between these grants of power; the executive can put his negative upon the acts of the legislature for other cause than that of want of conformity to the constitution; whilst the judiciary can only declare void those which violate that instrument. But the decision of the judiciary is final in such a case; whereas, in every instance where the veto of the executive is applied, it may be overcome by a veto of two-thirds of both houses of Congress. The negative upon the acts of the legislature, by the executive authority, and that in the hands of one individual, would seem to be an incongruity in our system. Like some others of a similar character, however, it appeared to be highly expedient, and if used only with the forbearance and in the spirit which was intended by its authors, it may be productive of great good, and be found one of the best safe-guards to the Union. At the period of the formation, the principle does not appear to have enjoyed much favor in the

State governments.   It existed in but two, and in one
of these was a plural executive.   If we would search
for the motives which operated upon the purely patriotic and enlightened assembly which framed the
constitution for the adoption of a provision so apparently repugnant to the leading democratic principle,
that the majority should govern, we must reject the
idea that they anticipated from it any benefit to the
ordinary course of legislation.   They knew too well
the high degree of intelligence which existed among
the people, and the enlightened character of the State
legislatures, not to have the fullest confidence that
the two bodies elected by them would be worthy of
such constituents, and, of course, that they would require no aid in conceiving and maturing the measures
which the circumstances of the country might require.
And it is preposterous to suppose that a thought could
for a moment have been entertained, that the President, placed at the capital, in the centre of the country, could better understand the wants and wishes of
the people than their own immediate representatives,
who spend a part of every year among them, living
with them, often laboring with them, and bound to
them by the triple tie of interest, duty, and affection.
To assist or control Congress, then, in its ordinary
legislation, could not, I conceive, have been the motive for conferring the veto power on the President.
This argument acquires additional force from the fact
of its never having been thus used by the first six
Presidents—and two of them were members of the

convention; one presiding over its deliberations, and
the other having a larger share in consummating the
labors of that august body than any other person.
But if bills were never returned to Congress by either
of the Presidents above referred to, upon the ground
of their being inexpedient, or not as well adapted as
they might be to the wants of the people, the veto
was applied upon that of want of conformity to the
constitution, or because errors had been committed
from a too hasty enactment.

"There is another ground for the adoption of the
veto principle, which had probably more influence in
recommending it to the convention than any other.
I refer to the security which it gives to the just and
equitable action of the legislature upon all parts of
the Union. It could not but have occurred to the
convention that, in a country so extensive, embracing
so great a variety of soil and climate, and consequently of products, and which, from the same causes,
must ever exhibit a great difference in the amount of
population of its various sections, calling for a great
diversity in the employments of the people, that the
legislation of the majority might not always justly
regard the rights and interests of the minority; and
that acts of this character might be passed under an
express grant by the words of the constitution, and,
therefore, not within the competency of the judiciary
to declare void. That however enlightened and patriotic they might suppose, from past experience, the
members of Congress might be, and however largely

partaking in general of the liberal feelings of the people, it was impossible to expect that bodies so constituted should not sometimes be controlled by local interests and sectional feelings. It was proper, therefore, to provide some umpire from whose situation and mode of appointment more independence and freedom from such influence might be expected. Such a one was afforded by the executive department, constituted by the constitution. A person elected to that high office, having his constituents in every section, State and sub-division of the Union, must consider himself bound by the most solemn sanctions to guard, protect and defend the rights of all, and of every portion, great or small, from the injustice and oppression of the rest. I consider the veto power, therefore, given by the constitution to the executive of the United States solely as a conservative power; to be used only,—first, to protect the constitution from violation; secondly, the people from the effects of hasty legislation, where their will has probably been disregarded or not well understood; and, thirdly, to prevent the effects of combinations, violative of the rights of minorities. In reference to the second of these objects, I may observe, that I consider it the right and the privilege of the people to decide disputed points of the constitution, arising from the general grant of power to Congress to carry into effect the powers expressly given. And I believe with Mr. Madison that repeated recognitions, under varied circumstances, in acts of the legislative, executive and judicial branches of the government, accompanied by indications in different modes of the concurrence of the general will of the nation, as affording to the President sufficient authority for his considering such disputed points as settled.

"Upwards of half a century has elapsed since the adoption of our present form of government. It will be an object more highly desirable than the gratification of the curiosity of speculative statesmen if its precise situation could be ascertained, and a fair exhibit made of the operations of each of its departments; of the powers which they respectively claim and exercise; of the collisions which have occurred between them, or between the whole government and those of the States, or either of them. We could then compare our actual condition after fifty years' trial of our system, with what it was in the commencement of its operations, and ascertain whether the predictions of the patriots who opposed its adoption, or the confident hopes of its advocates, have been best realized. The great dread of the former seems to have been, that the reserved powers of the States would be absorbed by those of the federal government, and a consolidated power established, leaving to the States the shadow only of that independent action for which they had so zealously contended, and on the preservation of which they relied as the last hope of liberty.

"Without denying that the result to which they looked with so much apprehension is in the way of being realized, it is obvious that they did not clearly see the mode of its accomplishment. The general government has siezed upon none of the reserved rights of the States. As far as any open warfare may have gone, the State authorities have amply maintained their rights. To a casual observer, our system presents no appearance of discord between the different members which compose it. Even the addition of many new ones has produced no jarring; they move in ther respective orbits in perfect harmony with the central head, and with each other. But there is still an under current at work, by which, if not seasonably checked, the worst apprehensions of our anti-federal patriots will be realized. And not only will the State authorities be overshadowed by the great increase of the power in the executive department of the general government, but the character of that government, if not its designation, be essentially and radically changed.

"This state of things has been in part effected by causes inherent in the constitution, and in part by the never-failing tendency of political power to increase itself. By making the President the sole distributor of all the patronage of the government, the framers of the constitution do not appear to have anticipated at how short a period it would become a formidable instrument to control the free operations of the State governments. Of trifling importance at first, it had, early in Mr. Jefferson's administration, become so powerful as to create great alarm in the mind of that patriot, from the potent influence it might exert in controling the freedom of the elective franchise. If such could have then been the effect of its influence, how much greater must be its danger at this time, quadrupled in amount, as it certainly is, and more completely under the control of the executive will than their construction of the powers allowed, or the forbearing characters, of all the earlier presidents permitted them to make. But it is not by the extent of its patronage alone that the executive department has become dangerous, but by the use which it appears may be made of the appointing power to bring under its control the whole revenues of the country.

"The constitution has declared it the duty of the President to see that the laws are executed, and it makes him the commander-in-chief of the armies and navy of the United States. If the opinion of the most approved writers upon that species of mixed government which in modern Europe is termed *monarchy*, in contradistinction to *despotism*, is correct, there was wanting no other addition to the powers of our chief magistrate to stamp a monarchial character on our government but the control of the public finances. And to me it appears indeed that any one should doubt that the entire control which a President possesses over the officers who have the custody of the public monies by the power of removal, with or without cause, does for all mischievous purposes, at least, virtually subject the treasure also to his disposal. The first Roman emperor, in his attempt to seize the sacred treasure, silenced the opposition of the officer

to whose charge it had been committed by a signifi-
cant allusion to his sword. By a selection of political instruments for the care of the public money, a
reference to their commission by a President would
be quite as effectual an argument as that of Cæsar to
the Roman knight. / I am not insensible of the great
difficulty that exists in devising a proper plan for the
safe-keeping and disbursement of the public revenues,
and I know the importance which has been attached
by men of great abilities and patriotism to the divorce,
as it is called, of the treasury from the banking institutions. It is not the divorce which is complained of,
but the unhallowed union of the treasury with the
executive department which has created such extensive alarm. To this danger to our republican institutions, and that created by the influence given to the
executive through the instrumentality of the federal
officers, I propose to apply all the remedies which
may be at my command.

/ "It was certainly a great error, in the framers of
the constitution, not to have made the officer at the
head of the treasury department entirely independent
of the executive. He should at least have been re-
movable only upon the demand of the popular branch
of the legislature. I have determined never to remove a secretary of the treasury without communicating all the circumstances attending such removal
to both Houses of Congress. The influence of the
executive in controling the freedom of the elective
franchise through the medium of the public officers

30

can be effectually checked by renewing the prohibition published by Mr. Jefferson, forbidding their interference in elections further than giving their own votes ; and their own independence secured by an assurance of perfect immunity, in exercising this sacred privilege of freemen under the dictates of their own unbiased judgments. Never, with my consent, shall an officer of the people, compensated for his services out of their pockets, become the pliant instrument of executive will.

"There is no part of the means placed in the hands of the executive which might be used with greater effect, for unhallowed purposes, than the control of the public press. The maxim which our ancestors derived from the mother country, that 'the freedom of the press is the great bulwark of civil and religious liberty,' is one of the most precious legacies which they have left us. We have learned, too, from our own, as well as the experience of other countries, that golden shackels, by whomsoever or by whatever pretense imposed, are as fatal to it as the iron bonds of despotism. The presses in the necessary employment of the government should never be used 'to clear the guilty or varnish crimes.' A decent and manly examination of the acts of the government should be not only tolerated but encouraged.

"Upon another occasion I have given my opinion, at some length, upon the impropriety of executive interference in the legislation of Congress. That the article in the constitution making it the duty of the

President to communicate information, and authorizing him to recommend measures, was not intended
to make him the source of legislation, and, in particular, that he should never be looked to for schemes
of finance. It would be very strange, indeed, if the
constitution should have strictly forbidden one branch
of the legislature from interfering in the origination
of such bills, and that it should be considered proper
that an altogether different department of the government should be permitted to do so. Some of our best
political maxims and principles have been drawn from
our parent Isle. There are others, however, which
cannot be introduced in our system without singular
incongruity and the production of much mischief;
and this I conceive to be one.

"No matter in which of the Houses of Parliament
a bill may originate, nor by whom introduced, a minister or a member of the opposition, by the fiction of
law, or rather of constitutional principle, the sovereign is supposed to have prepared it agreeably to his
will, and then submitted it to Parliament for their
advice and consent. Now the very reverse is the case
here, not only with regard to the principle, but the
forms prescribed by the constitution. The principle
certainly assigns to the only body constituted by the
constitution (the legislative body) the power to make
laws, and the forms even direct that the enactment
should be ascribed to them.

"The Senate, in relation to revenue bills, have the
right to propose amendments; and so has the execu-

tive, by the power given him to return them to the
House of Representatives with his objections. It is
in his power, also, to propose amendments in the existing revenue laws, suggested by his observations upon
their defective or injurious operation. But the delicate duty of devising schemes of revenue should be
left where the constitution has placed it—with the
immediate representatives of the people. For similar
reasons, the mode of keeping the public treasure
should be prescribed by them; and the farther removed it may be from the control of the executive,
the more wholesome the arrangement, and the more
in accordance with republican principle.

" Connected with this subject is the character of
the currency. The idea of making it exclusively
metallic, however well intended, appears to me to be
fraught with more fatal consequences than any other
scheme, having no relation to the personal rights of
the citizen, that has ever been devised. If any single
scheme could produce the effect of arresting, at once,
that mutation of condition by which thousands of our
most indigent fellow-citizens, by their industry and
enterprise, are raised to the possession of wealth, that
is the one. If there is one measure better calculated
than another to produce that state of things so much
deprecated by all true republicans, by which the rich
are daily adding to their hoards, and the poor sinking
deeper into penury, it is an exclusive metallic currency. Or if there is a process by which the character of the country for generosity and nobleness of

feeling may be destroyed by the great increase and necessary toleration of usury, it is an exclusive metallic currency.

"Amongst the other duties of a delicate character which the President is called upon to perform is the supervision of the government of the Territories of the United States. Those of them which are destined to become members of our great political family are compensated by their rapid progress from infancy to manhood, for the partial and temporary deprivation of their political rights. It is in this District only where American citizens are to be found, who, under a settled system of policy, are deprived of many important political privileges, without any inspiring hope as to the future. Their only consolation, under circumstances of such deprivation, is that of the devoted exterior guards of a camp—that their sufferings secure tranquillity and safety within. Are there any of their countrymen who would subject them to greater, to any other, humiliations than those essentially necessary to the security of the object for which they were thus separated from their fellow-citizens? Are their rights alone not to be guaranteed by the application of those great principles upon which all our constitutions are founded? We are told by the greatest of British orators and statesmen, that at the commencement of the war of the revolution the most stupid men in England spoke of 'their American subjects.' Are there, indeed, citizens of any of our States who have dreamed of their subjects in the Dis-

trict of Columbia? Such dreams can never be realized by any agency of mine.

—— "The people of the District of Columbia are not
the subjects of the people of the States, but free
American citizens. Being in the latter condition,
when the constitution was formed, no words used in
that instrument could have been intended to deprive
them of that character. If there is anything in the
great principle of inalienable rights, so emphatically
insisted upon in our Declaration of Independence,
they could neither make, nor the United States accept,
a surrender of their liberties and become the *subjects*,—
in other words, the slaves,—of their former fellow-
citizens. If this be true, and it will scarcely be denied by any one who has a correct idea of his own
rights as an American citizen, the grant to Congress
of exclusive jurisdiction in the District of Columbia
can be interpreted, so far as respects the aggregate
people of the United States, as meaning nothing more
than to allow to Congress the controling power necessary to afford a free and safe exercise of the functions
assigned to the general government by the constitution. In all other respects the legislation of Congress
should be adapted to their peculiar position and
wants, and be conformable with their deliberate opinions of their own interests.

"I have spoken of the necessity of keeping the
respective departments of the government, as well as
the other authorities of our country, within their appropriate orbits. This is a matter of difficulty in

some cases, as the powers which they respectively claim are often not defined by very distinct lines.

"Mischievous, however, in their tendencies, as collisions of this kind may be, those which arise between the respective communities, which for certain purposes compose one nation, are much more so; for no such nation can long exist without the careful culture of those feelings of confidence and affection which are the effective bonds of union between free and confederated States. Strong as is the tie of interest, it has been often found ineffectual. Men, blinded by their passions, have been known to adopt measures for their country in direct opposition to all the suggestions of policy. The alternative, then, is to destroy or keep down a bad passion, by creating and fostering a good one; and this seems to be the corner-stone upon which our American political architects have reared the fabric of our government. The cement which was to bind it and perpetuate its existence was the affectionate attachment between all its members. To insure the continuance of this feeling, produced at first by a community of dangers, of sufferings and of interests, the advantages of each were made accessible to all.

"No participation in any good, possessed by any member of an extensive confederacy, except in domestic government, was withheld from the citizen of any other member. By a process attended with no difficulty, no delay, no expense but that of removal, the citizen of one might become the citizen of any other, and successively of the whole. The lines, too, separating powers to be exercised by the citizens of one State from those of another, seem to be so distinctly drawn as to leave no room for misunderstanding. The citizens of each State unite in their persons all the privileges which that character confers, and all that they may claim as citizens of the United States; but in no case can the same person, at the same time, act as the citizen of two separate States; and *he is therefore positively precluded from any interference with the reserved powers of any State but that of which he is, for the time being, a citizen.* He may indeed offer to the citizens of other States his advice as to their management, but the form in which it is tendered is left to his own discretion and sense of propriety.

"It may be observed, however, that organized associations of citizens, requiring compliance with their wishes, too much resemble the *recommendations* of Athens to her allies—supported by an armed and powerful fleet. It was, indeed, to the ambition of the leading States of Greece to control the domestic concerns of others that the destruction of that celebrated confederacy, and subsequently of all its members, is mainly to be attributed. And it is owing to the absence of that spirit that the Helvetic confederacy has for so many years been preserved. Never has there been seen in the institutions of the separate members of the confederacy more elements of discord. In the principles and forms of government and religion, as well as in the circumstances of the several countries, so marked a discrepancy was observable, as to promise anything but harmony in their intercourse or permanency in their alliance; and yet for ages neither has been interrupted. Content with the positive benefits which their union produced, with the dependence and safety from foreign aggression which it secured, these sagacious people respected the institutions of each other, however repugnant to their own principles and prejudices.

"Our confederacy, fellow-citizens, can only be preserved by the same forbearance. Our citizens must be content with the exercise of the powers with which the constitution clothes them. The attempt of those of one State to control the domestic institutions of another can only result in feelings of distrust and jealousy—the certain harbingers of disunion, violence, civil war, and the ultimate destruction of our free institutions. Our confederacy is perfectly illustrated by the terms and principles governing a common co-partnership. There a fund of power is to be exercised under the direction of the joint councils of the allied members; but that which has been reserved by the individual members is intangible by the common government or the individual members composing it. To attempt it finds no support in the principles of our constitution. It should be our constant and earnest endeavor mutually to cultivate a spirit of concord and harmony among the various parts of our confederacy. Experience has abundantly taught us that the agitation by citizens of one part of the Union of a subject not confided to the general government, but exclusively under the guardianship of the local authorities, is productive of no other consequences than bitterness, alienation, discord, and injury to the very cause which is intended to be advanced. Of all the great interests which appertain to our country, that of union, cordial, confiding, fraternal union, is by far the most important,— since it is the only true and sure guaranty of all others.

"In consequence of the embarrassed state of business and the currency, some of the States may meet with difficulty in their financial concerns. However deeply we may regret anything imprudent or excessive in the engagements into which States have entered for purposes of their own, it does not become us to disparage the State governments, nor to discourage them from making proper efforts for their own relief; on the contrary, it is our duty to encourage them, to the extent of our constitutional authority, to apply their best means, and cheerfully to make all necessary sacrifices, and submit to all necessary burdens, to fulfill their engagements and maintain their credit; for the character and credit of the several States form part of the character and credit of the whole country. The resources of the country are abundant, the enterprise and activity of our people proverbial; and we may well hope that wise legislation and prudent administration, by the respective governments, each acting within his own sphere, will restore former prosperity.

"Unpleasant, and even dangerous, as collisions may sometimes be between the constituted authorities or the citizens of our country, in relation to the lines which separate their respective jurisdictions, the results can be of no vital injury to our institutions, if that ardent patriotism, that devoted attachment to liberty, that spirit of moderation and forbearance for which our countrymen were once distinguished, continue to be cherished. If this continues to be the ruling passion of our souls, the weaker feelings of the mistaken enthusiast will be corrected, the utopian dreams of the scheming politician dissipated, and the complicated intrigues of the demagogue rendered harmless. The secret of liberty is the sovereign balm for every injury which our institutions may receive. On the contrary, no care that can be used in the construction of our government, no division of powers, no distribution of checks in its several departments, will prove effectual to keep us a free people if this feeling is suffered to decay; and decay it will without constant nurture. To the neglect of this duty, the best historians agree in attributing the ruin of all the republics with whose existence and fall their writings have made us acquainted. The same causes will ever produce the same effects; and as long as the love of power is a dominant passion of the human bosom, and as long as the understanding of men can be warped and their affections changed, by operations on their passions and prejudices, so long will the liberty of a people depend upon their own constant attention to its preservation. The danger to all well-established free governments arises from the unwillingness of the people to believe in its existence, or from the influence of designing men diverting their attention from the quarter whence it approaches to a source from which it can never come. This is the old trick of those who would usurp the government of their country. In the name of democracy they speak, warning the people against the influence of wealth and the danger of aristocracy. History, ancient and modern, is full of such examples. Cæsar became the master of the Roman people and the Senate, under the pretense of supporting the democratic claims of the former against the aristocracy of the latter; Cromwell, in the character of protector of the liberties of the people, became the dictator of England; and Bolivar possessed himself of unlimited power with the title of his country's liberator. There is, on the contrary, no single instance on record, of an extensive and well-established republic being changed into an aristocracy. The tendency of all such governments in their decline is to monarchy; and in the antagonist principle to liberty there is the spirit of faction—a spirit which assumes the character, and, in times of great excitement, imposes itself upon the people as the genuine spirit of freedom, and like the false Christs, whose coming was foretold by the Savior, seeks to, and were it possible would, impose upon the true and most faithful disciples of liberty. It is in periods like this that it behooves the people to be most watchful of those to whom they have intrusted power. And although there is at times much difficulty in distinguishing the false from the true spirit, a calm and dispassionate investigation will detect the counterfeit as well by the character of its operations as the results which are produced. The true spirit of liberty, although devoted, persevering, bold, and uncompromising in principle, that secured, is mild and tolerant and scrupulous as to the means it employs; whilst the spirit of party, assuming to be that of liberty, is harsh, vindictive and intolerant, and totally reckless as to the character of the allies which it brings to the aid of its cause. When the genuine spirit of liberty animates the body of a people to a thorough examination of their affairs, it leads to the excision of every excrescence which may have fastened itself upon any of the departments of the government, and restores the system to its pristine health and beauty. But the reign of an intolerant spirit of party amongst a free people seldom fails to result in a dangerous accession to the executive power introduced and established amidst unusual professions of devotion to democracy.

"The foregoing remarks relate almost exclusively to matters connected with our domestic concerns. It may be proper, however, that I should give some indications to my fellow-citizens of my proposed course of conduct in the management of our foreign relations.

31

I assure them, therefore, that it is my intention to use every means in my power to preserve the friendly intercourse which now so happily subsists with every foreign nation; and that although, of course, not well informed as to the state of any pending negotiations with any of them, I see in the personal characters of the sovereigns, as well as in the mutual interest of our own and of the government with which our relations are most intimate, a pleasing guaranty that the harmony so important to the interests of their subjects, as well as our citizens, will not be interrupted by the advancement of any claim or pretension upon their part to which our honor would not permit us to yield. Long the defender of my country's rights in the field, I trust that my fellow-citizens will not see, in my earnest desire to preserve peace with foreign powers, any indication that their rights will ever be sacrificed, or the honor of the nation tarnished, by any admission on the part of their chief magistrate, unworthy of their former glory.

"In our intercourse with our Aboriginal neighbors, the same liberality and justice which marked the course prescribed to me by two of my illustrious predecessors, when acting under their direction in the discharge of the duty of superintendent and commissioner, shall be strictly observed. I can conceive of no more sublime spectacle—none more likely to propitiate an impartial and common Creator—than a rigid adherence to the principles of justice on the part of a

powerful nation in its transactions with a weaker and
uncivilized people, whom circumstances have placed
at its disposal.

"Before concluding, fellow-citizens, I must say
something to you on the subject of the parties at this
time existing in our country. To me it appears perfectly clear that the interest of that country requires
that the violence of the spirit, by which those parties
are at this time governed, must be greatly mitigated,
if not entirely extinguished, or consequences will en-
sue which are appalling to be thought of. If parties
in a republic are necessary to secure a degree of vigilance sufficient to keep the republic functionaries
within the bounds of law and duty, at that point their
usefulness ends. Beyond that they become destructive of public virtue,—the parents of a spirit antagonist to that of liberty, and eventually its inevitable
conqueror. We have examples of republics where
the love of country and of liberty, at one time, were
the dominant passions of the whole mass of citizens;
and yet, with the contour of the name and forms of
free government, not a vestige of these qualities remaining in the bosom of any one of its citizens. It
was the beautiful remark of a distinguished English
writer, that 'in the Roman Senate, Octavius had a
party, and Anthony a party, but the Commonwealth
had none.' Yet the Senate continued to meet in
the Temple of liberty, to talk of the sacredness and
beauty of the Commonwealth, and gaze at the statues
of the elder Brutus and of the Curtii and Decii.

And the people assembled in the forum, not as in the days of Camillus and the Scipios, to cast their free votes for annual magistrates, or pass upon the acts of the Senate, but to receive from the hands of the leaders of the respective parties their share of the spoils, and to shout for one or the other, as those collected in Gaul, or Egypt, and the Lesser Asia, would furnish the larger dividend. The spirit of liberty had fled, and, avoiding the abodes of civilized man, had sought protection in the wilds of Scythia or Scandinavia; and so, under the operation of the same causes and influences, it will fly from our capitol and our forums. A calamity so awful, not only to our country, but to the world, must be deprecated by every patriot; and every tendency to a state of things likely to produce it, immediately checked. Such a tendency has existed—does exist. Always the friend of my countrymen, never their flatterer, it becomes my duty to say to them from this high place, to which their partiality has exalted me, that there exists in the land a spirit hostile to their best interests—hostile to liberty itself. It is a spirit contracted in its views, selfish in its object. It looks to the aggrandizement of a few, even to the destruction of the interests of the whole. The entire remedy is with the people. Something, however, may be effected by the means which they have placed in my hands. It is union that we want, not of a party for the sake of that party, but a union of the whole country for the sake of the whole country— for the defense of its interests and its honor against foreign aggression—for the defense of those principles for which our ancestors so gloriously contended. As far as it depends upon me, it shall be accomplished. All the influence that I possess shall be exerted to prevent the formation at least of an executive party in the halls of the legislative body. I wish for the support of no member of that body to any measure of mine that does not satisfy his judgment, and his sense of duty to those from whom he holds his appointment; nor any confidence in advance from the people, but that asked for by Mr. Jefferson, to give firmness and effect to the legal administration of their affairs.

"I deem the present occasion sufficiently important and solemn to justify me in presenting to my fellow-citizens a profound reverence for the christian religion, and a thorough conviction that sound morals, religious liberty, and a just sense of religious responsibility, are essentially connected with all true and lasting happiness; and to that good Being who has blessed us by the gifts of civil and religious freedom, who watched over and prospered the labors of our fathers, and has hitherto preserved to us institutions far exceeding in excellence those of any other people, let us unite in commending every interest of our beloved country in all future time.

"Fellow-citizens! being fully invested with that high office to which the partiality of my countrymen has called me, I now take an affectionate leave of you. You will bear with you to your homes the remembrance of the pledge I have this day given to discharge all the high duties of my exalted station, according to the best of my ability, and I shall enter upon their performance with entire confidence in the support of a just and generous people.

CHAPTER XXIII.

HAVING now gone through all the requirements of the constitution necessary to qualify him for the discharge of the duties of President of the United States, General Harrison promptly set himself about the great work of correcting whatever abuses may have crept into the administration of the government, and of performing the pledges he had made before his election and in his inaugural address. These pledges had been made from an honest conviction that they were not only just, but demanded by the general good. Having therefore been made in good faith, he was determined to carry them out in the same, so far as it was in his power to do so. Investigations were instituted into the various branches of the public service with a view to those reforms which the country had so long demanded and he had promised to introduce, and many corrupt or injurious practices marked out for correction. And if he had been spared to the country to serve out the term for which the people elected him, there is no doubt that he would have redeemed all his pledges to the country.

Considering it a great abuse of power to bring

the patronage of the government into conflict with the freedom of elections, as has been seen both by his letters before his election and his inaugural address, and that such abuse ought to be corrected wherever it might exist, circulars were addressed to all the heads of the departments on the 20th of March, designed to effect this object. They were directed to furnish information to all officers and agents in their several departments, that partisan interference in popular elections, whether of State officers or officers of the general government, and that for whomsoever or against whomsoever it might be exercised, or the payment of any contribution or assessment on salaries, or official compensation for party or election purposes, would be regarded by him as cause of removal.

It was not intended that any officer should be restrained in the free and proper expression and . maintenance of his opinions respecting public men, or public measures, or in the exercise, to the fullest degree, of the constitutional right of suffrage; but persons employed under the government, and paid for their services out of the public treasury, were not expected to take an active or officious part in attempts to influence the minds or votes of others, such conduct being deemed inconsistent with the spirit of the constitution and the duties of public agents acting under it. He expressed his determination, that while the exercise of the elective franchise by the people shall be free from undue influence of official stations and authority, so far as depended upon him, opinion should also be free among the officers and agents of the government. He wished it farther announced and understood, that from all collecting and disbursing officers promptitude in rendering accounts, and entire punctuality in paying balances, would be rigorously exacted.

With a view of arresting what was feared to be a needless and extravagant expenditure of money upon the public works in the city of Washington, he appointed a board of commissioners or examination to investigate the subject rigidly. They were required to report upon the number of persons employed upon those works, exclusive of laborers, what was their respective duty, what compensation was paid them, and whether there was any just ground of complaint against any of these in regard to their diligence or skill, or in regard to their treatment of laborers. They were especially instructed to inquire into no man's political opinions, but to report if any one having the power of appointing and removing had abused that power, or in any way violated his duty for party or election purposes.

These evidences of the honesty and sincerity of his professions were received with lively demonstrations of satisfaction by the public at large, however little encouraging they may have been to the hopes and aspirations of the mere politician. They gave assurance that, under his administration, that system of prescription which had excluded every man from office, however deserving, competent or needy, whose

political principles did not accord with the ruling executive, was to be repudiated, and all the benefits of
the government to be shared by the people equally.
This he believed to be the theory of our government,
and so far as was consistent with the obligations he
admitted himself to be under to the party which had
placed him in power, he determined it should be its
practice.

As the case always had been, and as it is always
desirable it should be, under our democratic form of
government, upon so important an occasion as the
change of rulers, he was overwhelmed with visits of
all classes, actuated either by motives of pure friendship or personal interest; and no one was ever denied
an interview. Unlike the members of his cabinet,
and indeed the members of most American cabinets,
he could at all times be approached, and when approached, he assumed none of the airs which men, occupying minor positions, too frequently think it necessary to put on for the purpose of inspiring that
reverence and respect which their characters would
never command. He understood that real greatness
could not be affected by a familiar and free intercourse
with the people, and that it would never fail to restrain the impertinent and ill-bred. An assumption
of superiority, and that supercilious bearing so common to naturally vulgar minds, however high in office,
found no countenance in his practice, nor no sympathy
in his disposition. This practice of General Harrison,
of receiving visits from all who sought access to him,

and the multiplicity of public duties necessarily attendant on his first entrance into office, produced not only great fatigue of body, but anxiety of mind. In addition to this, he was overtaken by a violent shower in one of his usual morning walks, and his clothes became thoroughly wet. This was followed by a slight cold; but he paid little attention to it, although on the 25th of March he was really ill, and continued to receive visits from all, as when in health, refusing to postpone any of his official duties. Even when thus indisposed, and pressed with cares too great for a man in sound health to endure, he neglected no demand upon his friendship and benevolence. Accidentally meeting an old acquaintance in distress, he took him to the President's house, gave him a breakfast, and after conversing with him a while upon events long since passed, he wrote to the collector of New York the following (*his last*) letter, dated March 26, 1841, for the purpose, as will be seen, of aiding him in his adversity:

"The bearer hereof, Mr. Thomas Tucker, a veteran seaman, came with me from Carthagenia, as the mate of the brig Montidia, in the year 1829. In an association of several weeks, I formed a high opinion of his character; so much so, that (expressing a desire to leave the sea) I invited him to come to North Bend, and spend the remainder of his days with me.

"Subsequent misfortunes prevented his doing so, as he was desirous to bring some money with him to **commence farming operations. His bad fortune still** continues, having been several times shipwrecked within a few years. He says that himself and family are now in such a situation that the humblest employment would be acceptable to him. I write this to recommend him to your favorable notice. I am persuaded that no one possesses, in a higher degree, the virtues of fidelity, honesty and indefatigable industry, and I might add, indomitable bravery, if that was a quality necessary for the kind of employment he seeks."

On the 27th of March he was seized with a chill, and other symptoms of fever. The next day, pneumonia, with congestion of the liver, and derangement of the stomach and bowels, was ascertained to exist. In spite of all the efforts and skill of his physicians to arrest the disease, it continued to increase in violence until the 3rd of April, at three o'clock in the afternoon. A profuse diarrhea then came on, under which he rapidly sank; and at thirty minutes past twelve o'clock, on the morning of April 4th, 1841, he breathed his last. His last words were, as heard by Dr. Worthington, one of his consulting physicians: Sir, I wish you to understand the true principles of the government. I wish them carried out. I ask nothing more." Thus died General William Henry Harrison, the ninth President of the United States, at the age of sixty-eight years and twenty-six days, after having filled the office of President but one single short month.

This great national calamity fell upon the public mind with startling suddenness. Almost before the sound of the cannon which announced to the people that he had been invested with the office of President had died away, and before the news had spread scarcely beyond the District of Columbia, the sad intelligence was received that he had ceased to exist. The affecting event, feared, perhaps, by those who best knew General Harrison's enfeebled constitution, was at once officially made public in the following document, signed by the Secretary of State, and all the other heads of departments:

"An All-wise Providence having suddenly removed from this life WILLIAM HENRY HARRISON, late President of the United States, we have thought it our duty, in the recess of Congress, and in the absence of the Vice-President from the seat of government, to make this afflicting bereavement known to the country, by this declaration under our hands. He died at the President's House, in this city, this 4th day of April, Anno Domini 1841, at thirty minutes before one o'clock in the morning.

"The people of the United States, overwhelmed like ourselves, by an event so unexpected and so melancholy, will derive consolation from knowing that his death was calm and resigned as his life had been patriotic, useful and distinguished; and that the last utterance from his lips expressed a fervent desire for the perpetuity of the constitution and the preservation of its true principles. In death, as in life, the happiness of his country was uppermost in his thoughts."

Wednesday, April 7th, was selected for perform-

32

ing the funeral solemnities of the late President. The ceremony was as solemn as it was imposing. Every countenance was impressed with the most profound melancholy. The military portion of the procession was volunteer companies from Washington city, Georgetown, Baltimore, Philadelphia and various other cities, together with several companies of marines and United States artillerists, all accompanied by the mounted and dismounted officers of the army, navy, militia and volunteers. The civic part of it consisted of the municipal officers of the District of Columbia, the clergy, the judiciary and executive officers of the government, including the President of the United States and all the heads of bureaus. The procession occupied two miles in length. The religious ceremonies at the grave were performed by the Reverend Mr. Healey, of the Episcopal church.*

As the news of General Harrison's death spread throughout the Union, the profound respect which was entertained for his character, and the gratitude they felt for his important public services, begun to be exhibited in their full force. Every demonstration in the power of the people to show was bestowed upon his memory. All party animosity was at once forgotten, and the whole people united in the performance of ceremonies appropriate to the occasion. In almost every city and town in the Union funeral sermons were delivered, processions got up and addresses delivered; and the most profound grief was every-

*See Appendix (D).

where, and by all parties and sects, evinced. The nation for a time was almost literally clothed in mourning, and there was a general rivalry amongst those so lately his warm political opponents who should best show how little their political differences blinded them to his real merits and many noble virtues.

On the 31st of May following, Congress assembled in extra session, in pursuance of a proclamation issued by General Harrison; and on the 4th of June, passed the following resolutions in relation to the national loss:

" The melancholy event of the death of William Henry Harrison, late President of the United States, having occurred during the recess of Congress, and the two houses sharing in the general grief, and desiring to manifest their sensibilities upon the occasion of that public bereavement, therefore :

" *Resolved, by the Senate and House of Representatives of the United States of America in Congress assembled*, That the chairs of the President of the Senate and Speaker of the House of Representatives be shrouded in black during the residue of the session; and that the President *pro tempore* of the Senate, the Speaker of the House of Representatives, and the members and officers of both Houses, wear the usual badge of mourning for thirty days.

" *Resolved*, That the President of the United States be requested to transmit a copy of these resolutions to Mrs. Harrison, and to assure her of the profound respect of the two Houses of Congress for her person and character, and of their sincere condolence with the late dispensation of Providence."

But Congress went still further than this. On the 9th of June, John Quincy Adams reported a bill in the House of Representatives in favor of a grant of money to the widow of General Harrison. This had been suggested to Congress by Mr. Tyler, in his message at the opening of the session. He said, " that the preparations necessary for his removal to the seat of government, in view of a residence of four years, must have devolved upon the late President heavy expenditures, which, if permitted to burthen the limited resources of his private fortune, might tend to the serious embarrassment of his surviving family ; and it was therefore respectfully submitted to Congress, whether the ordinary principles of justice would not dictate the propriety of legislative interposition."

The measure was also urged upon Congress from various quarters as an act of simple justice to the family of Harrison. He had occupied positions in which he might have amassed an immense fortune, if he had chosen to avail himself of the advantages placed in his hands. It could have been done without any real injustice to government, and with but a very slight departure from the principles of rectitude. He chose not to enrich himself by any doubtful means. Poverty in his estimation was far preferable to riches thus acquired. These and other considerations, operating with the sympathy felt for the affliction of the widow of Harrison, an appropriation of $25,000 was finally made to Mrs. Harrison. The bill passed the House, on the 18th of June, by a vote of 122 to 66, and the Senate by a vote of 28 to 16.

General Harrison's personal appearance was commanding, and his manners prepossessing. He was about six feet high, of rather slender form, straight, and of a firm, elastic gait, even at the time of his election to the presidency, though then closely bordering on seventy. He had a keen, penetrating eye, denoting quickness of apprehension, promptness and energy. His forehead was high, broad and prominent, his lips rather thin and compressed, and his whole features strongly marked. His countenance was expressive of the genuine kindness and philanthropy which his whole life had practically exemplified. There was that in his personal appearance which indicated him as a man of not an ordinary character. The inherent honesty and integrity of his nature showed forth in his countenance.

The qualities which General Harrison displayed as a military chieftain are now universally admitted to be. of the very highest order. Indeed few were ever found, even during the violent political contest which resulted in his elevation to the presidency, hardly enough, and so reckless of his own reputation, as to deny him the merit of a great general. As commander-in-chief of the north-western army, he was intrusted with almost unlimited discretionary powers, requiring the exercise of military skill, science and ability, such as few commanders of American armies

32 *

have ever exhibited. The history of the last war with
England, and especially the misfortunes that befell
so many of our generals at the North and North-west,
as well as at the South, proves this to be true. While
most of the generals in command of our armies in that
war, no matter how eminent and how successful *generally* they may have been, sometimes meet with
reverses, General Harrison never lost a battle, and
never committed an error in his military movements.
This was the peculiar glory of General Harrison as a
commander. This uniform success was the result of
" an almost intuitive sagacity, great power of combination, with prudence, caution, promptness and energy,
combined with perfect self-reliance and self-control."
These qualities are necessary to form the great, or
what is equivalent, the successful general.

It has been claimed that in many points the military career of Harrison bears a striking analogy to
that of Washington,—that the same extent of discretionary powers and responsibilities were assigned to
both, that both had the same difficulty in procuring
supplies of troops and provisions, and, above all, that
they never hazarded the grand result of a campaign,
by any minor enterprise, however tempting. Both
exercised the extensive powers with which they were
invested without any invasion of the laws, or the
rights of citizens, and both retired to the peaceful
pursuits of agriculture when the objects which had
called them to the field had been effected. This is
high praise to General Harrison, as the parallel has,

at least, some ground to rest upon, though nothing must be admitted to stand almost without parallel.

The prominent feature of General Harrison's character was the most inflexible and rigid integrity, his devoted patriotism, his keen sense of honor, and his great love of justice. These noble virtues marked his whole life from youth to old age, in the field as well as in the council. No consideration of personal advantage, of whatever character, could induce him to swerve a hair's breadth from them. During twenty years of public employment he had numerous opportunities of enriching himself; but he sternly rejected them all, and retired from the service of his country poorer than he entered it. Of the three million dollars that passed through his hands as a government agent, not a single dollar ever adhered to them. So nice were his feelings upon these points that he even refused to make purchases of land, lest it might by possibility be charged that he had transcended his official authority. Equally sensitive were his feelings of honor, with the single exception of private secretary, he invariably refused to appoint any of his relatives to office.

General Harrison's mind was of a good order. He possessed excellent natural powers of mind, and they were thoroughly disciplined and well-directed. Few men possessed a sounder or better judgment, or had more sagacity and penetration. His scholarly attainments were far above mediocrity. In general history he was thoroughly versed, and his notes upon that important branch of education possess many valuable suggestions. With the public characters and leading events of both ancient and modern times he was intimately familiar. As a writer he ranks among the first public men of the country; and many of his compositions exhibit felicity of expression, strength of thought, and sound, practical common sense. As a speaker he was easy, graceful and fluent, often rising to real eloquence. He might have excelled as an orator had he failed as a soldier, and the renown he won in the field might have been eclipsed by that he possessed in the Senate, had his profession led him in that direction.

No man possessed a kinder or more benevolent heart. His feelings were ever alive to the sufferings or misfortunes of those about him, and his hand was ever open to relieve the necessities of the needy. His personal address and manners were well suited to win the favor of the people, as he was open, frank, and courteous in his intercourse with all. There was nothing of the aristocrat in his character; on the contrary, he was purely democratic in his tastes as well as in his inclinations. While President of the nation he was as easy of approach, and as free in his intercourse with the people, as when only the plain farmer of North Bend. Courtesy and a graceful condescension, united with ease and dignity of manners, relieved every one of embarrassment while in his presence.

His moral character was above reproach; though

perhaps not a professing christian, he entertained the highest and most profound regard for the christian religion. This he did not fear to declare as well in his inaugural address as upon all suitable occasions during the brief period he occupied the presidential chair. Such, imperfectly drawn, is the character,—and such, imperfectly recorded, are the great deeds and important public services,—of William Henry Harrison. There is much that cannot fail to be admired in the one, imperfectly as it has been sketched, and much to excite the gratitude of the people in the other, imperfectly as they have been recorded. General Harrison had his imperfections, like all other men, but that his virtues greatly outweighed them must be the verdict of impartial history. His errors, whatever they were, were never permitted to affect the public welfare, while his virtues and public services have contributed something, at least, to the happiness of the people, and much to the honor of the nation.

A single circumstance will illustrate his high sense of justice and his true nobleness of soul far better than any studied panegyric could do: A few years ago it was ascertained that a large tract of land near Cincinnati, which had been sold some time before for a mere trifle, under an execution against the original proprietors, could not be held by the title derived from the purchasers on account of some irregularity in the proceedings. The legal title was in General Harrison and another gentleman, who were the heirs at law. This tract of land was exceedingly valuable,

and would have constituted a princely estate for
both these heirs, had they chosen to insist on their
legal rights; or they might have compromised with
the purchaser. But General Harrison refused to do
either the one or the other. He had never yet suffered his own interests to blind him to other's rights,
and on being informed of the situation of the property,
he and his co-heir immediately granted deeds in fee
simple to the purchaser, without claiming any consideration except the trifling difference between the actual value of the land when sold and the amount paid
at the sheriff's sale. There were in this tract, too,
twelve acres of General Harrison's private property
improperly included in the sale, which he might have
retained both legally and equitably. But such was
his nice sense of honor and scrupulous regard for the
rights of others, that he suffered even his own rights
to be invaded rather than to vindicate them at the expense of others. Such instances of magnanimity and
chivalrous sense of honesty are bright spots in the
history of humanity, the more conspicuous, perhaps,
from being so seldom seen, but equally the objects of
our admiration, however often and whenever seen.

APPENDIX.

STATISTICS OF THE SIX CENSUS.

The following facts, compiled from the returns in the census office, will show the extent, population, resources, manufactors, and, above all, the growth of our country since General Harrison entered upon public life. They will also be of great and permanent interest as a matter of reference.

The seventh enumeration of the inhabitants of the the United States exhibits results which every citizen of country may contemplate with gratification and pride. Since the census of 1840 there have been added to the territory of the Republic, by annexation, conquest, and purchase, 635,988 square miles; and our title to regions covering 341,463 square miles, which before properly belonged to us, but was claimed, and partially occupied, by a foreign power, has been established by negotiation, and it has been brought within our acknowledged boundaries. By such means the area of the United States has been extended, during the past ten years, from 2,055,163 to 3,221,595 square miles, without including the great lakes which lie upon our northern border, or the bays which indentate our Atlantic and Pacific shores, all which has come within the scope of the seventh census.

In the endeavor to ascertain the progress of our population since 1840, it will be proper to deduct from the aggregate number of inhabitants shown by the present census the population of Texas in 1840, and the number embraced within the limits of California and the new territories at the time of their acquisition. From the best information which has come to hand it is believed that Texas contained, in 1840, 75,000 inhabitants; and that when California, New Mexico, and Oregon came into our possession, in 1846, they had a population of 97,000. It thus appears that we have received, by additions of Territory since 1840, an accession of 172,000 to the number of our people.

The increase which has taken place in those extended regions since they came under the authority of our government should obviously be received as a part of the development and progress of our population; nor is it necessary to complicate the comparison by taking into account the probable natural increase of this acquired population, because we have not the means of determining the rate of its advancement, nor the law which governed its progress while yet beyond the influence of our political system. The year 1840, rather than the date of our enumeration of Texas, has been taken for estimating her population in connection with that of the Union, because it may be safely assumed that, whatever the increase during the five intervening years may have been, it was mainly, if not altogether, derived from the United States.

Owing to delays and difficulties mentioned in completing the work, which no action on the part of this office could obviate, some of the returns from California have not yet been received.

Assuming the population of California to be 165,000 (which we do partly by estimate), and omitting that of Utah, estimated at 15,000, the total number of inhabitants in the United States was, on the 1st of June, 1850, 23,-246,301.

The absolute increase from the 1st of June, 1840, has been 6,176,848; and the actual increase per cent. is 36.18. But it has been shown that the probable amount of population acquired by additions of territory should be deducted in making a comparison between the results of the present and the last census. These deductions reduce the total population of the country, as a *basis of comparison*, to 23,074,301, and the increase to 6,004,848. The relative increase, after this allowance, is found to be 35.17 per cent. The aggregate number of whites in 1850 was 19,-619,366, exhibiting a gain upon the number of the same class in 1840 of 5,423,371, and a relative increase of 38.20 per cent. But excluding the 153,000 free population supposed to be acquired by the addition of territory since 1840, the gain is 5,270,371, and the increased per cent. 37.14. The number of slaves, by the present census, is 3,198,298, which shows an increase of 711,085, equal to 28.58 per cent. If we deduct 19,000 for the probable slave population in Texas in 1840, the result of the comparison will be slightly different. The absolute increase will be 692,085, and the rate per cent. 27.83.

The number of free colored in 1850 was 428,637, in 1840, 386,245. The increase of this class has been 42,-392, or 10.95 per cent.

From 1830 to 1840 the increase of the whole population was at the rate of 32.67 per cent. At the same rate of advancement the absolute gain for the ten years last past would have been 5,578,333, or 426,515 less than it has been, without including the increase consequent upon additions of territory.

The aggregate increase of population from all sources shows a relative advance greater than that of any other decimal term, except that from the second to the third census, during which time the country received an accession of inhabitants, by the purchase of Louisiana, considerably greater than one per cent. of the whole number. Rejecting from the census of 1810 1.45 per cent. for the population of Louisiana, and from the census of 1850 one per cent. for that of Texas, California, &c., the result is in favor of the last ten years by about one-fourteenth of one per cent. ; the gain from 1800 to 1810 being 35.05 per cent., and from 1840 to 1850 35.12 per cent. But without going behind the sum of the returns, it appears that the increase from the second to the third census was thirty-two-hundredths of one per cent. greater than from the sixth to the seventh.

The relative progress of the several races and classes of the population is shown in the following tabular statement:

Increase per cent. for each class of Inhabitants in the United States for sixty years.

	1790 to 1800.	1800 to 1810.	1810 to 1820.	1820 to 1830.	1830 to 1840.	1840 to 1850.
Whites..................	35.68	36.18	34.30	34.52	34.72	38.20
Free colored	82.28	72.00	27.75	34.85	20.88	10.95
Slaves	27.96	33.40	29.57	30.75	23.81	28.58
Total colored	32.23	37.58	29.33	31.31	23.40	26.16
Total population.....	35.02	36.50	33.35	33.92	32.67	35.18

The census had been taken previously to 1830 on the 1st day of August; the enumeration began on that year on the 1st of June, two months earlier, so that the interval between the fourth and fifth census was two months less than ten years; which time allowed for would bring the total increase up to the rate of 34.36 per cent.

The tables given below show the increase from 1790 to 1850, without reference to intervening periods.

	1790.	1850.	Absolute increase in 60 years.	Incr. per ct. in 60 years.
No. of whites.......	3,172,464	19,630,019	16,457,555	52,797
Free colored.......	59,466	428,637	369,171	61,744
Slaves...............	697,897	3,184,262	2,486,365	35,013
Tot. free col. & sl.	757,363	3,612,899	2,855,536	377
Total population...	3,929,827	23,246,301	19,316,417	491,152

Sixty years since the proportion between the whites and blacks, bond and free, was 4.2 to 1. In 1850 it was 5.26 to 1; and the ratio in favor of the former race is increasing. Had the blacks increased as fast as the whites during these sixty years the number on the first of June would have been 4,657,239; so that, in comparison with the whites, they have lost in this period 1,350,340.

This disparity is much more than accounted for by European emigration to the United States.

Dr. Chickering, in an essay on emigration, published in Boston in 1848, distinguished for great elaborateness of research, estimates the gain of the white population from this source at 3,922,152. No reliable record was kept of the emigrants into the United States until 1820, when, by the laws of March, 1819, the collectors were required to make quarterly returns of foreign passengers arriving in their districts. For the first ten years the returns under the laws afford materials for only an approximation to a true state of the facts involved in this inquiry.

Dr. Chickering assumes, as a result of his investigations, that of the 6,431,088 inhabitants of the United States in 1820, 1,430,906 were foreigners arrived subsequent to 1790, or the descendants of such. According to Dr. Seybert, an earlier writer upon statistics, the number of foreign passengers from 1790 to 1810 was, as nearly as could be ascertained, 120,000; and from the estimates of Dr. Seybert, and other evidence, Honorable Geo. Tucker, author of a valuable work on the census of 1840, supposed the number from 1810 to 1820 to have been 114,000. These estimates make, for the thirty years preceding 1820, 234,000.

If we reckon the census of emigrants at the average rate of the whole body of white population during these three decades, they and their descendants in 1820 would amount to about 360,000.

From 1820 to 1830 there arrived, according to the returns of the custom-houses, 135,986 foreign passengers; and from 1830 to 1840, 579,370; making, for the twenty years, 715,356.

During this period a large number of emigrants from England, Scotland, and Ireland, came into the United States through Canada.

Dr. Chickering estimates the number of such from 1820 to 1830 at 67,993, and from 1830 to 1840 at 199,130; for the twenty years together, 267,123. During the same time a considerable number are supposed to have landed at New York with the purpose of pursuing their route to Canada; but it is probable that the number of these was balanced by omissions in the official returns.

Without reference to the natural increase, then the accession to our population from foreign sources, from 1820 to 1840, was 982,479 persons.

From 1840 to 1850 the arrivals of foreign passengers in the ports of the United States have been as follows:

1840, 1841	83,504
1842	101,107
1843	75,159
1844	74,607
1845	102,415
1846	202,157*
1847	234,756
1848	226,524
1849	269,610
1850	173,011†
Total	1,552,830

As the heaviest portion of this great influx of emigration took place in the latter part of the decade, it will

* This return includes fifteen months, to wit, from July 1, 1845, to September 30, 1846.

† The report from the State Department for this year gives 315,333 as the total number of passengers arriving in the United States; but of these 30,023 were citizens of the Atlantic States proceeding to California by sea, and 5,320 natives of the country returning from visits abroad. A deduction of 106,879 is made from the balance for that portion of the year from June 1 to September 30. Within the last ten years there has probably been very little migration of foreigners into the United States over the Canadian frontier,—the disposition to take the route by Quebec having yielded to the increased facilities for direct passenger transportation to the cities of the Union; what there has been may perhaps be considered as equaled by the number of foreigners passing into Canada, often landing at New York, many having been drawn thither by the opportunity of employment afforded by the public works of the province.

probably be fair to estimate the natural increase during the
term at 12 per cent., being about one-third of that of the
white population of the country at its commencement.

This will swell the aggregate to 1,789,192. Deducting
this accession to the population from the whole amount of
the increase of white inhabitants before given, that increase
is shown to be 3,684,519, and the rate per cent. is reduced
to 25.95.

The density of population is a branch of the subject
which naturally first attracts the attention of the inquirer.
The following table has been prepared from the most authentic data accessible to this office.

*Table of the Area, and the number of Inhabitants to the square mile,
of each State and Territory of the Union.*

States.	Area in square mile.	Population in 1850.	No. of inhab. to sq. mile.
Maine......................	30,000	583,188	19.44
New Hampshire...........	9,280	317,964	34.26
Vermont....................	10,212	313,611	30.07
Massachusetts	7,800	994,499	126.15
Rhode Island	1,360	147,544	108.04
Connecticut	4,674	370,791	79.33
New York	46,000	3,097,394	67.66
New Jersey................	8,320	489,555	60.04
Pennsylvania	46,000	2,311,785	50.25
Delaware..................	2,120	91,535	43.64
Maryland	9,356	583,035	62.31
Virginia....................	61,552	1,421,661	23.17
North Carolina...........	45,000	868,903	19.30
South Carolina...........	24,500	668,507	27.28
Georgia	58,000	905,999	15.68
Alabama	50,722	771,671	15.21
Mississippi.................	47,156	606,555	12.86
Louisiana	46,431	511,974	11.02
Texas	237,321	212,592	.89
Florida....................	59,268	87,401	1.47
Kentucky	37,680	982,405	26.07
Tennessee.................	45,600	1,002,625	21.98
Missouri...................	67,380	682,043	10.12

(Continued from last page.)

States.	Area in square mile.	Population in 1850.	No. of inhab. to sq. mile.
Arkansas..................	52,198	209,639	4.01
Ohio......................	39,964	1,980,408	49.55
Indiana	33,809	988,6	29.22
Illinois	55,405	85,.4.0	15.36
Michigan.................	56,243	397,654	7.07
Iowa......................	50,914	192,214	3.77
Wisconsin................	53,924	305,191	5.65
California	188,981	....	......
Minnesota	83,000	6,077	.07
Oregon...................	341,463	13,293	.03
New Mexico..............	210,744	61,505	.28
Utah	177,923	....	......
Nebraska.................	136,700	....	......
Indian	187,171	....	......
North-West	587,564	....	......
District Columbia........	60	51,687	861,45
Total	3,221,595	23,080,792	

From the location, climate, productions, and the habits and pursuits of their inhabitants, the States of the Union may be properly arranged into the following groups:

States.	Area in square mile.	Population.	No. of inhab. to sq. mile.
New England States............	63,226	2,727,597	43.07
Middle States, including Maryland, Delaware, and Ohio	151,760	8,653,713	57.02
Coast planting States, including South Carolina, Georgia, Florida, Alabama, Mississippi, and Louisiana.........	296,077	3,537,089	12.36
Central Slave States, Virginia, N. Carolina, Tennessee, Kentucky, Missouri, and Arkansas	308,210	5,168,000	16.75
North-Western States, Indiana, Michigan, Illinois, Wisconsin, and Iowa............	250,000	2,735,000	10.92
Texas	237,000	212,000	89
California......................	189,000	165,000	87

There are points of agreement in the general characteristics of the States combined in the above groups which warrant the mode of arrangement adopted. Maryland is classed as heretofore with the Middle States, because its leading interests appear to connect it rather with the commercial and manufacturing section to which it is here assigned, than with the purely agricultural States. Ohio is placed in the same connection for nearly similar reasons. There seems to be a marked propriety for setting off the new agricultural States of the North-West by themselves, as a preliminary to the comparison of their progress with other portions of the Union. The occupations which give employment to the people of the central range of States south of the line of the Potomac, distinguish them to some extent from that division to which we have given the appellation of coast planting States. In the latter cotton, sugar, and rice are the great staples, the cultivation of which is so absorbing as to stamp its impress on the character of the people. The industry of the central States is more diversified, the surface of the country is more broken, the modes of cultivation are different, and the minuter divisions of labor create more numerous and less accordant interests. So far as Texas is settled, its population closely assimilates with that of the other coast planting States, but it would obviously convey no well-founded idea of the density of population in that section to distribute their people over the most uninhabited region of Texas. For the same reason, and the additional one of the isolation of her position, California is considered distinct from other States.

Taking the thirty-one States together, their area is

1,485,870 square miles, and the average number of their inhabitants is 15.48 to the square mile. The total area of the United States is 3,220,000 square miles, and the average density of population is 7.219 to the square mile.

The areas assigned to those States and Territories in which public lands are situated are doubtless correct, being taken from the records of the Land Office; but as to those attributed to the older States, the same means of verifying their accuracy, or the want of it, do not exist. But care has been taken to consult the best local authorities for ascertaining the extent of surface in these States; and as the figures adopted are found to agree with, or differ but slightly from, those assumed to be correct at the General Land Office, it is probable they do not vary essentially from the exact truth.

The area of some of the States, as Maryland and Virginia, are stated considerably below the commonly assumed extent of the territory, which may be accounted for on the supposition that the portions of the surface within their exterior limits, covered by large bodies of water, have been subtracted from the aggregate amount. This is known to be the case in regard to Maryland, the superficial extent of which, within the outlines of its boundaries, is 13,959 square miles, and is deemed probable with reference to Virginia, from the fact that many geographers have given its total area as high as 66,000 square miles.

It appears from the returns that during the year ending on the 1st of June, 1850, there escaped from their owners 1,011 slaves, and that during the same period 1,467 were manumitted. The number of both classes will appear in the following table:

Manumitted and Fugitive Slaves in 1850.

	Manu.	Fug.
Delaware	277	26
Maryland	493	297
Virginia	218	83
Kentucky	152	96
Tennessee	45	70
North Carolina	2	64
South Carolina	2	16
Georgia	19	89
Florida	22	18
Alabama	16	29
Mississippi	6	41
Louisiana	159	90
Texas	5	29
Arkansas	1	21
Missouri	50	60
Total	1,467	1,011

In connection with this statement, and as affecting the natural increase of the free colored population of the United States, it may be proper to remark that, during the year to which the census applies, the Colonization Society sent 562 colored emigrants to Liberia.

In our calculations respecting the increase of the free colored population, we have not considered that class of persons, independent of these two causes, which respectively swell and diminish their number.

The statistics of mortality for the census year represent the number of deaths occurring within the year at 320.194, the ratio being as 1 to 72.6 of the living population, or as 10 to each 726 of the population. The rate of mortality in this statement seems so much less than that of any portion of Europe, that it must at present be received with some degree of allowance.

Should a more critical examination, which time will

enable us to exercise, prove the returns of the number of deaths too small, such a result will not affect their value for the purposes of comparison of one portion of the country with another, or cause with effect. The tables will possess an interest second to none others in the world; and the many valuable truths which they will suggest will be found of great practical advantage.

Medical men accord to the Census Bureau no small meed of credit, for the wisdom manifested in an arrangement which will throw more light on the history of disease in the United States, and present in connection more interesting facts connected therewith, than the united efforts of all scientific men have heretofore acccomplished.

———

AGRICULTURE.

The great amount of labor requisite to the extraction of the returns of agriculture will admit at this time of presenting but limited accounts, though perhaps, to some extent, of the most separate interests.

The returns of the wheat crop for many of the Western States will not at all indicate the average crop of those States.

This is especially the case with Ohio, Indiana, and Illinois, from which, especially the former, the Assistant Marshals returned a "short crop" to the extent of fifty per cent. throughout the whole State.

The shortness of the wheat crop in Ohio in 1849 is verified by returns made during the subsequent season by authority of the legislature.

The period which has elapsed since the receipt of the returns has been so short as to enable the office to make but a general report of the facts relating to a few of the most important manufactures.

If, in some instances, the amount of capital invested in any branch of manufacture should seem too small, it must be borne in mind that, where the product is of several kinds, the capital invested, not being divisible, is connected with the product of greatest consequence. This, to some extent, reduces the capital invested in the manufacture of bar iron in such establishments where some other article of wrought iron predominates,—sheet iron, for example.

The aggregate, however, of the capital invested in the various branches of wrought iron will, it is confidently believed, be found correct.

The entire capital invested in the various manufactures in the United States, on the 1st of June, 1850, not to include any establishment producing less than the annual value of $500, amounted to, in round numbers $530,000,000
Value of raw material 550,000,000
Amount paid for labor 240,000,000
Value of manufactured articles............................ 1,020,300,000
Number of persons employed 1,050,000

The capital invested in the manufacture of cotton... $74,501,031
Value of raw material 34,835,056
Amount paid for labor... 16,286,304
Value of manufactured articles............................ 61,869,184
Number of hands employed 39,252

The capital invested in the manufacture of woolen
   goods amounted to.. $28,118,650
Value of raw material.. 25,755,98
Amount paid for labor....................................... 8,399,28
Value of product 43,207,55
Number of hands employed................................ 92,286

The capital invested in the manufacture of pig iron
    amounted to... $17,346,425
Value of raw material ..,..................................... 7,005,289
Amount paid for labor.. 5,006,628
Value of product.. 12,748,777
Number of hands employed.............................. 20,448

In making these estimates the Assistant Marshals did
not include any return of works which had not produced
metal within the year, or those which had not commenced
operations. The same is applicable to all manufactures
enumerated.

The capital invested in the manufacture of castings
    amounted to $17,416,361
Value of raw material 10,346,355
Amount paid for labor.. 7,078,920
Value of product 25,108,155
Number of hands employed 23,589

The capital invested in the manufacture of wrought
    iron amounted to $13,995,220
Value of raw material 9,518,100
Amount paid for labor.. 4,196,628
Value of product... 16,387,074
Number of hands employed 13,057

The statistics of the newspaper press form an interesting feature in the returns of the seventh census. It
appears that the whole number of newspapers and periodicals in the United States, on the 1st of June, 1850,
amounted to 2,800. Of these 2,494 were fully returned,
234 had all the facts excepting circulation given, and 72
are estimated for California, the territories, and for those
that may have been omitted by the Assistant Marshals.

From calculations made on the statistics returned, and
estimated circulations where they have been omitted, it
appears that the aggregate circulation of those 2,800 papers

and periodicals is about 5,000,000, and that the entire number of copies printed annually in the United States amounts to 422,600,000. The following table will show the number of daily, weekly, monthly, and other issues, with the aggregate circulation of each class.

	No.	Circulation.	No. of copies printed annually.
Dailies	350	750,000	235,000,000
Tri-weeklies	150	75,000	11,700,000
Semi-weeklies	125	80,000	8,320,000
Weeklies	2,000	2,875,000	149,500,000
Semi-monthlies	50	300,000	9,300,000
Monthlies	100	900,000	10,800,000
Quarterlies	25	20,000	80,000
Total	2,800	5,000,000	422,600,000

424 papers are issued in the New England States, 876 in the Middle States, 716 in the Southern States, and 784 in the Western States.

The average circulation of papers in the United States is 1,785.

There is one publication for every 7,161 free inhabitants in the United States and Territories.

The work, of course, has not been submitted to the public for its judgment; but where opinions have been at all expressed, by those deemed good authority, on the propriety of our classification, they have been invariably favorable. Some such have found their way into public documents. In the 32d Annual Report of the New York Institution for the Deaf and Dumb, made to the legislature of that State, the following language occurs with respect to our designed classification of such portion of the work as interested particularly the Directors of the Institution:

"Such a list will furnish valuable materials, never possessed to any extent before, for solving many highly interesting statistical questions, and its publication is looked for with much interest. We shall endeavor in our next Annual Report to set forth the results of a careful analysis of the census respecting the Deaf and Dumb."

So far as the judgment of the public press is concerned, its expression has been much more favorable than could be wished, with its imperfect knowledge of the plan, as expectations may thereby be raised which the results will not justify. None of the information, as imparted in the volume of statistics, has been promulgated, it being considered indelicate to make known to the world information due first to the Head of the Department, and through him to Congress; and it would not be decorous to forestal the dispassionate judgment of either.

It has seemed to me that a work, the expense of which is shared by the whole community, should be arranged, as far as possible, for general utility, and not a compilation of mere columns of figures, interesting only to the man of science, for legislative purposes, or for reference, but should be so adapted that, while it will furnish practical information to the statesman and philosopher, and useful data for the legislator, it will contain also matters interesting to every portion of the community, furnished somewhat in advance of those deductions from analytical investigations made years after its publication. To this end, if supported by the favorable opinion of Congress, it will be made to evolve all the instruction which zealous efforts, though limited ability, are capable of eliciting from the facts, within such period of time as it must be accomplished without retarding its publication.   J. R. ROCHE.

Census Office, Dec. 3, 5½ o'clock, A. M.

COTTON MANUFACTURES.—(COMPILED FROM THE CENSUS RETURNS OF 1850.)

A Table showing the capital invested, the bales of cotton and tuns of coal consumed, the number of hands employed, and their wages, in the manufacture of cotton goods in the United States, together with the value of the raw material, and the entire product.

States.	Capital Invested.	Bales of Cotton.	Tuns of Coals.	Value of all Raw Material.	Number of hands employed. M.	F.	Entire wages per month. M.	F.	Av'rage w'ges per month. M.	F.	Value of entire Product.	Yards Sheeting, &c., &c.
Maine	$3,300,700	3,531	2,921	$1,573,110	780	2,95	$22,945	$35,973	$29 35	$12 16	2,596,356	32,852,556
New Hampshire	10,050,500	83,326	7,679	839,428	2,511	9,211	75,713	124,131	25 45	13 47	6,830,19	113,106,247
Vermont	292,500	2,243		114,415	191	147	1,460	18,061	15 55	12 67	398,100	1,651,004
Massachusetts	23,45,000	225,07	46,545	3,894,309	9,292	19,457	212,892	264,514	33 01	13 55	13,712,461	198,751,392
Rhode Island	6,675,100	50,713	15,210	1,484,579	4,519	5,916	52,282	70,658	18 61	12 95	6,447,120	96,925,412
Connecticut	4,219,100	29,482	2,866	2,600,062	2,73	3,478	51,679	41,000	19 08	11 81	4,267,522	51,580,700
New York	4,174,929	33,575	1,528	1,985,973	2,602	3,688	48,244	35,609	18 33	9 08	3,591,989	44,901,475
New Jersey	1,483,500	14,457	4,467	669,645	616	1,090	11,078	10,487	17 98	9 56	11,109,524	8,122,5-0
Pennsylvania	4,52,925	44,162	24,187	3,152,580	3,549	4,099	64,642	40,656	17 26	9 91	5,322,299	45,746,790
Delaware	460,100	4,730	1,920	312,659	445	425	15,326	4,926	15 55	11 40	558,479	3,551,936
Maryland	2,260,000	28,725	2,212	1,165,579	1,008	2,014	15,246	19,108	15 42	9 53	2,120,501	27,883,628
Virginia	1,908,400	17,785	4,865	825,375	1,275	1,688	12,983	11,791	10 15	9 98	1,486,800	15,640,107
North Carolina	1,058,800	13,617		530,003	442	1,117	5,153	7,216	11 66	6 13	831,312	2,470,110
South Carolina	857,20	9,654		295,971	299	620	5,565	5,151	13 94	8 30	744,338	6,602,757
Georgia	1,735,156	29,220	1,000	900,419	873	1,390	12,725	10,755	14 57	7 39	2,135,044	7,207,292
Florida	840,00	640		20,000	28	67	960	335	32 15	5 00	49,920	634,000
Alabama	667,90	5,20	257,081	255,04	346	369	4,053	2,946	11 71	7 98	382,270	3,081,000
Mississippi	58,00	420		21,900	19	17	270	101	14 21	5 84	20,500	
Arkansas	16,500	170		8,975	13	18	190	106	14 61	5 83	16,637	
Tennessee	6 9,000	6,411	3,010	297,500	310	541	3,384	3,730	10 95	6 42	510,024	362,250
Kentucky	2 39,00	3,750	270	180,905	181	221	2,797	2,070	14 62	9 36	273,439	1,003,000
Ohio	2,97,400	4,270	2,159	225,040	152	269	2,191	2,534	16 60	9 05	384,700	280,000
Indiana	43,000	675	300	25,220	38	57	495	386	13 00	6 77	44,500	
Missouri	102 00	2,101	1,638	86,446	75	80	820	800	10 94	10 09	142,500	
District of Columbia	85,000	960		47,000	41	105	575	825	14 02	8 01	100,0 0	1,400,0 0
Total	74,501,031	41,246	121,069	$1,825,056	33,151	59,136	654,878	763,414			61,869,184	763,678,470

WOOLEN MANUFACTURE.

A Table showing the capital invested, the number of pounds of wool and tuns of coal consumed, the number of hands employed, and their wages, in the manufacture of woolen goods in the United States, together with the value of the raw material, and the entire product.

States.	Capital Invested.	Pounds of Wool used.	Tuns of Coals.	Value of all Raw Material.	No. of hands employed. M.	F.	Entire wages per month. M.	F.	Av'rage wages per month. M.	F.	Value of entire Product.	Yards of Cloth Manuf'd.
Maine	$425,100	1,459,464	3,400	$495,940	310	314	$6,698	$3,97	$22 57	$11 76	$755,300 00	1,025,620
New Hampshire	2,457,700	3,801,163	3,600	1,267,329	936	1,204	21,171	17,453	22 84	14 51	2,121,245	3,712,840
Vermont	886,200	2,958,100		850,634	683	710	16,712	8,388	24 50	11 80	1,579,161	2,605,400
Massachusetts	9,095,942	25,225,962	15,400	3,651,951	6,107	4,963	141,565	70,581	22 95	14 22	12,770,565	25,063,668
Rhode Island	1,013,570	1,467,360	2,072	987	771	20,431	11,762	20 70	15 18	2,313,825	5,612,400
Connecticut	3,772,950	6,414,100	7,912	3,335,769	2,907	2,581	70,141	33,159	24 12	13 28	4,359,163	9,408,417
New York	4,459,570	12,598,786		3,338,492	2,412	2,581	83,147	48,577	21 46	13 60	7,050,604	6,924,252
New Jersey	494,271	548,367	1,829	548,367	411	487	10,387	4,192	25 02	8 50	1,164,444	771,100
Pennsylvania	3,006,094	1,300,579	10,777	3,382,718	3,490	2,236	67,155	25,279	19 20	10 40	5,521,410	10,693,524
Delaware	148,500	365,000	45	203,172	122	18	2,933	312	18 79	10 75	251,010	152,000
Maryland	244,000	730,300	160	165,563	202	100	4,875	1,189	18 60	11 89	295,110	573,162
Virginia	392,640	1,564,110	357	486,809	478	268	8,688	1,184	18 50	9 00	841,043	2,057,423
North Carolina	18,000	20,600		13,950	15	15	270	105	18 00	7 00	23,750	34,600
Georgia	68,000	153,816		30,392	40	38	1,099	536	24 47	14 10	88,750	340,700
Texas	8,000	20,000		10,000	4	4	80	60	20 00	20 00	16,000	14,000
Tennessee	10,940	6,280		1,675	15		265	12	17 66	6 00	6,510	
Kentucky	249,830	672,900	2,110	205,287	266	62	3,915	689	15 29	11 11	318,819	875,024
Ohio	870,220	1,667,726		578,423	993	628	19,911	3,250	20 14	11 47	1,311,057	1,574,687
Michigan	94,800	162,250		43,402	76	51	1,649	585	21 65	10 05	66,242	141,570
Indiana	171,545	412,250	190	130,486	189	57	4,122	339	21 81	11 05	295,442	255,500
Illinois	154,500	206,964	987	115,367	124	64	2,728	676	22 00	12 52	206,672	200,965
Missouri	20,800	80,000	1,071	16,000	16	10	480	65	32 00	6 50	36,000	12,000
Iowa	10,040	14,500		3,500	7		78		11 42		15,000	14,000
Wisconsin	31,255	134,500		32,620	25		602		22 45		87,392	30,000
District of Columbia	700	5,000		1,630	2		60		30 00		2,400	10,000
Total	25,118,750	70,862,829	46,370	25,765,988	22,578	16,574	489,029	210,901			43,207,555	82,000,634

IRON MANUFACTURES.

A Table showing the capital invested, the number of tuns of pig metal blooms and ore used, and of coal, &c. consumed, the number of hands employed, and their wages, in the Wrought Iron Works in the United States, together with the value of the raw material and the entire product.

States.	Capital Invested	Tuns Pig Metal	Tuns Bl'ms Used	Tuns Ore Used	Tuns Min'l Coal	Bushels Coke and Charcoal.	Value Raw Material, Fuel, &c.	No. Hands Emp.	Average Wages per Month.	Tuns Wrought Iron made.	Value of other Products.	Value of entire Products.
Massachusetts	$110,300	1,030			22	78,500	40,624	40	$28.75	730		48,740
Connecticut	529,500	7,861	1,940		5,023	782,603	258,780	270	31.59	6,225	$5,500	672,000
New York	1,131,500	8,539	340	44,642	12,908	5,454,150	88,314	1,007	26.16	13,603	193,000	1,122,06
Delaware	13,000	310	30				19,534	50	21.19	150		25,639
Maryland	780,450	19,172	2,584		10,435	228,000	49,511	503	23.33	10,000		771,39
Virginia	791,211	17,296	2,600		96,615	163,100	301,448	1,293	23.62	15,328		1,251,905
Georgia	9,500	100				74,600	5,484	826	11.35	30		15,84
Tennessee	755,000	11,696	355	9,351	62,628	280,000	285,476	4734	15.30	10,748	$880	650,718
Kentucky	176,000	2,600	1,400			184,500	148,505	182	22.66	3,070		99,790
Ohio	630,800	13,675	2,500		25,755	466,900	60,449	748	23.61	14,416		1,07,192
Missouri	42,100	1,254			9,824		9,340	101	20.00	968		229,00
Rhode Island	208,000	3,000			6,000	111,750	111,750	210	26.00	2,650		6,500
Pennsylvania	7,620,005	163,702	20,105	14,549	325,997	3,939,968	2,438,391	6754	27.78	182,703	212,000	8,902,677
New Jersey	1,016,543	10,450			4,567	1,004,140	323,050	595	22.60	8,162		629,273
New Hampshire	4,000	145				50,000	5,660	6	22.00	110		10,00
Alabama	2,500	120		4,650		20,000	3,000	14	20.00	100		7,000
North Carolina	103,000			2,625		257,300	28,143	172	18.00			
Vermont	62,700	730	525	3,150		322,000	66,191	57	31.95	2,018		6,3,986
Indiana	17,000	50				83,000	4,425	22	27.45	175		11,500
Total	$13,915,229	251,491	33,344	78,767	525,062	11,536,388	3,513,109	12,978		272,044	$415,880	16,687,074

DECLARATION OF WAR.

The Message of President Madison to Congress, immediately preceding the Declaration of War against England, in 1812,—the Report of the Committee on Foreign Relations, to whom it was referred,—the Declaration of War itself,—and the President's Proclamation of that grave event,—are all documents that will ever possess deep interest to Americans. The two first give, in the most concise form, the causes that led to that war, and they therefore deserve to be often read and free to general access. For these reasons they have been incorporated in this volume. The President's message was communicated to Congress on the 1st day of June, 1812.

To the Senate and House of Representatives of the United States.

I communicate to Congress certain documents, being a continuation of those heretofore laid before them, on the subject of our affairs with Great Britain.

Without going back beyond the renewal, in 1803, of the war in which Great Britain is engaged, and omitting our repaired wrongs of inferior magnitude, the conduct of her government presents a series of acts hostile to the United States as an independent and neutral nation.

British cruisers have been in the continued practice of violating the American flag on the great high way of nations, and of seizing and carrying off persons sailing under it; not in the exercise of a belligerent right, founded on the laws of nations against an enemy, but of a municipal prerogative over British subjects. British jurisdiction is thus extended to neutral vessels in a situation where no laws can operate but the law of nations and the laws of the country to which the vessels belong; and a self-redress is assumed which, if British subjects were wrongfully detained and alone concerned, is that substitution of force, for a resort to the responsible sovereign, which falls within the definition of war. Could the seizure of British subjects in such cases be regarded as within the exercise of a belligerent right, the acknowledged laws of war, which forbid an article of captured property to be adjudged without a regular investigation before a competent tribunal, would imperiously demand the fairest trial when the sacred rights of person were at issue. In place of such a trial, these rights are subject to the will of every petty commander.

The practice, hence, is so far from affecting British subjects alone, that under the pretext of searching for these, thousands of American citizens, under the safeguard of the public and of their national flag, have been torn from their country and from everything dear to them; have been dragged on board ships of war of foreign nations, and exposed, under the severities of their discipline, to be exiled to the most distant and deadly climes, to risk their lives in the battles of their oppressors, and to be the melancholy instruments of taking away those of their own brethren.

Against this crying enormity, which Great Britain would be so prompt to avenge if committed on herself, the United States have in vain exhausted remonstrance and expostulation. And that no proof might be wanting of their conciliatory dispositions, and no pretext left for a continuance of the practice, the British government was formally assured of the readiness of the United States to enter into arrangements, such as could not be rejected, if the recovery of

British subjects were the real and sole object. The communication passed without effect.

British cruisers have been in the practice also of violating the rights and the peace of our coasts. They hover over and harass our entering and deporting commerce. To the most insulting pretensions they have added the most lawless proceedings in our very harbors, and have wantonly spilt American blood within the sanctuary of our territorial jurisdiction. The principles and rules enforced by that nation, when a neutral nation, against armed vessels of belligerents hovering near her coasts and disturbing her commerce, are well known. When called on, nevertheless, by the United States to punish the greater offences committed by her own vessels, her government has bestowed on their commanders additional marks of honor and confidence.

Under pretended blockades, without the presence of an adequate force, and sometimes without the practicability of applying one, our commerce has been plundered in every sea; the great staples of our country have been cut off from their legitimate markets, and a destructive blow aimed at our agricultural and maritime interests. In aggravation of these predatory measures, they have been considered as in force from the dates of their notification, a retrospective effect being thus added, as has been done in other important cases, to the unlawfulness of the course pursued; and to render the outrage the more signal, these mock blockades have been reiterated and enforced in the face of official communications from the British government, declaring, as the true definition of a legal blockade, "the particular ports must be actually invested, and previous warning given to vessels bound to them not to enter."

Not content with these occasional expedients for laying waste our neutral trade, the cabinet of Great Britain resorted, at length, to the sweeping system of blockades, under the name of Orders in Council, which has been moulded and managed as might best suit its political views, its commercial jealousies, or the avidity of British cruisers.

To our remonstrances against the complicated and transcendent injustice of this innovation, the first reply was that the orders were reluctantly adopted by Great Britain as a necessary retaliation on decrees of her enemy, proclaiming a general blockade of the British Isles, at a time when the naval force of that enemy dared not to issue from his own ports. She was reminded, without effect, that her own prior blockade, unsupported by an adequate naval force actually applied and continued, was a bar to this plea; that executed edicts against millions of our property would not be retaliation on edicts confessedly impossible to be executed; that retaliation, to be just, should fall on the party setting the guilty example, not on an innocent party, which was not even chargeable with an acquiescence in it.

When deprived of this flimsy veil for a prohibition of our trade with her enemy, by the repeal of his prohibition of our trade with Great Britain, her cabinet, instead of a corresponding repeal or a practical discontinuance of its orders, formally avowed a determination to persist in them against the United States, until the markets of her enemy should be laid open to British product; thus asserting an obligation on a neutral power to require one belligerent power to encourage, by its internal regulations, the trade of another belligerent, contradicting her own practice towards all nations, in peace as well as war, and betraying the insincerity of these professions which inculcated a belief that, having resorted to her orders with regret, she was anxious to find an occasion for putting an end to them.

Abandoning still more all respect for the neutral rights of the United States, and for its own consistency, the British government now demands, as pre-requisites to a repeal of its orders as they relate to the United States, that a formality should be observed in the repeal of the French decrees, no-wise necessary to their termination, nor exemplified by British usage; and that the French repeal, besides includ-ing that portion of the decrees which operate within a ter-ritorial jurisdiction, as well as that which operates on the high seas against the commerce of the United States, should not be a single special repeal in relation to the United States, but should be extended to whatever other neutral nations unconnected with them may be affected by those decrees. And as an additional insult, they are called on for a formal disavowal of conditions and pretensions ad-vanced by the French government, for which the United States are so far from having made themselves responsible, that, in official explanations, which have been published to the world, and in a correspondence of the American minister at London with the British minister for foreign affairs, such a responsibility was explicitly and emphatically disclaimed.

It has become, indeed, sufficiently certain that the com-merce of the United States is to be sacrificed, not as interfer-ing with the belligerent rights of Great Britain, not as sup-plying the wants of her enemies, which she herself supplies, but as interfering with the monopoly which she covets for her own commerce and navigation. She carries on a war against the lawful commerce of a friend, that she may the better carry on a commerce polluted by the forgeries and perjuries which are, for the most part, the only passports by which it can succeed.

Anxious to make every experiment short of the last resort of injured nations, the United States have withheld from Great Britain, under successive modifications, the benefits of a free intercourse with their market, the loss of which could not but outweigh the profits accruing from her restrictions of our commerce with other nations. And to entitle these experiments to the more favorable consideration, they were so framed as to enable her to place her adversary under the exclusive operation of them. To these appeals her government has been equally inflexible, as if willing to make sacrifices of every sort, rather than yield to the claims of justice or renounce the errors of a false pride. Nay, so far were the attempts carried, to overcome the attachment of the British cabinet to its unjust edicts, that it received every encouragement within the competency of the executive branch of our government to expect that a repeal of them would be followed by a war between the United States and France, unless the French edicts should also be repealed. Even this communication, although silencing forever the plea of a disposition in the United States to acquiesce in those edicts, originally the sole plea for them, received no attention.

If no other proof existed of a predetermination of the British government against a repeal of its orders, it might be found on the correspondence of the minister plenipotentiary of the United States at London, and the British secretary for foreign affairs in 1810, on the question whether the blockade of May, 1806, was considered as in force or as not in force. It had been ascertained that the French government, which urged this blockade as the ground of its Berlin decree, was willing, in the event of its removal, to repeal that decree; which, being followed by alternate repeals of the other offensive edicts, might abolish the whole system on both sides. This inviting opportunity for accomplishing an object so important to the United States, and professed so often to be the desire of both the belligerents, was made known to the British government. As that government admits that an actual application of an adequate force is necessary to the existence of a legal blockade,—and it was notorious, that if such a force had ever been applied, its long discontinuance had annulled the blockade in question,—there could be no sufficient objection on the part of Great Britain to a formal revocation of it; and no imaginable objection to a declaration of the fact, that the blockade did not exist. The declaration would have been consistent with her avowed principles of blockade, and would have enabled the United States to demand from France the pledged repeal of her decrees; either with success, in which case the way would have been opened for a general repeal of the belligerent edicts; or without success, in which case the United States would have been justified in turning their measures exclusively against France. The British government would, however, neither rescind the blockade nor declare its non-existence; nor permit its non-existence to be inferred and affirmed by the American plenipotentiary. On the contrary, by representing the blockade to be comprehended in the orders in council, the United States were compelled so to regard it in their subsequent proceedings.

There was a period when a favorable change in the policy of the British cabinet was justly considered as established. The minister plenipotentiary of his Britannic majesty here proposed an adjustment of the differences more immediately endangering the harmony of the two countries. The proposition was accepted with a promptitude and cordiality corresponding with the invariable professions of this government. A foundation appeared to be laid for a sincere and lasting reconciliation. The prospect, however, quickly vanished. The whole proceeding was disavowed by the British government without any explanations which could at that time repress the belief that the disavowal proceeded from a spirit of hostility to the commercial rights and prosperity of the United States. And it has since come into proof, that at the very moment when the public minister was holding the language of friendship, and inspiring confidence in the sincerity of the negotiation with which he was charged, a secret agent of his government was employed in intrigues, having for their object a subversion of our government, and a dismemberment of our happy union.

In reviewing the conduct of Great Britain towards the United States, our attention is necessarily drawn to the warfare just renewed by the savages on one of our extensive frontiers; a warfare which is known to spare neither age or sex, and to be distinguished by features peculiarly shocking to humanity. It is difficult to account for the activity and combinations which have for some time been developing themselves among tribes in the constant intercourse with British traders and garrisons, without connecting their hostility with that influence, and without recollecting the authenticated examples of such interpositions heretofore furnished by the officers and agents of that government.

Such is the spectacle of injuries and indignities which have been heaped on our country, and such the crisis which its unexampled forbearance and conciliatory efforts have not been able to avert. It might at least have been expected that an enlightened nation, if less urged by moral obligations, or invited by friendly dispositions on the part of the United States, would have found, in its true interest alone, a sufficient motive to respect their rights and their tranquillity on the high seas; that an enlarged policy would have favored that free and general circulation of commerce, in which the British nation is at all times interested, and which in times of war is the best alleviation of its calamities to herself as well as the other belligerents; and more especially that the British cabinet would not, for the sake of the precarious and surreptitious intercourse with hostile markets, have persevered in a course of measures which necessarily put at hazard the invaluable market of a great and growing country, disposed to cultivate the mutual advantages of an active commerce.

Other councils have prevailed. Our moderation and conciliation have had no other effect than to encourage perseverance and to enlarge pretensions. We behold our seafaring citizens still the daily victims of lawless violence committed on the great common and highway of nations, even within sight of the country which owes them protection. We behold our vessels freighted with the products of our soil and industry, or returning with the honest proceeds of them, wrested from their lawful destinations, confiscated by prize courts, no longer the organ of public law, but the instruments of arbitrary edicts; and their unfortunate crews dispersed and lost, or forced or inveigled, in

British ports, into British fleets; whilst arguments are employed in support of these aggressions, which have no foundation but in a principle equally supporting a claim to regulate our external commerce in all cases whatsoever.

We behold, in fine, on the side of Great Britain a state of war against the United States; and on the side of the United States a state of peace toward Great Britain.

Whether the United States shall continue passive under these progressive usurpations, and these accumulating wrongs, or, opposing force to force in defense of their natural rights, shall commit a just cause into the hands of the Almighty Disposer of events, avoiding all connections which might entangle it in the contests or views of other powers, and preserving a constant readiness to concur in an honorable re-establishment of peace and friendship, is a solemn question, which the constitution wisely confides to the legislative department of the government. In recommending it to their early deliberations, I am happy in the assurance that the decision will be worthy the enlightened and patriotic councils of a virtuous, a free, and a powerful nation.

Having presented this view of the relations of the United States with Great Britain, and of the solemn alternative growing out of them, I proceed to remark that the communications last made to Congress, on the subject of our relations with France, will have shown that since the revocation of her decrees as they violated the neutral rights of the United States, her government has authorized illegal captures, by its privateers and public ships, and that other outrages have been practiced on our vessels and our citizens. It will have been seen, also, that no indemnity had been provided or satisfactorily pledged for the extensive spoliations committed under the violent and retrospective orders of the French government against the property of our citizens, seized within the jurisdiction of France. I abstain at this time from recommending to the consideration of Congress definitive measures with respect to that nation, in the expectation that the result of unclosed discussions between our minister plenipotentiary at Paris and the French government will speedily enable Congress to decide, with greater advantage, on the course due to the rights, the interest, and the honor of our country.

JAMES MADISON.

WASHINGTON, June 1, 1812.

The committee on Foreign relations,—to whom was referred the Message of the President of the United States, of the 1st of June, 1812,—

REPORT,—That after the experience which the United States have had of the great injustice of the British government towards them, exemplified by so many acts of violence and oppression, it will be more difficult to justify to the impartial world their patient forbearance than the measures to which it has become necessary to resort, to avenge the wrongs, and vindicate the rights and honor of the nation. Your committee are happy to observe, on a dispassionate review of the conduct of the United States, that they see in it no cause for censure.

If a long forbearance under injuries ought ever to be considered a virtue in any nation, it is one which peculiarly becomes the United States. No people ever had stronger motives to cherish peace: none have ever cherished it with greater sincerity and zeal.

35*

But the period has now arrived when the United States must support their character and station among the nations of the earth, or submit to the most shameful degradation. Forbearance has ceased to be a virtue. War on the one side, and peace on the other, is a situation as ruinous as it is disgraceful. The mad ambition, the lust of power and commercial avarice of Great Britain, arrogating to herself the complete dominion of the ocean, and exercising over it a lawless and unbounded tyranny, have left to neutral nations an alternative only between a base surrender of their rights and a manly surrender of them. Happily for the United States, their destiny, under the aid of heaven, is in their own hands. The crisis is formidable only by their love of peace. As soon as it becomes a duty to relinquish their situation, danger disappears. They have suffered no wrongs,—they have received no insults, however great, for which they cannot obtain redress.

More than seven years have elapsed since the commencement of the system of hostile aggression by the British government on the rights and interests of the United States. The manner of its commencement was not less hostile than the spirit with which it has been prosecuted. The United States have invariably done everything in their power to preserve the relations of friendship with Great Britain. Of this disposition they gave a distinguished proof at the moment when they were made the victims of an opposite policy. The wrongs of the last war had not been forgotten at the commencement of the present one. They warned us of dangers against which it was sought to provide. As early as the year 1804, the minister of the United States at London was instructed to invite the British government to enter into a negotiation on all the points on which a coalition might arise between the two countries, in the course of the war, and to propose to it an arrangement of their claims on fair and reasonable conditions. The invitation was accepted. A negotiation had commenced and was depending, and nothing had occurred to excite a doubt that it would not terminate to the satisfaction of both parties. It was at this time, and under these circumstances, that an attack was made by surprise on an important branch of American commerce, which affected every part of the United States, and involved many of their citizens in ruin.

The commerce on which this attack was so unexpectedly made was between the United Utates and the colonies of France, Spain, and other enemies of Great Britain. A commerce just in itself, sanctioned by the example of Great Britain, in regard to the trade with her own colonies; sanctioned by a solemn act between the two governments in the last war, and sanctioned by the practice of the British government in the present war, more than two years having elapsed without any interference with it.

The injustice of the attack could only be equaled by the absurdity of the pretext alleged for it. It was pretended by the British government that, in case of war, her enemy had no right to modify its colonial regulations so as to mitigate the calamities of war to the inhabitants of its colonies. This pretension to Great Britain is utterly incompatible with the rights of the sovereignty in every independent State. If we recur to the well-established and universally admitted law of nations, we shall find no sanction to it in that venerable code. The sovereignty of every State is coextensive with its dominions, and cannot be abrogated, or curtailed in rights, as to any part, except by conquest. Neutral nations have a right to trade to every port of either belligerent which is not legally blockaded, and in all articles which are not contraband of war. Such is the absurdity of this pretension, that your committee are aware, especially after the able manner in which it has been heretofore refuted and exposed, that they would offer an insult to the understanding of the House if they enlarged on it; and if anything could add to the high sense of the injustice of the British government in the transaction, it would be the contrast which her conduct exhibits in regard to this trade, and in regard to a similar trade by neutrals with her own colonies. It is known to the world that Great Britain regulates her own trade in war and in peace, at home in her colonies, as she finds for her interest—that in war she relaxes the restraints of her colonial systems in favor of the colonies, and that it never was suggested that she had not a right to do it, or that a neutral in taking advantage of the relaxation violated a belligerent right of her enemy. But with Great Britain *everything* is lawful. It is only in a trade with her enemies that the United States can do wrong. With them all trade is unlawful.

In the year 1793, an attack was made by the British government on the same branch of our neutral trade, which had nearly involved the two countries in a war. That difference, however, was amicably accommodated. The pretension was withdrawn and reparation made to the United States for the losses which they had suffered by it. It was fair to infer from that arrangement that the commerce was deemed by the British government lawful, and that it would not be again disturbed.

Had the British government been resolved to contest this trade with neutrals, it was due to the character of the British nation that the decision should be made known to the government of the United States. The existence of a negotiation which had been invited by our government, for the purpose of preventing differences by an amicable arrangement of their respective pretensions, gave a strong claim to the notification, while it afforded the fairest opportunity for it. But a very different policy animated the then cabinet of England. The liberal confidence and friendly overtures of the United States were taken advantage of to ensnare them. Steady to its purpose, and inflexibly hostile to this country, the British government calmly looked forward to the moment when it might give the most deadly wound to our interests. A trade just in itself, which was secured by so many strong and sacred pledges, was considered safe. Our citizens, with their usual industry and enterprise, had embarked in it a vast proportion of their shipping, and of their capital, which were at sea, under no other protection than the law of nations, and the confidence which they reposed in the justice and friendship of the British nation. At this period the unexpected blow was given; many of our vessels were seized, carried into port and condemned by a tribunal, which, while it professes to respect the law of nations, obeyed the mandates of its own government. Hundreds of other vessels were driven from the ocean, and the trade itself in a great measure suppressed. The effect produced by this attack on the lawful commerce of the United States was such as might have been expected from a virtuous, independent and highly injured people. But one sentiment pervaded the whole American nation.

No local interests were regarded; no sordid motives felt. Without looking to the parts which suffered most, the invasion of our rights was considered a common cause, and from one extremity of our Union to the other was heard the voice of an united people, calling on their government to avenge their wrongs, and vindicate the rights and honor of their country.

From this period the British government has gone on in a continued encroachment on the rights and interests of the United States, disregarding in its course, in many instances, obligations which have heretofore been held sacred by civilized nations.

In May, 1806, the whole coast of the continent, from the Elbe to Brest inclusive, was declared to be in a state of blockade. By this act, the well-established principles of the law of nations, principles which have served for ages as guides, and fixed the boundary between the rights to belligerents and neutrals, were violated : By the law of nations, as recognized by Great Britain herself, no blockade is lawful, unless it be sustained by the application of an adequate force, and that an adequate force was applied to this blockade, in its full extent, ought not to be pretended. Whether Great Britain was able to maintain, legally, so extensive a blockade, considering the war in which she is engaged, requiring such extensive naval operations, is a question which it is not necessary at this time to examine. It is sufficient to be known that such force was not applied, and this is evident from the terms of the blockade itself, by which, comparatively, an inconsiderable portion of the coast only was declared to be in a state of *strict and rigorous blockade*. The objection to the measure is not diminished by that circumstance. If the force was not applied, the blockade was unlawful from whatever cause the failure might proceed. The belligerent who institutes the blockade cannot absolve itself from the obligation to apply the force under any pretext whatever. For a belligerent to relax a blockade, which it could not maintain, it would be a refinement in justice, not less insulting to the understanding than repugnant to the law of nations. To claim merit for the mitigation of an evil, which the party either had not the power or found it inconvenient to inflict, would be a new mode of encroaching on neutral rights. Your committee think it just to remark that this act of the British government does not appear to have been adopted in the sense in which it has been since construed. On consideration of all the circumstances attending the measure, and particularly the character of the distinguished statesman who announced it, we are persuaded that it was conceived in a spirit of conciliation, and intended to lead to an accommodation of all differences between the United States and Great Britain. His death disappointed that hope, and the act has since become subservient to other purposes. It has been made by his successors a pretext for that vast system of usurpation which has so long oppressed and harassed our commerce.

The next act of the British government which claims our attention is the order of council of January 7, 1807, by which neutral powers are prohibited trading from one port to another of France or her allies, or any other country with which Great Britain might not freely trade. By this order the pretension of England, heretofore claimed by every other power, to prohibit neutrals disposing of parts of their cargoes at different ports of the same enemy, is revived and with vast accumulation of injury.   Every enemy, however great the number or distant from each other, is considered one, and the like trade even with powers at peace with England, who from motives of policy had excluded or restrained her commerce, was also prohibited.   In this act the British government evidently disclaimed all regard for neutral rights.   Aware that the measures authorized by it could find no pretext in any belligerent right, none was urged. To prohibit the sale of our produce, consisting of innocent articles, at any port of a belligerent, not blockaded,—to consider every belligerent as one, and subject neutrals to the same restraints with all, as if there was but one,—were bold encroachments.   But to restrain or in any manner interfere with our commerce with neutral nations with whom Great Britain was at peace, and against whom she had no justifiable cause of war, for the sole reason that they restrained or excluded from their ports her commerce, was utterly incompatible with the pacific relations subsisting between the two countries.

We proceed to bring into view the British order in council of November 11th, 1807, which superseded every other order, and consummated that system of hostility on the commerce of the United States which has been since so steadily pursued.   By this order all France and her allies and every other country at war with Great Britain, or with which she was not at war, from which the British flag was excluded and all the colonies of her enemies, were subjected to the same restrictions as if they were actually blockaded in the most strict and rigorous manner; and all trade in articles, the produce and manufacture of the said countries and colonies, and the vessels engaged in it, were subject to capture and condemnation as lawful prizes. To this order certain exceptions were made, which we forbear to notice, because they were not adopted from a regard to natural rights, but were dictated by policy to promote the commerce of England, and, so far as they related to neutral powers, were said to emanate from the clemency of the British government.

It would be surperfluous in your committee to state that by this order the British government declared direct and positive war against the United States. The dominion of the ocean was completely usurped by it, all commerce forbidden, and every flag driven from it or subjected to capture and condemnation, which did not subserve the policy of the British government by paying it a tribute and sailing under its sanction. From this period the United States have incurred the heaviest losses and most mortifying humiliations. They have borne the calamities of war without retorting them upon its authors.

So far your committee has presented to the view of the House the aggressions which have been committed, under the authority of the British government, on the commerce of the United States. We will now proceed to other wrongs which have been still more severely felt. Among these is the impressment of our seamen, a practice which has been unceasingly maintained by Great Britain in the wars to which she has been a party since our revolution. Your committee cannot convey in adequate terms the deep sense which they entertain of the injustice and oppression of this proceeding. Under the pretext of impressing British seamen, our fellow-citizens are seized in British ports, on the high seas, and in every other quarter to which the

British power extends, are taken on board British-men-of-war, and compelled to serve them as British subjects. In this mode our citizens are wantonly snatched from their country and their families, deprived of their liberty and doomed to an ignominious and slavish bondage, compelled to fight the battles of a foreign country, and often to perish in them. Our flag has given them no protection ; it has been unceasingly violated, and our vessels exposed to danger by the loss of the men taken from them. Your committee need not remark that while the practice is continued, it is impossible for the United States to consider themselves an independent nation. Every new case is a new proof of their degradation. Its continuance is the more unjustifiable because the United States have repeatedly proposed to the British government an arrangement which would secure to it the control of its own people. An exemption of the United States from this degrading oppression, and their flag from violation, is all that they have sought.

The lawless waste of our trade, and equally unlawful impressment of our seamen, have been much aggravated by the insults and indignities attending them. Under the pretext of blockading the ports and harbors of France and her allies, British squadrons have been stationed on our own coast to watch and annoy our own trade. To give effect to the blockade of European ports, the ports and harbors of the United States have been blockaded. In executing these orders of the British government, or in obeying the spirit which was known to animate it, the commanders of these squadrons have encroached on our jurisdiction ; siezed our vessels and carried into effect impressments within our limits, and done other acts of great injustice, violence and oppression. The United States have seen, with feelings of mingled indignation and surprise, that these acts, instead of procuring to the perpetrators the punishment due to their crimes, have not failed to recommend them to the favor of their government.

Whether the British government has contributed by active measures to exercise against us the hostility of the savage tribes on our frontiers, your committee are not disposed to occupy much time in investigating. Certain indications of general notoriety may supply the place of authentic documents; though these have not been wanting to establish the fact in some instances. It is known that symptoms of British hostility towards the United States have never failed to produce corresponding symptoms among those tribes. It is also well known that, on all such occasions, abundant supplies of the ordinary munitions of war have been afforded by the agents of British commercial companies, and even from British garrisons, wherewith they were enabled to commence that system of savage warfare on our frontier which has been, at all times, indiscriminate in its effects on all ages, sexes and conditions, and so revolting to humanity.

Your committee would be much gratified if they could close here the detail of British aggressions; but it is their duty to recite another act of still greater malignity than any of those which have been already brought to your view. The attempt to dismember our Union and overthrow our excellent constitution by a secret mission, the object of which was to foment discontents, and excite insurrection against the constituted authorities and laws of the nation, as lately disclosed by the agent employed in it, affords full proof that there is no bound to the hostility of the British government towards the United States—no act, however unjustifiable, which it would not commit to accomplish their ruin. This attempt excites the greater honor from the consideration that it was made while the United States and Great Britain were at peace, and an amicable negotiation was depending between them for the accommodation of their differences, through public ministers, regularly authorized for the purpose.

The United States have beheld, with unexampled forbearance, this continued series of hostile encroachments on their rights and interests, in the hope that yielding to the force of friendly remonstrances, often repeated, the British government might adopt a more just policy towards them; but that hope no longer exists. They have also weighed impartially the reasons which have been urged by the British government in vindication of these encroachments, and found in them neither justification or apology.

The British government has alleged, in vindication of the orders in council, that they were resorted to as a retaliation on France, for similar aggressions committed by her on our neutral trade with the British dominions. But how has this plea been supported? The dates of all British and French aggressions are well known to the world. Their origin and progress have been marked with too wide and destructive a waste of the property of our fellow-citizens to have been forgotten. The decree of Berlin, of November 21st, 1806, was the first aggression of France in the present war. Eighteen months had then elapsed, after the attack made by Great Britain on our neutral trade, with the colonies of France and her allies, and six months from the date of the proclamation of May, 1806. Even on the 7th January, 1807, the date of the first British order in council, so short a time had elapsed after the Berlin decree, that it was hardly possible that the intelligence of it should have reached the United States. A retaliation which is to produce its effect, by operating on a neutral power, ought not to be resorted to till the neutral had justified it by a culpable acquiescence in the unlawful act of the other belligerent. It ought to be delayed until after sufficient time had been allowed to the neutral to remonstrate against the measure complained of to receive an answer, and to act on it, which had not been done in the present instance; and when the order of November 11th was issued, it is well known that a minister of France had declared to the minister plenipotentiary of the United States at Paris, that it was not intended that the decree of Berlin should apply to the United States. It is equally well known that no American vessel had then been condemned under it, or seizure been made. The facts prove incontestibly that the measures of France, however unjustifiably in themselves, were nothing more than a pretext for those of England. And of the insufficiency of that pretext, ample proof has already been afforded by the British government itself, and in the most impressive form, although it has declared that the orders in council were retaliatory on France for her decrees. It was also declared, and in the orders themselves, that owing to the superiority of the British navy, by which the fleets of France and her allies were confined within her own ports, the French decrees were considered only as empty threats.

It is no justification of the wrongs of one power, that the like were committed by another; nor ought the fact, if

36*

true, to have been urged by either, as it could afford no proof of its love of justice, of its magnanimity, or even of its courage. It is more worthy the government of a great nation to relieve than to assail the injured. Nor can a repetition of the wrongs by another power repair the violated rights or wounded honor of the injured party. An utter inability alone to resist would justify a quiet surrender of our rights, and degrading submission to the will of others. To that condition the United States are not reduced, nor do they fear it. That they ever consented to discuss with either power the misconduct of the other, is a proof of their love of peace, of their moderation, and of the hope which they still indulged, that friendly appeals to just and generous sentiment would not be made to them in vain. But the motive was mistaken, if their forbearance was imputed, either to the want of a just sensibility to their wrongs, or of a determination, if suitable redress was not obtained, to resent them. The time has now arrived when this system of reasoning must cease. It would be insulting to repeat it; it would be degrading to hear it. The United States must act as an independent nation, and assert their *rights* and avenge their *wrongs*, according to their own estimate of them, with the party who commits them, holding it responsible for its own misdeeds unmitigated by those of another.

For the difference made between Great Britain and France, by the application of the non-importation act against England only, the motive has been already too often explained, and is too well known to require further illustration. In the commercial restrictions to which the United States resorted as an evidence of their sensibility, and a mild retaliation of their wrongs, they invariably placed both powers on the same footing, holding to each, in respect to itself, the same accommodation, in case it accepted the condition offered; and in respect to the other, the same restraint, if it refused. Had the British government confirmed the arrangement which was entered into with the British minister in 1809, and France maintained her decrees, would the United States have had to resist, with the firmness belonging to their character, the continued violation of their rights? The committee do not hesitate to declare that France has greatly injured the United States, and that satisfactory reparation has not yet been made for many of those injuries; but that is a concern which the United States will look to and settle for themselves. The high character of the American people is a sufficient pledge to the world, that they will not fail to settle it on conditions which they have a right to claim.

More recently, the true policy of the British government towards the United States has been completely unfolded. It has been publicly declared by those in power that the orders in council should not be repealed until the French government had revoked all its internal restraints on the British commerce, and that the trade of the United States with France and her allies should be prohibited until Great Britain was also allowed to trade with them. By this declaration, it appears, that to satisfy the pretensions of the British government, the United States must join Great Britain in the war with France, and prosecute the war until France should be subdued, for without her subjugation it were in vain to presume on such a concession. The hostility of the British government to these States has been still further disclosed. It has been made manifest that the United States are considered by it as the commercial rival of Great Britain, and that their prosperity and growth are incompatible with her welfare. When all these circumstances are taken into consideration, it is impossible for your committee to doubt the motives which have governed the British ministry in all its measures towards the United States since the year 1805. Equally is it impossible to doubt, longer, the course which the United States ought to pursue towards Great Britain.

From this view of the multiplied wrongs of the British government, since the commencement of the present war, it must be evident to the *impartial world* that the contest which is now forced on the United States is radically a contest for their sovereignty and independence. Your committee will not enlarge on any of the injuries, however great, which have had a transitory effect. They wish to call the attention of the House to those of a parliamentary nature only, which intrench so deeply on our most important rights, and wound so extensively and vitally our best interests, as could not fail to deprive the United States of the principal advantages of their revolution, if submitted to. The control of our commerce by Great Britain in regulating at pleasure, and expelling it almost from the ocean; the oppressive manner in which these regulations have been carried into effect, by seizing and confiscating such of our vessels, with their cargoes, as were said to have violated her edicts, often without previous warning of their danger; the impressment of our citizens from on board our own vessels, on the high seas, and elsewhere, and holding them in bondage until it suited the convenience of these oppressors to deliver them up, are encroachments of that high and dangerous tendency which could not fail to produce that pernicious effect, nor would those be the only consequences that would result from it. The British government might for a while be satisfied with the ascendancy thus gained over us, but its pretensions would soon increase. The proof which so complete and disgraceful a submission to its authority would afford of our degeneracy, could not fail to inspire confidence that there was no limit to which its usurpations and our degradations might not be carried.

Your committee believing that the freeborn sons of America are worthy to enjoy the liberty which their fathers purchased at the price of much blood and treasure, and seeing, in the measures adopted by Great Britain, a course commenced and persisted in which might lead to a loss of national character and independence, feel no hesitation in advising resistance by force, in which the Americans of the present day will *prove* to the *enemy* and to the world that we have not only inherited that liberty which our fathers gave us, but also the *will* and *power* to maintain it. Relying on the patriotism of the nation, and confidently trusting that the Lord of Hosts will go with us to battle in a righteous cause, and crown our efforts with success—your committee recommend an immediate appeal to ARMS.

AN ACT

Declaring War between the United Kingdom of Great Britain and Ireland, and the dependencies thereof, and the United States of America and their territories.

Be it enacted by the Senate and House of Representatives of the United States in Congress assembled, That

WAR be, and the same is hereby declared to exist, between the United Kingdom of Great Britain and Ireland and the dependencies thereof, and the United States of America and their territories; and that the President of the United States be, and he is, hereby authorized to use the whole land and naval force of the United States, to carry the same into effect, and to issue to private armed vessels of the United States commissions, or letters of marque and general reprisals, in such form as he shall think proper, and under the seal of the United States, against the vessels, goods and effects of the government of the same United Kingdom of Great Britain and Ireland, and of the subjects thereof.

June 18, 1812.

Approved,—JAMES MADISON.

On the final passage of the act in the Senate, the vote was 19 to 13—in the House 79 to 49.

———

By the President of the United States of America.

A PROCLAMATION.

Whereas the Congress of the United States, by virtue of the constituted authority vested in them, have declared by their act, bearing date the 18th day of the present month, that war exists between the United Kingdom of Great Britain and Ireland, and the dependencies thereof, and the United States of America and their territories: Now, therefore, I, JAMES MADISON, President of the United States of America, do hereby proclaim the same to all whom it may concern; and I do especially enjoin on all persons holding office, civil or military, under the authority of the

United States, that they be vigilant and zealous in discharging the duties respectively incident thereto; and I do moreover exhort all the good people of the United States, as they love their country,—as they value the precious heritage derived from the virtue and valor of their fathers,—as they feel the wrongs which have forced on them the last resort of injured nations,—and as they consult the best means under the blessings of Divine Providence, of abridging its calamities,—that they exert themselves in preserving order, in promoting concord, in maintaining the authority and the efficacy of the laws, and in supporting and invigorating all the measures which may be adopted by the constituted authorities, for obtaining a speedy, a just, and an honorable peace.

          In testimony whereof I have hereunto set my hand,
L. S. and caused the seal of the United States to be affixed
          to these presents.

Done at the City of Washington the nineteenth day of June one thousand eight hundred and twelve, and of the Independence of the United States the thirty-sixth.

(Signed)   JAMES MADISON, *President.*
(Signed)   JAMES MONROE, *Secretary of State.*

GENERAL GEORGE ROGERS CLARK.

This gentleman, though his history has never yet been written, was undoubtedly one of the most eminent men and purest patriots the country has ever produced, fruitful as it has been in great men and disinterested patriots. And for decision, energy, forethought, good sense and intrepidity, he will compare favorably with any general of the Revolutionary War. In the West he was one of the best, if not the best, soldier that ever led an army against the savage force. He has been esteemed, too, the most extraordinary military genius which Virginia, of which State he was a native, has ever produced, although the field of his operations was the remote wilderness of the West. Judge Hall, a biographer of General Harrison, declares him to have been a man of extraordinary talents and energy of character, and possessed of a military genius, which enabled him to plan with consummate wisdom, and to execute his designs with decision and promptitude.

His great mind readily comprehended the situation of the country, and he made himself acquainted with the topography of the whole region and the localities of the enemies forts, as well as the strength of their forces. He possessed the rare faculty of penetrating the designs of his antagonist, thus becoming informed of the actual condition and movements of the enemy. He could therefore deduce his subsequent operations and his ulterior designs, and hence was enabled to anticipate and defeat all his plans and movements before they were matured. In the execution of his plans, his movements were made with such precision and celerity, and conducted with such consummate judgment, that success was always doubly ensured. General Washington entertained the highest opinion of his character, talents and military genius, and long hesitated whether he would appoint him or "Mad" Anthony Wayne to the command of the army designed to chastise the north-western Indians after the defeat of General St. Clair. He only selected General Wayne because he was *compelled* to make a choice between them—not because he believed either possessed superior qualifications or claims as a general.

General Clark, it has already been stated, was a native of Virginia, and was born in 1742. In his personal appearance he was commanding and dignified, and was well calculated to attract attention. His personal appearance was rendered particularly agreeable by the manliness of his deportment, the intelligence of his conversation, and, above all, by the vivacity of his manners and the boldness of his spirit for enterprise.

Early in the Revolutionary War, while a private citizen, holding no commission, civil or military, he distinguished himself by his efforts to protect the frontier settlements of Virginia and North Carolina against the incursions of the Indians. He led the party which made the first settlement at the falls of the Ohio, where an improvement was commenced, from which the splendid, flourishing and wealthy city of Louisville has grown up.

General Clark was the leading commissioner in negotiating a treaty between the United States and the chiefs and warriors of the Shawanee nation, including a part of the Delawares, at the mouth of the big Miami, in January, 1786, by which the United States were acknowledged to be the sole and absolute sovereigns of all the territory ceded by the treaty of peace with Great Britain, in 1783.

This treaty was negotiated at Fort Washington, where there were, at the time, a garrison of only seventy troops. All the Indians in council appeared peaceable, except three hundred Shawaneese, whose chief made a boisterous speech, and then placed on the table his belt of black and white wampum, to indicate that he was prepared for peace or war.

37

This act of daring and defiance of their chief was applauded
by the three hundred Shawaneese warriors, by one of
their terriffic war-whoops. At the table sat Commissary-
General Clark and General Richard Butler. Nowise intim-
idated by this war-like demonstration, General Clark with
his cane coolly pushed the wampum from the table, and
then rising, as the savages muttered their indignation, he
trampled the belt under his feet, and with a voice of authority ordered them instantly to quit the hall. His boldness,
assumed superiority, and disregard of the savage threat, had
such an effect upon them that they returned the next day
and sued for peace.

After the massacre of Wyoming, in 1778, he took command of a body of troops designed to operate against the
Indians, and to protect the frontiers against their murderous
incursions. His vigilance extended to the borders along
and near the Monongahela and southward to the Kanhawa.
In that year he superintended the construction of Fort Fin-
castle, afterwards Fort Henry, for the protection of the inhabitants in the vicinity of Wheeling Creek, as well as
other settlements north and south of that point, near the
Ohio River. His expedition to the Mississippi, in the same
year, with the view of taking possesion of it on behalf of
Virginia, was conducted with so much skill, judgment and
boldness as to give him a rank amongst the first military
men of his day.

When the commonwealth of Virginia sent him a colonel's commission, accompanied with a warrant to raise a
regiment of volunteers, and for that purpose to make con-
tracts on the credit of the State, they did not furnish him
with funds for that purpose, but left him to procure them

in the best way he could, either on their credit or on his own. Yet such was his perseverance and energy, and so unbounded was his confidence in the honor of his native State, and such was his influence with the people of the West, who knew his bravery and military talents, that he soon raised a regiment of hardy Kentuckians, whom he inspired with his own spirit; and having attached them warmly to his person, led them to the Mississippi, and captured the posts at Kaskaskia and Cahokia. The inhabitants of those villages, on receiving a promise of protection, took the oath of allegiance to the United States.

At the same time Governor Hamilton was at Fort Vincennes, making his arrangements to capture Clark and his band of heroes, which he expected to accomplish with but little difficulty. He was aware, however, of Hamilton's purpose, and also of the danger of his own situation, and determined to anticipate his enemy. Having left a sufficient number of men to ensure the safety of the conquests he had already made, he proceeded with the residue by a forced march through swamps and quagmires to the Wabash, where he arrived without the loss of a man, though the country was so flooded that they were sometimes compelled to swim. The advance of the troops was so arranged as to bring them to the village before the dawn of day, and before the governor was advised of their movement from the Mississippi. The consequence was, the post was carried by storm, and the governor and his troops made prisoners of war. The expedition was not excelled in difficulty and suffering, or in daring courage, by the memorable march of Arnold to Quebec, in 1775.

General Clark, in starting on the enterprise against

Kaskaskia and Cahokia, embarked with his regiment at the Falls, and descended the Ohio to some point not far from the mouth of the Wabash, where he landed a part of his men; and, having ordered the residue to proceed with the boats and baggage to the mouth of the Ohio, and thence to Kaskaskia, proceeded across the country by the most direct route to the same place. When he arrived in sight of the village, the inhabitants were as much surprised as if they had seen him descend from the clouds. As the provisions brought in the knapsacks of his men were nearly exhausted, and many days must elapse before the arrival of his boats, he was admonished to act promptly and without delay.

For the purpose of magnifying his force in the estimation of the town and garrison, as soon as he came in sight he ordered his men to march in such a circuitous manner that the formation of the intervening ground led the enemy to see and count them twice or thrice, without discovering the deception. He then halted, and with a part of his men and a flag, advanced to the fort, and demanded an immediate surrender, on the penalty of receiving no quarter in case of a refusal. The inhabitants at once submitted. The commandant of the fort, in the surprise of the moment, followed the example, and surrendered the garrison prisoners of war without firing a gun. Having thus captured Kaskaskia, he proceeded to Cahokia, thirty miles distant, which surrendered at once.

These conquests were achieved before the arrival of the boats, and were immediately made known to the British governor of Vincennes, by some friend, who stated at the same time, the diminutive force by which the object was accomplished. The governor immediately projected a plan to surprise the Americans, and re-take the posts. In the meantime the boats arrived with the residue of the regiment, when General Clark, leaving a sufficient number of men to retain the posts he had captured, marched without loss of time to Vincennes. Having waded through mud and water for several days, he approached the Wabash River, which was so flooded that his men were frequently up to their arm-pits in water; yet they were not disheartened, nor did their devotion to their heroic leader in the least degree abate until Vincennes, its garrison and governor, were in their hands, as already seen.

General Clark succeeded in retaining military possession of that extensive country till the close of the war of the revolution, and by that means secured it to the United States. The fact is well known that in arranging the articles of the treaty of peace, at Paris, the British commissioners insisted on the Ohio River as part of the northern boundary of the United States, and that the Count de Vergennes favored that claim. It appears also from the diplomatic correspondence on that subject, that the only tenable ground on which the American commissioners relied to sustain their claim to the lakes, as the boundary, was the fact that General Clark had conquered the country, and was in the undisputed military possession of it at the time of the negotiation. That fact was affirmed and admitted, and was the chief ground on which the British commissioners reluctantly abandoned their pretensions.

These, however, are only a few of the many great and valuable services rendered his country by this noble-minded man and true-hearted soldier. And all this was accomplished, too, almost literally on his own credit, and by his

37 *

own unaided enterprise.   Virginia neither sent him money
nor means when she sent him a commission, with permission
to raise men and money as he might be able.   The State
having no credit, he was compelled to rely solely on his own
efforts to raise and equip troops, and to feed and clothe them
during the term of their service, which continued to the
end of the war.   The task was a herculean one, and few
other men could have accomplished it.   Nothing but the
most devoted attachment to the country could have prompted
him to undertake it, and to persevere as he did; and, at all
events, nothing else could have prompted him to persevere
in his patriotic labors after the indignities to which he was
constantly subjected.

   Though holding conclusive evidence of the authority
upon which he acted from the legislature of Virginia, his
drafts upon that State in favor of those who had advanced
means to enable him to equip, feed and clothe his troops,
were dishonored, and for reasons, too, of the most humiliating character; but even this did not shake his purpose, or
induce him for a moment to relax his patriotic efforts.   As
his difficulties multiplied, his resolution gained strength;
and when his credit failed, and he was cut off from every
other resource, he resolved to sustain his troops, and preserve his conquests, by the strong arm of power.

   After weighing all the consequences both to himself and
his country, he resorted to force loans, and by that hazardous expedient accomplished the object nearest his heart,
which was the preservation of his conquests until the close
of the war.   He issued an order, as commandant of the
regiment, directed to two or three of his officers, commanding them to enter on the premises of the persons designated

in the order, requested the property there found, and remove it to the public store, for the exclusive use of the
troops. An exact inventory and careful valuation of the
property was ordered to be made, that the amount might be
made good by the legislature of Virginia. By this expedient, and this only, he was enabled to maintain the posts he
had conquered on the Mississippi and the Wabash till the
termination of the war, and thus save to the nation the
vast territory lying between the Ohio River and the lakes.

The persons whose property was sold under this order
of General Clark, commenced suit against him, obtained
judgments, and portions of his own private property were
sold to satisfy these demands contracted for the exclusive
benefit of the country. After the close of the war the legislature of Virginia made an appropriation of one hundred
and fifty thousand acres of land lying on the Ohio River,
opposite to Louisville, for the use of the officers and soldiers
of General Clark's regiment; but at that day it was of but
very little value, and was long since disposed of at mere
nominal prices.

Thus it appears that one of the most distinguished and
valuable officers of the revolution, who had performed services of the most incalculable importance, was not only
treated with cold neglect, but was subjected to the payment
of debts and claims incurred for the support of his troops,
to a very large amount. The cruel ingratitude to which he
was doomed, for which no justifiable cause can be assigned,
and the comparative poverty which made him almost a pen-
sioner on the bounty of his relatives, was more than he
could bear.

A person familiar with the lives and character of the

military veterans of Rome, in the days of her greatest power, might readily have selected this remarkable man as a specimen of the model he had formed of them in his own mind. But he has fallen a victim to his extreme sensibility, and to the ingratitude of his native State, under whose banner he had fought so bravely, and with such eminent success. But the time must come when the people of Louisville and of his native State, at least, will render the debt of gratitude they owe to the memory of this distinguished man, however forgetful the nation may be of his eminent services. It is a reproach upon the character of his native State, that she will not easily rid herself of; and never, except by a full and ample atonement for the base ingratitude done to this most worthy son.

The above particulars of the life of General Clark are principally taken from Burnet's Notes on the North-western Territory, and Monette's Valley of the Mississippi. With the example of such an uncle before him, it is not very strange that Colonel Croghan should *know how to fight*. The sketch, meager as it is, compared with his pre-eminent merits, it is thought will be found interesting, and fully to justify general reference to him. It is only to be regretted that one who has done so much for his country could not have found a biographer worthy his deeds and his fame. This evil should have been corrected long since. The life of scarcely any man in America would be found more replete with sterling and brilliant events than that of George Rogers Clark, or to afford a brighter example for the imitation of the rising generation.

GENERAL HARRISON'S DEATH AND BURIAL.

The following detailed account of General Harrison's last illness and burial was compiled principally from the Washington "Intelligencer" and "Madisonian," and the New York "Observer." It will undoubtedly possess a permanent interest as a chapter in the history of the times, long after the generation in which the melancholy event to which it refers shall have passed away. The general particulars of his death have been elsewhere given.

ACCOUNT OF THE PRESIDENT'S LAST HOURS.

Saturday, 1 o'clock, P. M.—Dr. Alexander of Baltimore has just visited the President's chamber, and pronounces him better, giving all his friends reason to indulge in hope. The good news spreads all over the city with joyful alacrity.

2 o'clock.—The favorable symptoms continue.

3 o'clock.—The symptoms are becoming alarming; a diarrhea is threatened.

Half-past 3 o'clock.—The alarm of General Harrison's friends are very great: the symptoms grow worse, and his case becomes more dangerous than ever. The medical men begin to doubt, if not to despair, and to speak in a manner and tone that hardly give us hope.

4 o'clock.—The news of increased danger flies over the city, and all are inquiring, and in all directions.

5 o'clock.—The President wanders, and is at times quite insensible. All his symptoms are worse. His family hanging in anxiety over his bedside, his physicians watching

every motion.   His diarrhœa grows worse, and leaves hardly
a hope, so rapidly does it prostrate his strength.

6 o'clock.—The members of the Cabinet have been
summoned to the President's; Mr. Granger just gave the
alarm to his associates.   The symptoms all worse.   His
physicians give him up.   The dreadful report fills all with
consternation.   The danger of losing the good and venerable man now breaks fully upon us all.

10 o'clock.—Reports from the sick chamber for the last
four hours have all been worse.   The pulse beats feebler
and feebler every minute.   His flesh has become cold and
clammy.   During this time, General Harrison has spoken
his last words, after which he fell into a state of insensibil-
ity.   At a quarter of nine, Dr. Worthington at his bedside,
he said (and it is presumed he was addressing Governor
Tyler),—

SIR,—I WISH YOU TO UNDERSTAND THE TRUE PRINCI-
PLES OF THE GOVERNMENT.   I WISH THEM CARRIED OUT.
I ASK NOTHING MORE.

This is the dying injunction of the good old man, made,
Dr. Worthington says, in a strong tone of voice.

All the members of the Cabinet, except Mr. Badger,
for three hours past, have been in a chamber near the President's sick room.   Their spirits, of course, are sadly de-
pressed by this melancholy event, but they are preparing
for the mournful duty that devolves upon them.

11 o'clock.—The President yet lingers.   The White
House has been thronged by citizens of all classes, fearfully
inquiring into the President's health.   He is insensible,
feeble indeed, and no one now indulges in hope.   All preparations are making as for a man already dead.   The con-

solations of religion have all along been administered. He has been calm, and manifested no fear of death. The physicians are just using the last remedies their skill devises, but with no hope of any favorable result.

12½ o'clock.—General Harrison has just breathed his last, and without a struggle. He has been insensible for a long while, and the last words he spoke were to Dr. Worthington. Most anxious and deeply affected friends are weeping around his chamber. What a dreadful blow has struck the land!

1 o'clock, A. M.—The members of the Cabinet, after performing their last mournful duties to the departed President, are preparing a letter to the Vice-President, announcing the fact officially. The chief clerk of the State Department, Fletcher Webster, Esq., is dispatched with it, and he will reach Mr. Tyler by Monday noon, who will probably be here Wednesday or Thursday the latest.

OFFICIAL LETTER TO THE VICE-PRESIDENT.

WASHINGTON, April 4, 1841.

"To JOHN TYLER, Vice President of the United States.

"Sir:—It has become our most painful duty to inform you that WILLIAM HENRY HARRISON, late President of the United States, has departed this life.

"This distressing event took place this day, at the President's mansion in this city, at thirty minutes before one in the morning.

"We lose no time in dispatching the chief clerk in the State Department, as a special messenger, to bear you these melancholy tidings.

" We have the honor to be, with the highest regard, your obedient servants,

> DANIEL WEBSTER, Sec'ry of State.
> THOS. EWING, Sec'ry of the Treasury.
> JOHN BELL, Sec'ry of War.
> JOHN J. CRITTENDEN, Attorney-General.
> FRANCIS GRANGER, Postmaster-Gen."

ARRANGEMENTS FOR THE FUNERAL.

WASHINGTON, April 4, 1841.

The circumstances in which we are placed by the death of the President render it indispensable for us, in the recess of Congress and in the absence of the Vice-President, to make arrangements for the funeral solemnities. Having consulted with the family and personal friends of the deceased, we have concluded that the funeral be solemnized on Wednesday, the 7th instant, at 12 o'clock. The religious services to be performed according to the usages of the Episcopal Church, in which church the deceased usually worshiped. The body is to be taken from the President's House to the Congress Burying Ground, accompanied by a military and civic procession, and deposited in the receiving tomb.

The military arrangements to be under the direction of Major-General Macomb, the General Commanding in Chief of the Army of the United States, and Major-General Walter Jones, of the Militia of the District of Columbia.

Commodore Morris, the Senior Captain in the Navy now in the city, to have the direction of the naval arrangements.

The Marshal of the District to have the direction of the civic procession, assisted by the Mayors of Washington, Georgetown, and Alexandria, the Clerk of the Supreme Court of the United States, and such other citizens as they may see fit to call to their aid.

John Quincy Adams, ex-President of the United States, Members of Congress now in the city or its neighborhood, all the members of the Diplomatic body resident in Washington, all officers of government, and citizens generally, are invited to attend.

And it is respectfully recommended to the officers of government that they wear the usual badge of mourning.

> DANIEL WEBSTER, Sec'ry of State.
> THOS. EWING, Sec'ry of the Treasury.
> JOHN BELL, Sec'ry of War.
> JOHN J. CRITTENDEN, Attorney-General.
> FRANCIS GRANGER, Postmaster-General.

ARRIVAL OF THE VICE-PRESIDENT.

At 12 o'clock, all the Heads of Departments, except the Secretary of the Navy (who has not yet returned to the city, from his visit to his family), waited upon the Vice-President to pay him their official and personal respects. They were received with all the politeness and kindness which characterized the new President. He signified his deep feeling of the public calamity sustained by the death of President HARRISON, and expressed his profound sensibility of the heavy responsibilities so suddenly devolved upon himself. He spoke of the present state of things with great concern and seriousness, and made known his wishes that the several Heads of Departments would continue to fill the places which they now respectively occupy, and his confidence that they would afford all the aid in their power to enable him to carry on the administration of the government successfully.

The PRESIDENT then took and subscribed the following oath of office:

I do solemnly swear that I will faithfully execute the office of President of the United States, and will, to the best of my ability, preserve, protect and defend, the Constitution of the United States.   JOHN TYLER.

April 6, 1841.

DISTRICT OF COLUMBIA,
City and County of Washington, } ss.

I, William Cranch, Chief Justice of the Circuit Court of the District of Columbia, certify that the above-named JOHN TYLER personally appeared before me this day, and, although he deems himself qualified to perform the duties and exercise the powers and office of the President on the death of WILLIAM HENRY HARRISON, late President of the United States, without any other oath than that which he has taken as Vice-President, yet, as doubts may *arise*, and for greater caution, took and subscribed the foregoing oath before me.   W. CRANCH.

April 6, 1841.

FUNERAL CEREMONIES.

It was not until Wednesday, that the full force of the bereavement was felt by the public mind, when to all who about five weeks before had witnessed the spectacle of the inauguration, there was now presented the very different spectacle of a funeral—and the funeral of that very inaugurated Chief Magistrate. The day itself—the clouds covering the heavens—resembled the Fourth of March. The numerous flags at half-mast, and hung with crape, met the eye wherever it was turned; while the ear was saluted with the deep thunder of heavy cannon, as at short intervals the melancholy sound came through the air. The stream of human beings continued to pour into the city from all quarters until 12 o'clock, and although it was supposed all the States of the Union sent the materials that constituted the host at the Inauguration, there seemed really to be as many to-day in the city as on the Fourth of March.

At sunrise the sound of cannon from the several military stations in the vicinity of the city heralded the melancholy occasion which was to assemble the citizens of the district and its neighborhood, and minute guns were fired during the morning. In entire consonance with those mournful sounds was the aspect of the whole city, as well its dwellings as its population. The buildings on each side of the entire length of the Pennsylvania avenue, with scarcely an exception, and many houses on the contiguous streets, were hung with festoons and streamers of black, not only about the signs and entrances, but in many cases from all the upper stories. Almost every private dwelling had crape upon the knocker and bell-handle of its door, and many of the very humblest abodes hung out some spontaneous signal of the general sorrow. The stores and places of business, even such as are too frequently seen open on the Sabbath, were all closed. Everything like business seemed to have been forgotten, and all minds to be occupied with the purpose of the day. The great point of attraction was the President's Mansion. Toward that, all steps, all

thoughts were tending. The northern portico of the Mansion was hung with long banners of black, extending from
column to column. The iron gates of the enclosure in front
were closed, save when the Foreign Ministers, Members of
the Cabinet, the attending Physicians, the Clergy, the Judiciary and ladies, were admitted, preparatory to their taking
the places assigned them in the funeral procession.

At the entrance of the Mansion, the dressings of black
presented themselves on every side, descending from the
lofty ceiling to the floor. The great chandelier, with the
immense mirrors of the east room, and other articles of
furniture, were enveloped in the sable symbols; while in
the centre of the room reposed the illustrious dead—the
body being contained in a coffin covered with rich silk velvet, over which was thrown the pall of similar material.
Under the lid of the coffin was a glass, through which could
be seen the face of the late President. The expression was
calm and natural : his white hair lying close to his head, and
his features regular and peaceful, as if they had been quietly
composed to their last long sleep. It was impossible to escape contrasting this moveless repose of death with the
incessant activity of the living individual, when receiving
the visits of the people, or transacting business with those
who called. What little of form or ceremony remained
about the Government was extinguished by the late President.

The first semi-circle around the coffin was composed of
about forty clergymen of different denominations in and
near the district. Opposite to these, encircling the head
of the coffin, sat the Vice-President and the Cabinet, except
Mr. Badger, who had gone to North Carolina. On the

left of the Cabinet were Messrs. Forsyth, Poinsett and
Paulding, also Mr. Adams. In their rear sat the Foreign
Ministers, in their gorgeous dresses of gold and silver lace,
stars, epaulets and other insignia peculiar to monarchical
governments, and strongly contrasting with the severe simplicity of all around, especially the *simplicity of death.*
Immediately behind the clergy were the mourners, about
fifteen or twenty in number, including the "faithful women,"
who "did what they could" to minister to the last wants of
their departed relative and friend. The next semi-circle was
composed of the attending and consulting physicians, and
the twenty-four pall-bearers, all with white sashes. Officers
of the government of various grades, ladies and others, who
had the privilege of admission, filled the room, which was
not crowded, the thousands of the people being outside even
the gates of the great front lawn, and maintaining the most
profound stillness and exemplary order. In fact, the population had, as if by common consent, extended itself in
very equal masses along the whole distance of a mile and
a half from the Mansion to the Capitol. The passage-way
within the spacious front lawn was filled with mourning-
coaches, in waiting for the Family Mourners, the Cabinet,
the Clergy, Members of Congress, Foreign Ministers, &c.

At half-past 11 o'clock, the Rev. Mr. Hawley, Rector
of St. John's Church, arose, and observed that he would
mention an incident connected with the Bible which lay on
the table before him (covered with black silk velvet).
"This Bible," said he, "was purchased by the President
on the 5th of March. He has since been in the habit of
daily reading it. He was accustomed not only to attend
church, but to join audibly in the church service, and to

38 *

kneel before his Maker." Mr. H. stated that had the President lived, and been in health, he intended on the *next Sabbath* to become a communicant at the Lord's table. A part of the 15th of 1st Corinthians was then read, some selections from the Psalms, and a short prayer. No address or particular appeal was made to the assembly or to any portion of it.

It was after 11 o'clock, when the procession in front of the Presidential Mansion presented a complete line, and a few minutes before twelve, a funeral car entered the square, and drew up within the portico. It was of large dimensions, in form an oblong platform, on which was a raised dais, the whole covered with black velvet. From the cornice of the platform fell a black velvet curtain outside of the wheels to within a few inches of the ground. From the corners of the car a black crape festoon was formed on all sides, looped in the centre by a funeral wreath.

Precisely at 12 o'clock, a detachment of musicians, which had been marched up in front of the portico, played the Portuguese hymn, during which the body was moved, and placed on the car. The coffin was covered with a rich velvet, on which were placed two swords, laid across (the Sword of Justice and the Sword of State), surmounted by the scroll of the Constitution, bound together by a funeral wreath formed of the yew and cypress. The car was drawn by six white horses, having at the head of each a colored groom, dressed in white, with white turban and sash, and supported by pall-bearers in black. The effect was very fine. The contrast of this slowly moving body of white and black, so opposite to the strong colors of the military around it, struck the eye even from the greatest distance, and gave a chilling warning beforehand that the corpse was drawing nigh.

The most impressive portion of the military part of the procession consisted of the dismounted and mounted officers of the Army, Navy, Militia, and Volunteers. Seldom has there been exhibited within a space so limited so many distinguished military men, the sight of whose well-known figures led back our thoughts to many a bloody field, and many an ensanguined sea, on which the national honor has been well and nobly maintained.

Next to the military were the clergy of the district and elsewhere, (dressed with scarfs, and with crape on the hat and left arm), about forty in number, in carriages.

Then followed the attending physicians, in their private vehicles.

Immediately *behind* the hearse were the male relatives of the deceased, including his old and faithful friends, Colonels Todd and Chambers.

Immediately after them President Tyler, in a carriage with the Secretary of State; then the several other Heads of Departments, and Mr. J. Q. Adams. Several members of the Judiciary Department followed, and then all the Ministers of Foreign Governments, now present, or their Secretaries.

Next followed officers and soldiers who had served under General Harrison in the late war. Another division of the procession consisted of public societies and associations preceded by their banners, and wearing their respective badges.

On the firing of the signal gun at the appointed hour, the procession moved along Pennsylvania avenue, under the fire of minute guns near the President's House, repeated at the City Hall, on the head of the column arriving opposite to it, and at the Capitol on its reaching the western gate of the enclosure. The music was excellent; several fine bands playing mournful airs, giving place, from time to time, to the muffled drums of the military, beating slow marches.

The solemnity of the scene was beyond description.

Among the most touching incidents which occurred during the procession was its meeting the Maryland Legislature about half-way down the avenue. Having just arrived in the cars, the members, preceded by their officers, marched on to meet the funeral train of the President, and were immediately assigned their proper and honorable rank in the multitude of public mourners.

Having reached the Capitol Square, passing on the south side of it, the procession advanced over the plains eastward till it reached the space in front of the Congressional Burying Ground.

Here the car halted, while the line was formed by the military; and then passed slowly on, being saluted as it passed with a dirge, with colors lowered, the troops presenting arms, and the officers saluting it in military form. Having reached the principal entrance, the car was again halted; the coffin was taken down and placed on the shoulders of the bearers; the clergy advanced, and the Rev. Mr. Hawley, reciting the solemn funeral service of the Episcopal Liturgy, the procession advanced down the principal avenue of the cemetery until it reached the receiving vault, where a space had been kept open by sentries under arms, and where a hollow square being formed, the coffin was lowered in the public vault, which was hung with festoons of black crape and muslin. It is a spacious arched apartment at the extremity of the ground, perfectly dry. There were about eight coffins in it before that of General Harrison was received into it. In the centre of this vault, a mahogany shell had been placed, and into this shell the coffin was fitted, and the lid was then placed upon it, when, in an interval of "expressive silence," the coffin was conveyed down into the tomb, and all that remained on earth of the President of this great Union was laid in its narrow bed; near the other coffins almost unnoticed, and altogether unknown to us, how did all earthly grandeur dwindle to its real insignificance, and how impressively did the tomb teach it in that hour! The immortality of Fame! How did the bubble burst in the atmosphere of that house of death! And when I saw TYLER, WEBSTER, EWING, BELL, CRITTENDEN and GRANGER enter that house, to take their last view of the coffin, and to emerge again with the weight of a nation's cares, added to present affliction upon them who could help exclaiming: "What shadows we are, what shadows we pursue!" Among the last things which I observed were the tears of his old comrades in arms on many a hard-fought field, as they ascended out of the vault, and left their brave and beloved General in the embrace of the Universal Conqueror, adding another trophy to the triumphs of Death, and another portion to the spoils of the Grave.

A signal being given to the troops outside, the battalion of Light Artillery, who were placed on an adjoining eminence, fired a salute, which was immediately followed by the several military bodies in line, who commenced firing from the left to the right, and had continued the salute till it had thrice gone up the whole line.

The Vice-President appeared to be much affected. Mr. Ewing, the Secretary of the Treasury, was, at times, almost unmanned by the excess of his grief. Mr. Webster, Mr. Bell, Mr. Granger, and Mr. Crittenden evinced by their deportment that they felt their loss.

The entire procession occupied two full miles in length, and was marshaled on its way by officers on horseback carrying white batons with black tassels. The utmost order prevailed throughout; and, considering the very great concourse of people collected, the silence preserved during the whole course of the march was very impressive.

The procession returned by the same route to the city, where the troops were dismissed, and the citizens retired to their several abodes. By five o'clock, nothing remained but empty streets and the emblems of mourning upon the houses, and the still deeper gloom, which oppressed the general mind with renewed power after all was over, and the sense of the public bereavement alone was left to fill the thoughts.

It was the universal impression, that the procession was larger, and the whole effect more imposing, than that of the pageant of the Inauguration. In regard to solemnity, the two occasions of course admit of no comparison. The one was a nation in joy; the other a nation in tears.

REFLECTIONS IN THE EAST ROOM—April 7, 1841.

The great East Room of the President's House,—that room in which I have seen a thousand gay and joyful faces glowing in the light of ponderous chandeliers, radiating the light of a hundred burners,—was now the scene of death! Those brilliant fountains of light were hid in the dark robes of mourning. The splendid mirrors, which rose almost to the lofty ceiling, reflecting on every side the brilliant crowds which often thronged this room, now refused to look upon the scene before them, and buried their polished bosoms in the habiliments of sadness. In short, this magnificent room, in every part of it, spoke in the appropriate language of silent grief, announcing to all—Death is here!

The coffin rested in the centre of the room, and was richly and beautifully dressed. Closely attached to it was a covering of black velvet. The edges where the top rested were delicately traced with fine gold lace, and on either side and at each end of the coffin the same material was formed into beautiful squares. A gorgeous velvet pall hung gracefully over the whole, with a deep rich fringe appended to a border of gold lace. On the top of all rested two elegantly wrought swords in mourning, buried in a profusion of lovely and fragrant flowers, which Flora had consecrated to this sad and melancholy service, as if to express the idea that sweetness and beauty could conquer the sword and survive death itself!

Around the coffin, and at an appropriate distance, was formed a circle composed of the new President of the United States, the heads of departments, the clergy of every denomination, judges of courts, and members of the bar. The next circle contained the foreign ministers in their rich and varied court dresses, with a number of members of both Houses of Congress, and the relatives of the deceased President. Beyond this circle a vast assemblage of ladies and gentlemen filled up the room. Silence, deep and undisturbed, even by a whisper, pervaded the entire assembly. The solemn event which they were now gazing upon fixed every eye and hushed every tongue. When, at the appointed hour, the officiating minister rose from his seat, and as he rose in solemn tones announced these words, " *I am the resurrection, and the life!*" one simultaneous move placed this vast assemblage upon their feet on the first sound of the ministers voice, and a feeling of deeper awe rested upon every countenance, as he uttered the above sentence. Never before did I realize the grandeur and sublimity of these words—never before did I feel the thrilling effect which the enunciation of this glorious Christian truth is capable of inspiring.

At the close of these religious ceremonies, the coffin was conducted to the funeral car specially constructed for the occasion, where it was met and saluted by the solemn dirge of appropriate music; and the procession moved off under the discharge of funeral artillery, which uttered loud and long the nation's grief.

THE MOURNFUL INTELLIGENCE.

As the news of the decease of the venerable President of this republic spread from city to city, there was every demonstration of the deep grief which the nation feels, at the removal by death, of the chief officer of the republic. In the smaller towns on the route of the mail hither, the persons always waiting at the railroad depots, heard the intelligence in silence, and turned away to communicate it to their friends, in that suppressed tone which is the indication of true feeling.

In Baltimore, on Sunday, the bells of the city were

tolled throughout the day, and the flags from various edifices floated at half mast, trimmed with the "insignia of woe." In several of the churches, the ministers took advantage of the occasion, and made most impressive and affecting allusions to the national bereavement, in the decease of the President.

In Philadelphia, the slip signed by all the heads of the department, announcing the fact, was read at the Exchange to about 500 persons, all of whom evinced much feeling, and without uttering a word left the room. In less than two minutes after the announcement not three persons of the dense crowd that had so lately filled the apartment were to be seen.

The news was received in New York a little before midnight, by the evening train. At that hour, on account of the storm with which the afternoon closed, few persons were stirring, but as the intelligence was announced by the passengers, it was received with the same demonstrations of grief and respect for the deceased, which had marked its reception in other cities. The news was circulated through a large part of the city; but still could not be said to be generally circulated, until the appearance of the morning papers, dressed in the proper marks of mourning.

New York is emphatically a reading city. The proportion of houses at which a morning paper is served in the city is probably as eight to ten, if not larger. Consequently almost the first thing that met every man's eye was the indication of the national loss, in the turned rules, and funeral appearance of the newspapers, which, with one exception only, paid this mark of respect for the deceased. Made in a manner so striking, the announcement could es-

cape no one, and men walked abroad to their daily avocations, with faces which betrayed what every honest man's
heart felt.　Our daily avocations make us among the ear-
liest of early risers, and had we been, by any chance, unap-
prised of the intelligence, we could have read in the faces
of those whom we met, the unanimous declaration that some
grief, for the general weal, oppressed our fellow-citizens.

The method of striking fire alarms in this city prevents
the use of the bells to toll an unexpected announcement.
None were therefore struck, but at the usual hour of hoist-
ing flags, the city standard, and the national ensign were
displayed at half mast upon the City Hall.　All the principal hotels, the political head quarters of both parties, and
the other public buildings upon which flags are usually
hoisted on public occasions, displayed them yesterday at
half mast; and the shipping at the piers and in the harbor
wore the same testimonials of national grief.　We never
felt before so proud of our citizenship, as we did in exchang-
ing remarks of sincere condolence with our friends of the
opposition party, who thus testified that love of country is
superior in American hearts to devotion to party.

The courts met only to adjourn; and the Common
Council was convened to take measures for testifying the
public sympathy and respect.

All the flags in Albany were displayed at half mast;
the Supreme Court and Court of Chancery adjourned, and
an extraordinary meeting of the Common Council was convened at 12 o'clock.

The Governor of the State sent a message to the legislature, which immediately adjourned after appointing com-
mittees of arrangements.

At Hartford, and at all other places, reached by steam-boat hence, the news was divined by the half-mast flag, before a word was spoken; and many citizens turned away without asking or waiting to hear one word. There was agony in that telegraphic sermon.

At Boston, the news of the death of the President of the United States was received on Tuesday morning. The shipping at the wharves hoisted their colors at half mast, and the Revenue Cutter Hamilton, Captain Sturgis, at anchor in the harbor, fired minute guns for an hour. This was done in compliance with the recommendation and instructions of the Collector of that Port. The courts adjourned, and the Common Council was convened to take proper measures for a municipal observance of the occasion.

In every place, indeed, throughout the land, the intelligence was received with mourning, dismay and solemnity. No event that has ever occurred since the death of Washington has ever filled the nation with such sincere and universal grief.

FUNERAL CEREMONIES ELSEWHERE.

In addition to the ceremonies at Washington, there was, on the day and during the hours of the funeral obsequies, a cessation of business, with other demonstrations of solemnity, in the great cities of Baltimore, Philadelphia, New York and Boston.

After due arrangements had been made, during the same or the following week, the afflicting dispensation was further solemnized by the delivery of addresses and large funeral processions in all the principal cities and many other places. The procession in *New York* occupied a space of four miles, and was many hours in passing, with its large concourse and funeral tread. In *Albany* there was a torch-light procession. The procession was accompanied by a full band of music, and the funeral urn, covered with its pall—the whole illuminated by the light of upwards of 600 torches. It passed through the principal streets of the city between 8 and 10 o'clock. The night was still, and very dark; and the effect produced by the long array of mourners at that unusual hour,—the funeral emblems, the solemn music, and the strong red glare of the torches, revealing from the gloom and lighting up with picturesque effect the houses and crowds of spectators which thronged the windows as they passed,—left an impression which will not soon be effaced from the memory of those who beheld the scene.

Accounts are still coming in from every quarter of the very many public testimonies of the grief of the people, for the loss of their venerable and beloved Chief Magistrate.

GENERAL HARRISON'S FAMILY.

1. The following relatives of Gen. HARRISON were present in the city on the day of the funeral, viz :

Mrs. Jane Harrison, of Ohio (son's widow), and two sons.

Mrs. Taylor, of Virginia (niece), a daughter and two sons.

Pike Harrison (grand-son), son of J. C. Harrison, and grand-son of Gen. Pike.

Mr. D. O. Coupeland, of Ohio (nephew).

Mr. Benjamin Harrison, of Berkley (nephew).

Henry Harrison (grand-nephew), son of the preceding, who has acted as confidential secretary of the President.

Dr. John Minge, of Charles City, Va (nephew).

We may also add the name of *Mrs. Findley*, of Ohio, who adopted Mrs. Jane Harrison as a daughter, and who almost invariably occupied the right hand of the President at his table.

2. The following are the surviving relatives who were absent :

Mrs. Harrison, the General's bereaved widow.

John Scott Harrison, the only living son.

Mrs. Judge Short, eldest daughter.

Mrs. Dr. Thornton, daughter.

Mrs. Taylor, daughter. All these are living at or near North Bend.

Mr. Taylor and his wife and family were expected to become members of the President's family, for the whole term of his service.

3. The following are the names of the deceased members of the family :

Lucy Harrison, a daughter, married Judge Este.

J. C. S. Harrison, a son, married Miss Pike. Both dead.

Wm. H. Harrison, Jr., married Miss Jane Irvine. His widow presided at the President's table, and her personal graces have commended her to the affections of all who have had the pleasure to know her.

Dr. Benjamin Harrison, a son. Died the last summer.

Carter B. Harrison, who was a lawyer of fine talents, and accompanied General Harrison to Colombia. Died two years ago. All the sons left children.

Mrs. Harrison, the President's widow, has been for many years a member of the Presbyterian church. The

39 *

rest of the family are also Presbyterians, except Mr. Benjamin Harrison, who is an Episcopalian, and Mrs. Taylor, of Richmond, who is a member of the Baptist church.

GENERAL HARRISON DEAD.

BY ANN S. STEPHENS.

Death sitteth in the Capitol! His sable wing
Flung its black shadow o'er a country's hope,
And lo! a nation bendeth down in tears.
A few short weeks and all was jubilee,—
The air was musical with happy sounds—
The future full of promise—joyous smiles
Beam'd on each freeman's face and lighted up
The gentle eye of beauty.
The Hero came—a noble good old man—
Strong in the wealth of his high purposes.
Age sat upon him with a gentle grace,
Giving unto his manhood dignity,
Imbuing it with pure and lofty thoughts
As pictures owe their mellow hues to time.
He stood before the people. Their's had been
The vigor of his youth his manhood's strength,
And now his green old age was yielded up
To answer their behest.
Thousands had gathered round the marble dome
Silent and motionless in their deep reverence,
Save when they gushed the heaving throb
And low tumultuous breath of patriot hearts
Surcharg'd with grateful joy. The mighty dead
Bent gently o'er him with their spirit wings,

As solemnly he took the earthly state
Which flung its purple o'er his path to Heaven.
The oath was said, and then one mighty pulse
Seem'd throbbing through the multitude—
Faces were lifted upward, and a prayer
Of deep thanksgiving wing'd that vow to Heaven.
Time slept on flowers and lent his Glass to Hope—
One little month his golden sands had sped
When, mingling with the music of our joy,
Arose and swell'd a low funeral strain,
So sad and mournful, that a nation heard
And trembled as she wept.
        Darkness is o'er the land,
For lo! a death flag streams upon the breeze,—
The Hero hath departed!
Nay, let us weep, our grief hath need of tears—
Tears should embalm the dead, and there is one,
A gentle woman, with her clinging love,
Who wrung her heart that she might give him up
To his high destiny.   Tears are for her,—
She lingers yet among her household gods
And knoweth not how low her heart is laid.
From battle-fields where strife was fiercely waged,
And human blood-drops fell a crimson rain,
He had returned to her.   God help thee, Lady,
Look not for him now!
. Thron'd in a nation's love he sunk to sleep,
And so awoke in Heaven.

NEW YORK, April 5.

VICE-PRESIDENT TYLER'S RECOMMENDATION OF A NATIONAL FAST.

OFFICIAL.

To the People of the United States.

A RECOMMENDATION.

When a Christian People feel themselves to be over-taken by a great public calamity, it becomes them to humble themselves under the dispensation of Divine Providence, to recognize His righteous government over the children of men, to acknowledge His goodness in time past, as well as their own unworthiness, and to supplicate His merciful pro-tection for the future.

The death of WILLIAM HENRY HARRISON, late Presi-dent of the United States, so soon after his elevation to that high office, is a bereavement peculiarly calculated to be regarded as a heavy affliction, and to impress all minds with a sense of the uncertainty of human things, and of the dependence of nations, as well as of individuals, upon our Heavenly Parent.

I have thought, therefore, that I should be acting in conformity with the general expectation and feelings of the community in recommending, as I now do, to the People of the United States, of every religious denomination, that, according to their several modes and forms of worship, they observe a day of Fasting and Prayer, by such religious ser-vices as may be suitable on the occasion ; and I recommend Friday, the fourteenth day of May next, for that purpose ; to the end that, on that day, we may all, with one accord, join in humble and reverential approach to HIM, in whose hands we are, invoking him to inspire us with a proper spirit and temper of heart and mind under these frowns of His providence, and still to bestow His gracious benedictions upon our Government and our country.

JOHN TYLER.

WASHINGTON, April 13, 1841.

CONCLUSION.

Thus the national bereavement, so signal and so overwhelming, has been acknowledged by many sincere demonstrations of sympathy and grief—and finally by an executive recommendation of a day of national fasting and prayer. President Tyler has done well to enter upon the honors of office by honoring our fathers' God and ours! The public solemnities attending the late fearful dispensation are appropriately concluded by the humiliation of the whole people before the majesty of Heaven.

Christians! the voice of God summons you to Zion! Prepare ye to assemble at her solemn places with humiliation and prayer. The national visitation demands national penitence; and the garment of our praise must be wrapped in the spirit of heaviness.

Now therefore, our God, the great, the mighty, and the terrible God, who keepest covenant and mercy, let not all the trouble seem little before Thee, that hath come upon us, unto this day. Howbeit Thou art just in all that is brought upon us; for Thou hast done right, but we have done wickedly. We have not kept Thy law, nor hearkened unto Thy commandments and Thy testimonies, wherewith Thou didst testify against us!

To the Lord our God, belong mercies and forgiveness. O Lord, hear! O Lord, forgive!